The Top of the Octagon

by

Colleen Lumadue

authorHOUSE®

AuthorHouse™
1663 Liberty Drive, Suite 200
Bloomington, IN 47403
www.authorhouse.com
Phone: 1-800-839-8640

First published by AuthorHouse 5/12/2008

ISBN: 978-1-4343-5575-1 (sc)

Library of Congress Control Number: 2007910176

Printed in the United States of America
Bloomington, Indiana
This book is printed on acid-free paper.

For Audrey

Acknowledgments

My very special thanks to my grandson Justin Lumadue for transporting me into the computer age and making the technical challenges of writing this book so much easier. I couldn't have done it without you, Justin. A big thank you to my dear husband Bill for all of his loving support and patience and for taking over the ordinary chores of daily living while I was consumed with the writing of this novel. My deep gratitude to my daughter Jeanine and her husband Ken Womack for their wonderful editing and encouragement toward getting my book published. I owe a debt of thanks to Ken and his brother Andy for their efforts at designing my book cover. I am grateful to Steven J. Murdoch for generously allowing me to reprint his splendid photograph of Ely Cathedral. I will always remember the loving interest given to me in the writing of this novel by my dear sons Paul and Steven; my grandchildren Ryan, Rebecca, Victoria, and granddaughter-in-law Mellissa; and my brothers Bunt and Richard. Thanks to the friends who read through the loose pages of the manuscript, including Ken Smith, Don, Terry, Maureen, Patty, Ann, Mary Alice, Kelley, Peggy, Dorie, cousin Fleeta, and nieces Joan, Maggie and Julie. Their enjoyment of the book was for me a great delight. Thanks to Keith Pesto, Esq., for advice on legal matters mentioned in the book and to AuthorHouse's Ryan Wilke and Kathy Moriarty, who encouraged me to publish. Last, but certainly not least, I want to thank Heidi and Don Maier, whose first names I used for characters in this novel. The real Heidi and Don first took me to Ely and gave me Ely Cathedral. This I will never forget along with one heartfelt thank you to my sister Audrey.

Chapter 1

"Attention, please. All passengers kindly fasten your seatbelts."

Fran surfaced from the mental fog of agony she had been feeling during the entire flight. When she had looked at the white clouds the plane was flying above, in her mind, they turned to black. They seemed to seep through the window and permeate her being. She tried desperately to listen to the words of the stewardess.

"We will be starting our descent and landing at Heathrow Airport soon. Our captain and crew wish to thank you for flying British Air. It has been our pleasure to serve you. We hope you have had a pleasant flight and that you will continue to choose British Air for your travel needs. Please follow the directional signs at the terminal. They will assist you in finding the luggage stations, customs, layover areas, etc. If we can be of further help to you, please tell us. Again, thank you and do enjoy your stay in England."

The light and happy inflection Fran heard in the voice of the stewardess was so beyond her inner being. Could she ever again approach any of life with such a feeling? Yes, she needed help. Something she could ask no one for. Something for which there are no directional signs. The last two years of her life had brought her to this feeling of being emotionally dead. The only thing that kept her coping with the necessary things of living was her parent's need of her during her mother's illness. Now, her mother was well; the need was not there. It was time that she had to begin a direction for her life, a fresh start, but she didn't know how to begin. For such a long time she had forced herself to feel nothing and to bury the little spark of a wish to be the happy, exuberant person she was before she married Jeff.

The plane was down. Fran stood, smoothed her skirt and put on her light purple suit jacket. It did nothing to stop the chill that was shaking her body. Her inner voice was muttering, "I shouldn't have come, I shouldn't have come, I shouldn't have come." It was time to start the airport routine and look for Heidi who would be waiting for her. Dear, warm, caring Heidi phoned so many times and begged her to visit, knowing that Jeff had died and that Fran had other problems with her mother's illness. Still, Heidi could have no idea of Fran's real inner state or that her heart was broken, not at the time of Jeff's death, but from the beginning of their marriage.

While Fran stood waiting by the luggage belt she kept promising herself to act as a guest should, for Heidi and Don's sake, all the while fearing she shouldn't have come. She wished she could feel some happy response, some excitement at being in this busy terminal and at the thought of seeing England. England had always been for her a longed for place to see. Fran was through customs and began to look through the crowd for Heidi. There she was with her beaming smile and looking even six years prettier, if that was possible. She came running toward her and soon that welcoming hug made Fran feel a momentary jolt of happiness that she hadn't expected. It almost broke her control and tears were near the surface. Fran tried to put on a carefree and happy smile and act as if everything was fine. Somehow she didn't think she could win an Oscar. Heidi held her at arm's length and studied the face of her dear friend.

"Fran, why are you smiling with your mouth but not with your eyes? Do you think you have to pretend with me?"

"Heidi, you know me so well. I am so glad to be with you. That isn't pretending."

Heidi squeezed Fran's hand as she answered, "Of course, Fran, but honestly sharing of good and bad times has always been a part of our friendship. We'll keep it that way. Ok? You haven't said much in your letters. I know that your mom was ill, and that things haven't been good. How is she now?"

"Mom is feeling fine now. She and Dad have moved to Florida. The milder climate will be easier for both of them. They loved their home in Pennsylvania but the winters can be hard there. My mind is relieved about them. My own emotional state is quite another story." Fran felt the tightness in her throat; her shoulders were hunched up like a vulture's wings. She swallowed hard and moved her tightened muscles around before she could continue. "I don't want to burden you and Don with this low feeling of mine but I need a release, so I probably will—but enough about me for a while. How are you and Don and little Bryan?"

By this time they had reached the car and were ready to start the long ride on the crowded highway from Heathrow to the American Air Force base housing. Heidi almost felt reluctant to tell Fran of her own happiness but couldn't hide the joy in her voice. "Fran, this assignment to England was the greatest thing that could have happened to us. Don and I have loved living here. Everything is so new and exciting. We still feel much like tourists. Everything we have seen from Big Ben to the cathedrals has been wonderful. We are going to see that your visit includes them all. Don said he would baby-sit with Bryan while we girls sight see. He has some leave time coming up. He is so thrilled with the baby and loves being with him. Oh, Fran, Bryan is the most beautiful baby. He is only five months old and I can't imagine life without him. I can't wait for you to see him."

Fran tightened her hand on her purse strap and silently stared out of the window for a few moments. Wanting a baby was one of the wounds to her spirit that happened in the months of marriage to Jeff. Seeing little Bryan and being asked to hold him was a thing Fran was dreading most. She roused herself from her thoughts and said, "I'm sure he is beautiful and wholly loveable with the parents he has. Does he look like you and have your big brown eyes and gorgeous black hair or does he look like Don, that handsome blond with sky blue eyes?"

Heidi was smiling as she described him. "Right now he doesn't have much hair but I think it's coming in dark. His eyes are blue but darker than Don's are. You know, Fran, he has about your shade of eyes, almost a violet color. I always loved your dark brown hair; I've wished mine was like yours, with highlights, instead of black."

Fran looked surprised and said, "Heidi, I always wanted black hair like yours. All through high school I envied yours. I would have dyed mine if Mom wouldn't have had a bird." For a few minutes they were laughing and remembering old high school times. "Heidi, it's so strange to laugh. It has been such a long time. I didn't remember what it felt like."

"We'll have many laughs, Fran. That is what I'm here for. Though I should keep quiet a while and let you look at the English scenery." They stayed silent for a little. Fran's lighter moment had passed. Her feeling of any joy just didn't seem real. She was wishing she hadn't come. For Heidi's sake she tried to give attention to the passing scenery.

After a while Fran said, "I've been noticing so many sheep in the fields. They're interspersed with old charming villages and some very new developments. It's so different from anything I've seen. Of course, I didn't do much traveling even at home in the States."

Heidi asked, "Didn't you travel a lot with Jeff on his concert tours?"

Heidi looked at Fran whose expression suddenly was one of pain and felt pain herself when Fran replied in a flat voice, "I wish to God that I could just forget them. Some tours I was not *allowed* to accompany the great man. And when I did go, we saw very little of the country. They were all hurry and work. My real word for them was misery." Fran closed her eyes and remained silent for the rest of the drive.

Heidi parked the car in front of the pretty, neat, buff brick row house and turned to Fran. "We have a lot of talking to do," Heidi said in a gentle tone. "First we will get you settled in and have a nice cup of tea." She reached out and took Fran's hand and said, "You know that is the English cure-all for everything, hot strong tea in a pretty china cup. Well, if it doesn't help, it can't hurt."

Fran said, "You are the help, Heidi, and the tea sounds lovely."

The evening passed slowly. Don and Heidi couldn't believe the difference in the exuberant person that Fran had always been. They kept a light chatter going and Fran tried hard to allow a response to Don and Heidi's warmth. Yet, little of the tension they were all feeling was eased. Seeing and holding their precious baby was less traumatic than Fran had anticipated. His warm little body felt comforting against her; until the thought of Jeff and her hurt surfaced. Damn Jeff, she almost said aloud. She felt a sharp anger toward Jeff; a feeling she hadn't allowed to surface through the guilt she hugged toward herself. She forced these feelings from her and tried to think only of these dear friends who deserved all happiness. Fran was truly glad for them. Yet, when Heidi asked Fran if she did want to settle down for the night, Fran was very grateful. Physically she was tired and quite exhausted emotionally.

When Fran went to her room, the large beautiful black cat she had seen earlier was now on her bed. Heidi said, "Oh, I don't know what I'm going to do with Scooby. He has adopted this room and won't stay in any other. Ever since we got our little dog Dottie, two weeks ago, Scooby has been so scared of her that he won't risk contact. I know you like cats Fran. Would it be all right if he stays with you?"

Fran picked up Scooby, hugged him and assured Heidi that she would love his company and would find him the perfect roommate. Scooby purred loudly and it was obvious he felt the same about Fran.

"Problem solved," said Heidi. "I'm so glad you are an understanding cat person. See you in the morning, Fran dear. Pleasant dreams! If Scooby gets annoying call me."

"We are fine, Heidi. Sweet dreams to you too. Goodnight."

Alone at last, except for her quiet furry friend, Fran gave into the tears she had so often held back during this most stressful day. Holding Scooby close, Fran sat down on the window seat. She gazed up at the star-filled night sky for a little while until the physical exhaustion overtook the emotional one. Finally she turned down the coverlet of the bed. The linens smelled of English lavender, so inviting. She stretched out between the cool, fragrant sheets and was soon in a deep sleep.

Chapter 2

"Ely!—my beloved Ely!" A surge of joy went through the inmost being of Etheldreda. St. Etheldreda had felt for hundreds of years only concern and tenderness for others and unspeakable joy in her eternity with God. Yet, now she felt the most human emotion of delight at being in a place that was so dear to her in life. For many centuries her spirit had been close to Ely. Oh, the many times she had interceded to the Lord Himself on behalf of those who prayed for help, in special needs, in this holy place.

Somehow, someway, this moment in time was different. Shocking was the awareness that she was part of earthly time again. No prior knowledge was given her that this would happen. She could feel with her sandaled feet the cool, damp earth and smell the air of the soft summer night. With joy, she could feel the sweet breeze on her face.

"Why is this happening to me?" Her voice spoke quietly but aloud. To hear the sound of her own voice, to feel her lips as she moistened them with her tongue was astonishing. She looked down at her body, so alive. She kicked a pebble with the toe of her sandal and picked it up and felt the smoothness of the stone with her delicate fingers. Why? Again, her heart and soul and voice asked the question. To know all the senses in their fullness, once again, was stunning; but her heart remained in peacefulness. She knew, with certainty, the purpose was of God. The why would be answered in His good time.

Suddenly she was remembering people, things, and feelings that had been part of her earthly years. These memories seemed to flood over her as standing under a waterfall. She was remembering a walk with her husband, Ecgfrith, on a summer night, so long ago. The recall of this was as brief as it was vivid. Deep within her, awareness grew that something in her memories would help her give direction to someone in the present time.

Once more her confused thoughts overwhelmed her. She knew this place so well. Yet, it was vastly different. Standing on a small space of neatly clipped grass, she looked around at the few lovely tall trees and the neatly trimmed bushes. There were buildings nearby. She walked down closer to the river and found herself walking on a smooth surface. So much of the ground was covered with this. Its name, unknown to her, was cement.

Her feet, now only damp and cool, would have been wet with the ever-present water of the Fens. The tall rushes would have tugged at her skirt and the night air would have been filled with the ever-pungent odor of must from the swamp. She missed also the sweet fragrance of the summer wild flowers that had grown, in the Fens, in such abundance.

Etheldreda looked down at her dress. It was neither the queen's dress of fine linen trimmed in braid nor the habit of rough wool that she had worn as an abbess. There was no veil or crown upon her head. There were no beads around her throat, such as she had worn as a young woman. Her throat—how plain the remembrance of the tumor that grew there shortly before her death and the pain of the lancing. She felt her neck in its wholeness and the smooth young feeling of her skin. She felt her long hair and looked at its end. It was silken and fine, a pale yellow, as when she was young. The dress she was wearing was a simple one of soft material. It was light brown in color with small yellow flowers. It reached only to the middle of her legs. It had a squared neckline and short sleeves. It was gathered softly at her waist. So unlike any clothing she had ever seen. She knew that it must be a dress of this new time and necessary for what she was to do. She wondered if she would be visible to others and, if so, why?

The sky was beginning to lighten a little and the flight of the meadow pipit, its small zeep sound, broke the silence of the night. She saw a barn owl, on the wing, returning to its roost after the night's hunt. She thought there still must be farming land near.

The breaking of dawn and the ordinary sounds of the earthly world were causing her sheer delight. She touched her small perfect ears and blinked her eyes. She marveled at the abilities that once again were hers.

What would this day mean to her, what would the day's activities be for the people in this place? *Wait.* Be patient, Etheldreda, her silent voice within her spoke.

She was now so fully aware that this place was all so different from her memory of it. She knew that her beautiful Fens must have been, somehow, drained because even in the midst of summer, such as this, the ground would have been wet and marshy. Her sandaled feet would have been muddy during a nighttime walk. She turned her back to the river and looked up toward the rise. She knew the big Cathedral would be there where her abbey had once been, so long ago.

The rosy breaking of dawn was lighting the sky, revealing the distant outline of the majestic Cathedral. So familiar this noble building that enshrined the memory of her. Because of this, her spirit had known this place, always. Yet, today it was so different. How thrilling to see it standing high above the flat lands by the river. She felt an irresistible urge to be near it, to touch its splendid stone. She wished to see it in her earthly presence this splendor of man's creation, this work of genius given by the great God.

As she walked toward the rise, her mind and spirit felt as open and new as the dawn itself. She would relish each new wonder until the purpose for being here would be revealed. She walked steadily toward the Cathedral and went up the paved walk, known as Jubilee Terrace, then on through the green of the Dean's Meadow, preferring to walk on the soft earth. She stood in the Meadow for a long time, gazing up to the magnificent Octagon and Lantern. She went on and found her way to the right until she was on the Palace Green, in front of the Cathedral. She experienced the feelings of awe in the same mortal way that thousands of people have felt when being in this place.

The huge, impressive doors were locked when she tried to enter. In her mortal form Etheldreda could not move through them. She continued to walk all around the Cathedral. She thought of its beginning in the year 1083, four hundred and ten years after her monastery had been built here. How different, how humble her monastery had been in comparison. It had begun, at that time, to make this spot, in Ely, a holy one that enlivened faith and brought people closer to the wonder of God. She knew she had a definite purpose in dedicating her life to God during her earthly existence.

Yet, during her young years there were indeed moments of self-doubt. She began to remember, again, the walk with Ecgfrith. He was a dear, kind man and her fondness for him was real. He had truly loved her and had been so tender in his pleading, that night, for their marriage to be a total one. She had promised her life to the service of God. This he had known and agreed to from the beginning of their marriage. His wanting to change her mind could well be understood. His love and desire for her had grown along with his longing for an heir for his kingdom. Yet, for her there could be no "yes." Her doubts that she was right in this for his sake, the desire of her young body and the constant denial of maternal longing for a child made this moment in her life one of deep misery. Yet, there could be no Yes." Why think of those things now? Things so far in the past. Things so long over and well resolved. To understand someone else? Who?

The spell of this time of solitude ended. She was still alone in this morning. Her thoughts now became less introspective as she took her eyes from the Cathedral and began to look at other things around her, things so vastly different and confusing. She was standing on firmly paved walk. She followed the walk out of the grounds and saw more paved stretches, which seemed to be roads. No earth paths beaten firm or cobbled stones. What were the many large things of different colors standing on the roadside? She returned to the Cathedral grounds and walked far to the rear. There she saw a large paved place. She looked on in amazement as one of the large bright things came moving into the place and stopped. She went closer and knew it to be some kind of carriage of this time, one that didn't need horses.

The man got out of his car and Etheldreda went toward him to say good morning and ask about the carriage. She felt confused about things but not about people. People were the same in any time. All were God's children. She felt no fear at approaching him.

There was no response to her good morning greeting. Etheldreda was directly beside him. He was locking his car door with a key. He turned and said nothing. He did not see her. He had no awareness of her presence. He was carrying his keys as he started walking toward the Cathedral. She knew them to be keys but they were not at all like the ones she had once carried on a large round ring.

Etheldreda had believed that with her present mortal image and mortal limitations that others would see her. If the man could have seen her now, he would have noticed her stunned expression. Confusion grew. What good would she be here if she would not be seen? She watched the man as he walked away and noticed his clothes. He was wearing a plain short sleeve shirt and jeans. She then fully realized that, although through the years she had been spiritually aware of the needs and prayer of others, she had no knowledge of the trivialities of change on Earth. Leaving the Cathedral grounds, she returned to the public roads. She walked on the paved walks along the streets and gazed with awe at the large buildings of brick and stone as well as wooden buildings that were painted bright colors. Oh, how different from the wooden structures in the Fenland she knew. Those broad boards soon weathered to black and brown. She looked in amazement at glass covered windows with so many things displayed, most of them unknown to her. Some windows were filled with clothes and shoes of many kinds. Again, she looked at her clothing on herself. The dress and sandals were similar to some she was seeing in the windows.

She crossed the street from the Cathedral side and as she walked she came upon a large open space that she knew was surely the Ely marketplace of her day. She remembered the selling of crops and animals and wares of her time. Was this place still used as a market? What would be offered for sale? By now there were many people about. The streets had become filled with cars and trucks and buses. Everything was moving around her. There was so very much of everything. Etheldreda trusted that she would be given time to adjust to all this before her mission would be made known to her.

She walked back to the Cathedral grounds with a group of people. Her presence was completely unknown to them. She waited in front of the great doors and watched them entering. When she was quite alone she put her hand on the heavy handle and opened the door the mortal way.

Once inside she went along as a guide took the group throughout the Cathedral. They went from the southwest transept to the Prior's Door with its Norman carvings, to the side chapels, to the bays of the choir, to the shrine set aside for her memory, on to the superb Octagon and so many other wonderful things, and to the Lady Chapel. Oh, yes! She knew it all. Her spirit had been here since its beginning and she knew of all of the Cathedral's changes and growth. But somehow in her otherworldness she was unaware of the appearance of the present living people. Her spirit had been open to them. Her intercession was not sought in vain. Now, it seemed her heavenly intercession was not to be enough. Someone would seek her help in someway, right here in Ely. She simply must wait.

Chapter 3

Fran woke suddenly from a dreamless sleep. A surge of hope and expectation went through her before she could even assemble waking thoughts. She got up swiftly and put on her pale peach-colored robe and crossed the room to again sit on the window seat and look out at the night sky. The stars had faded and the first touch of dawn was apparent. What was it that seemed to speak of a new day in her life? Was it being with dear friends in a new place? No, this was like a force beyond her defining. As the dawn of the new day unfolded, her sense of peace grew. Somewhere, out there under the skies of England, something or someone would help her. Comforted and relaxed, Fran returned to her bed and fell asleep again.

Fran roused from her sleep when Scooby gave a loud, hungry mew. She was still for a few minutes as the remembrance of her early morning experience filled her mind. She thought she must have been having a wishful, half dream. Yet, a sense of wonder and puzzlement was with her.

Fran opened the door when she heard a soft knock. She found a radiant Heidi with a baby in one arm and a dish of cat food in her other hand. Scooby soon relieved her of that. "Good morning, Fran, breakfast is any time you want it. Bryan had his and is going for his morning nap." Fran took Bryan's little hand and kissed it. "Fran, you look rested. It must have been a good night."

"It was, Heidi. Maybe Scooby's company was relaxing," Fran said laughing. She could not have begun to tell Heidi of the strange feeling that came to her in the early morning.

They were in the kitchen, lingering over coffee. The baby was back in his bassinet and sleeping soundlessly. "Fran, would you like to talk a little now about what has been wrong or leave it for awhile?"

"Heidi, it is truly one of those long stories. I don't know where to begin."

"Well, Fran, for a long time your notes have been just the keep-in-touch kind, without saying anything. The last really happy letters you wrote were while Don was stationed in Texas and we were living there. That was years ago when you were studying voice at the conservatory."

"I remember your letter telling how excited you were about meeting Jeff. The next letter gave us the news of your plans to marry him. That seemed so sudden, for you couldn't have known him long. We were glad to know you planned to continue serious study because your voice is truly beautiful. I can still hear the sound of it in my mind. Not only did you do all the leads in our high school musicals, you simply couldn't keep quiet anywhere. Even walking to school or in parking lots, you would break into "Oh, What a Beautiful Morning" or "September Song" or "Winter Wonderland," depending on the season. Singing was so much a part of you." Heidi squeezed Fran's hand. "Now you seem as if there is no song inside."

"Heidi, I haven't sung at all for a long time. I've no desire to. You are right; there is no song inside. When I wrote to you during those years at the conservatory I felt on cloud nine. Yes, I loved singing. I loved the building of voice and the trying ever to perfect the music I was given to work on. The times I was given parts in the productions at the conservatory were exciting beyond words. Many of my teachers thought I could have gone on to an important career. However, I was leaning more toward the desire to teach and perhaps do solo work in choirs or choruses. I still felt I would be singing always. The truly professional reach the top at any price; that sort of career was not something I longed for. So it wasn't a sacrifice, my career for his kind of thing, which made life with Jeff so awful." Fran's eyes filled with tears and she folded and unfolded her napkin nervously. She couldn't bring herself to continue.

"Hon," Heidi said sympathetically, "we have all the time in the world when you want to tell me more. Why not go out to the backyard and enjoy some of that bright sunshine. When it is like this in England you have to take advantage of it."

"That sounds good to me, Heidi. I think I'll see if Scooby will let me carry him out of the bedroom and into the yard. Maybe he would like some sunshine too."

"Fran, there is some catnip growing in the herb patch. It might help him relax. I'm going to wash baby clothes and get things ready for Don's day of babysitting tomorrow. We want to start seeing something. Right now I think I hear Bryan. Just do what you want and remember this is your home in England. Enjoy!"

Heidi's graciousness was warm to Fran and she went up to fetch Scooby. As long as he was in Fran's arms, he didn't seem to mind going downstairs; and once in the yard, surely enough, he headed for the catnip. Fran stretched out on the soft padded lounge and closed her eyes. She wanted to recapture the feeling of promise she had felt in the early morning. It had been so real. Her thoughts were muddled. Why couldn't she continue telling about her marriage to Jeff? She felt she had to talk it out with someone. She never talked it out with anyone—even her parents. During the time she went home to take care of her mother, she felt she couldn't worry them and kept her deep unhappiness to herself. When they saw sadness in her, they assumed it was because of losing Jeff in the car accident.

Too restless to stay still, Fran got up and walked around the small yard. It was so pretty, boxed in with pink hedge roses and its beds of purple cosmos and Shasta daisies. Its loveliness seemed to reflect the gentle, honest affection that she knew existed between Don and Heidi. She realized now that no real love was ever there in her relationship with Jeff. She had loved the man she thought Jeff was. The reality of the man was completely different. She opened her mind to memories she hadn't allowed to surface for a long time. She could see herself and the other students in the cafeteria and hear the buzz of excitement. It was April 17th, of her third year. She, too, felt excitement at the anticipation of the violin concert to be given at the Conservatory that night. The soloist was Jeff Amberson. His picture held a place of honor in the lobby of the auditorium for years. It was a very professional, posed black and white portrait of a man handsome enough to be a model. The hair was dark and thick, parted far to the side and brushed straight back from a broad forehead. The eyes, light, were looking off to the side. The mouth was thin and unsmiling, creating a thoughtful look if not a warm one. Handsome, he was. The picture evoked admiring remarks daily from the female students.

Jeff Amberson had graduated from this conservatory ten years ago. He was indeed a brilliant violinist. His career had constantly advanced. From his first year of concert tours, he was in demand as soloist for major orchestras in the States and in Europe. He was also recording and selling well. What a prestigious event for the Conservatory to have his return for a concert and to have him stay with them until the end of the term, in late May, for evaluations of their violin students

When the lights dimmed, the accompanist Fredrick Hendermer was already seated at the concert grand piano. Frederick was a mature, pleasant looking man of about fifty, whose talent as an accompanist was well known. After what seemed a long wait, Jeff Amberson entered from the wings. The welcoming applause was deafening at the sight of this slender, handsome man. His solemn acknowledgment was a simple nod of his head. There he stood very erect. He placed his priceless instrument under his chin and held the bow in his arched right hand for a silent moment.

Fran felt intoxicated by the end of the concert. Never had she been as overwhelmed as with the exquisite beauty of his music. It was so easy to be infatuated with his handsome self and the beautiful spirit that she was sure he had to possess. No one could play with such feeling she thought, if one's depth of soul did not equal it. She attributed his unsmiling and remote reaction to his audience as something necessary to his time of performing. She told herself he had to be in a world apart. For the final selection, Jeff had played Corelli's "La Folia Sonata." Jeff made this difficult and complex work seemingly effortless. Every full-blooded romantic passage, every sweet high tone was exquisite.

When the last sweet sound of the rich low tone faded away, the audience was completely hushed for a moment. Then, as if one body, they stood and gave him a prolonged standing ovation. Still, no warm communicating smile, only one gracious bow was his acceptance of their tribute. Had Fran thought about it then she might have read his thought that this was no less than was his due. Fran had no room for logical thoughts at that moment. She had been invited to the private reception, to be held at Dean Ratchford's home; there she would actually be meeting Jeff Amberson. She felt almost giddy with anticipation, a feeling she was trying to put under control. She wanted to appear calm and sophisticated. Being so warm and open in her emotions, this seemed a hard thing for Fran. Jeff had seemed so reserved. She didn't want him to think her flighty, if he thought of her at all. "Silly goose," Fran told herself, "you are just one of many people shaking that beautiful, artistic hand. He does not know the thrill you are feeling at the thought of it."

At last the meeting took place and at last the smile came to his face. His hand lingered on hers for sometime beyond that introduction. Her dark shining hair was gently pulled back and curled, framing her beautiful, oval face. Her large violet blue eyes were alive with excitement and admiration. Her skin smooth and white as alabaster against the deep blue velvet, demure, simply cut gown. Oh yes, his physical attraction to her was immediate and overwhelming. He liked his women beautiful and this was a rare find, even among the many Jeff had known. He decided at once that she would be a delightful diversion for him while he had to remain at the Conservatory. He really hadn't wanted to come, much less to stay and be part of the student evaluation. When the request had been sent to him, during his concert tour in Spain, his response was a screaming "no." However, his agent felt it was advantageous for publicity reasons, since he was to be back in the States preparing for his first concert in Carnegie Hall in the coming October.

Because of this and because he thought it a good way to break off his current relationship with an attractive, but clinging, slightly older Spanish woman (of whom he was totally bored), he agreed to make this commitment.

Fran was delighted when Jeff said he would like to have a quiet, longer time to talk with her. He asked her to please make a point of saying goodnight to him before leaving the party. During the refreshments and small talk the evening passed as unnoticed by Fran as were the many other admiring looks that came her way.

Finally, at what she deemed an appropriate time for leaving, Fran approached Jeff to say goodnight. She was truly surprised when he once again took her hand in both of his. He asked her if she would go to lunch with him the next day and fill him in on current news and activities of the Conservatory and anything a student might think it good for him to know, since he was to be a part of it for a while. It sounded to Fran as if it were almost a business-type lunch he was planning. Fran's delighted acceptance assured him he was using the right approach.

As Fran closed the door to the Dean's house, Frederick Hendermer, who had been watching the good-bye scene, walked over and with a direct gaze into those cold blue eyes said, "Jeff, leave her alone. She is, quite obviously, a very nice and very inexperienced young woman, beautiful, yes, but far too good for you. You don't need to add her to your list of conquests."

"Fred, you can mind your own damned business. Keep your eyes on the musical score, not my personal one. If you can manage to do that, I'll see you to begin rehearsals for Carnegie on the tenth of June, in New York."

Fred walked slowly to the waiting cab. He breathed deeply of the night air, as if trying to rid a stench he had smelled. He would soon be settled back into a plane seat and on his way to his own New York apartment, which held his real world, his precious wife Susan and their two young sons. He had flown home whenever there had been a long enough break between concerts. But this last tour had been so long, too long. He so loved being with his family. He thought of Jeff and wondered if he would have been different if he had been a part of a real family while growing up. Jeff's parents had died in a plane crash when he was four years old. He didn't even remember them. The older uncle, who was his guardian, had shown maximum interest in his schooling and development of his rare talent. But on a personal level he had no time, or love, to give. Poor Jeff. Fred knew that he and Pete, Jeff's agent, were the nearest things to friends Jeff had. Sometimes they both found him hard to take.

Back in her room that night, Fran wondered why Jeff had never married. She was not so naïve to think that he hadn't been involved romantically over the last ten years. However, knowing the demands of a musical career such as his and his moving about, she thought, perhaps he simply didn't have time to give to such a special love. Oh, she was sure, with the beauty of the spirit he must possess; his love for a woman would be as strong and true as his music. If she could have heard the remarks after she left the party, it certainly would have saved her from such delusion and from all the sadness that was ahead. Fran would never know of the many other scenes played out during their dating, revealing Jeff's real self. She did not, of course, have them in her memories as she paced the yard on that summer afternoon. But they had been there, like black threads being woven through the fabrics of her joyful delusion.

Fran now walked the garden in an accelerated gait. Her mind a kaleidoscope of brightly colored scenes of places they went and things they did and saw and ate on the many dates and meetings of that next few weeks. Jeff being charming and thoughtful and witty conversations filled with interesting things about his career and the places it took him. The first time he gently kissed her goodnight. Oh, his pedestal was growing higher and higher. She was absolutely lost in her admiration of him and blindly attracted to his handsome self. This noble man, to think that he might be falling in love with her was delicious. He never mentioned love, at least not yet. *This Jeff of her illusion.*

Then the bits of her memory became a darker shade.

They had gone to see a movie and then stopped to pick up some audiotapes at Jeff's apartment. He knelt down at a storage cabinet and pulled her down beside him. He kissed her lightly on the nose and they were both laughing when they stood up. Jeff took hold of her arms tightly and said "Don't you think it is time to go to bed?" Fran felt startled and confused and tried to keep it light.

"It is getting late and I have an early class tomorrow. Jeff, it is time you take me home." Jeff's face looked cold and angry but just for a moment. Then he tried to put on his charming smile, somehow it didn't quite happen. He released his hold on her arms and slid his hand gently but firmly down her hair and the back of her neck.

"We have had such a wonderful time together, Fran. I want you to want me. It's as simple as that. You will not say no, *to me,* my little Fran. His lips on hers were hard and hurtful. Fran pushed him away. The look on his face was actually one of surprise, what a slap to his ego. Fran's look of disappointment was beyond his grasp. He went to the door and opened it, saying he would take her home. Fran said coolly that she preferred to be alone.

Hot tears scalded her face in the cool night air. She literally ran back to her dorm. She felt grateful that no one was about and that her room was private. How could she have been so wrong about Jeff? The sleepless night of confused thoughts finally passed.

Jeff, too, had a sleepless night. Not because of hurt but anger. Why hadn't this "diversion" worked out as he had planned?" He had enjoyed her company. She was musically literate and enjoyed many of the things he liked. Most of all she seemed to enjoy *him*. That was understandable to Jeff. Oh, let her go—the silly little thing. However, his attraction to her was a strong reality. There had been so many beautiful *diversions* in his life, more than willing to be delightful companions and fulfill his needs for all comforts. Damn! This little Miss Goody probably wanted a declaration of love. Well he would play it her way. *Lust. Love.* They were both only words. He would choose the one that would appeal and appease her. But she would give in. By this time his ego was sure of that.

Two days later Fran was sitting on a bench on the Campus green. Although confused and hurt, she was sick with longing just to see him. When Jeff approached her with such a gentle and contrite look on his handsome face, her heart was beating wildly with joy. Jeff said all the things he knew Fran wished to hear. "How could she ever forgive him? Did she understand her loveliness caused him to be carried away? He has no right, etc., etc. and of course, 'I can't lose you. I love you dearly, Fran.'" Fran, who deeply loved her illusion of Jeff, had believed every word. Jeff, however, was totally unprepared for Fran's response to his little speech. Fran told him how she did believe him. Knowing now, how he truly loved her; she smiled tenderly as she said, "I know that you would never really expect the total intimacy of our love outside OF marriage."

Marriage—Jeff almost laughed—that stupid state that he always had made fun of. He caught himself and said he was late for an appointment with the Dean and said they would meet for lunch the next day. Fran understood his need to leave. She sat for a long time feeling a glow. How could she have been so critical of him?

Marriage. Jeff tried to put the whole silly thing out of his mind. He had to concentrate on his conversation with the Dean concerning the student violin competition. After the discussion was over—lo and behold!—Dean Ratchford remarked about Jeff's close friendship with Fran. "Why, everyone on campus thinks that you make a great couple." The Dean went on to sing Fran's praises. Then, with a fatherly handshake said, he rather hoped they might be heading to the altar. Marriage. Was the whole world nuts?

He was back in his apartment for an hour when his agent Peter Norce called. Peter knew Jeff's every amorous dalliance and just how much of an egotist he was. It was surprising to Peter that Jeff admitted to a no conquest. Jeff was feeling the situation to have taken a comical turn and related the whole story, including the Dean's remark. Jeff had expected much laughter at the other end of the phone. To his surprise there was none. To his dismay, Peter said, "I strongly feel, although your playing is brilliant, that your personal image could stand a face lift. Considering the musical circles you will be encountering and your summer Eastern Tour, and with the Carnegie concert coming up, a decent, beautiful, intelligent wife wouldn't hurt. But then again, I shouldn't wish that on the poor girl."

Jeff retorted with a, "Go to Hell" and hung up.

Jeff angrily threw open the doors to his small balcony, it was early May and the evening was warm with soft fragrant air. He calmed a little. That he was insanely attracted to her, he couldn't deny. Nor could he deny that he never would possess her, outside of marriage. Would it be good for his career? Well, maybe so. His calculating thoughts continued. It might also be useful to have someone to arrange the nitty-gritty things of daily living. Peter Norce had said he had rented an apartment for him in New York. That meant there would be no hotel staff on call for all of that stuff. The more he thought about it, marriage, at least for a while, might work out for his good. With a smirk on his face, he softly closed the doors. Why take it so seriously? Back in the room, he poured himself a drink. He said aloud, "Well I guess they have themselves a groom."

Once Jeff had decided on marriage, the plans were set as he wished. They could leave for New York in early June. With the ending of school and many things to tend to, May flew quickly by. Jeff played the devoted fiancé, with loving concern for everything important to her. He was so sorry her parents were not well enough to make the trip for her wedding. He would just insist when they were in New York that she would make the time to continue her musical studies. She had such a beautiful voice Oh, yes, she must go with him on his tours. "He couldn't play as well if he didn't have his precious one close." Thinking back on those weeks, Fran had often mused that if Jeff had not been such a brilliant violinist, he could have been a great actor.

The Dean's wife Marion had been so sweet and helpful planning the wedding to be held in their home. She helped Fran choose her dress. It was of white silk, simple in design but elegant. It was straight and ankle length with a long cut tight bodice, a wide cut squared neckline and short, tight sleeves. She wore one white gardenia, caught at the back of her dark hair. It was a small wedding with just close friends from the conservatory attending. But it was as bright and beautiful as the springtime itself. How sincere Jeff looked when he made the vows; how much she had meant them with all her heart. "Oh, Dear God," Fran now silently cried, "Why couldn't it have been real?"

Soon after the buffet and the cutting of the cake and champagne toast, they said goodbye to their friends and changed their clothes at the Dean's home. They immediately left for the airport. Jeff was eager to be off for New York and away from all of this.

Fran's thoughts of memories suddenly stopped. Her head ached. It was as if her whole being couldn't bear the pain of continued remembrance. She felt exhausted. Fran looked at her watch. Why, she had been here in the yard for only half an hour. Her thoughts had gripped her so completely that it seemed she had been locked into them for hours. She looked around again at the peaceful garden. Scooby was curled up in a contented cat's sleep by the bed of catnip. Fran walked over to the lounge and sat on the edge. Her body shook with a chill, although the day was warm and lovely. She buried her face in her hands. Then memories of the deeply unhappy relationship with Jeff enveloped her mind.

Keeping up a smiling, jovial mood, with people who meant nothing to him, had tired Jeff completely. He had paid little attention to Fran on the flight and slept most of the time. When they entered the large apartment on Central Park West that Peter Norce had arranged for them; Fran was delighted and thought it beautiful. Jeff glanced around and said, "I thought it would be bigger," giving a sneering look.

Peter had taken the trouble to have a bedroom furnished and to have a few major pieces of furniture, as well as the piano in the living room.

Dear Frederick and Susan had the kitchen ready. There was a coffee pot, toaster, china and flatware. The cupboards were stocked with food and other necessities, to make their first few days of living there easier. There was a lovely bouquet of fresh flowers with a beautiful card on the table. This was all a gift from these friends. Fran was simply thrilled, and went on to joyfully exclaim how wonderful it was of them to be so thoughtful.

Jeff said, "Don't be so silly. Fred has made enough money off of me. Why shouldn't they?"

Fran felt her first put-down and, his cold, cynical reaction to his friend's gifts was unbelievable. It made her feel uneasy with him. Fran almost spoke up to Jeff about this, but didn't want to spoil their first time together. Within herself she tried to excuse his comment. He was tired and perhaps uptight about his coming schedule. No, she didn't want her little glimpse of the real Jeff to open her eyes. Fran quietly left the kitchen. She unpacked a little, then showered and put on her beautiful, sheer white negligee. When she came into the living room, she found Jeff, busy sorting his music. It had to be ready for his first practice session with Fred. When Jeff looked up he felt, again, overwhelmed by her beauty, a desire for her surged within him. At that moment, he did want her more than anything on Earth. He drew her close and kissed her hair and her face with tenderness. Their arms around each other, they walked slowly into the bedroom. While Jeff showered and changed, Fran lay on the still made bed, her whole being pulsed with anticipation. To Jeff's credit he was the gentle, sweet lover that she needed. Her attraction to this handsome man and the tender, idealized love she felt for him made her response warm and thrilling. Her total inexperience was, at that time, a different delight for Jeff.

For a few weeks Jeff found it very nice to have her there when he needed her. He was mildly amused by her exuberance at seeing New York City for the first time. Still, each and every day there were more put-downs. Fran was so careful not to interrupt any of his practice times or rest times. However, if he was there, and Fran would burst into song or work on her music, there was always a snide remark of obvious annoyance. Any thought of her continuing voice studies was definitely to be put on hold. Most of the remarks Jeff made were delivered in a domineering voice. "We are going to be much too busy going on the summer tour. I need you to make the way smooth for *me* as I prepare for the October Carnegie Concert." Finally, "You have a pretty voice, Fran, but not a great one, certainly. It really is not important if you study further and why on Earth would you want to do church music?"

Fran knew her voice was unusually good and that she had much to give. However, it was easy for her to feel her talent inferior to his brilliance on his instrument.

Jeff had been living alone for years and never had come even close to loving anyone enough to enjoy day after day in constant company. He was finding this way of living irksome, to say the least. True, Fran did the daily chores and saw to the care of his clothes and all the other little things that made his life run as he wished. But he thought, an efficient housekeeper or hotel staff could do the same and you wouldn't have to smile while you had your morning coffee, or pretend an interest in unpacking wedding gifts, or in apartment decorating. Most of the time he didn't even pretend an interest in the ordinary things of their life together. This lack of caring and sharing hurt and was crushing to Fran's warm and sensitive spirit. Their intimate life had become infrequent, occurring only to satisfy Jeff's most physical needs. Gone were the loving, tender moments. Still, the excuses were made for him. He was such a gifted man who had to be so focused and his stress was so great right now.

One evening they were invited to Fred and Susan's home for dinner. Fran had been grateful for Susan's friendship. It had helped often to lighten her moods during this time of mounting tension. Fred, for all his great talent, was as warm as Jeff was cold in disposition. He obviously loved and was proud of his pretty wife Susan. He was proud of her work as a free-lance writer. Their son Robert was fourteen years old and their son Doug was ten. Both boys were fun to be with and reflected the love in their home. Fred was proud of his boys and showed it. Doug seemed to be following his dad in his talent as a pianist. Fred was overjoyed with this. Jeff seemed to enjoy that evening, but as always, stayed only long enough to be polite.

During the taxi ride home, Fran's thoughts were filled with Fred and Susan and their sons. Fran wondered if they had a child, if Jeff had that special extension of himself, would he be proud, loving and giving. Would he be thrilled if his child was likely to be a gifted violinist also?

Fran was seated at her dressing table when Jeff came into the bedroom that night. She stood up and Jeff drew her close to him. Fran pulled back a little and looked lovingly at Jeff, and asked, "Jeff, what will it be like when we have a child? Will you be happy as a father like Fred is? You know I'm not doing anything to avoid becoming pregnant."

The warmth that had shown on Jeff's face was gone instantly. It was replaced by an absolute sneer. He threw back his head and laughed in a condescending way. "Are you so dumb? There will never be children. I took care of that a long time ago. If I wouldn't have, I'd probably have brats throughout two continents. *No*, Fran, I never wanted children cluttering up my life. I don't now and never will." Fran lowered her head. Her body felt ice cold. She turned and walked across the room, away from him.

"Fran, be reasonable." His words were cut short, when she turned and fixed her look upon him. It was a look beyond hurt. It was a look of disgust. A look that showed she had admitted to herself, at last, the knowledge of the real Jeff. As she silently walked past him, her look turned to one of pity. Her feelings were beyond tears. She felt physically ill. She went into the dark living room and sat quietly for hours, numb to even her own emotions. She heard the closet doors and the drawers of his chest being banged. She heard the loud profanities directed at her "stupid" self. Yes, she thought, "I have been stupid Until Tonight."

The next morning Jeff came out of the bedroom to find Fran sleeping uncovered, on the sofa. She was so beautiful, but this life wasn't for him and he knew it. He also knew that what she felt for him was dead. Damn. What a time to complicate things. He had to have her go with him on the first of his summer concerts. They were to leave for Pittsburgh, Pennsylvania, in three days. Arrangements had been made for them to stay in the home of good friends of Dean and Marian Ratchford. Jeff and Fran had received a letter from their soon to be hosts, telling them how delighted they were to be having the "lovely newly-weds" visit with them. "We have heard so much about you from the Ratchfords." Fran awoke to see Jeff sitting across the room, his head in his hands. He looked up and actually smiled as if nothing had happened. There was still just a cool, knowing look from the silent Fran. Jeff knew then that Fran would never buy an attempt at an apology or a charming plea for her to understand him. He said, coldly, "You are my wife. You wanted to be my wife. Remember?"

"I am the wife of Jeff Amberson, yes. I wanted to be the wife of the man Jeff Amberson pretended to be. That man does not exist. But, tell me, Jeff, how can a man be so selfish, have no beauty of soul; yet, you make your violin speak with the exquisite beauty that reaches the soul of others?"

"Soul, Fran, has nothing to do with it. It is my talent, my superior skill, brought about through years and years and years of practice and focus that gives life to my violin. I don't want the brilliance of my concerts to get lost in criticism about my personal life by over-emotional and boring yokels. So, since you are expected to be with me, I expect you to go to Pittsburgh."

Fran went into the kitchen to make coffee before answering. "I don't think anything I would ever do, Jeff, would help make you a finer person. But I won't do anything to hurt your career. I will go as we planned."

The memories of the following months, of the concerts in Pittsburgh and the one in Boston, were a blur of bitterly unhappy days—days of pretending all was well and happy in front of strangers. There were countless times of feeling sorry for Fred. So often, Jeff vented his anger and frustration on him at their rehearsals. Fred, a very professional person, wouldn't think of not honoring his contract. Fran had been glad, for she needed the kindness of his friendship throughout this trying time. During the time spent in New York, Susan and Fred helped her through as much as they could. They had grown to love Fran and, at first, had hoped that Jeff would be capable of changing.

At the reception after the concert in Boston, they were introduced to an attractive blonde woman who was the wife of a U.S. Senator. She had been visiting the area, but lived in Washington, DC. She was rather gushing about, "how thrilled," she would be to see Jeff in Washington. "How wonderful it would be to hear him play again, etc." Fran had observed Jeff's charming side emerging, as she saw them together. Fran had not been at all surprised when Jeff told her that he didn't need her to go to Washington with him. "No one in Washington would think it strange if his wife was not along." Fred had returned to New York the day after the Washington concert. Jeff, of course, did not. Jeff's rehearsals with the full orchestra didn't begin for four more days for the Carnegie concert. Jeff remained in Washington for three days.

When Jeff returned, Fran and he saw little of each other. Jeff's practice sessions and rehearsals and a radio interview consumed most of his time. Fran was grateful for this. It was getting harder each day to be in his company.

The Carnegie concert was scheduled for a Wednesday evening. It was to be an important event. There was even to be a live telecast. On the Sunday prior to the concert there was no rehearsal scheduled. Jeff left the Hall after the afternoon rehearsal on Saturday. He rented a car and drove to Washington.

He told Fred to call Fran and tell her he would be home Sunday night. He hadn't told Fred what his plans were. However, Fran was sure she knew. It was hard for her to believe Jeff would risk losing so much rest before the most important concert of his career.

It started raining on Sunday morning and continued through the day. The temperature fell to an unusual low for October; it was just at freezing by eight o'clock, in the evening. The rain turned to an icy glaze. At nine-thirty o'clock the doorbell of the apartment rang. "Are you Mrs. Jeff Amberson?" one of the policemen asked, in a solemn voice, when Fran opened the door.

"I am Mrs. Jeff Amberson," Fran replied, as she stood aside to let them enter.

"Mrs. Amberson, there has been a fatal accident. A man driving a rented Buick car apparently lost control on the icy roads and skidded off the highway and smashed into a tree. He was found dead in the car. His wallet and papers seem to identify him as Jeff Amberson. But you will have to go to the City Morgue for a positive identification. I'm sorry, Mrs. Amberson."

Fran's pacing had stopped. She was standing quite still. Her every muscle was tense. Just as she had stood between Fred and Susan, waiting for the sheet to be pulled away from the still face of the form on the litter. She could, again, see that handsome face, all bruised and cut and swollen. She could feel again the horror of that moment—not at the sight of Jeff or the reality of his death, but at her own heart's reaction. No sorrow. Only a sense of release. Had she become as cold and unfeeling as the Jeff she despised? She was silent at that moment in the morgue. Then in a calm, quiet voice she had confirmed Jeff's identity. Now, standing here in this garden, her voice broke into screams and sobbing. Her tense body shook. She knew this was what she had been afraid of facing. The thought that her warm, loving self had become as cold and cruel as Jeff's, the belief that she was not deserving of happiness, the fear that she could never again be an open, giving woman. This was the mourning that had overwhelmed her these many months.

Heidi heard the screams of anguish and came running into the yard. She held Fran close until the sobbing stopped. Her heart was breaking for her friend but she asked nothing. Fran felt grateful for this comfort. She allowed herself to be calmed. Scooby was quite disturbed by all of this and wandered over to rub gently around Fran's ankles. She picked him up and buried her face in his warm, catnip scented coat and allowed this to give her comfort too.

Fran was much too spent to talk, so the three went back into the house. Fran held Scooby and went straight to her bedroom. She fell across the bed in total exhaustion. Scooby jumped up to the window seat and began his bath. She watched him for a little, trying to think of nothing but how cute he was. She finally relaxed and fell into a merciful sleep.

Chapter 4

Fran didn't waken until dinnertime. The smell of roast beef and sage filling was permeating the house. Despite the trauma of her day, Fran now rested, felt hungry. She combed her hair, washed and touched up her make-up.

Scooby yawned and went with her to the door. "Why, Scooby, are you going downstairs? Are you trying to face your fears too?" Scooby went down right beside her; he only glanced at the dog and went with all the dignity that only a cat can show over to the stove and meowed up at Heidi who was putting the beef on a platter. He, of course, got the first serving.

Dinner conversation was filled with all of the exciting things that Heidi was planning to show Fran the following day in London. Fran did not dampen the enthusiasm and hid well the thoughts of her self-revelations during her afternoon in the garden.

After dinner Don took Bryan into the living room to give him his bottle while he watched television. Heidi and Fran talked of trivial things while they cleared the table. By then it was time to give Bryan his bath and put him to sleep for the night. When Heidi had him settled, she suggested to Fran a walk around their neighborhood. She just knew it was the right time for Fran to really talk things out. On the walk, Fran told Heidi everything she had been remembering that day. She ended describing her feeling of self-condemnation. They stopped walking and stood very still. Heidi took Fran's hands and looked with all tenderness and understanding into that beautiful but oh so troubled face. Heidi's sorrow for her precious friend was extreme. Finally she spoke, "Fran, there is no use in my telling you what we know, that you are still the same warm, wonderful person you have always been. You must come to love yourself and forgive yourself any imagined faults. You must know that you are indeed worthy of a life of love and loving. Don and I will help all we can. We hope that seeing new and different things will help to put the memories of the hell you have been going through far behind you."

Fran lowered her head. Heidi cupped Fran's chin with her hand and lifted it. "Believe me, Fran, it will happen. You will stay with us 'til there is a real smile on that pretty face and until you can't stop singing. When that happens, you might wake Bryan; then, you would have to move on," Heidi laughed.

That bit of humor did bring a smile for Fran and broke the tension for both of them. Yes, Fran felt the burden was a little lighter, finally sharing it with her friend. They walked the remaining block back to the house in silence.

"Heidi, I don't think I even saw your neighborhood," Fran said, when they had reached the door.

"No, Fran. Neither did I," Heidi responded. "We will take Bryan for a walk someday and you can look around. Tonight we needed a talk not the walk. Now we'll have a glass of wine with Don. We both need to relax a bit before going to bed."

Later, when Fran went to her room, she sat in the window seat and looked out at the sky. Was it just the morning of this day when she had that strange and vibrant feeling of hope and promise? How long ago it seemed. She wondered would she ever feel it again. Well, she thought, best get some sleep. Heidi had said tomorrow was to be their first day in London.Fran was wide awake before her alarm clock buzzed. She lay still, hoping to recapture the feeling of yesterday morning but only the remembrance of that feeling filled her thoughts. Her spirit seemed as cold and gray as the foggy morning she saw through the window.

Heidi said the fog would lift when Fran went down to the kitchen for coffee. She said it was to be a sunny and very warm day in London. Determined to show happy anticipation for Heidi's sake, Fran said, "I can't wait to get my first glimpse of Big Ben."

Heidi said they would buy and enjoy an early lunch on the grounds at Westminster Abbey before they took their tour. Fran thought Heidi was teasing. "Yes," Heidi said, laughing. "There are lunch-wagons set up right on the grounds. I was surprised the first time I was there. I expected everything to be oh so formal around that wonderful and awe-inspiring Abbey. However, I'm mighty glad they have refreshments right there because by the time we reach London and sightsee a little, we will be starved. We will need food before doing four hours in the Abbey. Oh, Fran, you will just love it." Fran agreed and began to feel an excitement mount. Fran went to dress and found Scooby waking and stretching. He purred and rubbed around Fran's ankles for a minute, then marched to the door. He was now going downstairs again. His breakfast had been put out for him and he soon found it. Completely ignoring the bouncing, tail wagging little dog, he proceeded to eat happily. He was in control again, feeling sure of himself, as cats should.

Don and baby Bryan were not awake when Heidi and Fran were ready to go. Heidi had dressed in a pretty sleeveless white pantsuit and had put a white band to hold her long black hair in place. She went close to the bed and looked down at her beloved Don. She leaned over and kissed his nose and said, "Goodbye, darling." He smiled at her sleepily and said, "Have a good time, luv ya. Gee, honey, you look pretty. Don't worry and don't hurry; Bryan and I will be fine." After another longer kiss, Heidi went into Bryan's room. She looked tenderly at her darling baby but didn't disturb him. She gently touched his tiny hand. She said a silent prayer of thanksgiving for the blessings that were hers.

Fran was ready to leave; she had chosen to wear a full-skirted, pale blue sundress with a white jacket for the chill of the morning hours. Her hair was caught back in a large blue barrette.Don by this time was up and said, as the girls were going out the door, "No one is going to look at the sights of London when they see you two. Have fun."

"What a great start to the day!" Heidi thought at hearing this.

Chapter 5

They parked their car at Cockfosters station and took the short train ride to get the tube. By the time they were getting off, Fran said to Heidi, "It's a good thing I'm with you. I would still be lost and on the wrong trains. What a maze. I loved hearing at every stop, in that English accent, 'Mind the gap.' England is fun."

When they walked up the steps onto the sidewalk and Fran looked up and saw Big Ben right in front of her, she didn't have to pretend excitement.

They crossed the street to the riverside where they took pictures with the Thames as their background. Also, more pictures were taken of each other standing by a red phone booth. Fran marveled at the size and beauty of the Parliament building; there were many pictures taken there. Her joyful response to everything she saw was so rewarding for Heidi who had hoped so much for this. They crossed to the Abbey grounds. First, they toured St. Margaret's Church; it was small, as English churches go, but oh so beautiful. Fran and Heidi walked on to the food wagons, on the grounds closer to the Abbey. While sitting on a round, stone wall surrounding a large old tree, they lunched on hot dogs, muffins and tea. All things were so different, so new for Fran. Heidi was already knowledgeable about much of the history of the Abbey, even though she had lived in England such a short while. Her interesting chatter about what they would be seeing kept Fran from thinking of herself and her problems. Fran and Heidi walked slowly around the magnificent exterior of the Abbey. With silent awe they entered through the massive doors between its west towers. Fran felt a sense of unreality, as many visitors must, at being in such a place. The very atmosphere was pregnant with a feeling of things past and present and to come. Walking among the seemingly countless tombs, Fran was thinking, "what was the real history of those who lay asleep here? What were their hopes, their dreams, and their times of laughing and loving and crying?" So much more was here than the historical facts of their names and times of birth and death. There was so much to see—the marvelous monuments, the sculptures, the choir stalls with the thirteen shields carved in the aisles. The Coronation Chair and the beautiful Lady Chapel were but a few of the wonderful things they saw. The Poet's Corner was the final spot they visited. To be at the very place where Chaucer and Tennyson, among others, were buried was thrilling. Fran stood for a long time looking at the monument to Handel. She remembered the many times she had the privilege of singing his *Messiah*. She heard in her mind her own voice as she had soloed the *Recitatives* and *I Know That My Redeemer Liveth*. Suddenly her heart ached. She felt she no longer had voice to sing or faith to proclaim the message. Once she had sung those words with all the meaning from her heart. Now her troubled thoughts returned. Her heart was as cold as the stone of the tombs around her. Why couldn't she feel grief for Jeff, or at the very least for his music that was silenced?

Heidi touched Fran's arm and said, "It's time to go. You will come back again. Four hours is a very little time to spend here. One has to come to Westminster Abbey many times to begin to absorb its history and its holiness."

Fran was glad to be out in the sunshine again and on to lighter things. They went back to the tube for a short ride. Next they took a refreshing walk through St. James Park with its lovely flowers, ponds, quaint bridges and interesting waterfowl. It was hard not to linger. They reached the square in front of Buckingham Palace. Seeing the great gates was quite a thrill. After taking some pictures, they walked back through the park. Neither of them would admit to any tiredness. Heidi suggested a quick trip to Harrods Department Store. She and Fran were soon on the tube on their way to Knightsbridge and Brompton Road. They stayed a very short time at Harrods. Just long enough for Fran to arrange to send Bryan a Pooh Bear three times his size. Hunger was beginning to consume their thoughts. They went across the side street from Harrods to an Italian restaurant. Heidi strongly recommended The Spaghetti House. She told Fran that friends had eaten there who said it was the best Italian food they ever had, surpassing any they had as they traveled throughout Italy. The Spaghetti House lived up to the praise. Heidi and Fran were impressed.

Getting back into the car at Cockfosters, Fran tried to thank Heidi for this wonderful day. Heidi said, "We are just beginning."

Fran didn't have any trouble sleeping that night. She had disturbed a sleeping Scooby but he yawned and stretched and went right back to sleep himself.

Fran spent the next day grocery shopping with Heidi, playing with Bryan, and giving Don a much detailed and glowing account of her day in London. Don enjoyed seeing Fran behave more like the girl he remembered. Some of her exuberance had returned to her voice, and her love for the language of description was flowing. Don used to tease her that she was the queen of adjectives. Don knew, as Heidi did, that this little diversion wasn't enough to give Fran the help she needed to be back on track and able to move on to a happy life. Don had mentioned to Heidi about a great guy who would appreciate a girl like Fran. His name was Tom Hart.

Heidi told Don it was much too soon for Fran to be interested in meeting anyone. She had a lot of emotional healing to do first. Hearing some of what Fran told Heidi, Don agreed completely.

Chapter 6

Etheldreda had spent two full days and nights at Ely. She stayed inside the Cathedral during the nights. Even though it was still summer, the huge stone building felt damp and cool at night. That she would feel a physical response to this was so strange to her. It was not a feeling of comfort and yet it was exciting. The first night she walked through the choir stalls she found, folded on one of the seats, a large warm throw. It was of a soft blue color. For whatever reason it was there, she knew a caring God provided it for her use. With the warm throw wrapped around her, even covering her sandaled feet, she slept in the mortal way. She returned it to the choir stall in the morning. The second night it was still there.

When she was inside the Cathedral she watched the people taking tours and praying at the side altars. She watched some lighting prayer candles near her statue. Knowing their silent prayers, she offered her prayers for them.

She spent some time during these two days walking about the town of Ely. She delighted at the things new to her and yet, tired of them quickly. Oh, the noise! She thought she would never get used to it. She was still amazed at paved walks, the cars, the trucks and large buses filled with people.She went back down to the River Ouse to see it in the light of day and delighted in seeing the many colorful, cruising boats on the water. She now understood that they were powered by motors just as the cars, trucks and buses were. Like the town of Ely, its river was now such a busy place. It was hard for her to believe that this neatly cemented riverbank with its evenly placed docking boards was part of the very place where she used to walk. In her time, she enjoyed the coolness of the Fens while meditating and watching the slowly drifting water. She tried to picture the little boats or bats as they were named back then. They had been carved from hollowed out trees. The bats with their rough handmade oars would be tied to large round, weathered posts, sunk firmly into the edge of the Fens. Sometimes there would have been rafts made of logs lashed together that brought supplies to the Monastery. How calm it was. How quiet. How different! She sighed and walked slowly back to the calm of the Cathedral.On her second day, Etheldreda walked a long distance from the Cathedral. She saw an expansive building with many cars in the large paved place around it. It seemed to be another busy place with many people going in and out. The ones coming out were carrying bags or pushing carts. She went close to its glass doors, thinking she would enter when other people did. Oh, she was startled when the door swung open without anyone touching it. She thought it must have done that just for her. However, once she was inside she noticed it did that for everyone, coming in and going out. Oh, the astonishing things that the present-day people lived with and took for granted. She found these new things fascinating in the mortal sense. Yet, she thought, as she looked at the people, they are still the ones to be astonished at the grandeur and freedom of spirit and wholeness that one has living in eternity with God.

She walked on through the supermarket and watched the many people going through aisles, picking bright packages from shelves. She saw countless jars and bottles filled with so many different foods and drinks. She walked past large places where food was packaged, cold and hard to the touch. Standing by them she felt the store to be colder in this spot. She went by places where fresh fruits and vegetables were displayed. Oh, so very many! Some she recognized, many more she didn't. She remembered eating apples and berries. Orange balls and long yellow things in bunches were among the many other things she had never seen. She wondered at their taste. Now, however, this mortal looking body that she was in did not require food or drink. She was beyond the need or desire of earthly sustenance.

She went on to the large bins of all kinds of packaged meats and fish. She remembered, from her day, the hanging carcasses of freshly killed hogs and lambs and the almost continuous smell of the roasting meat from the large stone pits. During her life as a princess in Northumbria there had been feasting and drinking, almost nightly, in the great hall built of logs. Etheldreda was called upon to sit beside her husband Ecgfrith during these evenings of noisy, vulgar excess. How she had hated it. Now, she looked at this packaged meat that seemed so remote from the creature killed. Still, she doubted that if she was living in the normal, mortal way today, that she could bring herself to eat of this flesh.She remembered her constant, austere fasting from food during her life as an abbess. She had thought this a penance, pleasing to God. Now she wasn't sure that decision she made had mattered. When she made her transition to her heavenly life, she became aware that her finding and following God's purpose for her individual life and the goodness and kindness she had shown to others during her earthly span were the requirements for her eternal joy. She went on to the milk and butter and eggs and cheeses, then to shelf after shelf of breads of all kinds and cookies and cakes and pies of such variety. She thought of all these things and the countless things she had seen that she couldn't begin to know the use of. In complete awe, Etheldreda pondered how the great God provided for the vast amount of people here on Earth today. He gave his children of this age the knowledge and ability to preserve and fix this food in ways to feed so many. She likened it, in her mind, to the Lord's miracle of the loaves and fishes, no less necessary, no less wonderful. She wondered if the people of today thought of this as she did. Did their hearts swell with thanks, or were they all too busy as they appeared to be?

She went to the front of the store and stopped to watch by the counters on which people put their purchases. The person behind the counters punched numbers at a machine. Suddenly she knew this was to add the cost of the things the people had gathered. Then the people would pay for their things and put it into bags. She began to have complete knowledge of all she had seen. The concept of Earth, as it now existed, began filling her mind. Knowledge of the different lands, the different nationalities, the tremendous amount of people on the Earth, the industrial age, the methods of travel were clear to her. The knowledge of the present day world was being completely given to her as she stood, watching the activities of these busy people. She knew now of all that had changed since she lived on earth so many hundreds of years ago. All was in her mental grasp. She knew this to be necessary. She could only give help to this special person as the mortal she appeared to be. Still, she was visible to no one. Not one person was aware of her presence as she stood close and watched them.

It was early Saturday morning. When the caretaker of the Cathedral unlocked the great doors, Etheldreda went outside and felt pleasure at finding the sun already warming the air. She walked slowly through the Almonry gardens. She admired the lavender shrubs along the walk and the many roses planted behind them. Praise was on her lips for the beauty of God's creation here and in heaven. Suddenly she heard His voice, clearly, in her mind. "My daughter Etheldreda of Ely, today you will meet and begin to help another daughter of mine. She needs help in finding me again and finding faith in herself." Etheldreda stood quietly while feeling the total communion of this mortal world and her eternal world.

There were a few people entering the Cathedral when Etheldreda reached the doors. She looked at them and knew with certainty that the woman she was to meet was not among them. They were unaware of her, even when pushing against her.

People gathered to begin the first tour of the day. Etheldreda's eyes were drawn to the guide. He was of medium height and build. He was good looking with regular features. He had gentle, blue-grey eyes that seemed to possess a beauty of spirit and a perpetual twinkle of humor. His eyebrows were straight and light brown as was his hair. It was evenly cut and brushed straight back. His lips were beautifully shaped and had a kindly look about them. It was such an open, honest face that it simply spoke of the sincerity of the man himself.

Etheldreda moved through the group of people and came close enough to him to read the name on his pin. Tom Hart, she said aloud. Of course, she was not seen or heard by Tom. As she observed him, she knew that this man would be a part of the reason for being here. Etheldreda went with the tour. She was deeply impressed with Tom's knowledge of the history of Ely Cathedral, his reverence, and his most apparent love of God and this holy place. The tour guide delivered his lecture with greath warmth and humor.

Etheldreda left the tour as they entered the Bishop West's Chapel, with its beautiful vaulted ceiling. She made her way back to the main entrance of the West Doors. She was experiencing an intense feeling that the woman she was to meet would soon be here at Ely.

Chapter 7

Heidi was up early tending to Bryan. It felt so good to hold him. She said to Don, "I missed being with him and really hate to leave him for another whole day. I want Fran to go to Ely. It's such a beautiful day. Don, could you drive Fran there and take her to lunch at the Almonry?" Don took Heidi and Bryan in his arms, "Hon, I don't like going without you. Couldn't we take Bryan and all go together?"

"I don't think that would be a very relaxing day for any of us, Don dear. I've been to Ely many times. I think it would be better if Bryan and I stayed home."

"Okay, Hon, if that's what you really want, I'll escort Fran to Ely. I can't pretend I'm not looking forward to lunch at the Almonry. Their tomato basil soup is worth the drive."

Fran got up and showered and dressed before going down for breakfast. Scooby was still stretching when Fran was ready to go downstairs. He blinked at her and gave a hungry mew. Having received his good morning kiss, he hurried down in front of her.

Heidi told Fran of the plans for the day. Fran demurred at first, not wanting to break up Heidi and Don's day together. Finally convinced, this was what they wanted for her, Fran agreed.

Don and Fran set out right after breakfast. The drive to Ely was indeed beautiful and very relaxing. They parked the car in the lot. Slowly, they walked around the Cathedral, admiring its splendor and the beauty of the gardens. Don sensed Fran's quietness and wondered if she needed some time alone. "Fran, I've been in the Cathedral many times. Do you mind if I go outside the Almonry walls and across the street to browse through the market, while you spend some time alone in the Cathedral? I'll meet you inside in a little while."

"Don," Fran replied, "I really need to do that. You are a dear friend and very perceptive." Don gave a knowing smile. "Try to relax. I'll meet you inside at the gift shop in about an hour."

Fran walked up to the great West Doors. She stood for a moment before entering. In that moment, she experienced the same lifting of the spirit and hopefulness she had felt while looking out of the window, on that first early morning in England. The intensity of that feeling lasted but an instant. After entering the Cathedral, and feeling awe at the grandeur of the whole, she noticed a statue of Christ to her left. It was of bronze. It was a newer addition to the Cathedral, a twentieth century statue. The hands of Christ were opened and reaching out. Fran saw in this statue what the artist had tried conveying—a message to modern man. God was here for man in this century, just as He had been for man hundreds of years ago. Fran felt a flatness and sorrow that the faith that was once such a part of her existed no longer. She lowered her eyes and tried to concentrate on something practical. She forced her attention to the gray marble floor with its large white diamond design and on the different patterns on the other parts of the entrance floor. Startled, Fran saw a pair of sandaled feet standing close to her. She hadn't heard or noticed anyone approaching. The woman standing beside her had eyes the color of cornflower blue. She looked at Fran with such warmth and kindness that Fran felt bewildered. The woman was wearing a light brown dress with a small yellow flowered print. The simplicity of the dress was perfect for her. Her hair was straight and long, to the shoulder. It was a natural pale yellow, worn plainly back. Her skin was pale and soft and her features were classically beautiful. At first, Fran thought the woman to be young, about her own age. Yet, there was a serenity about her that made her seem older—or ageless.

Etheldreda had been standing close to the entrance, watching as Fran came in with the other visitors. She soon realized that Fran was not a part of the group but was quite alone. She observed Fran's movements and saw the look of strained sadness on the face of the lovely young woman; without question, this was the time. This was the special person who needed her help. Their eyes met. Fran felt somewhat disconcerted that the woman's stare was so intense and personal. Fran could not know the joy Etheldreda was feeling that this meeting had happened and she was finally being seen.

Etheldreda said, "Good morning." Her voice was soft and well modulated. Her warmth, in that "good morning" seemed to Fran to sound like a blessing. Fran's tension completely left her. She was thinking, such a charming lady, as she returned the greeting.

Etheldreda's accent was British and cultured. The pronunciation of words and the mode of speech she would have used in the seventh century were replaced effortlessly in the manner of today. Fran and Etheldreda engaged in a few ordinary remarks about the beauty of the Cathedral and the loveliness of the day. Etheldreda noticed people coming back toward the West Doors. Knowing Fran couldn't be seen talking to no one, she said good-bye. Fran watched her leaving through the doors and wondered at the woman's sudden departure. Fran was just about to ask her name, being intrigued by this interesting person; a stranger, yet someone with whom she felt already comfortable.   Fran decided to go into the gift shop, where she would meet Don. There wasn't time now to do a tour before lunch. What a great little shop! She picked up a folder on the Cathedral and bought a booklet on the life of St. Etheldreda, the foundress of the first monastery here at Ely. She bought a clever book, *Cats and Cathedrals*, for Heidi, a fellow cat lover. Etheldreda, all the while, was watching Fran, eagerly hoping for another time alone with her; Fran, it seemed, would see her only then. Don came into the shop, found Fran and announced that he was starved. They left for the restaurant. Etheldreda was wondering who this young man was and what part he played in Fran's life? She had to know all about Fran. She found she was unable to do that except in the mortal way of observing and listening and from conversations with Fran herself. Unseen, she was with them when they went to lunch. Etheldreda learned that Fran was from the United States of America, one of the countries that didn't exist when she lived in Ely. She learned that Don was a good friend, along with his wife Heidi. She learned that Fran was visiting them and heard about little Bryan

There was a lot of trivial talk but nothing, absolutely nothing to inform her of Fran's need of her. Etheldreda decided to stay close to Fran and watch for the opportunity to talk alone. Would it be today? She had been given a feeling that she would meet Fran that day, but in no way could she predict the future.

Don said he would take an official tour with Fran. They returned to the Cathedral. They waited with others for the next guide. Coming toward them, through the Norman nave, was Tom Hart. Don had completely forgotten that Tom had mentioned to him, at one time, that he volunteered as a guide twice a month at Ely Cathedral. Don was thinking that it must be fate. After a hearty handshake with Tom, Don introduced Fran.

In such a natural setting and with such an uncontrived introduction, Fran showed pleasure in meeting Tom. Her smile was relaxed and genuine, mirroring the real Fran. Tom's immediate thought was she is something special.

They started down through the Norman nave with its wonderful painted ceiling, and onto the sublimely inspired Octagon. Next, they spent considerable time in the choir with its elaborately carved stalls. There were so very many wonderful things to be shown; each and everyone fascinating, as Tom shared his thorough knowledge of the Cathedral. Fran observed in him much of the quality that had been seen by Etheldreda. They finished the official tour in the Lady Chapel. Even though Tom had described it many times, his face registered a look of sad disbelief when he drew attention to the smashed and defaced statues, which had occurred during the reign of King Henry VIII. He shook his head and said sadly, "I guess it's easier to comprehend the lack of understanding and the madness of that day, than man's ongoing inhumanity to man in this age of communication and quote 'enlightenment' unquote." There was a general murmur of agreement from the group. The tour being at an end, Tom urged the people to continue to enjoy their time in the Cathedral and mentioned that Evensong would be held later that day.

When the group left the Lady Chapel, Tom stopped Don and Fran and said, "I haven't had a lunch break yet. Would you be my guests at the Almonry?"

They told Tom that they had had lunch already. Tom looked truly disappointed. Fran suggested Don go with Tom for company. She said she wanted to stay longer and look a little more. Don thought this a good idea, as he wanted to start home in an hour. Tom still looked a little disappointed as he said to Fran, "I hope I have the pleasure of your company at lunch sometime soon."

Fran smiled sweetly but only replied, "Thank you." Fran especially wanted to return to the shrine of St. Etheldreda. It was almost an urge she couldn't understand.

When Fran walked toward the statue of Etheldreda, she found the lady she had met in the morning, standing by it, with a touch of a humorous expression. Etheldreda had just been thinking, she had never remembered herself looking all that serene during her lifetime. She heard Fran approaching, she turned and smiled warmly. Indeed, at this moment, there was no resemblance to the solemn, majestic statue. "Have you enjoyed your day here," she asked Fran?

"Yes, very much," Fran replied. "Did you enjoy yours? I didn't see you with our tour group. Our guide Tom Hart was terrific."

"I've been in the Cathedral many times and I always enjoy it. I had been with a tour, once, that Tom Hart gave. Yes, he is a really good guide and seems to be a very fine person."

Fran nodded her head in agreement then shrugged her shoulders just a little and said, "But things are seldom what they seem."

Etheldreda was sorry to see this bit of cynicism in Fran and felt the deep desire to help and comfort her. First, Fran would have to confide in her. She remembered times when she was Mother Abbess and her young, troubled novices needed to talk with her. She would suggest a walk together. Often in this feeling of companionship a trusting communication would develop; she must aim at this with Fran. Then, she would have to ask some leading questions.

"Is this your first trip to England?" Etheldreda ventured.

"Yes, I'm from the U.S. and this is my first trip to Europe. I'm Fran—Amberson." Fran never could say the last name without feeling a sickening chill through her. She had not yet taken the legal step needed to use her maiden name of Colbert. Fran saw that the lady had noticed her hesitation. The smile had changed to a look of concern.

Etheldreda had given some thought to a name she would use, knowing there would be a need. "I'm Ethel Fenman," she said to Fran. "I've been wondering if you have walked down from the east side of the Cathedral to the river. I'm from Ely and that is one of my favorite walks. To the south there are farms about. Even though the Fens are drained, there are still some wonderful and beautiful moisture-loving plants to be found. Of course, there is the untouched Fenland at Wicken but that is quite a distance; would you like to go on a walk with me now?"

"I wish I could, but today there isn't time. My friend, who is driving, needs to start home soon. I will be coming here soon again. I feel so drawn to this place. I would love to have you as my guide around the area. It was so kind of you to offer. Could I phone you and arrange to meet when I know I'll be back?"

Etheldreda said to Fran, "I'm sure we will find one another when you visit again. I'm here at the Cathedral often. It would just be impossible to reach me by telephone."

Fran felt a little uncomfortable. Perhaps, she had been forward in suggesting a phone call but Ethel Fenman had seemed so friendly. A walk together had been her idea.

Fran walked over to the metal stand that held the small prayer candles. She looked at them and was lost in thought. She glanced up to find Ethel beside her. "Ms. Fenman," she asked, "do you believe in this kind of thing?"

Ethel seemed as warm and friendly as ever as she replied. "Do I believe that lighting a candle makes a prayer more special of more efficacious? Oh no, it's just a little sign of communication between earthly life and eternal life. It's very nice. I'd liken it to taking a little gift to a friend, of whom you asked a favor. It would be your response to the friend, not theirs to you." Then Ethel smiled broadly, and said, "It does give a very small offering for the support of the Cathedral." Fran smiled at that. Then she grew very serious as she asked, "Ms. Fenman, do you really believe God exists and really cares for us?"

Ethel put her hand, lightly, on Fran's shoulder. Her face and voice showed joyful conviction when she replied, "*Yes*, I know that *God exists* and really loves us, Fran. I'll call you by your first name. Please call me Ethel. We were meant to be good friends."

"I should like that, Ethel. I will be coming back to Ely soon and hope so very much to see you here."

Etheldreda watched as Fran glanced at her watch. Knowing that the Cathedral would soon have people coming for Evensong and that Tom and Don would be returning, Etheldreda said, "I'll see you on your next visit, Fran. I hope it will be soon." She turned and walked back behind the main altar, out of sight.

Fran went back to the West Doors to wait for Don and Tom. When they came, Tom said to Fran, "Would you like to stay for Evensong? I'll be going back to London right after and I would gladly take you down to Don and Heidi's."

Fran thanked him but honestly told him she was too tired to stay on tonight. Tom was truly sorry to hear her answer. He brightened considerably when Fran added, "I would like to attend Evensong sometime and I do intend to return to Ely. Perhaps we could arrange for another time."

Tom said, "I'll look forward to that. Don has my phone number. I hope to hear from you soon, Fran. Don told me that you seem to be really enjoying England. I hope your visit will be a long one."

Don said graciously, "Heidi and I are keeping her here as long as we can. We love having her and our cat has adopted her; I don't think she could ever leave without him. It's been nice seeing you, Tom, but we have to start home. I miss my Heidi and Bryan. Tom, you haven't seen him yet. You will have to visit us soon."

"Give me a call anytime. I'll make it suit, Don."

Good-byes were exchanged, and Fran said a silent good-bye to this place that, in this one short time, had possessed her as nowhere ever had. She remembered reading the phrase, a sense of place. All of her senses responded to Ely. This *place* was hers.

Chapter 8

Tom thought about Fran almost constantly during his drive home. It was so unlike him to be so interested in someone at a first meeting. They hadn't had time to talk at all. Yet, he could hardly wait to see her again. Don had told him that her husband had been killed in a car accident. He had indicated that it hadn't been a happy marriage and in no way was that her fault. Don's point being, that she still wasn't grieving a lost love. Maybe he did have a chance she would be willing to get to know him. She had seemed politely friendly toward him but that was all. He hoped Don would call with that invitation to see the baby soon.

Tom had driven down to his chemist shop in London. Instead of staying over he drove back up to his home in the Village of Ashwell, Hertfordshire County. It had made for a very long trip. He was feeling extremely tired. Yet, he felt a pleasant sense of well-being as he turned the key in his door.

He had loved this old, large, long, wonderful farmhouse the moment he saw it. The house had its beginning in the fifteenth century. Its wide gabled cross-wing was an addition in the seventeenth century. Most likely the timbers had always had their protective coating of plaster and lime-wash. Its appearance had always been much the same as it now was. Its many small-paned windows, now all set a little crooked, the shaped brackets supporting the jetty timbers and the squared doorway, framed simply with strong English oak, had spoken to Tom as clearly as a voice. *You are home.*

The house had been updated many times with heating, lighting, baths and kitchen. The work had been done in such a way as not to spoil its charm and look of antiquity. The open hearth remained in the kitchen and the shelving was left open without doors. Its floor was stone with braided rugs. It even boasted an ancient trestle table with benches.

Tom had longed for a house with a lot of ground, as a child. He had lived with his parents in a large, pretty flat in London, near his father's chemist shop. Tom had loved his dad so much. Jody was warm and fun loving.

Tom spent much of his boyhood in The Hart Chemist Shop, to be near him. It delighted Jody Hart that his son always wanted to become a chemist, too.

Now, Tom owned three Hart Chemist Shops. The original one in London had been his since his father's death. His Uncle Cliff Hart had managed it while Tom grew up and finished college. With the insurance money that Jody had put on trust for Tom, he was able to open shops in Ashwell and Ely. It meant a lot of traveling right now, but he wanted to maintain the high standards that Jody's shop had always kept. His Uncle Cliff wanted to retire soon so Tom had a lot of organizing to do. He wanted to have the shops managed well so he could spend more time as the chemist in the shop at Ashwell. He wanted so much to really live here, to really be home.

Inside his home, he put on the lights and sat down on the comfortable over-stuffed sofa. He took off his shoes, laid back and looked around the room. The room was sparsely furnished. The fireplace was cold. There hadn't been time to furnish or decorate. He knew the bareness that suddenly struck him was not caused by the lack of things in the room; it was not having a special someone in the room with him.

Tom got up and went into the kitchen. His afternoon lunch at the Almonry was many hours ago. He made some coffee and fixed two cold beef sandwiches; he wanted horseradish but found none. He always seemed to be out of something. His cooking was strictly the bachelor kind and the kitchen held the bare necessities. He looked around the room and felt an emptiness here that he had never felt before. It had nothing to do with things.He took his supper on a tray into his favorite room. This large, bright room had been chosen for his studio. Tom's avocation was art. He had always loved to draw and paint. Mostly he loved to paint scenes of the English countryside; lately, though, he had begun painting portraits, recently finishing one of his mother. She had visited for a while after he had bought the house six months ago. They laughed at how difficult it had been for her to sit still and pose. She was always a busy person and would have preferred cooking something wonderful for her Tom.

Tom's mother Susanna was still such a beautiful woman. Her thick auburn hair was just beginning to gray a little; it was softly pulled back in a twist. She had a distinctly Irish look with fine bones and a faintly aquiline nose. Her eyes were wide set and gray blue. She looked much younger than her sixty-two years. Her figure was still slender and she always dressed with a gentle sophistication. Mostly, her beauty was in the consistent warmth of her expression because of the beautiful spirit within.

Tom had hung the picture on the wall. As he ate his supper, he studied her face. How precious she was. Susanna had been through many times of sadness in her life. Yet, she never became bitter, Tom reflected.

Susanna was four years old when her mother died. Shortly after her mother's death, her father, Peter Moran enlisted in the British army. It was the time of the Second World War and Ireland had declared neutrality. Still, Peter, like many Irish men, had chosen to go into British service. Susanna was sent to England to live with her mother's aunt and uncle. Susanna's mother Nancy was English. Peter and Nancy had lived in Belfast, Ireland, from the beginning of their marriage. Susanna was born there. However, her mother's England was the country of her heart.

Chester and May Hargraves, an older couple, were childless. Their niece Nancy had been very dear to them. They loved having her little daughter with them and raised Susanna as their own. When the war was over, her father remarried. Susanna had never felt close to her father. He had a withdrawn disposition, possessing none of the Irish warmth or humor. He was never a man to show affection. Still, at first Susanna's heart felt hurt by his most infrequent communications with her. They grew totally apart during their years of separation. Susanna felt only relief when her father's new wife urged that she stay in England with the Hargraves. She was so happy with Uncle Chet and Aunt May and loved the beauty that was everywhere in the Yorkshire Dales. This, to her, was home. Tom was thinking, of the many things his mother told him about those times. The Hargraves owned a small dairy farm in the Village of Warfedale in North Yorkshire. Being in the northern part of England, Susanna as a child was somewhat cushioned from the full terror of the war. Yet, there were nightmare times. Uncle Chet and Aunt May were unable to always hide the deep anguish in their hearts. Their beloved England was at war. Their anxiety for their fellow countrymen, including some relatives and close friends in London, was too great to hide, even to shield Susanna.

Susanna was a sensitive child. She was aware enough to hate the war. Her thought of humans killing one another was terrifying.

The one wonderful, beautiful thing that happened in Susanna's life, because of the awful war, was meeting Jody. She often told of the day they met. It was a bright but cold day in early April of 1940. She was holding Uncle Chet's hand, walking across to the edge of their pasture to pet the noses of the grazing cows. The farm animals were her playmates. There were no children living near. When they reached the dividing fence Susanna couldn't believe her eyes. There were other children in a cluster. The biggest one was a handsome fellow with a slightly round face and sky-blue eyes. The wind was brisk and had smarted his cheeks to a rosy red. His sweater was quite caught in the fencing but he was laughing, as were the smaller boy and two little girls. They were trying to help him get free. They seemed to be almost in a pile and with the laughing, not much progress was being made. Uncle Chet quickly came to the rescue and Jody's sweater was freed. Susanna was four years old and Jody nine years; but Susanna always said, "It was the beginning of one of the truest loves there ever was."

Jody Hart and his younger brother Clifford and the three-year old twins Edith and Emily had been sent to live with their grandparents. Clifford was six years old and was of a more slender, wiry build than Jody. His hair was a lighter brown but his eyes were the same sky-blue color. The girls were truly identical with soft blond ringlets and violet blue eyes. It was strange how Susanna quickly knew them apart. Their grandparents were sometimes confused.Their grandparents were Joseph Hart, Sr. and his wife Elizabeth, mostly known as Betsy. They owned the pastureland next to the Hargraves. They raised stock, mostly sheep.

With heavy hearts the children's parents had sent them to live with their grandparents. Joseph Hart, Jr. had opened his chemist shop in the nineteen twenties and had to remain in London. He and his wife Janice knew they had no choice but to try to keep their children safe, though, the separation seemed unbearable. During those war years it was so difficult to travel so the visits couldn't be frequent. When they could manage a visit there was unspeakable joy at being together.Susanna and the Hart children were soon like brothers and sisters. They played together everyday. Eventually they went to school together and attended the same Anglican parish church. The parish church was in the major surviving structure of Bolton Abbey. Susanna was to love this small but romantic ruin all her life.

Susanna would always be overcome with emotion when she told of hearing that blessed news on the radio, on May eighth of nineteen forty-five. *The war was over!* The indescribable relief, the unmitigated joy, the village celebrations. Oh yes, she remembered all of this. She remembered too, feeling glad that her father had survived. Most of all, her joy was for her friends. Their parents would be safe. Their family would be back together. The torture for her precious England was over.

Despite her joy, having her friends move was a personal sorrow for Susanna. She loved them all so much but especially Jody. He was thirteen now; she was nine. The love that was to grow was already rooted in their hearts. Always, Jody was gentle and caring, never treating her like a little kid. They had been the best of friends. The day they were to leave for home, their families had gone together to the church at the Abbey.

After the service Jody and Susanna had walked opposite the Abbey and stood on the footbridge that crossed the river. Jody said he wanted to stand and look at the beautiful view of this country from there, one more time, before going back to London. They stood and looked for a long time. Both young faces had tears. "I shall miss this place," Jody said. He took Susanna's hand and said, "most of all I'll miss you." He kissed her quickly on her cheek. Then with both of their eyes blinking back tears, they ran back to join their families.

Tom had been utterly lost in his thoughts for a long time. How grateful he was that his parents had found one another. He loved life. He was glad to be.

Glancing down at the empty coffee cup he was still holding; he started back to the kitchen. The phone rang; it startled him, by breaking the absolute silence of the house. It was late and he answered with some apprehension. He felt relief that it was a wrong number. He remembered then, that he hadn't checked his phone messages. There was one from his mother. She said she wanted him to call her but it wasn't urgent. Tom, however, heard a tension in her voice that usually wasn't there. He couldn't call now. It was far too late. He would call first thing in the morning.

Chapter 9

It was after seven o'clock in the evening. All the people had left the Cathedral after the beautiful Evensong service. The great doors were locked. The darkened Cathedral was totally silent.

Etheldreda walked to the choir stalls to look for the throw she had used. Tonight it was not there. Had someone removed it before all the Saturday tourists came or before Evensong?

She sat down in one of the choir seats and pondered the happenings of that day, thinking there still hadn't been enough time with Fran to help her. She had to know so much more about her. Also, she wondered if Tom Hart was to be an important part of Fran's life. She had noticed that during the tour Tom's gaze was frequently on Fran. She saw also that Fran had shown no special interest in Tom, even having had the personal introduction to him. Fran appeared, to Etheldreda, as one going through, politely, that which was expected of one, nothing more. Yet, there were times when Fran was talking with her at her shrine, especially about believing in God, that she saw in Fran a desire to break the numbness of spirit that she was locked in. She would see Fran again she knew, but when? Her thoughts drifted to memories of the time she had lived at Ely as Mother of the Abbey. She remembered giving advice to Elsa, a young, new novice, who was deeply troubled. The girl's father had decided on a husband for her, an older man, wealthy but rough and vulgar and given to drink. The girl so loved a fine young man, William, from her village. Elsa was afraid for his very life at the hands of the man her father had chosen, were she to marry him without her father's consent. The girl sought to solve the problem by entering the convent. Etheldreda was sure that Elsa had not been called by God to this convent life. This was not the life she was meant to live. Etheldreda counseled the girl. She had made Elsa understand that to embrace a life that gave you no joy was wrong. It was wrong not to listen to the direction the spirit gave deep in your soul. Only in being honest and open with the mind and heart, Etheldreda told her, could one live the life God intended. Etheldreda smiled to herself, remembering the day the girl emerged from the fear that held her.

Etheldreda had been walking in the direction of the Fens. She found her meditation came easily when surrounded by the natural beauty of this place. She had walked quite a distance, and was startled by someone running rapidly behind her. She heard a voice calling loudly, "Please, Mother Abbess, please wait." When she stopped and turned, the owner of the voice stumbled, causing a slight collision between Abbess and novice.

Elsa was embarrassed to the point of tears. She breathlessly stammered, "Oh, I'm sorry, so sorry, Mother Abbess."

"Calm, child." Etheldreda said, as she gently lifted the lowered head. "Whatever is the problem? How can I help you?"

Elsa touched Etheldreda's flowing sleeve and pleaded, "Please, Mother Abbess, send to the village a message for William to come here. Please, I want you to meet him."

Etheldreda had done just that. Upon meeting with William, she had been convinced that his love for the girl was true as Elsa's love was for him.

Etheldreda was now thinking how fortunate that she hadn't been caught; because it was she, who helped to arrange the couple's secret marriage. She also had provided a safe escort, with the help of some trusted friends, for the couple to escape the area. She had sent them north to stay with friends of hers at Whitly. Nothing bad had ever come of it. Always, she felt it was the will of God. Oh yes, there was much more to the monastic life than prayers and the practice of austere penance. There were many practical needs to see to and many problems to be faced at her monastery.

Etheldreda wondered why that event in her life had come to her so clearly now. The underlying trouble then had been fear. That must be the key, she thought. Fear. Fran seemed to be locked in some kind of fear. She was so anxious for another meeting with Fran. Again, she would have to wait. The Cathedral was beginning to seem quite cool. She didn't have her throw for tonight. Etheldreda laughed, thinking the discomforts she imposed on herself during her years as Abbess were far greater than being chilly.

"What am I to do while I wait?" she asked aloud. Suddenly the dark Cathedral shone in brilliant light. An answering voice said, *"You will come home, my daughter, and wait."*

Etheldreda felt a thrill charging through her mortal body. At that moment the physical presence of Etheldreda left Ely.

Chapter 10

Susanna sat gazing at the fire. The flames leapt and danced in the hearth. Her stillness belied her inner turmoil. Her body was rigid with every muscle tense. She had started the fire for the house was damp and chilled. It was exceptionally cool and the rain had been constant throughout the day. Mostly, though, her chill was from her very self. The fears and worries that gripped her during the past few weeks were mounting. She lowered her head and covered her face with her hands as if to shield herself from some unbearable reality.

Was she wrong to call Tom and worry him? She had put this off but knew that soon she would have to talk about Brendan, Tom's half-brother, and about her fears. Maybe she was imagining things. Was she reading more into Brendan's behavior during these past few months than needed? No, there had to be something wrong—something seriously wrong. This precious youngest son of hers—this handsome, tall, slender young man so like his father with the thick, sandy colored hair and ready grin, was surely in trouble. They had always been able to talk to one another even if they disagreed. His personality had been so open and fun loving. His conversation sparkled with a quick Irish wit. Now, his communication with her was at a minimum of necessity. He completely ignored his life long friends, even Kitty McCauley, the girl he truly seemed to like. He had planned to start college in the fall, now he refused to go. Brendan had always been so sure that he wanted to become a veterinarian like his father had been. He loved animals, especially horses. Three summers were spent away from home at a breeding stable in Connermara on Ireland's west coast. Susanna had agreed to let him go. She and Dermod, her second husband, had known the Hagans, who owned the stable, for years. Knowing Brendan would be with fine people, she had given into his pleading. He loved those summers working with the horses and he loved Connermara. His letters had been filled with the pleasure he found in the beauty of the coastline with its rocky cliffs and sandy bays. He had been determined to move there, near the little town of Clifton, as soon as he was through his schooling. Now, no one or no thing that had been a part of his life seemed to matter.

Brendan had felt so free this past summer, so grown up. Accepted, along with his younger friend John Hobson, by the group of older men; he hadn't had to explain to anyone his late hours or nights at the pubs. He had reveled in the songs and jokes with their anti-English feeling. They talked of protesting, maybe some kind of demonstration. Being part of it made him feel important. When had it all started to escalate? Sean Devlin started his militant preaching and forced on all of his friends the hate-filled, violent pamphlets to read. He should have backed out then. Sean no longer exhibited the persuasive charm and charisma that had once held him. Sean was drinking more and more and on drugs besides. Brendan felt it was over for him; still, he had to go on to the meeting tonight. He had to see John. He simply had to talk him out of staying with the group. Part of him hated the thought of this break, for he still felt a friendship with Pearse and Dennis and Michael, and knew that John felt the same.

Earlier in the day, Brendan had come into the living room while Susanna was writing at her desk. She looked up and glanced at his face. She lowered her eyes for she felt like crying. His eyes, those beautiful blue eyes, had a cold, angry look. His jaw was set in a grim determination, making his raw-boned face look almost haggard, for one so young. Susanna couldn't know that part of the angry look on Brendan's face was caused by his mixed emotions.

Susanna tried to ask, lightly, "Where are you going tonight, Brendan?"

"I'm going to meet my friends. We have things to discuss. Mom, just because I'm not going to college, doesn't mean I'll be staying here. I'll be moving soon." Before Susanna could answer, he opened the door and was gone.

Susanna shivered still, even though the fire was blazing. She feared so much the kind of friends Brendan had mentioned. She had found the propaganda pamphlets in the trash bin; written by extremists, the fringe hate groups of the IRA. How, in God's name, could Brendan have been taken in by such stupid ideas. Brendan had been raised with ideas so different. If only his father Dermod, good and intelligent man that he was, hadn't died when Brendan was ten. *Maybe. Maybe.* The maybes could go on forever. Thoughts raced through Susanna's troubled mind.

How dearly she loved her two sons. Tom, her oldest, was so much like his father, her dear Jody. He possessed that same kindness and warmth. He had a rationality of mind and an understanding of other's needs. Even in his own immense grief, when he lost his own beloved father, when he was twelve years old, he was a bulwark of strength for her. He had discernment far beyond his years.

Susanna's thoughts went back to the time of Jody's death. The fatal heart attack was so sudden. Jody had always seemed so strong and well. Her grief had seemed unbearable. During the months that followed, she and Tom tried desperately to console and help one another, but to little avail. The memories that spoke to them from every corner of the home that they had shared with their precious Jody made keener the reality of their loss each day. Susanna then had reached the decision to move to Warfedale, the beloved place of her childhood.

She thought now of the dear family members that had lived there; some of them now dead or moved away, some were still there with their children. Jody's parents had gone to live in Warfedale when they retired and Jody and she had taken over the London Shop. They were elderly and lived until their deaths in a small cottage near their daughter Edith. Edith and her husband, Ben Phillips, now owned and managed the farm that had belonged to Edith's grandparents. They had one daughter they had named Betsy after the great-grandmother. Jody's other sister Emily also lived in Warfedale. She had married Robert Lindsey, who was a partner with her brother Clifford in the Warfedale Chemist Shop. Cliff had not married and was willing to move to London to take over Jody's shop until Tom grew up. Dear Cliff. A smile came to Susanna's face as she remembered him. It had proved a happy move for Cliff. He met his pretty Berniece and was happily married within his first year in London. Emily and Robert had bought Susanna's Uncle Chet and Aunt May's home. Aunt May had died first and Uncle Chet stayed on at the home, after selling it to Emily and Robert. He was happy with them and shared their joy when their two little boys were born.

Susanna thought of the visits that she and Jody had made to "the clan." Tom had loved every minute of those visits. The little cousins were much younger than he. He always tried to entertain them and they were delighted with their big cousin Tom. Tom's love for the Yorkshires had grown during those visits and from the stories she and Jody had told him about their happy times there. Jody and Susanna had each gone back to the area many times during their growing up and college years. Their dream to be married at Bolton Abbey had come true in June of 1962.

Susanna remembered how happy Tom had been when he learned of her plans to move there. She too had felt lightness at the thought of the move.

She needed the comfort of being close to people that loved them, and had shared their love for Jody.

This anticipated joy was short-lived. The letter had arrived from a neighbor of her father. The letter stated that Peter Moran's second wife had died a year before and that he had no one to care for him now that he was ill. He had undergone surgery for an advanced cancer condition. The prognosis was not a good one.

Susanna had tried to keep in touch with her father; but letters went unanswered and visits not encouraged. Jody and she had taken Tom for a short visit, when he was a small child, to meet his grandfather Moran. The time was more strained than happy. They had not seen each other since.

Despite the lack of caring on her father's part, Susanna's heart had gone out to him. She could not ignore his need. Her time was free and in her compassion she knew she must go to him. She agonized over the disappointment it would be for Tom. Still, her sense of duty had compelled her to move to Belfast, Ireland instead of Warfedale in the Yorkshires.

How different their lives would have been if that letter had never come. She wouldn't have had those happy years with her dear Dermod. Her precious son Brendan would not have been. Her love for him was equal to her love for Tom. She recalled the sick feeling when she and Tom approached the door of that dreary row house in West Belfast. Most of the neighboring houses were in poor condition, but some had been kept up and freshly painted. This was not the case of her father's house. Was this due to her father's later years of ill health? Was it his lack of caring spirit that he seemed to have always toward everything and everyone? Susanna did not know. Still, she was not sorry that she had come and vowed to herself to make these remaining months of his life as bearable as possible.

They entered through the unlocked door. Peter was sitting, half-asleep, in the darkened room. He looked with surprise when he saw them. Susanna put her hand on his shoulder and told him gently, that they had come to help him. He nodded weakly. A look of gratitude was unmistakable in his eyes.

As well as caring for her father, Susanna had much physical work to make the house clean and pleasant for them to live in. She was often numb with a blessed tiredness. It served to drive the intensity of her grief for Jody to a bearable level.

Susanna was so lost in her memories that she was surprised when she noticed the fire was almost gone. She still felt cold and worked with it until it was blazing again. It was useless to go to bed; sleep would never come in the state she was in. She sat down on the floor, close to the fire, and tucked her legs under her pale green skirt. She was wearing her lovely Aran-style sweater with its beautiful diamond design. These fine Irish sweaters lasted a very long time. It had been Dermod's last gift to her. It was comforting to have it about her. Susanna's thoughts were soon back to those early days in Belfast. Her heart and mind didn't believe then that there ever could be another man in her life but Jody. Strange, how circumstances change things.

During the second week at Belfast she was in the little back yard hanging clothes. She was wondering which plumber she should call to fix a problem with the kitchen sink. Over the short fence she noticed a man coming out of his back door. That was the first time she saw Dermod Patrick McKenna. She judged him to be about her age. He was tall and lean with sandy colored short cut hair.

The house he came out of was one of the painted, neat and well kept ones. The small yard, neatly trimmed, held small flowerbeds and what appeared to be a young crabapple tree. Susanna thought of the contrast to this unkempt house and yard of her father's. Surely the neighbors would resent the condition of this place. She felt embarrassed to call him but thought he might be willing to help her find the right plumber. She called, "good morning."

He looked across and saw her and nodded politely. She crossed to the fence. His smile softened the firm lines of his manly, well-tanned handsome face. His eyes were the Irish blue that always seemed to sparkle. Susanna introduced herself, explaining about her father's need of her. He didn't seem to be aware of the situation. He told her that he found Peter Moran to be a very private man who seemed to reject a neighbor's friendliness. "I have been in this house only a year. When I first moved in I met him and tried to know him; but I soon knew he wanted none of it."

Susanna said, "I thought perhaps it was your wife, a Mary Kate Dennis, which had written me concerning my father."

"No, Mary Kate lives in the house on the other side of his. She has been away for a week or you surely would have met her. Even your father couldn't keep Mary Kate out." Dermod laughed a little, "even if he wanted to. My name is Dermod McKenna. My wife is gone, Mrs. Hart. She died close three years ago. My twenty-year-old son Matthew moved to the States to stay with some relatives in Washington, DC. He is attending Georgetown University. He is thinking he might have a vocation for the priesthood. At any rate he has to find himself. He wanted to leave Ireland."

"You must miss him very much. Do you have other children?"

"He's the only one and I do miss him terribly, but I could understand his going. He was so opposed to the prolonging of the ancient hatred, and the violence was unthinkable to him. He got that message strong and clear from his mother and me. When he left I needed to make a change. I have taken over a veterinary practice in this area for a friend of mine who is ill. When he is well I'll be moving. There is still such unrest in Belfast; violence can occur at any time. Be careful, Mrs. Hart, anywhere you go. Be aware that your father is not liked, by some around here, because he had served with the British Army in the Second World War."

How well Susanna understood his need for a change. She told him of Jody's death and the need for Tom and herself to make a change in their living. The common grief they were feeling made conversation easy for both of them. Susanna remembered her reason for calling to him and explained the drain stoppage and leaking pipe and her need to find a plumber.

"Mrs. Hart, I'm off work today. I'm rather handy with things. I'll be glad to look at the problem. Perhaps I can fix it."

Susanna started to demur not wanting to impose. Dermod made a stopping gesture with his hand and said, "Please allow me. I'm at such loose ends today; it would give me something to do."

What a small ordinary thing and yet it led to the friendship that would change both of their lives.

Dermod went into the house with Susanna. While she tended to her father's lunch he went about checking the plumbing. He said it was no trouble to go for the new parts and he would be back within the hour.

When he returned Susanna's father was sleeping and she and Tom were having fresh apple-crisp and tea in the kitchen. Dermod was pleased to join them. He took an interest in Tom at once and asked Tom what he was doing to pass the time in this new place.

Tom said he had spent most of his time, so far, helping his mother do the scrubbing, reading and watching a little on the telly. He said his grandfather didn't like it on much. Tom added, "I miss my friends."

Dermod smiled and said, "I'm sure you do, Tom. You will meet other friends but while you are living here in Belfast, I think it best that you stay close to home. If you would like, I'll work with you and help you to fix up the backyard a little." Tom had been thrilled. He had thought when he had first seen the yard that he would like to make it nice but didn't know how to start. Dermod was pleased with his response. "Tom, if it is alright with your Mom, I could teach you to play golf. I taught my son to play; now, he is better than I am. I play every chance I get. That's why I'm so tan even in Ireland." Dermod grinned and gave a warm ripple of Irish laughter.

It was so good for Susanna to see Tom happy and excited. He had been so good through everything but joy hadn't been a part of their lives for many months.

During the next few months, Dermod was indeed a blessing in their lives. His help in so many practical ways and his caring warmth and humor gave to Tom and Susanna comfort and a sense of well being beyond the telling.

Then, of course, there was Mary Kate Dennis, the neighbor from the other side.

Her heart was as big as her round self. Strictly, in the Irish way, she could be mournful one minute and filled with optimism, letting loose with a hearty laugh, the next. She was a busy lady, spending a lot of her time caring for her daughter's children. She attended daily Mass and was a loyal member of the ladies guild that took care of the church cleaning and altar linens. Yet, she found time to drop in and visit and stay with Peter while Susanna did shopping. "You need a getting out, girl," Mary Kate would say. On Sunday mornings she would go to the earliest Mass so that Susanna and Tom would be free to attend the Anglican service at St. Anne's Cathedral. Susanna was thrilled at seeing it. The first time they went, when service was over, she and Tom toured the Cathedral. They studied the fine sculpture decorating the west doorways. They marveled at the beauty of the mosaic ceiling of the Baptismal Chapel. Tom loved all forms of art even at this young age. Susanna thought of her mother's being here. She had only one or two misty memories of her. Susanna had been told by her Aunt May that her mother had always attended church here at St. Ann's.

Some Sundays Dermod would go to early Mass and accompany Susanna to the Cathedral. He loved the beauty of this great Cathedral. He felt a peace of spirit worshiping with Susanna and Tom. He was a devout Roman Catholic but was sickened by the lack of respect and love that was held in the hearts and actions of some of his countrymen. That anyone in this present, educated age, could clothe hatred and political extremes with the banner of religion was, to Dermod, the greatest blasphemy. Anyone on either side of the religious fence who thought their approach to God gave them the right of hatred, injustice, condescension, or worse, violence, could not begin to be called Christian. To Dermod it was a mockery. Often Susanna and Tom and Dermod would talk together on these lines. How much we think alike, thought Susanna.

Susanna's father was grateful for her help and was not a demanding man. His quiet, withdrawn nature seemed to serve him with a stoic attitude toward his illness. He slept a goodly amount of time. He did allow Tom to read to him, mostly history of ancient Ireland and the daily newspaper. He appeared to come close to enjoying these times.

Susanna's heart was heavy when the more severe pains started to be manifest. Shortly before he had begun the time of being deeply drugged for the pain, he took hold of Susanna's hand when she was removing his luncheon tray. His eyes were sad and tear filled. "Sit down beside me, daughter. I have a say to you." Susanna pulled a chair close to his bed. She tenderly reached and held his hand. "I've not been a real father to you, lass, more the pity, my great loss. May the Lord forgive me! You've come to me as an angel itself, holdin no grudge, though you've many a reason to. I wish you to know that even if you wouldn't have come, you had been named my heir. I've this house and not a fortune, but a tidy sum in the bank. It can't make up for time not spent, but it eases my mind that I've something to leave you."

Susanna was deeply moved, "thank you, father. Your real gift to me has been your "Say to me" today. I'm glad I can be with you now. I am your daughter." Susanna leaned over and kissed her father's brow. Their eyes met and held for a moment before Peter's closed in exhausted sleep.

In less than three weeks, Susanna, Tom, Dermod, Mary Kate Dennis and the parish priest stood by Peter's open grave. Susanna saw that her mother had been buried next to his grave. She hadn't known where her mother rested before this.

Susanna was grateful that God had released Peter from his suffering. Still, she felt a sadness in this goodbye to the father she had just come to know. This funeral, of course, renewed so intensely the grief that was still in her heart for Jody and the remembrance of that awful time. Tom and Dermod had both put their arms around her, tenderly, as they walked away.

They returned to the house. Mary Kate busied herself getting them sherry, hot tea, and lunch. "Ya need the comfort of good warm food at a time like this. Ya must eat, girl," Mary Kate said in her authoritative voice.

Susanna squeezed her hand and said a silent prayer. "Thank God for the Mary Kates of this world."

In the next few weeks, Susanna had many things to settle. Mary Kate helped her. She often knew neighbors that needed things and could put to use most of the small amount of furniture and household items. Susanna had been surprised by the sizeable sum in the bank. Her father had worked always as a laborer in the shipyard. He had preferred saving to spending. With Jody's insurance, her share in the Chemist Shop and this inheritance, Susanna had no financial worries, at least.

She was planning again to move back to England to Warfedale. However, she didn't feel the same need or longing as she had felt before her time in Belfast. As the time was drawing near to leaving, she saw that Tom was growing very quiet and obviously unhappy.

Susanna had started preparing their dinners daily at Dermod's house. Most kitchen things and dishes were moved away from their home. When Dermod came in from the clinic and Tom came in from school, they enjoyed those times, much like a family.

One evening, after dinner, when Tom was in the living room watching the telly, Dermod reached over the table and took Susanna's hand in both of his. She didn't pull hers away. "Susanna, I haven't spoken of this before and I know it is soon upon your loss of Jody; but I can't bear the thought of losing you in my life. I love you so, Susanna. Young Tommy seems a very son to me. Please tell me there is a chance for me in your feelings."

Susanna had tried to chase this very thinking from her mind, time and again. She still loved Jody and all they had meant to each other and always would. Yet, Dermod's presence in her life had become so important to her. Could she admit to herself that she had fallen in love with Dermod? Guilt would overtake her at the thought and she would try desperately to think of other things. Also, Dermod was in their lives as a caring friend, not once did he speak of feelings beyond.

Now, looking across the table into Dermod's eyes, Susanna knew what Jody would wish. She almost could hear his voice saying, "This is a fine man, Susanna. Live the life now that God wants you to live. Your grief does me no honor. Be free, Susanna. Be free." Susanna gently moved her hand from Dermod's. She stood and walked to the back window. In silence she gazed at the little crabapple tree that had been in summer green when they met. Now, it was bare and stark but it will bloom and be green again she thought. Life goes on. Life must be lived by the living. She thought of Tom and how he loved Dermod already and was sad at the thought of moving away from him. No, Susanna thought, it must have nothing to do with Tom. Dermod crossed the room, his mind filled with anxiety. Had it been too soon to speak of love? Did she care for him at all? He put his hand gently on Susanna's shoulder. At that moment she admitted to herself the feelings she had locked inside. She turned and rested her hand on Dermod's face; she smiled and said, with a calm joy in her voice, "I can't bear the thought of losing you in my life either, Dermod. I love you."

They held each other tenderly and lightly kissed. Dermod buried his face in her thick auburn hair and whispered, "I promise to try to make you happy, Susanna, for the rest of my life. Shall we now go to ask Tommy's blessing?"

Tom liked that Dermod called him Tommy. Somehow it made him feel that he was special to Dermod. When Dermod would say, "Tommy, ma' boy, that was good," when he was teaching him to play golf; Tom was happy all through.

Dermod and Susanna went into the living room. "May I turn off the telly, Tommy? Your mom and I need to talk with you."

"Sure," said Tom as he moved over to make room on the sofa for his Mom. They seem so serious, Tom thought.

"Well, Tom, it's like this—during these past months—we have been together a lot. Your mom is a wonderful woman—I—I've grown to care for her deeply."

Tom had never known Dermod to stammer like this. "Oh, Tom, blast it all, I'm in love with Susanna and she loves me. We are going to be married. I hope you—"

Tom cut Dermod short by throwing back his head and laughing. "I thought something was wrong when you came in. This is wonderful. It's what I've been hoping for."

Dermod's friend, Patrick Kelley, was well again, ready to take over his own clinic. Dermod's clinic, in the little village of Glaslough in Monaghan County, had been kept open by his older partner, who wanted to retire. Dermod had to move back soon.

Those next weeks had been busy ones, Susanna remembered. There were trips to Glaslough, house-hunting. She had to arrange for Tom's school change, pack all the rest of their things and shop for the pale mint-green, lace dress she would wear for the wedding. The wedding itself was small and took place in the rectory of Dermod's parish church. Patrick Kelley and Mary Kate Dennis stood up for them. After the ceremony, Mr. and Mrs. McKenna, their son Tom, Patrick, Mary Kate, and Father Flynn all went to The Culloden Hotel for what Mary Kate called, "a mighty grand breakfast."

That very day they left for their own house. This house that she now was in; how thrilled she had been when they found it. It was a roomy, pink washed, two story, L-shaped house. It had fancy, white wooden trim around the roof. Its solid door was painted spring green. Its deep-set windows had flower boxes. There was ground all around it with a lovely old, low stone wall. When the spring came, the glorious cherry tree and wild flowers were beautiful as the life she and Dermod and Tom were sharing. Then, joy of joys, there was a baby on the way. Tom was fifteen when Brendan was born. How he loved him. Tom was the best of big brothers. Blest they all were with one another. What very happy years they had been.

Chapter 11

The clock chimed. It was one a.m., Sunday morning. The fire was out completely. Susanna walked to the front door and put her hand on the latch. She so loved this place. It was filled with memories of quiet contentment. Even after losing Dermod, being in this house had given her comfort. She had been at a different age, a different time in her life from when she had known the loss of Jody. Then, she had to run, to leave the place that they had shared. After Dermod's death she had to stay here, not just because Brendan loved living in Ireland, but to let the continuity of life and death and life permeate her soul.

Susanna opened the door and breathed deeply of the fresh night air. She loved the pungent, earthly smell. The rain had stopped. She stood at the open door for a long time, thinking. This land, this very Earth, the dividing of it leads to man's killing one another. Oh, dear God, why couldn't it be accepted as your gift to all and dealt with in true justice. She closed the door and walked, sadly, to her bedroom. Still unable to sleep, she changed to a soft warm robe. She tried to read but couldn't keep focused on the words. Her memories had absorbed her for a while but now, her worry for Brendan increased with every chime of the clock.

Susanna was seated at the small oak table in the dimly lit kitchen. A cup of tea, now cold, was in front of her. She heard the heavy steps on the back porch and watched as Brendan pushed open the door. "Mom, what are you doing up?" asked Brendan in a thick, slurred voice.

"Brendan, where have you been? It's after three in the morning."

"You wouldn't want to know, Mom." Brendan started to leave the kitchen without looking directly at her.

"Brendan, please—please come. Sit down and tell me what is going on with you." She looked more closely into his eyes. They were glazed and his movements were clumsy. He was more intoxicated than she first had thought. She had never seen him in this state. "You never used to drink while driving, Brendan. I think you have had much too much tonight for safety."

Brendan shut his eyes tightly and shook his head as if trying to clear it. "I—I went with friends. I didn't drive. My tires are bad—you know that. Then I walked. I walked a long, long way."

Susanna watched him as he stood in the doorway. He stayed perfectly still as if he had forgotten how to move. She startled him when she asked, "Brendan, what is wrong? What did happen to you this past summer?"

Brendan moved toward the table and pulled out a chair, turned it around and straddled it. He took hold of the top rail. He clinched it so tightly that the knuckles of his slender fingers turned white. His head hurt. His thoughts were so muddled. After a long pause, he straightened from his slumped position. His words began to spill out feelings that were no longer his. "Mom, what I've been about this summer is facing the injustice our country is living under and the injustice of hundreds of years. I'm finding I have no stomach for the filthy English Protestants. They've gotta be shown."

Susanna felt the knot in her stomach tighten. The exhaustion of her body was making it difficult not to cry. With an iron will, she held back the tears, and in a calm voice asked, "Brendan, does that include your mother? I am half-English and consider England to be my country. Also, I am Anglican, as is your brother Tom, whom you've always loved."

"Damn it, Mom, you're not the English powers that be. You know what I meant. Brendan was near a point of rage. He banged the table hard with his fist. Then feeling completely spent he folded his arms across the chair's top and laid his head on them. He continued to hear his mother's voice and sometimes had an understanding of her words but at the same time he kept imagining Sean was there and was screaming at him telling him what to say.

Susanna, of course, was unaware that Brendan was hallucinating. While he sat there with his head resting on his arms, she continued trying to reason with him. "Brendan, hatreds from the past cannot lead to peace and justice for the future. We are just now beginning a fresh new start with the Agreement. Ordinary people want peace and the stopping of this bloody murder that we have had. They want it for themselves and for their children. Even many of those who have been involved in political murders and violence are urging a stop to the way it had been."

Brendan raised his head and spate out Sean's words, "Oh, the Agreement—the damned Agreement might be signed, but there are those of us that haven't gotten soft."

"Your own dear father would be heartbroken if he were here to hear you, Brendan. The Catholic faith of your father's that you were raised in gives no condoning to murder and violence. Surely to heaven, you and your new friends aren't that confused or unintelligent. You have been filling your mind with propaganda from both sides, written by people who preach hate and bigotry. They are unwilling to let go of the past, often for their own evil gains. Haven't we yet reached an enlightened age? When will espousing a cause swamped in hatred be considered madness, not nobleness?"

Brendan's body was trembling. He was feeling like a small boy being scolded by his mother. Sean's voice was making fun of him and screaming in his mind. "Jesus Christ—can't a man have opinions of his own? Can't he stop being a milk-sop, without you trying to talk him down, Mom?"

"Brendan, Brendan—your new flung ideas may be far from His message of peace and love, but I'll not stand for your using His holy name vainly, in this house." Their eyes met, Susanna's were sad but piercing. Brendan's were hostile but in a moment he lowered them and mumbled, "I'm sorry." He stumbled up off the chair and left the room.

Susanna went into her bedroom. Still, in her robe, she laid across the bed. She pulled the warm coverlet around her. She was completely fatigued. Saying a silent prayer of thanks that Brendan was at least home and safe for now, she finally went to sleep.

After only two hours, she was wide-awake. She showered and dressed before going to the kitchen. When she went through the kitchen door, she could almost hear again the hurtful words that were spoken in this room a few hours ago. She made some coffee and toast and drank a little of the coffee but tossed the toast onto the back yard, for the birds. She looked over to the driveway. Brendan's blue car was parked beside her own. It had been gone yesterday, now it was here. How, she thought, in God's world did he drive last night? He said he had a ride with friends—another lie?

There was an early Mass at the Catholic Church. She had sometimes attended there with Dermod and in later years with Brendan. She felt she might feel close to Dermod if she went this morning. She needed that. The freshness of the morning air and the necessity of thinking only of the driving helped her to relax a little.

Surely, she thought as she slipped into the pew in the back of the church, I shouldn't get too emotional. Yet, the fervent, pleading of her prayers for Brendan, instead of bringing the peace she sought, made her nervousness heighten.

Susanna wept silently at the time of Communion. She longed to receive at the altar, the bread and wine, which she believed to be the true presence of her Lord. She had always believed this as an actuality in the Anglican denomination, in which she was raised. The presiding priests of both churches say the prayer "Heavenly Father, we ask you to bless this offering, work of human hands that it may become for us, The Body and Blood of your Divine Son, Jesus Christ." Would God deny the prayer of either priest? Would He not be present in the bread and wine to those who believed and loved him? NO, she couldn't believe that. Why could there be no unity, even at the table of God? If differences of theological opinions of men kept His followers so apart in their worship of Him, how could lesser matters ever be met with unity? It was beyond her understanding. In her weariness, she simply prayed, "Dear God, I'm sure You feel oneness in us and Your great love is for all." After Mass, Susanna waited until the church was emptied. She knew she would see friends. One warm encounter would see her crumbling into tears. Before leaving, she looked up to the altar praying. "Come Holy Spirit, help me to help Brendan. Help me to know what to say. Please comfort me."

When Susanna came out of the church, the sun was full out. The warmth of its rays felt like a blessing. When she reached home she was relieved that Brendan's car was still there. She went into the house quietly, not wanting to disturb him. She saw his bedroom door was open and the bed was empty. She called out to him. There was no answer. Going into his room, she found some of his clothes and things gone. His shaving things, he kept in the bathroom, were missing. A needless look in the storage confirmed that a piece of his luggage was not there. Susanna went into the kitchen expecting to find a note on the table; that was the usual place for leaving communications between them. There was no note.

Tom woke early. His first thought was of Fran and his hope to see her again. Don had promised to call him soon and invite him to meet the baby. It would be presumptuous for me to call today and invite myself, he thought. However, he had a feeling he would do just that. Fran was so on his mind and the desire to see her again that he didn't think of his mother's call until he saw the phone on his nightstand. He put a call through to her at once. There was no answer. Tom began to feel uneasy. Where could his mom be so early? She always attended church on Sunday but the service wouldn't be starting for two hours. Where was Brendan, he wondered? If anything had been wrong with their mom, surely Brendan would have called him. Tom tried to call many times in between showering, dressing and breakfast. He wished his mother had moved back to England. Maybe she would, now that Brendan was to leave for college.

Susanna hurried to answer the ringing phone hoping it would be Brendan. When she heard her dear Tom's concerned voice, she gave into the tears she had been holding back.

"Mom—Mom, what is wrong? Tell me." His first fear was that Brendan had been in an accident and was hurt—or worse.

Finally, Susanna was able to control her voice. She explained about Brendan's leaving and about her fears for him during these past few months. "I couldn't be sure, Tom, until he came home at three a.m. this morning." She told Tom, in detail, of Brendan's conversation with her. "Now, I know there really is a reason for me to be fearful and worried."

Tom listened without comment, feeling heartsick. "Mom, I'm coming up. I would have come sooner if I had known—you know that. I wish you had told me. Maybe I could have talked with him." Tom's throat was tight. "You know how much I love you and I've always loved Brendan."

"Tom, maybe I should have talked about this sooner; but I didn't want to worry you unnecessarily. I understand how unusually busy you have been and what stress you have had organizing things with the shops. Tom, please don't come right now. I don't even know where Brendan is. There is absolutely nothing you can do."

"I could be with you, Mom. I don't like you to be alone with all this worry. Are you eating? Do you want to come here and stay with me a while? I could come though, I'm sure Uncle Cliff would stay on in the London shop, if he knew you needed me."

"No, Tom, it really isn't necessary, dear. I haven't had anything to eat today but I promise you I will. I'll take care of myself. Seriously, there is no need for you to come and I don't want to leave here. Brendan will surely be in touch with me here. Besides, I'm still working at the hospital dispensary four days a week. I can't leave them short handed. Working is a blessing; my mind will be occupied. That's what I need. I feel better just having talked it out with you and I'll call the minute I hear from Brendan or know anything."

"Mom, I expect to be home the rest of today. If I do go anywhere I'll give you a number where you could reach me."

"That will be good, Tom. Now please don't be fretting. I love you. God bless you, Son. Bye for now."

"I love you too, Mom. We'll talk soon."

Tom thrust his hands into his pockets and walked from room to room. His mind tried to assimilate what his mother had told him. Of all the problems that could have happened to their family, he thought, this was the most unlikely one. Brendan might be going through a confused time and talking stupidly, but he would come to his senses before any real involvement with violent groups. Tom just couldn't believe otherwise. If there had been any activity with a group like that and Brendan didn't go along with them, would he then be in danger from them? This nagging fear began to fill Tom's thoughts.

Tom remembered his elation at meeting Fran. How happy he was this morning at the thought of her. Now worry over Brendan and his mom was overwhelming, rather like from heaven to hell, he thought.

Tom began his jobs for the day. He started his laundry and then went out to mow the sizeable lawn. The sunshine felt good and the work was therapeutic. His mom was right, work of any kind helps.

Chapter 12

Don and Heidi and Precious Pumpkin, as Bryan was now often called, were up early. Heidi remarked to Don that Fran had seemed quiet and thoughtful to her, when they came back from Ely. "Fran did say how she loved it there. She mentioned meeting such an intriguing woman who had been so easy to talk with. She said she is going back to Ely soon and hopes to see her again. The woman's name is Ethel Fenman. Did you see her?"

"No," Don replied, "of course, I wasn't with Fran all the time she spent in the Cathedral. She didn't mention her to me. Come to think of it, Fran was rather quiet on the way home. You know how the adjective queen usually sparkles after she has been excited by something new—that certainly wasn't the case yesterday. I was hoping she might say something about meeting Tom. I could tell he was interested in her."

"Don, are you trying to promote something? I've told you it is too soon."

"Well, not exactly promote but it would seem a perfectly natural thing if a good friend of ours was invited to dinner sometime soon. Tom hasn't met Bryan yet." Don made that last statement with an impish grin.

Heidi took Bryan out of his infant seat and laid him the bassinet. She went over and sat on Don's lap and kissed him. "My darling, it is nice to know," she said while running her fingers through his hair, "That you want everyone to be as happy as we are." Another kiss, and Heidi said, "Okay, you win. I'll call Tom soon."

When Fran had gone to her room on Saturday night she felt restless and not at all tired. Her thoughts of Ely and Ethel were constant. Then there was something else that bothered her. Tom, that friend of Don's, had seemed nice. There had been something about him that stirred an attraction from her. She pushed that from her mind at once. She would never allow herself to be vulnerable again. Also, there was that nagging feeling that her bitterness toward Jeff made her unworthy of love in her life.

Fran curled up on the bed with a lap desk. She wrote a long overdue letter to her parents. She told them about going to Ely and her feeling of being drawn to that place and her intention to move there. Move there, she almost surprised herself in making the statement; yet, she had thought of nothing else on the drive back. Now the decision was final.

Fran didn't waken early. She probably would have slept longer if Scooby wouldn't have patted her face with his velvet paw and mewed loudly. She hugged him and said, "All right, my furry friend, I know it's time for your breakfast."

Fran and Scooby went down to the kitchen. Heidi and Don were enjoying another cup of freshly made coffee. They were still in their robes and seemed thoroughly relaxed. When Fran saw them, she knew her decision was the right one. They always made her feel so welcome, as they were doing now, but they deserved this alone time. She felt her visit had been long enough. Fran fed Scooby who had been constantly rubbing her ankles. She put some bread in the toaster and poured her coffee. Heidi got her a glass of orange juice. "Thank you, dear, I'm going to miss this kind of service when I move."

"Move! Fran, you're not going to leave us this soon? You are surely not going back to the States already. Why, we haven't taken you to see all the things we planned." Heidi went on sounding like a tour guide. "There's Warick Castle, Stratford-Upon-Avon, Sandringham, The Lavender Farms, Peterborough Cathedral."

Fran laughed and cut in. "No, no, I'm not going back to the States. I'll be in England, and I'm sure we will see many of those things together. I am going to move to Ely."

Heidi and Don were speechless. Don finally got out the single word, "*Why?*"

Fran shook her head and said, "I really can't say why. It's just that I've fallen in love with that place. I never had such an urge to be any place as much in my life. I'll probably have to impose on you to help get me there and find a place to live. I would like to find an apartment close to the Cathedral."

Don said, "Helping you wouldn't be an imposition, Fran. You know you are welcome to stay on with us for as long as you want."

Heidi said, "I'll miss you." She grinned, "I'll give even better service, if I can coax you to stay."

Fran laughed and hugged them both. "I'll miss you, too, and darling little Bryan." She glanced down at Scooby, "I'll miss you too. I really must do this. Please understand."

"Fran, if that is what you really want, we will start the ball rolling this week." Don hadn't lost his good old American expressions.

Fran left the kitchen to go upstairs. Heidi said to Don, "I've been thinking of that Ethel Fenman. She told Fran that she would see her again and had seemed to really want to. Yet, she wouldn't give a phone number where she could be reached. I thought that a little strange. Maybe she could have helped Fran find a place. She said she is from Ely."

Don said with a broad smile, "I have another idea. Good old Tom has one of his shops in Ely. He would be the one to help. Hon, how about calling and inviting him to dinner for tonight?"

Heidi smiled back, "Good old Cupid doesn't want to lose this opportunity, does he?" Don tried to look innocent as he said, "Who me?"

Tom had finished his mowing and was back in the house folding clothes when the phone rang. He picked it up, hoping to hear his mother's voice with good news concerning Brendan. Still he was thrilled when he found the caller was Heidi. She said she hoped she hadn't disturbed him. Tom told her no; he was just a bachelor doing his laundry, one of his Sunday jobs. Heidi laughed, and then issued the invitation to dinner. Tom sounded very pleased as he said, "I'd love to come. I'll be there. Heidi, my mother might need to reach me; could I give her your number so she could call me there or leave a message while I'm on my way? I left my cell phone in London."

"Of course, Tom, no problem." Heidi gave the number and said they couldn't wait to see him.

On the drive down, Tom had to keep reminding himself that he was going to visit Don and Heidi and baby Bryan. Fran just happened to be a guest there. There was no use pretending, Fran was most on his mind. He turned on some music and was determined to enjoy the drive on the quiet Sunday roads. I can't do a thing about Brendan and this invitation is just what I need.

Heidi was taking chicken breasts from the freezer when Fran came down to the kitchen. Fran was dressed in a white, full skirted, peasant style dress. It was slightly off the shoulders and banded by a deep turquoise colored American Indian print on the bodice and on the skirt's ruffled bottom. Her hair was caught back with a large silver and turquoise gem clip. Heidi looked at Fran and said, "Don't you look gorgeous? You are already dressed for company."

"I'm just dressed," said Fran. "Are you having company?"

"Yes, Don has been after me to invite a good friend of his to see the baby. Don met him when he first came to England, through some friends at the Base. I've met Tom a couple of times. He's very nice. You might have had him as your guide yesterday at Ely. Don said he saw him there." Heidi tried to sound casual.

Fran, trying to sound casual also, said, "Yes, he was our guide for the tour." She made no other comment. However, the news of his visit was somewhat disquieting.

Heidi went on talking about the menu, "I'm keeping it simple. I'll do the chicken with mushrooms and green onions in white wine. Steamed rice and green beans almandine will go good with that. Cherry pie would do for dessert—there's one in the freezer. A tossed salad might be nice too. Fran, will you make that? What do you think for wine—Chardonnay or Rosé?" Fran raised her eyebrows, "I thought you were keeping it simple, it sounds like a feast. Either wine would do but the Rose looks so pretty on the table. Of course, I'll be glad to make the salad."

Fran helped Heidi with the preparation for dinner and set the table. Bryan had been napping and Don had been working in the yard. When Heidi and Don were ready to go get presentable, as Heidi put it, Bryan woke.

"By this time I know how to take care of him," Fran said. She gently picked Bryan out of his crib. "I'll have him changed and in his cutest suit and give him a bottle in no time. Then I'll take him out back for some sunshine. Go on, you two, get ready."

Heidi grinned at Don and said, "Now that she knows all that, I think we should make her stay as a nanny. No helping her move to Ely."

All the good humor of the afternoon and the need to keep busy helped Fran to keep her thoughts in proper prospective. Tom was coming to see his friends and see their baby. Her being here was of no importance to him, she told herself.

The front door opened as Tom started up the short walk. Don and Heidi were both there to greet him. They exchanged the usual pleasantries. Don suggested a cold beer, after offering a chair in the living room. Tom saw nothing of Fran and couldn't ask. Maybe she isn't here today he thought and was already very disappointed. Heidi took Tom's empty glass and announced that it was time for Tom to meet Bryan.

They walked through the kitchen and dining area to the back door. Tom pushed the door open to allow Heidi to pass. He then looked out into the yard. On the ground he saw a square of blanket on which a laughing baby was wiggling. Sitting beside the baby and looking toward the doorway, directly at him, was the most beautiful woman he had ever seen. She was here! Heidi picked up the baby. Tom reached out his hand and helped Fran to stand. Just her smile and simple thank you were worth the crown jewels to Tom. Heidi lost no time in saying, "Tom, this is our son Bryan."

She gave him to Tom to hold. Tom focused his attention on the baby. Bryan was indeed sweet.

"I can't tell which of his good looking parents he looks like; but he really is beautiful."

Don and Heidi beamed, as all parents do, over praise of their child.

Tom picked up the baby's little hand and let its fingers curl around his. He hadn't held many babies, yet it seemed to him a wonderful thing to do. Suddenly, he remembered the only baby he had held a lot. It was his brother Brendan. That had been eighteen years ago, when he had been just fifteen. How he had loved Brendan right from the start. He experienced a pang of worry that diminished even the joy of these moments. He pushed such thoughts away and handed the baby to Don, smiling and saying, "I'm very happy to know your son. Much joy always, to all of you."

Fran watched Tom with the baby. What a contrast from Jeff. Easy girl, she thought, men aren't always what they seem.

Tom and Don sat down on the blanket and enjoyed watching Bryan, while Fran and Heidi went into the house to finish dinner. By the time it was ready, Don carried in a sleeping Bryan, along with the blanket. He stretched it out on the living room floor and, bless his heart, Bryan stayed asleep.

Fran was about to light the candles when Tom came beside her. Tom grinned and took the matches from her. "Allow me please, Madam," he said with a mock gallantry. Their hands touched ever so slightly, when he took the matches. Yet, for a moment, Fran felt a flame brighter than the candle from the warmth of his presence. She immediately tried to snuff it out. She said nothing and went to the other side of the table. Tom would have been joyous had he known her reaction, but he thought, gee—I didn't cut any ice that time. However, Tom enjoyed her gracious smile as they toasted little Bryan, their hosts and general happiness for all.

Tom remarked about the loveliness of the table and the most delicious dinner. "Cooking is certainly not one of my talents. I'm usually on the go and stopping at fast food restaurants. A dinner this great and served so beautifully is a wonderful treat for me."

The dinner conversation flowed smoothly. Don asked Tom how his newest Chemist Shop in Ely was doing.

Tom replied that it was doing well, beyond his expectations. "Sometimes I think, loving Ely as I do, I should have bought my house there instead of close to my smaller shop at Ashwell. I really like my house, though, and couldn't give it up. It's every thing I ever dreamed of in a house. Ashwell is a really nice little place. I'll take over in the shop there as full time chemist when I get everything organized."

"Tom, what's your house like?" Heidi asked.

"It's very old and charming. As soon as I get to spend more time there I'd like to have you come up. It's not totally furnished yet. Even the kitchen isn't too well supplied. My mom visited a few months back and had to buy a few things she needed for the cooking she did for me. I'm good at making sandwiches," Tom said, laughing.

Fran spoke of her instant love for Ely Cathedral and the little town. Her face was glowing as she talked of it. She asked, "Tom, do you know of anyone that might have an apartment for rent? I'm planning to move to Ely."

Tom looked greatly surprised at that announcement.

Fran continued, "Tom, would you happen to know a woman there by the name of Ethel Fenman? She seems to spend a lot of time at the Cathedral. She is a small woman, very slender, very genteel looking, with a look of the Anglo-Saxon English. She has straight, light yellow hair and clear blue eyes and is very memorable."

"No, I don't remember her, but then, I see so many people during the tours at the Cathedral."

"I met her and talked with her twice yesterday. She said she is from Ely. I would have asked her help in finding a place but I have no way of contacting her."

"Fran," Tom said, as he looked at her with puzzlement, "Do you really want to move to Ely, after being there but once? It's a very quiet little place. I would have thought if you were going to get your own apartment in England, you would have chosen London. There you would have so many things to see and do. However, if you are serious about a move to Ely, I might be able to help you."

"I'm very serious, Tom. I—I can't explain exactly why I feel I must go there."

"Well, I think I might be able to help you. I know an elderly lady, an Emma Pickens, who owns a house not far from the Cathedral. She turned her second floor into an apartment—or flat, as we call it. A few days ago it became vacant. She has asked at the shop, if anyone could recommend a tenant. She didn't want to advertise. I could call her now, if you would like."   Tom was getting his first glimpse of the animated side of Fran; that was so much a part of her true self. "That would be absolutely, positively wonderful," she said.

Don and Heidi had remained silent during this exchange between Tom and Fran. Don looked across the table at Heidi, with a smile, and raised his eyebrows. Heidi pursed her lips and blinked her eyes, with a look that said, "Don't get too cocky, Don."

Bryan had napped, soundly during their long dinnertime. Now, he was letting it known, it was time for his. Don and Heidi went to take care of him.

Fran started to clear the table. Tom used the kitchen phone to call a friend in Ely for help in getting Mrs. Pickens's number.

Mrs. Pickens was called. The apartment was still available. Yes, she would hold it until Fran could see it. Tuesday would be fine. Tom told her Fran would be there late Tuesday morning.

When Tom hung up, Fran said," I'm delighted it can be so soon, but I'll have to work out how to get there. Don will be at the Base and Heidi has a check-up appointment for Bryan. I'd rent a car, but I've no experience with the different side driving yet. I've never driven a lot even in the States. If you would help me plan public transportation, Tom, I would appreciate it. I'm sure I can get a bus or train but I need some help working it out."

"Fran, do you think I'd take the liberty of making an appointment for you without planning to take you there?"

"Tom, I couldn't impose on you for that."

"No imposition at all. It's my pleasure to help a fellow Ely lover settle there. Besides, you might do shopping at Hart's Chemist Shop. I always have to be on the look out for new customers. I have to be in London tomorrow and I'll spend the night there with Uncle Cliff and Aunt Berniece. I'll come here in the morning and pick you up about 8:30. I have to go onto Ely anyway. You will have to spend the afternoon there. I can't leave until early evening. Would that be all right?"

"Oh, Tom, you would have the long drive back here. I just couldn't put you out like that—really—I"

"Really—really, Fran," Tom said smiling, "you are not putting me out, *really*." He pressed his finger gently on her lips to silence her reply. That did nothing to silence the rapid beating of her heart.

"It's settled then," said Tom. Don and Heidi with the baby came into the kitchen. She gave him to Fran while she opened baby food. Tom explained the plans for Tuesday. Tom and Fran had no idea why Heidi gently poked Don in the ribs, and said, "Get that silly grin off your face."

Tom hated to leave. What a beautiful time this had been; not only because of Fran, but also because of the warmth of home with Don and Heidi and little Bryan. The loveliness of things—the way life should be—what he hoped would be his life someday. He was thinking this as he drove the first few miles. Then, like a thud, his mind dropped the comfort of the afternoon and his thoughts were of Brendan and his mother.

Tom drove up the drive to his house. This was the first time he felt no particular joy in seeing it. He was just glad the long drive was over. He called his mother hoping for good news. There was none; Brendan hadn't called.

Chapter 13

———⇒●⇐———

On that Sunday morning, Brendan woke feeling worse mentally and physically than he ever had felt in his life. He tried to recall coming home. Finally he remembered walking home. Then he remembered getting out of Pearse O'Neill's car and seeing his car. His hand had been shaking—he couldn't open his car door. Pearse told him to walk home. There was just Pearse, the others weren't there. He could see himself standing by his car and Pearse taking the keys to drive his car to his house.

"I walked," Brendan thought to himself. "I wanted to walk, I felt sick to my stomach." He could see himself at the side of the road, about three houses away from his own, shaking and vomiting and retching until hot tears had fallen down his face. There was considerable space between the houses and it had seemed like forever till he reached his own. Pearse had put his car in the driveway but hadn't waited for him. Brendan closed his eyes. What happened then? He couldn't think, he couldn't remember. Maybe he didn't want to.

Brendan opened his eyes with a start; his mother would be up. It seemed they had a fight. He couldn't recall what they said. He turned over and noticed the clock beside his bed. God! He hadn't set the clock. It was late and Sean Devlin would be waiting to take him down to Dublin. Damn! He wished he had gotten new tires. He hated having to go with Sean, but he had to see John. He *had* to talk with John. He got up, everything in his body hurt. His mouth felt like cotton and tasted like sour milk. He took time only to throw water on his face and brush his teeth. He was still in the clothes he had worn yesterday. Logic penetrated his befuddled mind. He'd have to take some things. Making an enormous effort to concentrate, he finally gathered his needs, stuffed them into his bag and left the house. He was glad his mom wasn't home.

He walked the distance of almost a mile to the agreed place for meeting Sean. It was the understanding that none of the group should be seen together by people who would know them. When he got there, Sean was waiting. There was no greeting, but a snarl: "you're late." Sean got out of the car to open the boot for Brendan's bag. He pulled away from Brendan and said, "You stink." He slammed the lid down and growled, "Sit in the back. I don't see how I'll be standing the drive down to Dublin with you"

Brendan couldn't tell Sean to go without him or go to hell. That is what he wanted to do. He had to get to John and he felt too miserable to go by bus.

Brendan got into the back of the car. "I didn't have time to shower and change. I don't remember going to bed, let alone not setting the clock."

Brendan had never disliked anyone in his life as much as he disliked Sean. Most of all he detested Sean's extremes of hatred. During last evening's *meeting*, Sean had expressed his views in such a fanatical, bigoted way. "The filthy English Protestants" was a direct quote of Sean's. Brendan felt appalled when hearing it. If only he could have remembered parroting those very words to his precious mother, he would have wanted to die. If he could have remembered, all the ranting and raving about the nobility of "the cause," and his allegiance to it, he would have been amazed and horrified. It was the complete opposite of his clear-headed decision of the day before.

Brendan laid his head back and closed his eyes. His head still throbbed. He was still trying to recall the events of last evening. It was like working his thoughts through a maze. He would picture just so much, and then be at a blank. He forced himself to stay focused and go on. This caused even more acute pain to his throbbing head. Pearse had picked him up last night. Pearse had told him John and Michael didn't come up from Dublin and that Sean, who already was there at his house, was furious. They had driven directly to Pearse's house It was a row house in the same area of Belfast where his Grandfather Moran had lived. He knew he had been close to there before. His mom and dad had brought him, when he was little, to visit a friend of theirs. A Mary Kate—Mary Kate—something—an old lady. It was a long time ago. He couldn't remember that last night—he certainly couldn't remember now.

Pearse and he had been stopped at the border on their way to Belfast but there was no trouble. When they arrived at the house Pearse shared with his friend Denis Flemming, Denis and Sean were both there.

Under Sean's self-appointed leadership of the group of friends, their social encounters were now referred to as "meetings." First it had been just friends gathering, usually at a pub, where they always drank too much. They'd sing and laugh over the virtues of the Irish. They'd get mellow and melancholy over the sad plight of Irish people during the past hundreds of years. Now it had become a group dwelling on ancient hatreds, with intent to disrupt the fragile peace. This thrust was mostly from Sean and Michael Griffith, Sean's lifelong friend from Dublin. Sean had told Michael and Pearse the plans he had formulated. He had planned to tell the others at the Belfast meeting. Brendan's involvement was to be an important part of his plans. Now Sean was getting worried. Brendan had made several comments that showed his gradual disenchantment with the group and the more radical ideas. Sean remembered them well. He was feeling sorry that he hadn't put an end to Brendan's association with the group. But most of the others seemed to like Brendan and he wasn't that sure of his control over them, as yet. He considered John and Brendan to be fringe members. Yet, Denis and Michael and Pearse approved of them. With his egotistical nature, he still thought, surely, he could convince Brendan and John of the righteousness of his ideas. If he could do that, Brendan with his connections in England would be useful.

Brendan was beginning to see the events of last evening more clearly. Denis had met them at the door. Denis was possessed of a warm Irish wit and a love and fascination for Celtic history and Celtic language. He had greeted them with "Dia dhuit—Failte." Hello, welcome.

Sean, however, was in a tense and surly mood. He hadn't acknowledged Brendan's presence or replied to Brendan's "Hello." Shortly, though, Sean had gotten up from his chair and taken two bottles of Guinness from the fridge. He handed one to Brendan and said, "Have a good Irish brew; it'll put a smile on your face." His face had a mocking smile.

Brendan took it from the pudgy hand and said to Sean, "I think you have had enough to take that smile off yours."

Sean shrugged his shoulders and didn't respond. Sean was in his thirties. He was tall and impressively built, but was already developing a bloated look about him, due to much overindulgence. With a different attitude he could have looked ruggedly handsome. There was none of the jovial about him last night. His big hulk merely seemed menacing. His look was one of pent-up anger. Brendan heard in his mind the loud angry voice of Sean's. "I don't know how much good this meeting will accomplish. John and Michael couldn't get up from Dublin. We are ready to plan for a major move. Now we will have to have a meeting in Dublin tomorrow night. Not like here. We can't all be seen together at a house there. I don't want any trail leading to us as a group."

Sean noticed Brendan's look of dislike. Thinking to himself, "damn it, I need him," Sean said in a more normal tone, "You'll have to be there tomorrow, Brendan."

"Yes, I'll go to Dublin, if someone can't give me a ride, I'll take a bus."

"I'm staying here tonight and leaving early tomorrow morning. It'll be out of my way but I'll pick you up." Sean told him the time and place. "Be there on time."

Brendan agreed to this knowing he had to see John; he had to convince him to back off. His own decision to do so was unshakable. There would be no meeting for him tomorrow night and he had to save John from this stupidity.

John Hobson lived in Dublin now; he was from Connermara. Brendan had been best of friends with John during the summers he had spent there. They had met in their early teen years and had really grown up together. John had moved to Dublin with the intent of attending Trinity College in the fall. He was living with his sister and her husband. Brendan had gone, in the early summer, to visit John. That visit began their association with the "friends."

Brendan opened his eyes and tried to look out of the car window, but the sun was too bright for comfort, he closed them. Again the thoughts of last night filled his mind. Denis had left the house shortly after Pearse and Brendan's arrival. He said he had a more important *meeting* with his girl friend. Sean had sneered and said, "A fine help you'll be in getting things started."Denis gave a wide Irish grin, cocked his head, shaking his full head of light red-colored, curly hair and said, "I'm having a hard enough time getting things started with Maggie." He left.

Brendan by now was clearly and effortlessly remembering what his own thoughts had been last night. He had been wishing he were spending the evening with Kitty McCauley. He missed her; she wasn't even speaking to him at this point. They had looked forward to having time together this past summer. Then he had to go and mess it up. He felt sorry that he had agreed to move to Dublin and find a job and share living expenses with John. John didn't want to stay on at his sister's home. Brendan couldn't let him down; he had promised and that was that. There wasn't time now for him to start the fall term at college. He had messed up that, too. What was important now was talking some sense into John. Deep inside, he was afraid that John was more and more taken in by Sean's preaching.

Last night Pearse hadn't said much. He had been busy in the kitchen, fixing corn-beef and cabbage and cornbread. Sean got three more Guinness. All three men were starved and the first part of the meal was passed in silence. Then Sean started his often told stories, he had heard as a boy, of his grandfather's patriotism and heroism during the 1916 Easter Monday Dublin Rising. He went on and on back to the bravery of his great-uncle that had been a member of the Invincibles in 1882. Sean had held close to his heart every family story of injustice and of bravery, no matter how misguided, since his childhood. Sean could sound mellow and sad, then proud, then violently angry and righteous. Sean could talk, switching his moods like a faucet being turned on and off. Yes, indeed Sean had that gift. His rhetoric could become very persuasive. Through it all Brendan had been thinking, wasn't that the way with mad men who wanted to control others—to get them to follow?

Sean had finally stopped his tirade. "Let's have another drink. Pearse, do you have something beside beer?"

Pearse and Brendan were clearing the table. Pearse said," I think you have had enough but there is whiskey in the cupboard under the sink, help yourself."

"I like mine straight but I'll mix one with soda for you, Pearse."

Pearse declined, "I have to drive tonight. I'll take Brendan home then go onto Dublin. I'll stay with Michael tonight. Denis will be driving down later tomorrow. Brendan, I want to leave soon, are you ready?"

"More than ready," was Brendan's reply. He went into the living room to get his jacket.

Sean stayed longer in the kitchen. He came into the living room and shoved a mixed drink at Brendan.

"I've had too much Guinness. I don't want it, Sean. *I don't want it*!"

"You're not drivin. I've made it; now damn ye, drink it."

Brendan remembered the smirk on Sean's face when he shoved the glass at him. Finally he took it. He felt too sick of Sean to argue with him. It tasted horrible, strong and bitter. He made a face when the repulsive taste filled his mouth. He could see Sean standing close to him, laughing. He had gulped the rest of it fast. Pearse was ready and all he wanted was to be away from Sean.

Brendan was thinking now, how strange he had felt on the drive back home last night. His body was almost numb. He had feelings that he was outside of his body looking at himself—the self that kept trying to tell an imagined Sean what he really thought of him and couldn't. The sound of Sean's preaching was pounding and resounding in his ears. Then he must have slept. When he woke, they were still driving but his body had felt like it was floating. He had crazy thoughts of beasts and big tigers. The tiger's faces kept turning into Sean's. Thinking back, he knew he had more to drink than he should, but never had he felt like that. Never had he lost coherent thought nor had such weird feelings in his mind and body. Once again he tried to recall what had happened when he got home. His mother was there. He guessed she was angry with him—she should have been. Still, he couldn't remember what she said or what he had said. It seemed his mind wouldn't let surface something so terrible.

They were getting close to Dublin. Brendan opened his eyes and stared at the back of Sean's head. He wanted to scream, "What the hell did you put into that drink last night?" When the words came out of his parched throat, his voice was a cracked whisper.

Sean tilted the rearview mirror to see Brendan's distressed face and laughed. "I read once about a nutmeg high. There was nutmeg in Pearse's cupboard. I've always wanted to experiment with a mighty strong amount of it in an extra strong drink. I just didn't want to experiment on me. I take it you did feel out of things for awhile, but you don't seem to have enjoyed it much. Looks like you're feeling sicker than I'd like to be. I'll stick with what works for me."

Brendan didn't respond to Sean's admission. His words would have been inadequate to express the anger and loathing he felt toward Sean. He knew of Sean's drug use. There were times when it would have been apparent to anyone. Sean used stronger drugs than the marijuana he offered during the fun-filled evenings at the pubs. Brendan had smoked on two occasions, but was firm in refusing more. That refusal had met with Sean's derisive sneer. He knew that none of the others were really hooked on drugs and John hadn't allowed Sean's influence to push him into it. Brendan thought that's one good thing Sean doesn't have a drug hold over John.

The drive was over at last. The three hours had seemed an eternity to Brendan. His feeling of nausea had passed and now he desperately wanted coffee. More, he wanted a place to bathe and take care of his needs. He had planned to go to John's sister's house when he got to Dublin. That wasn't possible. He had to have time to get decent. "Sean, take me to some inexpensive hotel. I'll check in for tonight. I can't go to John's place like this."

"You're right, I don't think you would be very welcome anywhere. We're close to Michael's place. I'm going there to meet him and do some planning about the meeting tonight. He'll let you in—he has a strong stomach."

Brendan thought he must have to, to be a friend of yours. He said, "I really would prefer a hotel."

"I don't have time. We're here." Sean stopped the car near one of the new buildings of flats that were being built to replace old tenements, on the north side of Dublin.

Michael Griffith was close to Sean in age but looked almost as young as Brendan. He was of medium height and slender build. His skin was the palest of ivory with a scattering of freckles. His hair was the color of flame, cut short but with a thick ridge of side bang on his forehead. He was surprised to see Brendan with Sean. He extended his hand in greeting. "Hello, Brendan, it's good to see you. I thought you were going to be dropped at John's."

Brendan explained his situation to Michael.

Sean laughed and said, "Yeah, he stinks."

"Don't be so hard on the lad, Sean. There have been times when you have been none too pretty. Have you no pity, Man? Brendan, make yourself at home. Just look around and find what you need. Sean and I will be off to a pub at Temple Bar for some food and talk."

Sean said, "When you're ready to go to John's, call a cab from the phone booth, not from here."

Michael frowned at Sean and asked, "Do you truly think that's necessary? Aren't you getting a little bit more than paranoid?"

"No, I'm not. We have to be careful. This isn't fun and games we're planning. There won't be any talking over plans at the pub. The damned bloody walls have ears. We'll talk on the way. Brendan, John knows where to come tonight. Pull yourself together and be there." Sean and Michael left.

Brendan, thankful to be alone, went into the kitchen and started coffee. He went to shower and change. The cleansing water felt like a blessing. He thought, if only I could cleanse my mind of this mess and be free of this. I'll talk to John and then be through with it. He firmly resolved to leave Dublin and return home that night. Brendan poured his coffee and got some eggs from Michael's almost empty fridge. He scrambled them, salting them heavily. His body craved the salt. There was no juice but he found an over ripe banana on the counter. After eating that and having more coffee, he felt much better.

He gathered his belongings and left the flat. He would have ignored Sean's stupid demand to use a public phone booth but he wanted to call his mother and didn't want an out of city call on Michael's charge. A phone booth was found about a block from the flat but then he discovered he had only enough change to phone for the cab. He'd have to call his mother later.

John was on the front stoop of his sister's house when the cab stopped at the curb. He walked toward Brendan, "I thought Sean was dropping you. Is there a problem?"

"Not really, I just had to stop at Michael's before coming here. It's a long story."

"Well, come in, come in and tell me about it. Sure is good to see you, man."

John pushed back his wind blown straight black hair. He was the shortest and thinnest of the group. He was close to Brendan's age, just a little younger. The thinness of his face and features gave his eyes a somewhat piercing look. His lips were thin but with an upturn that softened his young face. John's dark blue eyes were shining now with pleasure at seeing his close friend. "My sister and brother-in-law are away. We have the place to ourselves so we can talk for awhile, but we'll have to leave soon and go to O'Shea's. We are to see Sean and Michael there in a casual way. Sean will let us know then where the meeting will be."

Brendan was grateful that they were alone. He'd have this time to really talk to John. He followed John into the living room, thinking how much their friendship meant. They had been companions through so many summers. Brendan felt as close to John as he did to his own brother Tom. Dear God, he didn't want to see John mess up his life. He would have to make him listen to reason; he knew it wouldn't be easy. John was having his first time away from his home in the small town of Clifton. He had always been somewhat shy, now he felt surer of himself. There was a feeling of importance at being part of this group with the older men accepting him as an equal. Brendan knew this, because at first he had felt this himself even though in many ways he seemed much older than John. His own life had included more traveling and he had been raised in a home with ideas much different from those that had been imparted to John. John was raised, steeped in the love of the "old ways" and stories of ancient hatreds. He was easy prey for Sean's ideas.

"John, I've got to talk to you—really talk to you." Brendan sat on the very edge of a chair.

John saw the strained and grave look on Brendan's face. He sat down on a chair directly across. "God, man, what is it?" He had never seen or heard Brendan look or sound like this.

"I won't be going to the meeting tonight, John. I'm backing out and I must convince you to do the same."

John stared at Brendan in utter disbelief. "There's no way you can stop me from protesting a divided Ireland. Shame on you, Brendan. Have you forgotten the bravery of our ancestors? Are you a coward at heart?"

"I'm brave enough to face the truth and to see the logic of peaceful negotiations. I'm sure, in my mind and heart, that ancient hatreds should be buried and forgotten as the rotting things they are." Brendan continued by stating every logical reason he could. He asked John if he hadn't seen the change in Sean, the mood swings caused by the drugs and drinking. Could he not see the evil of his hate? Did he still want to follow a mad man? Still there was no convincing John. Finally he said, "If you won't give this involvement up, this is the end of our plans for me to stay in Dublin and help you during your first school term. I'm sorry but I see no way." Brendan's handsome young face looked haggard and sad as he looked into John's angry eyes.

"I haven't told you, Brendan, but your help won't be needed. I'm not entering Trinity this session, or ever. I've got a job and can manage on my own. I'll be moving from here into Mike Griffith's place tomorrow. The

Invincibles II, that's our official name now, is going to be very busy this fall. I don't know yet what Sean has in mind. But it's big. That will be discussed at the meeting tonight."

"Do you remember, John, that the Invincibles of 1882 was a small group of rebels who were all killed and achieved nothing? Did Sean mention that in the stories about his great-uncle?"

John looked at Brendan like he hated him but made no reply.

"I'm leaving now, John." Brendan walked toward the door and picked up his bag. He opened the door and looked back at John, who was still standing at the other side of the room. Brendan felt hurt all through when he saw the look of disdain on his dear friend's face. He shook his head sadly, "My friend, God help you before it's too late." Brendan closed the door quietly behind him.

Despite his angry determination to ignore Brendan's pleading, John's thin frame shook with sadness and confusion. He felt even younger than he was. He was vulnerable to the hurt of losing his friend's caring and respect. Also, he was feeling fear that he was set on a dangerous course. "They were right, weren't they, Sean and the friends?" They were brave and the cause a noble one. They weren't really going to hurt anybody. Something would be done in a way to upset the bloody English and let them know the hearts of young Irish people still had fight in them. That's all they really wanted. No, he wouldn't back out.

John left the house to go where Sean had told him. When he was close to O'Shea's, at Temple Bar, he thought of Sean's face and the anger he'd show on learning of Brendan's decision. Again, he felt fear—fear for Brendan and for himself.

When they were in the car Michael asked, "Where are we headed, Sean, O'Connell's?"

"Not O'Connell's, we've been seen there too much. I've told the others to meet at O'Shea's. We'll blend with the crowd there and don't have to act too chummy. We'll do our talking later. Right now I'm starved and O'Shea's has good substantial Irish food." Sean and Michael had been served their dinner when Denis and Pearse arrived. They merely nodded a greeting and sat at another table.

Sean began ordering whiskey straight up and Michael lingered over his pint of stout after their meal. Making light conversation, they blended well with the local and tourist trade. However, Sean was aware of the time and was feeling impatient that Brendan and John had not arrived.

When John came in alone, looking worried and upset, he went immediately to Sean and Michael's table.

Sean, not feeling the least bit humorous, gave John a big smile. "Well, hello there. Sit down, my lad, sit down." When an amazed John sat down, Sean said, still smiling through gritted teeth, in a sotto voice, "order something to eat. Don't leave with the others or us. Meet casually outside the passage at Merchants Arch." Sean and Michael stood and Sean pleasantly said, "Enjoy your dinner, Lad," and left.

Sean said nothing as they walked down the newly cobbled streets. He made a pretense of looking at the shops in the eighteenth century buildings. He was so determined to blend with the crowd that Michael laughed and said, "Your acting is getting to me, Sean; I'm finding your cloak and dagger routine a little silly."

It was near dark when they were at the Merchants Arch. Denis and Pearse came soon after. In a short while John arrived. Sean said to the others, "Separate and go across the Ha' Penny bridge, and then hang around. We'll meet there." Sean held John's elbow in an iron grip. "You wait with me." When the others were out of sight he released his hold. As they walked, he asked, "Where the hell is Brendan? What's happened?"

John saw the anger in Sean's face. He felt a lump in his stomach. The sandwich he had just eaten felt like lead. He was about to answer—

Sean growled, "Speak up, you know something, you young twerp."

"Brendan is backing out. He wouldn't come tonight. He doesn't want to be one of us, that's all there is to it. I guess he's going home."

"That's all there is to it? Like hell, that's all there is to it. A damned informer he'll be. It's too late for the bloody yellow slime to back out now."

John spoke up, "Sean, he really doesn't know much of what is planned. Had he come to tonight's meeting and found out more, it could have been much worse."

"He knows enough, blast him. He'll not be goin home or anywhere." Sean was restraining his voice. In truth, he wanted to scream. His impotent rage was not at the fear of Brendan's knowing too much, but at the reality that he—Sean Devlin—couldn't control him.

When they reached the others, Sean told Denis and Pearse, "Drop this skinny kid at his sister's. There can be no meeting tonight. You might as well go back to Belfast." Turning to Michael he said, "You come with me."

They headed back to where Sean had parked his car. He tossed the keys to Michael and said, "You'll drive." He told Michael of Brendan's back out and of his intention to return home.

Michael expressed similar thoughts to John's.

Sean, again almost exploded with anger, "Use your bloody, muddled mind. He could inform on us with what he does know. I'm not taking any chances. Head to the busaras and make it fast."

When they reached the busaras, a bus was boarding for Dundalk, the stop nearest Brendan's home. Brendan had decided to take this bus that far and call his mother from there if he couldn't make other connections.

Sean saw Brendan at the end of the boarding line. "Michael, stay with the car." He got out and ran toward the bus. The motor of the bus was already running. Sean thudded into Brendan's back. He shoved his pocketed gun tightly into Brendan's ribs, "You're goin nowhere, you slimy sneak."

Brendan's first reaction was to kick at Sean and get away. Sean grabbed his arm and pushed the gun harder at his back. The people ahead, noticing what seemed to be the starting of a fight, hurried into the bus. The driver got up from his seat, "Hurry, man, I'm ready to go." He s saw the terrified look on Brendan's face. "Are you all right? Be there a problem?"

Brendan felt another push of the gun and smelled Sean's breath, strong of whiskey. He knew that, as maddened as Sean was at this moment, the threat was not an idle one; even though there would be no escape for Sean. "I've changed my mind; I won't be taking the bus." The driver stood for a moment with a concerned look. Brendan knew he couldn't take the risk and said, "Everything is all right. I've just changed my mind." Sean stepped back a little but the gun was still at Brendan's back. Brendan picked up his bag. The driver returned to his seat and closed the door. The bus was gone.

"Don't try to make a run for it. Michael is in the car. We'll walk over easy and you'll get in the back, understand? Answer me, damn you." Brendan looked full on at Sean; he wouldn't deign to answer him, even if Sean killed him on this very spot. His loathing superseded his fear.

They reached the car and Brendan opened the back door. He got in himself not wanting the feel of Sean's hand touching him. Sean was beside him; the gun was now in full view. "Drive the car to a deserted spot," he ordered Michael, "and make it quick."

They drove a short distance to a dark alley behind some deserted, ready to be demolished, row houses. Sean kept the gun pointed at Brendan while he slowly got out of the car. He stood at the open door glaring down at Brendan. At this point Brendan thought Sean was going to kill him there and then. Sean kept his voice low, "Michael, get some rope from the boot."

"Come now, Sean, I don't think that's necessary."

"Don't argue; I'm not taking any chances. Get the rope."

Brendan's hands and feet were tied and his forearms tightly to his body. Satisfied that Brendan couldn't try anything, Sean slammed the door and got into the front seat of the car. Michael said, before closing the other rear door, "I'm sorry, Brendan. He has a lot in him right now. When it wears off he'll be more reasonable. We'll work this out."

Brendan made no reply. He knew there would be no change for the better in Sean, concerning him.

Michael got into the drivers seat. "Where to, my flat or yours, Sean?"

"Hell no! We're takin him to my Uncle Jack's abandoned place near Maynooth. Go North-West, take N.4."

"I know the way. Sean, I've been there, remember? It's quite a piece away, and I have to work tomorrow, man."

"There is no choice. You can turn around and drive back tonight. I'll stay with this monkey till I figure what to do. I'll call you to come for me." The drugs and whiskey overtook Sean and he fell into a loud snoring sleep, which continued until they reached the dilapidated place.

The long, low cottage was of whitewashed stone. Now the wash was almost completely gone, peeled and worn by the weather. The once red painted door was as rough and worn as the slab that held the stones above it. A room on one side was partly caved in along with its thatched roof. However, the other part with its rusted tin roof remained waterproof and usable. The place was built upon stony, uneven earth at the base of a hilly ridge.

Michael had to shake Sean awake when he stopped the car. It was a dark night and Michael got a torch from the boot. Sean was groggy and unsteady on his feet. He ordered Michael to get Brendan inside. Michael said, "First I'll be getting you inside." He pushed Sean inside and onto a cot. He flashed his light around and saw a kerosene lamp on the table; finding some matches in his pocket, he lit it. The glow of the light revealed a couple of old straight chairs and a few basic needs for existence. There were blankets on the bottom of the cot. Sean had stayed here occasionally. Sean's bicycle with a basket attached was leaning against a wall. There was a hearth but no wood or coal to build a fire. The old one door cupboard revealed a few dishes and pans but no stock of food. The place was very cold and damp.

Michael untied Brendan's feet enough to hobble. Once inside, he pushed a small chair in Brendan's direction. Michael tightened the rope then tied a piece of rope securely to the chair. "There would be hell to pay if you made a break for it. Maybe he will be more reasonable tomorrow." Brendan still remained silent.

Michael threw a blanket over the sleeping Sean and tucked one around Brendan, saying, "This damned place isn't fit to be in." He placed his cell phone and torch by the cot and left.

Chapter 14

The next morning, when Sean woke, it took a few minutes for last night's happenings to surface in his mind. He looked at the still tied Brendan with disgust. He went out of the cottage and to the back of it and relieved himself. Returning to the cottage he was hoping to find a bottle of water, but there was none. It had been a long time since he had been here. The old well was dry; the pump hadn't worked for years. He felt into his pocket for gum or something and found one cough drop—anything would be better than the taste in his mouth. He growled at Brendan, "Do you need to go outside? This guesthouse doesn't have a toilet inside—or outside for that matter." He laughed at his own joke.

Brendan looked at Sean and thought, how could I have been taken in by this man and what he preached? Of course, Sean had appeared so different when he first met him. Sean's ongoing drug use and over drinking had all but demolished the persuasive charm that he had once possessed. His mean and hateful side was now fully exposed. His physical appearance had changed too. The florid pudginess of his face was more visible each day.

"Answer, do you need to go out?"

Brendan nodded his head, yes, and tried to stand. Sean untied the ropes from around the chair. Brendan's arms were still tied across his chest and his hands and feet bound so tightly that the ropes cut into his skin. Sean loosened the ankle ropes enough for Brendan to move slowly. When they finally reached the back of the cottage, Brendan tried to fumble with his tied hands to undo his pants. Sean roared with laughter. This lack of personal dignity during this necessity was almost unbearable to Brendan. He was wishing Sean had shot him last night.

Back inside, Sean tied Brendan again to the chair. He inspected his bicycle. The tires seemed fine. It would do for the trip to the little town of Maynooth.

Sean thought, as he was going down the dirt road, he'd better call the boat building and repair business where he was to work this week, and tell them he wouldn't be in. He worked there off and on. This fine business had once belonged to his father. It could have been his, but when his father died, he sold it. Sean's mother had been dead for many years and Sean had been the only heir. He hadn't wanted the responsibility of the business and with the money he got from the sale and what else his father had left him, he had no money worries, at least for a long while.

He could devote all his time to the cause—his cause. However, he did like working with boats and knew them inside and out. It was said, "no one knew more about boats than Sean Devlin." He kept his own boat. She was a medium-sized cruiser—a real beauty! Having his boat would help him in carrying out his plans.

His plans—he had them all worked out, now he'd have to make some changes. Damn them—the others—they didn't seem to him to be as committed as they should have been, Michael and Pearse maybe, perhaps Denis. John seemed to be, but he was so young, a bit wet behind the ears, but easily controlled; that was a good thing. John might come in handy. Then his thoughts turned to Brendan. If only there wasn't this damned mess with him. What to do with him? Could they keep him hidden at the cottage for a few more weeks? Would threatening to harm his family make Brendan keep his mouth shut if he left him go free? Should he shoot him now and bury him deep at the back of the cottage. No one was ever around. No, not at this moment, since he was not completely mad with drugs or drink, did he think he could do that. Unless Brendan tried to escape before he knew what to do with him—maybe he could kill him, then. Trying to keep him hidden would be best, but how? Sean had planned to use the cottage as a place for Pearse to come to make the bombs. The bloody fool couldn't be kept there.

Sean reached the town of Maynooth and locked his bike outside a small pub. His first need was to use the rest room to wash his face and rinse his mouth. He tried vainly to get a little more presentable. He ordered coffee, eggs and potatoes and bacon, then a pint of beer before he left. He went into a small general store and bought a shirt and some under things for himself. He got some bottled water, a pound of coffee, bread and sliced ham and cheese, all that the bicycle basket would hold. His final purchase was three bottles of whiskey. He made room for that.

All the mental agony and physical discomfort didn't stop Brendan from feeling hungry and thirsty. He hadn't eaten or had anything to drink since the afternoon before, at Michael's flat. He was feeling weak, his head was hurting, and there was absolutely no way he could free himself. Had Sean just left him to die? His thoughts were of his mother and the worry she must be going through. He started to pray, something he hadn't done for a very long time. His parched lips mumbled through the Hail Mary—his heart cried, oh, Dear God, help me.

Sean came back, having been gone several hours. He put his purchases on the little table and gave Brendan a contemptuous look. "Aren't you the man of leisure sitting around all day?" He went back outside and brought some wood for starting a fire on the hearth. He placed an iron grill, with legs, on top of the fire. He poured some of the bottled water into an old tin percolator added the coffee and placed it on the grill.

Brendan so wanted the water, it broke his reserve, "Sean, may I please have some water?"

"Look—saints be praised—it can talk," Sean said, with a sneering grin. He poured a small glass and placed it in Brendan's tied hands and laughed watching the effort it took Brendan to bring it to his mouth.

Brendan was beyond caring about Sean. The water tasted wonderful. In his heart he said, Thank You, God.

Sean opened the whiskey and swigged it from the bottle while making ham sandwiches. He pushed one into Brendan's hands. Even from Sean's hands, Brendan was grateful. The fire was giving the cold room a little heat and soon the smell of coffee was masking the musty odor. Funny, Brendan thought, how good a small thing can be. He knew, if he ever got out of this, he would never again take for granted the ordinary creature comforts. Never again would he take for granted his loving mother and family and the beauty and goodness that had surrounded him, all of his life, until now. Sean put the mug of hot, strong coffee in Brendan's hands. He took his own and went outside. Brendan was glad to enjoy this without Sean's presence.

Sean returned with more wood to keep up the fire. This effort was for his comfort not Brendan's. At best the room was far from warm. Sean again checked Brendan's ropes in case the movement in eating loosened them. This time of nothing to do was really getting to Sean. Every time he looked at Brendan he hated him more. He hated him for all the things that were going wrong with his plans, and now, because of this miserable inconvenience.

Sean flung open the door, he'd take a walk around but his legs ached from the long bike ride. His bicycle—he looked at it and thought to bring it inside, the sky looked rather cloudy. Having done that, he grabbed his bottle of whiskey and drank most of it. He lay down on the cot and gave in to the boredom and liquor induced tiredness and slept for a short while. When he woke, he angrily paced about the cold room, threw some logs on the dying fire and finished off the bottle. He sat down on the edge of the cot, hunched over with his hands spread on his knees, and stared at Brendan. "I don't know yet what I'm going to do with you, you turncoat. You're a mighty disappointment to me. I shoulda known better than ta trust ye." Sean's speech was beginning to slur. "Ye with your English blood. I'd plans fer ye, with your English connections." Sean, certain that Brendan would never get away from him, kept on talking. "That Cathedral ye talked about, the one yer brother spends sa much time at—the one in Ely." Sean rocked his body from side to side with a look on his face like he was savoring each word he uttered. "Yerself talked about how they have a harvest time in early October—and how they take big flowers and bundles of wheat inside to decorate the pillars. Well, this year there is to be a surprise—in the pretty bundles, Sean Devlin will see to that. It would have been easier with ye havin the trust of yer brother, getting the surprise in the bundles, it'll be harder ta figure now—but it's goin to happen just the same."

A look of total disbelief and horror registered on Brendan's face. "Dear God, Man! You are completely *mad*. How could you imagine that I'd betray my brother's trust, in anyway. To bomb a place of worship is unthinkable? I thought when we had talked of protest we were speaking of organizing marches or demonstrations near the border, not bombs and vile destruction. You are *sick*, you should get help. There is *no* feel in me for *your cause*. It's evil—it's *stupid*!"

Hearing Brendan's reply enraged Sean to the point of no control. He lunged at Brendan. He beat his face and head with his big hands, over and over and over, until Brendan's face was swollen, bloodied and bruised. His nose was bleeding. Blood filled his mouth and ran down his torn lips. His eyes swelled shut and his head was exploding in pain. Brendan was silent through it all. Sean wouldn't have the pleasure of hearing his screams. With the final blows, Brendan lost consciousness.

Sean sat on the cot and buried his face in those big reddened and bruised hands. Hot tears of rage, remorse, and uncontrollable sadness came with a deep groan from his throat. "You're like him. You're just like him—my brother—my younger brother. His name was Dillon. He was all for talkin peace. Doin positive things to promote peace, That was his preaching. He moved up to Belfast and started in helpin at a youth recreation place, for both the Protestant and the Catholic kids. Some peace-lovin priest's idea." Sean spat on the floor. "Well, Dillon was walkin to his flat one night. There had been a bit of trouble, a bit of bombing and some windows broken by some IRA fringe group; the bloody English soldiers were after them. My brother just got in the way of it all. They didn't ask any questions—they just shot him." All the years of anger, at the English—and at his brother—and the grief at the loss of him, colored his words.

Had Brendan heard Sean, he might have had some understanding of him and maybe, just maybe, a little pity. He heard nothing of what Sean had said.

Sean didn't even look at Brendan. Totally spent, he stretched out on the cot and slept.

It was morning when Sean woke. He looked at the still unconscious Brendan. For a moment he studied him closely, thinking he might be dead. Brendan's breathing was so shallow. Sean was wishing he had died. It would have been a problem solved. He looked down at Brendan again thinking, no such luck; he's young and strong, he'll make it. He shrugged his shoulders and crossed the room to build another fire, then made coffee and a sandwich for himself.

Sean took his sandwich to the door. He needed to be out of this place, away from looking at that battered, blood-smeared face. It had started to rain hard. "Damn, I feel like a prisoner myself." Sean slammed the door and paced the room like a caged lion. Damn Michael, he wouldn't come with Sean's car and take a turn here with Brendan 'til tomorrow night. Sean made up his mind not to wait for Michael. Tomorrow, early, he'd go into Maynooth and take a bus to Dublin. He needed to see his contact bad. He'd go today if the blasted rain would stop. He'd just leave Brendan tied to the chair as he had done before. There was no way he could try anything; no matter how much time he was alone. Sean thought, I'll get my car and some supplies for here and come straight back.

Sean looked at Brendan, again, whose breathing was a little stronger. His bloodied, swollen eyes were still shut but Sean noticed his wincing and heard his low moan. Brendan was regaining consciousness. Sean tried to put a mug of cold coffee into Brendan's hands. He couldn't manage even a sip of it with the horrible pain of his swollen, torn mouth. It was impossible.

The long day dragged on. Sean cleaned the hearth and built another fire. He spent most of the day cursing the rain, that never stopped, and eating and drinking. The whiskey helped to quiet the small touch of guilt that started to jab his conscience when he looked at Brendan. He'd have none of that. He'd feel nothing for that damned wimp.

Brendan was in and out of consciousness all through that day and throughout the following night. When he did surface, the pain was monstrous through his head, his face, his ears and mouth. The feeling of terrible thirst added to the misery.

The night was over; it had seemed like an eternity to Brendan. Hearing Sean moving about, with great effort he opened his painful eyes a slit. He managed to speak, "water."

Sean poured the small amount of water that was left in the bottle into a glass and put it into Brendan's hands. It hurt so badly to drink and it seemed to take forever to finish the couple ounces of water.

"Can you talk? You had better be able to—and force yourself to sound normal. You are going to talk with your mother. I don't want her to start someone looking for you. You'll say what I tell you or you'll never be talking again." Sean got his gun and directed it at Brendan's head while he held the phone up to it with his other hand.

After the short call was finished to Sean's satisfaction, he went to the door. The rain that had continued through the night had stopped. It was early, the sky was still cloudy and the fog was thick but Sean didn't want to wait. He locked the cottage door and left on his bicycle for Maynooth. Leaving his bicycle at the local pub, he took the bus to Dublin. He did what he needed to do there and drove his car back. He stopped at Maynooth and tied his bicycle onto the car. He was back at the cottage shortly after noontime. He unloaded his supplies, and then drove to park his car at a distance from the cottage. The cottage was in such a remote place; it wasn't likely that anyone would be about, but he wasn't taking any chances.

When he went into the cottage, the room was colder and damper than ever, and there was no more dry wood to start a fire. Sean put his hands on his hips and stood looking down at the pathetic, shivering figure. The face was still so badly swollen and covered with dried blood. A feeling of almost pity momentarily touched Sean. He pushed that thought away and muttered to himself, "Don't be feelin soft. Remember what this damned bastard is puttin you through."

Sean poured himself a glass of whiskey and gulped it. He untied the ropes that held Brendan to the chair and shoved a glass of cola into his hands. With extreme effort Brendan drank some of it. Sean, of course, had not brought milk or broth or anything that might have given nourishment to Brendan, who was still unable to eat.

Sean had seen his contact in Dublin. With the drugs and whiskey, he felt tired. He lay down on the cot and was soon in a heavy sleep. Shortly after, he was wakened by Brendan's weak voice, "Sean, Sean. Sean, I must go outside. Sean, Sean, I really have to go. Sean—"

Sean came to with a curse. He put on his shoes and jacket. He loosened the ropes at Brendan's feet, enough for the trip outside. The rain that had been a drizzle off and on through the morning was now pelting. The ground was saturated and the mud paths slippery. They finally reached the area to the side of the cottage. Muddy water was rushing down the rise to the back.

"Sean, I can't manage with my hands tied, this time, I need to sit down."

"Damn," Sean gave an exasperated sigh. "I don't want to be near your stinkin shit." Sean had his gun in his jacket pocket. "Just don't try anything. Hold still. Sean undid the knot. While loosening the rope, he held the gun with his other hand. "Go up close the dirt ridge. I've put some wood and logs there to make some kind of a seat." They were both soaked. Sean growled, "Be quick about it" Brendan tried to walk up the mound of mud and running water but with his feet tied and the weakness he felt he simply couldn't do it. "Stop, damn ye, reach down and undo your ankle ropes—but don't pull anything funny," Sean ordered as he kept his gun on Brendan.

Brendan finally climbed the short but steep distance, sometimes trying to hold onto logs on the pile beside the muddy path. When he was through and his clothes fastened, he started down the steep grade. Close to the bottom, where Sean was standing holding the gun pointed at him, his foot caught on a rock that gave loose with the mud. He fell, full weight, onto Sean. The gun went off. The bullet whizzed into the air past Brendan. Sean's head had struck a large jutting rock on the side of the path when he fell. The impact was hard. Sean was unconscious. Brendan scrambled to his feet. He realized that Sean was knocked out—but for how long? But it was a chance. "Dear God, help my legs to run." He saw the gun in the mud, flung from Sean's hand. He grabbed it and ran past the cottage and down the dirt road.

Suddenly he thought if he reached the main road, Sean would be looking for him there. He cut to his right and ran through the muddy, stony fields, then across the main road to the fields on the left. Surely there would be farms somewhere within a few miles. It hurt him to think. His head and face throbbed with pain. He had to keep running. He was terrified at the thought of Sean's coming to and finding him. With his heightened fear, his body's adrenaline surged. He forced himself to run, on and on, far beyond what his weakened state should have taken him. Finally he fell. He could go no further. He crawled close to an old stone wall with thick bracken grown about. The rain stopped and the sun was starting to shine, but all was muddy and wet. He tried to pull the tangled brush and weeds around himself. He had to hide. He had to rest. He was so cold. He felt himself going under. He couldn't feel. He couldn't think.

"Ben, don't be running off," the pretty young girl on horseback called to the large fluffy black and white dog. "Ben," she called louder. Ben raced off, going about a block from the firmly packed path. Anne stopped the horse and watched Ben as he tore toward the old stone wall. She didn't want to follow. The field was muddy. "Ben," she called again. Ben didn't come; instead he barked and kept barking and jumping around a place by the wall. It wasn't like Ben to ignore her call, even when chasing rabbits. Still he didn't come and the barking continued. "Mud or no mud, we'll have to be going to see what the matter is, Bright." Anne lovingly patted the horse's neck and started over the field. Ben stopped barking and jumping and now waited quietly for Anne to come.

Anne screamed, "*Oh, Dear Holy Mother of God*!" At first terrified at the sight of the bloody, hideous face, like a horrible mask, she was about to race away. But seeing how still he was, she dismounted. Still trembling, she knelt beside Brendan. At first she feared him dead but saw his body quiver. She noticed his beautiful young hands and thought; he's not too many years older than myself. The poor hurt lad! "Can you hear me?" There was no answer. Anne pulled her sweater off and pushing the brush away, gently tucked it around Brendan. "Stay here with him, Ben. I'll go for Dad." Anne mounted Bright. Ben stood up and came beside the horse. "No, Ben. Stay, Ben, stay." Ben lay down by the man and whimpered and stayed. When Anne reached the road, she set Bright a fast pace and raced to the farm. "Thank God," she said aloud as she saw her father was home.

She threw herself into her father's arms and sobbed out what she had found. "Come, father, right away."

"I'll call the Gardai—or an ambulance."

"No, no. It would be too long. He is near dead. He can't be alone."

Pat gave into her frantic pulling.

Anne quickly tethered her horse at the fence and jumped into the pickup truck beside her father. When they reached the place in the road, they looked across the field. Ben was still keeping his vigil. They drove through the field and stopped closed to where Brendan was.

Pat Quinn saw that the man was not much more than a lad. He shook his head sadly when he saw the battered face and bruised and cut wrists and ankles where the ropes had been. He gently felt and thought no bones were broken, except perhaps the nose. "We'll have to get him on the truck bed. You will have to help me, Anne." Between the two of them, Brendan was soon stretched out on Bright's blanket that Anne had tossed into the truck. Anne again put her sweater over him. Pat Quinn took off his own jacket and placed it over Brendan.

Brendan stirred and flung out his arms. "Don't let him get me. Help me."

"It's all right, lad. No one is going to hurt you," Pat said in a soothing voice.

Brendan was asleep again. Ben jumped on the truck and lay beside him.

"We'll have to take him to the hospital, Anne."

"It's so far away, Father. Can't we take him home and call Dr. Tim?"

Anne was about to get into the cab when she saw something in the mud. It was almost hidden by the brush. She picked it up and held it out to her father. "There's been trouble."

Pat took the gun. "Anne, finding this, I guess we'll have to take him to the hospital and notify the Gardai." All of Pat's logical thoughts were for doing that at once. If it was pity he felt for the young lad or a reaction to a most strange urging from somewhere outside himself, he'd never know, but suddenly he knew he just couldn't. "He can't be dangerous now. I'd like to hear this lad's story first. I'm for taking him home. Is it still alright with you, Anne?"

"Ah, father, I think we must. He has been hurt so. He needs our help now. You said his breathing seemed even. He'll be alright at our house. Besides, Ben thinks he's a good man, too," she said smiling at the vigilant Ben.

When they reached the road, Pat glanced at his daughter and said, "I'm still a bit worried that he might be needing hospital care. But if he has run from someone, maybe he wouldn't want that, with the Gardai involved. He must have had the energy to come from somewhere. We'll see how he is and I'll call Dr. Tim. I feel very responsible for him, you know."

They parked the truck in front of the neatly kept farmhouse. Pat had driven over the ground and close to the door. When they tried to lift Brendan he seemed to come to a little. "Can you put your legs down over the back, man?" Pat asked.

Brendan managed that but was not strong enough to put his weight upon his legs to walk. Pat and Anne put his arms about their shoulders and carried him through the door. "We'll take him into my bed, Anne, and then you go fix him some hot broth," said Pat.

When Anne had gone, Pat stripped Brendan of the wet muddy clothes and covered the shaking Brendan with warm blankets. He got a basin of warm water and gently bathed Brendan's face and wiped the dried blood from his nose, mouth, and chin.

Brendan's eyes flickered open and looked at Pat. He managed a whispered, "Thank, you."

"Don't try talking now, my lad. Oh, here is Anne with some broth."

Anne sat down beside Brendan. Pat propped his head up with pillows so that Anne could feed Brendan the broth, spoonful by spoonful. After, she gave him strong hot tea with lots of milk and sugar, in the same manner.

Brendan kept his hurting eyes closed and was just gratefully accepting this kindness as he swallowed painfully.

It was apparent to Pat that Brendan was developing a fever. Pat called his friend Doctor Tim Madden. Doctor Tim agreed to come at once. His own home was only three miles from the Quinn farm.

When Dr. Madden came, before seeing Brendan, he spoke of his concern. "Pat, from what you've told me, I'm thinking it isn't safe for you and Anne to bring a stranger like this into your house. You and Anne could be in danger from him or someone who is after him."

"I've had the same thoughts, Tim; but I can't explain a knowing that this is the course I must be taking. I know he's no danger to us now, you'll see. I won't let Anne alone with him ever. I'll keep my gun handy in case he would come to and seem violent. But somehow I simply don't believe this will happen."

Brendan slept heavily after having the broth and tea. When he woke he was only partially coherent. He was hot and yet he felt like there were rivers of ice coursing through his veins. His eyes fluttered open. He was vaguely aware of three people standing by him. The heavy lids of his eyes shut again. He heard voices; they seemed far, far away. He was asleep again.

Dr. Tim pulled the stethoscope from his ears, turned to Pat, and said, "His lungs seem somewhat congested. I don't think the hospital is absolutely necessary but he's going to need a lot of care. I'll give him an antibiotic injection and will leave more for him to continue. He should be sponged with cool water now. When he is conscious he should be given lots of liquid. If he can't wake enough to drink, he'll have to be moved to the hospital for intravenous feeding. "Poor lad," Dr. Madden shook his head and looked at Brendan's bruised and scraped wrists and ankles, "it looks like he has been a prisoner for days." He touched gently around the swollen face, "nothing is broken.. I'll leave some salve for his skin and bring something to swab the inside of his torn mouth. I'm coming back early tomorrow. Pat, I'll help you sponge him tonight. As I said, he's going to need a lot of care—for several days at least." "Tim, I can't give him care during the day. I'm shorthanded on the farm now. Anne will be at school and as I said I won't let her alone with him. She is too young to even help as a man's nurse. She can feed him but that's all I'll allow. I don't want to send him to the hospital if he can get better here. I want to know his story and what this trouble has been. I don't want to be causing the poor lad more trouble. Do you know of anyone who could come and stay here and do for him?"

Dr. Tim looked thoughtful, then said, "Yes, I do, Pat. Amy McGill is a retired nurse, a no-nonsense lady, still very strong and able. She would be free to come and to stay here, I'm sure; but she would want a good wage."

"Of course, Tim. I'll take care of that," Pat looked with pity at Brendan's young, battered face. "He could stand a Good Samaritan right now. This gives me a chance to be one."

Dr. Tim and Pat bathed an unresponsive Brendan and got him into Pat's nightshirt. Dr. Tim left the house, saying he would contact Amy McGill and they would both come early in the morning.

It was almost two hours until Sean opened his eyes. He felt confused as he lay there staring up at the sunny sky. After a few minutes the reality of where he was and what had happened entered his consciousness. He looked at his watch and saw what time had passed. He got to his feet in a rage of cursing and profanity. The gun was not in his pocket. Kneeling down he crawled in the mud and felt around, it was gone. His head throbbed. He felt the back of it. His thick black hair was sticky with matted blood. Giving a cursory look about, he went inside the cottage, knowing it was useless to look for Brendan. He washed and changed clothes. The wound had stopped bleeding. Noticing Brendan's bag was still there, Sean thought, the damned bastard couldn't get far with no money. In the condition he was in, he couldn't get far anyway. Sean got into his car and went down the dirt road toward the road to Maynooth. He half expected to find Brendan lying about somewhere. God!—What if Brendan had gone to the main road and got a ride into Maynooth, to the gardai? He couldn't risk checking. He had better get out of here fast.

When Sean reached his apartment in Dublin, he phoned Michael and told him he was back to stay for a few days. "I got someone I can trust to watch the bloody bastard." He couldn't admit to Michael that he had failed—that Brendan had escaped. He'd have to call Pearse though, and get him down to watch Brendan's mother's house. If on the outside chance that he got in touch with her and she arranged to get him home, Sean knew he'd have to know. Brendan knew too much now, and he'd have to be silenced. Pearse hadn't known about Brendan being taken to the cottage. He wouldn't give Pearse any details. He'd just tell him that Brendan knew all the plans and backed out and had to be found.

Chapter 15

As Fran buttoned the pale purple suit that she had worn on the flight here, she was thinking, it was just one week ago today that I was packing to come. It seemed to her an age ago. So much had happened to her. She studied her reflection in the mirror. The woman looked the same as the woman who boarded the British Air flight on that Tuesday evening. The changes in this woman only the soul could see. This woman no longer felt total flatness of spirit. In its place was the small budding of hope. The thought of moving to Ely filled her with excitement, an emotion that had been dead for so long.

Fran was putting on her light cream raincoat as she came into the kitchen. Heidi was giving Bryan his cereal and strained peaches. He gave Fran a big smile. Fran leaned over and kissed his fuzzy, warm head. Heidi, said, "Don't get too close; he might get some of his breakfast on your clothes, Fran."

"It would be worth it; I'm going to miss him. I just didn't know how fast a baby could wrap you around his tiny finger. Heidi, you know I'm going to miss being here with all of you; but I have this pull toward Ely and I feel this need to start taking control of my life. It's a good feeling—one I haven't had for quite a while; for so long I've just been going through the motions."

"I know, Hon, and I'm glad for you. Won't you have at least a cup of coffee before you go? Tom said 8:30; it's only twenty after."

"I can't resist the smell; I'll have a cup, thanks. Tom said we are going to stop for breakfast at a "Little Chef." He said it's a restaurant chain here and I should think of it as England's "McDonald's.""

"It's a shame it had to rain today for your drive. We have had such an unusually prolonged hot spell for England. Since you came it has been nice until today."

"I don't mind, Heidi. A soft rainy day is a welcome respite after the intensity of the sun. It makes me think that it's freshening everything."

Fran opened the back door. "The rain is gentle and the air smells clean and sweet."

There was a knock at the front door. Fran's heart did the little flip at the thought of being with Tom again. Again, she hurriedly pushed away that feeling. She opened the door and experienced another flutter upon seeing Tom's smile. Heidi was standing behind her with Bryan in her arms. Tom put down his opened umbrella and reached in and took Bryan's little hand. Bryan responded with his own toothless grin.

"Have fun, you two," Heidi said, as Tom picked up the umbrella to cover Fran. "Hey, you two are match-mates," Heidi said, noticing the pale cream jacket Tom was wearing.

"Yes, we are," Tom, said, laughing. He thought—I hope it's more than the color of our coats.

Fran relaxed against the soft plush of the seat in the small white car. "This is the first time I've been in an English car and sat on the passenger side on the left. Heidi and Don still use the car they brought with them I guess if I stay in England, I'll have to learn to drive here. I would like to get a car like this."

"Fran, I would be glad to help you choose a car and ride with you until you're comfortable driving here."

"I don't want to be a pest and impose on your kindness, Tom." Fran was thinking I must not get too involved.

Tom glanced over at her. "My dear American girl, helping you would never be an imposition. Please believe me."

Fran studied Tom's face and realized in spite of his smile and good humor; he looked very worn and tired today. "Tom, you don't need more responsibility with anything right now. You look tired. Maybe you shouldn't be making this drive today."

"Fran, Fran, I had to go to the Ely shop today. Your being with me is making it a pleasure. You are really intuitive though; I didn't sleep well for the last two nights. I've had some worry about my mother and my eighteen-year-old brother. He seems to have gotten off track a bit. I think I will feel less tired after a good breakfast." Tom continued to talk a little of the situation that was worrying him and lovingly of his mother. Soon they found a Little Chef. Over breakfast, they were soon deep in conversation of memories about their childhood and school years. It was so comfortable. Fran thought, Jeff and I never shared talk like this. She couldn't bring herself to mention Jeff, or that part of her life. She wasn't ready to admit what to her was such a horrible mistake to Tom.

The rest of the drive was relaxing. The light rain had stopped and the sun broke through the clouds. They talked and laughed and learned a little of each other's likes and dislikes. The times of silence were not strained.

They came into the small town of Ely. At the first sight of the Cathedral towers, Fran longed to be in it again. Her thoughts, immediately, were of Ethel Fenman. How she wanted to see this mystery woman again. This is how Fran had come to think of her: The Mystery Woman.

Tom did not stop at the Cathedral. He drove around the old charming business part of the little town. Fran was delighted by the quaint look of everything. "How beautiful!" she exclaimed when she saw the Old Lloyds Bank. "Look, Tom, at that wonderful front with the two bayed, long windows. Just look at the beauty of the cream colored, decorated stone and aged red brick."

Tom smiled at her and reached for her hand, giving it a gentle squeeze. "Fran, I'm afraid I took that building for granted. I'm going to love seeing my England through your eyes. I hope you'll let me. There are so many things I'd like to show you here and in London."

A part of Fran wanted so much to say yes to this suggestion, but again the old fear gripped her. She had felt so relaxed now she felt tension all through her. Even her voice sounded tight as she offered logical excuses. "Tom, you are so busy and I must get this move of mine underway. Neither of us really has the time for sightseeing."

Dear God, thought Tom, what is it? She seems almost afraid of something. Fran's mood had been so different. They had been having such a great time together until now. Tom tried to keep his own voice very casual, when he answered, "I guess you're right. These next weeks will be busy ones."

Tom drove back again in the direction of the Cathedral. He parked the car in the rear lot. They walked up the long path toward the Cathedral. A split-rail fence bordered the grassy field, of the Paddock. Tom got his camera from his jacket pocket. "Fran, hop up on the rail and let me take your picture. I can get you and the top part of the Cathedral. It will be a great shot; your first picture taken in Ely."

"Wonderful, I'd love to have some pictures to send Mom and Dad. I have a few from my day in London, but I really want some from here. I never thought to bring my camera."

"Wait, you can't get your skirt dirty." Tom pulled out his large white handkerchief and spread it on the rail and helped her up. With the posing and camera focusing, they were both soon laughing. The tension of a short while ago was gone.

Tom helped her down and handed her the camera. "Put it in your purse. You might like to take some pictures while you spend your time this afternoon. We don't have time for more now; Mrs. Pickens will be expecting us."

They walked on up the path and went out onto High Street through the opening in the wall to the right of the Cathedral's grounds. They went a few blocks to the west and turned down a charming street of very old row houses. They were not pretentious but neat. Some were of buff colored brick, some of red. Not being uniform in size, the roofs were of different heights. Most had small paned windows. Some had shutters. In the middle of the row was a front, the width of two houses. It was painted cream with flower boxes and hanging plants on its lower sills. A thick red band of wood crossed its length, with large gold letters announcing it to be the Prince Albert. Delicate wrought iron extending from the top level had a picture of the prince and announced the same.

"Oh! A real English pub, it's darling. Do we have time to go in, Tom?"

Tom was delighted at seeing her so happy and carefree. "Not now, but after I'm through this afternoon at the shop, we'll come here before we start back. Now, we'll have to hurry on down to Mrs. Pickens."

They walked briskly down a few more blocks. The very last house, on the turn of the corner, was Mrs. Pickens'. The old wooden door was painted a shiny black with polished brass fittings. It was attached to the other row houses but it was different. The lower part of the house was buff brick but the top part, to the high-pitched roof, was stucco with wooden beams. The side of the house, at the turn of the corner, had two lovely bay windows on the lower and upper levels. The windowsills had bright red geraniums in dark wooden boxes that matched the wooden beams of the house. Between the two lower bays was a large trellis covered with fragrant white roses, growing from a large cement pot at its base. At the rear of the house was a small English garden with shrubs and flowers. On a flagstone floor was a welcoming small table with chairs of weathered wood that matched the dark beams.

"Tom, it's superb! It's beyond my wildest expectations. Oh, I hope Mrs. Pickens likes me. I'd love living here."

"Not a chance she won't, Fran. I think you'll like her too. She is quite the old fashioned English lady; somewhat reserved, but warm once she gets to know you."

"If her house speaks for her, I'm sure I'll like her." Fran took the brass knocker in her hand and gently tapped it. There was no response.

"Knock again, Fran, a bit harder this time. Mrs. Pickens is just slightly hard of hearing."

"I didn't want to be rude. I'll try again." She gave an eager, repeated knock.

The door was opened wide by a pleasant faced, but prim lady, in her early eighties. Her white hair was neatly done with a soft wave to the side and pulled back in a tight bun. She was short, small boned and very thin. Yet, she still had a straight carriage. There was nothing feeble looking about Mrs. Pickens. The light blue eyes that looked out of the glasses with their small gold frame were clear and young looking. She was dressed in a shirtwaist, straight line, house-dress; its self-material belt was tied around her small waist. Fran was to always picture her in this type of dress. Mrs. Pickens had many different colors and prints in this same style. This kind of clothing was simply a part of Mrs. Pickens.

Her warm smile as she patted Tom's arm belied her primness. "Good to see you, Tom, and this must be the lovely young lady you told me about. Come in, come in, I'm brewing some tea and have some fresh hot scones ready. Let's go into the living room and talk before I show Miss Amberson the flat."

"It's Mrs. Amberson, Mrs. Pickens," Fran said, as they were shown into the living room. Fran noticed the quick glance Mrs. Pickens gave Tom. Fran rapidly added, "I'm a widow."

Mrs. Pickens nodded understandingly, "I'm sorry, my dear, and you are so young. I've been a widow myself for fifteen years—but I'm quite old now. I still do miss Mr. Pickens. He was a good man. We were not blest with children. Sometimes, I'm very lonely. Oh, you don't have children, do you? I don't think the flat would be suitable for children."

"No, Mrs. Pickens, I was married only a short time. My hus"—Fran couldn't bring herself to say husband. She said, in Mrs. Pickens's formal way, "Mr. Amberson died in an automobile accident."

The tension in Fran's face was correctly read by Tom, to be one of revulsion at having to speak of her husband. Mrs. Pickens read it to be one of grief.

They talked about the details of renting the flat while they had their tea and delicious warm scones. Fran was greatly disappointed when Mrs. Pickens said the flat wouldn't be ready for two weeks. "I'm having it completely painted and papered before you can move in, Mrs. Amberson. I hope this won't inconvenience you. It really needed to be done. The painters will be starting tomorrow. I have the paper rolls upstairs; you can see them. It's not too late to change the paper, if it wouldn't be to your liking."

They went upstairs to the flat. It was the entire upper level of the house. The lovely bays were out of the living room and bedroom. Mrs. Pickens was a woman of good taste. The fresh paint was to be the same soft light color that the rooms were presently done. Mrs. Pickens had chosen paper, for certain areas, that could have been chosen by Fran herself. Fran was delighted. She hadn't thought much about the kind of place she would like; her thoughts had just been the need to move to Ely. She also hadn't given thought to needing furniture. "I have only my personal things, Mrs. Pickens. I'll have to buy a bed and chest of drawers before I move in. I'll take my time in choosing other things after I come. Do you know what store, here, would be best?"

Mrs. Pickens gave her the name of a store. Tom said he hadn't been in it but knew where it was and knew it to be a good store. "I'll be coming back to Ely this coming Saturday. Fran can come along and shop then."

Fran said, "I'll call you to arrange a time for the furniture to be delivered. I love the flat. I'm so anxious to make the move. By the way, Mrs. Pickens, do you know a woman by the name of Ethel Fenman? She is from Ely."

Mrs. Pickens looked thoughtful for a minute before answering, "No, I don't—I've never known anyone by that name."

Good-byes were exchanged. As they walked back toward the Cathedral, Fran said to Tom, "I think it's odd that Mrs. Pickens doesn't know Ethel Fenman. She has lived here all her life and seems to know most everyone. Ely is such a small place."

"As I said, Fran, I never saw her in the shop; but I'll ask around for you. You really sound like she made quite an impression on you. Maybe you might see her at the Cathedral today or on Saturday. I don't have to be there to guide. I'll be at the shop; but you can spend some time there, after we shop for the furniture. By the way, it is a good store that Mrs. Pickens mentioned but rather expensive. We could look somewhere else too."

"Tom, I have more than a comfortable amount. The agent Jeff had, insisted and arranged for a very large insurance policy on him, naming me as beneficiary. Peter Norce, Jeff's agent was also his business manager. Jeff left things up to Peter entirely. I'm not sorry I have this security now. I've been too distraught to function well, as far as working and setting up my own life. However, having the money from the insurance might be adding to my sense of guilt. I've got so much to work through; enough of that." Fran shook her head as if to get rid of all the thoughts that were causing her pain.

Tom wished that Fran would open up to him about the trouble she was having. Don had said very little to him about it; he had given no details. Tom, still, was so in the dark about her former marriage and the problems she was having emotionally. He had no idea who Jeff had been or what was behind Fran's self-acknowledged guilt. Tom simply knew, deep in his heart, that no fault could be Fran's.

"Fran, other than this coming Saturday at Ely, I'll have to be mostly at the London shop until the end of the next week. By that time the management should be set up and my trips to London will be infrequent. Since you can't make your move for two weeks, will you let me show you some of London?" He couldn't resist taking the slender hand he had been so aware of at his side.

She didn't pull away but said she would like to see more of London, in a noncommittal way. Tom still didn't hear in her words or voice, what he wanted to hear, that she wanted to see more of him.

Chapter 16

Tom said goodbye to Fran at the west front of the Cathedral before going to his car. "I'll be at the shop for a while and then we'll go to the Prince Albert for supper. Will you be all right here at the Cathedral and just walking about? I'll try to make it back here by five-thirty."

"Tom, I'll be fine, don't hurry. I could meet you at the Prince Albert."

"It looks like rain again, I don't want you caught in it."

"I'll go to the car with you and retrieve my raincoat and umbrella. I don't mind the walk at all."

"The rains are scheduled to get rather hard this after—"

"Stop worrying, Tom, I'm not sugar, I won't melt."

Tom smiled down at her. All he wanted to do was kiss that sweeter than sugar face, but resisted, fearing it wouldn't be welcome.

They went on down to the parking lot. Fran got her things and said a second goodbye to Tom. She walked back to the Cathedral and entered feeling anticipation. Was it a hope of seeing her mystery woman again? She didn't exactly know. There were fewer people about than on Saturday. Fran took a sweeping glance around. She didn't see Ethel Fenman. The small gift shop was open. She went in to browse and found a special key chain for Tom. It had the name Hart and a crest. She saw the copies of the thin paper book entitled *St. Etheldreda Queen and Abbess*; it had been written by C. J. Stranks and published by Ely Cathedral Shop. She had purchased a copy of this on her first visit but didn't bring it with her. She hadn't taken the time to read it. She thought of the conversation she had with Ethel Fenman when they were standing close to the statue of this saint. Fran purchased the book and decided to spend her time reading it while sitting near the statue. Fran walked slowly the distance of the nave. All the while she gazed upward at the wonderful Victorian Ecclesiastical painting on the ceiling. She stood for a long time in the center of the famous Octagon looking up at the figure of Christ. She was realizing that in her heart her belief in God still did exist. Her denial was past. She wandered on through and thought of the many artists and architects and masons and engineers that had designed and created and worked here through the many centuries. All surely were given the light of God Himself, to create this magnificent Cathedral. She thought too of all the gifted people who still worked daily to restore and maintain this wonderful place. Suddenly these thoughts lost their objectivity. Didn't God give Jeff the creative ability to play music that lifted souls to heaven, despite his human failings? What blackness of spirit did she possess—not to grieve at this loss for the world?

She felt a surge of guilt overtake her. Tears ran down her cheeks. Not just tears of self-loathing but tears because her guilt wouldn't allow happiness with Tom. She had tasted lightness and fun in his presence. She was convinced by now that he was just as he appeared to be—a kind, intelligent and gentle man, a man worthy of a woman better than her. She walked on to the shrine of St. Etheldreda. The Cathedral felt cold and damp; Fran put her coat around her. She went close to the statue. It was a beautiful work of art—but that's all it meant to Fran. It was no warmer than the cold she felt within her. Finding no pews or chairs in that part of the Cathedral, she returned to the Octagon and crossed to the right where the prayer chapel of St. Dunston was located. Her folder had stated that it was available for private prayer. No one was in the chapel or around it; placed there were a prie-dieu and a small chair.

She knelt for a while and closed her eyes, not trying to pray, just trying to empty her mind of all concerns. When she felt composed enough to read, she sat on the chair and opened the little book on the life of St. Etheldreda. Fran found her life fascinating and absorbing. Etheldreda had truly been a member of the royal house of East Anglia over thirteen hundred years ago, a woman of strength that had known her purpose in life from a very young age. How little she had cared for the queen-ship that was thrust upon her. How meaningless, to her, the two arranged marriages in her life, marriages in name only. One that would give to her this very land of Ely and one that would crown her a queen. Finally God had permitted what He always wanted of her and what she had always longed for. She gave her life to Him as a nun. She founded a monastery at this very place in Ely in the year 673. As Abbess she had been loved and revered by her followers at the monastery and by the town people for her goodness and kindness. After her death, her incorruptible body and the miracles that were attributed to her intercession gave to her the title of Saint. Fran found it interesting that after many centuries Etheldreda's name had been shortened to Audrey. Audrey had always been a favorite name of Fran's. Fran closed the booklet and walked back to the other side of the

Cathedral, to the little rack of candles. She lit one and whispered a silent wish that she would be given direction for her life and find peace from this terrible guilt. This was as close to a prayer as Fran had said for a long time. Fran looked at her watch and couldn't believe the late hour. It was several blocks to walk back to the Prince Albert. As she walked back to the West Doors, Fran noticed preparation for Evensong. She had to leave but promised herself to stay for this service on Saturday. Fran was glad she had her coat and umbrella and that her pumps had closed toes. It must have rained hard during the afternoon. Everything was quite saturated. Fran walked rapidly, constantly side stepping the puddles.

When she reached the Prince Albert, she was grateful to be inside. She hung her dripping coat on the peg close to the door and put her umbrella into one of the tall china containers kept there for that purpose. Looking about, she immediately liked this warm and cozy place. A plump older woman, wearing an allover apron, came up to her. "Would you like a booth or table, Miss.?"

"I'd like a booth, please. Someone is going to be joining me soon."

"Right over here, dear. Can I get you something while you're waiting—a nice glass of sherry or hot tea?"

"Good hot strong tea sounds great," Fran said, as she slid into the padded, leather booth. She noticed the small brass lamp with its tiny pleated shade. She was glad they decided to come here.

"Yer right, luv, hot tea on a cold day is the real pick-me-up. I'll get it right away." The woman quickly returned with a pot of steaming tea, a tall china mug, and a plate with cream and sugar and sliced lemon. "I didn't know how you like your tea, dear, most like their cream in their cup first—unless they just take lemon."

"I'll have a little cream and sugar, please." The woman fixed it for her in the English way of cream in the cup first. "Thank you so much," Fran said, delighted with this little extra caring.

"You're so very welcome. Take your mug in both of your cold hands, that'll help you feel warm," she said with a smile. "Anything else, dear, just call May and I'll be right with you."

Fran smiled and did as May suggested; she held the hot mug with both hands, indeed, it did feel warming. She closed her eyes and enjoyed this small comfort.

Fran was almost finished with her tea when the door opened and Tom came in. He looked over and smiled his joy at seeing her. She couldn't deny the thrill she was feeling at seeing him.

Tom and Fran both ordered the beef pie and salads and light red wine. May was all smiles as she took their order, thinking to herself, what a lovely young couple.

"Fran, I don't think we should linger long. The rain is to get heavier and the wind is to be strong. I was going to take you around to the shop but I think it best to do that on Saturday."

Fran agreed. They finished their meal hurriedly, watching through the window as the storm increased.

The rains became pelting, the visibility poor. They were silent as they watched the road. Tom had hoped to drive out of the rain, but it only worsened the further they went. With the oncoming night the visibility became worse. Fran looked at Tom, his dear face showed the tension of his concentration. "Tom, could we find a place to stop over tonight? You look so tired."

"I am tired, Fran. This is miserable to drive in. If you wouldn't mind, we are about twenty miles from my house in Ashwell; we could stay there. You could call Heidi so she wouldn't worry."

Much as Fran hated it, she thought of the stop at Jeff's apartment, that terrible time so long ago. *No—no—no*, she pushed the thought away. Tom was different. She looked at his dear face, even if nothing could come of her feeling because of her own unworthy self, she knew in her heart at this moment that she loved Tom tenderly and always would. She answered in a very matter of fact voice, "I think that would be the intelligent thing to do."

As they parked in the long side drive, Tom said, "someday I'd like to make a curved drive to go in the front of the house but that's a long way off. I couldn't resist this house when I saw it for the first time. I'm anxious for you to see it in daylight." They huddled together under one umbrella and hurried to the door.

"I'll turn up the thermostat then I'll start a fire in the fireplace and get this place warm for you, Fran. It feels so damp." Tom was happy to see the delighted look on Fran's face as she looked about the house and hear her comments about its charm. Tom disappeared for a minute then returned with a large, soft robe. "Here, this will fit over your suit and help till the house warms."

"Tom, you have to be one of the most thoughtful people I've ever known, thank you." Fran quickly slipped into the robe and tied it tightly around her. It being his it had the feel of his arms around her, a thought she quickly dismissed.

"This way to the kitchen; let's get some coffee going. I haven't been shopping for ages." He opened the refrigerator, "there are some muffins here, and would you like to toast them? There's jam or peanut butter for on them. If you make them, I'll start the fire."

"Remember, Tom, I'm from the U.S.A., where peanut butter is a way of life; it sounds delicious. I've found the toaster. Tom this beautiful open kitchen hearth, is it useable? Could you build a fire in here? This room is wonderful!—I'd love eating here at this beautiful old table."

"I've never made a fire out here but there's no reason why we couldn't. Your wish is my command, my lady." Tom made a little mock bow. They were both laughing. Tom left to bring wood from the living room hearth.

Fran peeked into the cupboards and found blue and white dishes of the onion-skin pattern. While looking for a knife she found two cream linen place mats. They were on the table with paper napkins, folded neatly, when Tom came back carrying the basket of wood. Tom knelt and started the fire; when he turned and saw the table set, his pleasure was obvious. "Fran, this is nice. It's the first time I've eaten at this table since my mother's visit. She brought the place mats. You probably noticed; I'm not too well supplied. I just haven't had the time. Do you want to call Heidi now so they won't worry?"

"Yes, I should do that before it gets later."

Tom picked up the phone and touched the message button. Fran saw the worried frown that crossed his face. His mother had said, "I'm alright, Tom, but I still haven't heard from Brendan. Please call tomorrow. Love you, Dear, and please pray."

He handed the phone to Fran and told her there was no news from Brendan, adding, "I don't see how he can worry Mom like this." A thoughtful look crossed his face and he added, "but then Brendan is very young."

Fran didn't know what to say to comfort him. She put her hand gently on his arm and her look told him of her deep concern for him in this worry. Her very presence helped.

Heidi was relieved when she heard Fran's voice and said she was glad they were smart enough to stop. The weather, she said, was just as bad there. She added that Scooby was in a very bad humor. "He won't settle down. He keeps wandering, in and out of your room, and mewing."

Fran laughed, "Give him a hug for me and tell him I'll see him tomorrow."

Hearing that last sentence, Tom looked at Fran and asked, "Is someone visiting you at Heidi's?"

"No, we were talking about Scooby. He misses me."

Tom felt relieved. He didn't consider Scooby as competition.

When they finished their snack, they sat a longer time in the cozy kitchen, sipping some warming sherry. Tom excused himself and when he returned he said, "I put fresh linens on the bed, Fran. I think it's time to get some sleep." They went into the living room. Fran saw that the couch was made into a bed for Tom.

"Tom, I could have taken the couch. You had all that driving and really need a good rest."

"This couch is really comfortable. I'll have no problem sleeping. Don't be worrying." Tom led Fran over to the stairs, "the room is the first on the right at the top. It has its own bath. There's a new toothbrush on the sink. If you need anything else, let me know. I want to be a proper host," he grinned.

They stood at the bottom of the stairs. For a moment their eyes met with mutual tenderness. Fran was first to lower hers. Tom fought the urge to give her even the slightest goodnight kiss. He murmured, "Good night, Fran, sweet dreams." He turned and walked to the couch.

Fran threw herself across the bed, his bed, and wept. She had wanted that kiss. Nothing could come of it—no, nothing could ever have come of it. She was glad it didn't happen. It would have put a strain on their friendship. Friends, that's what they must always be. Yes, she loved him; he was the dearest person she had ever known. But he didn't kiss her. Maybe, even if she was free inside, she was just a friend in his thoughts. Maybe he didn't find her attractive. Confused thoughts and feelings tumbled in her mind.

Finally she dried her eyes and got out of her clothes. She smoothed them and hung them. Tomorrow she would have to wear all of what she had worn that day. She snuggled again into Tom's warm robe and in exhaustion was soon asleep.

It was very early morning when Tom knocked on Fran's door. "Hate to wake you, Fran," he called, "but we have to leave soon. Coffee is in the making."

"I'll hurry, Tom. I won't be long." Fran took a quick shower and splashed cold water repeatedly on her face. She didn't want a puffy look to be a give away of last night's tears. She had no makeup except a powder compact and lipstick in her purse. She did her best in getting presentable. Her hair was not of her liking after the rain yesterday. She tied it straight back using a handkerchief, rolled, that she found in her purse.

Fran might not have felt at her best; but Tom's thought, when she came through the kitchen door, was that she was the most beautiful girl he had ever seen. He handed her the mug of coffee, being careful their fingers did not touch. He was fighting the desire to kiss her good morning. "We'll stop for breakfast on the way. You'll think of this place as Mother Hubbard's, the kitchen with the bare cupboards."

"I'll think of this kitchen as the most charming I've ever seen," Fran was glancing at the empty shelves, picturing them with that wonderful blue and white striped English pottery. She asked Tom if he liked it.

"Yes, I know what you mean," following her gaze, he said, "you're right, that would look great there."

As he picked up his keys, Fran noticed they were on a chain exactly like the one she had bought at the gift shop. "Oh, Tom," she said, taking it from her purse, "I got you a Hart key chain yesterday and I see you already have one like it."

"This is one I bought myself. I'd rather use the one you're giving me." He took time, at once, to switch his keys. "Thank you, Fran; I'll like having something special from you to keep with me all the time."

Such a little thing, Fran thought, yet he made it sound so very special to him.

Outside the house, they took a few minutes to look at this wonderful old place. Tom gave her a brief history of it and told her how much it had meant to him from the first time he had seen it. Fran understood his enthusiasm about it. She was hoping she would return to this house, as they drove away.

They drove for over an hour, and then turned in the direction of a small village to stop for breakfast. Fran went into the restaurant and waited as Tom walked to the red booth by the roadside to call his mom.

When he heard his mother's tense voice, he knew immediately that there had been no call from Brendan.

"Mom, I'm going to arrange things here and I can be in Dublin, probably the day after tomorrow. I'll start searching there."

"No, Tom, please don't just yet. We'll wait a little longer. This is only Wednesday morning and he left on Sunday. It isn't really a long time for his not calling. I know you're worried too, but I don't want this fear I'm feeling to make things harder for you. This panic of mine might be quite unnecessary. If he doesn't call within a day or two, I'll ask you to come. For now we'll wait a bit and keep praying. If anything happens I'll call one of the shops."

"Good, Mom, they can reach me on my cell phone anytime, after I pick it up at Uncle Cliff's. I forgot it. Mom, I still think most of this with Brendan is big talk and he'll be all right and coming to his senses. Try to hold on to that, Mom."

"I'll try, Tom, really I will. I love you."

"I love you, too, Mom, and I'll call you tonight."

"Tom sighed wearily as he sat down in the booth. "Fran, Mom still hasn't heard from Brendan. I might have to go to Dublin and try and find him and help straighten this out. He might call and, depending on what he has to say, I might not have to go right away. However, I do want to see him soon and have some good talks together. I think he needs me."

"I know you could get through to him, Tom, if anyone could."

"Well, I'll have to try. If he calls and is all right, I'll go after I have things completed in London. If we don't hear, I'll go in a few days. Then I'd have to cancel our plans for Ely on Saturday. Maybe Don and Heidi would take you up to shop for your furniture."

"Oh, my goodness, Tom, don't be worrying about a little thing like that. I just wish you would hear from Brendan for your sake, not mine. I wish I could help in some way; but I know there is nothing I can do."

"Remember him in your prayers, Fran, that's the best thing."

Fran did not answer, she couldn't admit to Tom that she no longer prayed; and yet she had a little at the Cathedral yesterday.

In blissful ignorance of the abhorrent situation and the terrible danger Brendan was in, Fran and Tom relaxed and enjoyed the rest of the drive on this beautiful, washed-clean morning.

Tom stayed only a few minutes at Heidi's when they arrived. Heidi and Scooby met them at the door. In no time Fran had a purring Scooby in her arms. Lucky cat, Tom was thinking, as he said goodbye and arranged for a time to leave for Ely on Saturday, if he didn't have to go to Dublin.

Fran excitedly told Heidi that she got the flat. "Oh, Mrs. Pickens is a dear. The flat is the entire upstairs of the house and is just charming. I can't wait till you see it. There's a wait, though, before I can move in. Mrs. Pickens is having it all painted and re-papered. I'm afraid you are going to have to put up with me a while longer."

Heidi was all smiles, "I know you are anxious, Fran, but I'm really happy that we will have you with us for awhile. We had expected your visit to be at least that long. Now, tell me all about your flat, and your adventure in the rain, Tom's house, and everything."

Tom went directly to the London shop. There was a message waiting to call his mother. Uncle Cliff told Tom it was good news, Brendan had called her.

Tom felt greatly relieved as he dialed the number. Susanna's voice still sounded tense as she repeated the conversation. "Brendan said he was fine, just staying with some friends in Dublin. But, Tom, his voice didn't really sound like he was all right. He told me not to worry. Yet, he wouldn't tell me where he was calling from or give me a number where I could reach him. He said he would be moving around and that he would be in touch with me. His sentences were rather disconnected. I don't know—he simply didn't speak very clearly. I knew it was his voice—maybe he had been drinking or had taken something. At least I know he's not hurt and lying somewhere in a hospital. He assured me he was all right."

"That's something, Mom, and he said he would keep in touch. That's a good sign. If you think I should come now Mom, I will."

"Tom, dear, you still wouldn't know where to begin. Wait until he calls again, as he said he would. I might be reading more into everything than I should. As I said, I know he's not hurt."

"I'll call you tonight, Mom. In the meantime, call me here or at Uncle Cliff's apartment, if you change your mind about my coming. Bye for now. I love you, Mom."

Tom phoned Fran with the news of Brendan's call. He said he felt somewhat relieved but still had reservations that all was really well with Brendan. "I won't be going this week. I'll wait until he calls again as he said he would. So, Fran, our plans are still on for Saturday."

"Tom, you aren't putting off going because of me, are you? You know I wouldn't want that."

"No, I'd try to fly out tonight if I thought it would do any good. But I will like being with you on Saturday. It will help keep my mind off things I can't fix right now. As far as I know, I'll see you very early Saturday. I'll call right away if things would change."

Fran hung up, happy that Tom would make it on Saturday but wishing he had found Brendan's call to be more reassuring. She felt anger toward this Brendan she didn't even know. He was causing so much unhappiness for Tom.

In and out Bryan's needs, the afternoon flew with all the things the girls had to talk about. As Don often said, "There never is a conversational lull with those two."

Later it was agreed that Don would baby-sit the next day. Fran and Heidi needed a shopping trip. There were so many little things Fran had to have for her apartment. First on her list though was some blue and white crockery for Tom's kitchen.

Chapter 17

Fran's days, from Wednesday until Saturday, were passed with ambiguous feelings. Sometimes it would seem to her, forever, till she would be with Tom again. Other times, remembering so much that had occurred between them, and so much within her unresolved; she wished she could have more time until their next encounter. Keeping busy helped some.

She and Heidi took a shopping trip to the Peterborough mall. Before going there, Heidi drove her to the wonderful St. Peter, St. Paul and St. Andrew Cathedral at Peterborough. The Cathedral held the tomb of Katharine of Aragon, King Henry VIII's first queen, as well as many great and impressive things. The Cathedral was almost as old as the one at Ely. Fran thoroughly enjoyed being there and seeing its many wonders. Yet, it did not touch and possess her spirit as Ely had.

Fran and Heidi had tea at the Cathedral café. Fran was delighted that the tea was served in delicate china cups, no plastic here; the scones were warm and delicious.

Then on to the mall at Peterborough where Fran found the blue and white striped pottery that she wanted for Tom. The pottery was a copy of the antique kind. She chose one very large bowl and one medium size and set of six small ones. There was a butter dish and cheese keeper she couldn't resist. She also chose a juice pitcher and a creamer and sugar bowl. Then she saw the salt and peppershakers and bought those, too.

Heidi laughed, "Fran, I thought you were going to shop for your apartment kitchen."

"Oh, I don't need as much or such special things for my apartment. Tom has those wonderful open shelves to display these lovely items."

Heidi thought, Tom is only one person too. He had no real need for the pottery. She smiled to herself and thought that Fran won't let herself admit it but she is mentally furnishing Tom's house with the lovely things she likes best.

She won't let it surface in her mind but deep down inside she is preparing for that someday. Heidi didn't mention these thoughts, of course, to Fran.

They went on to the kitchen utensils, flatware, towels, dishes and glasses, etc. that Fran would need to have for her move. They made four trips back and forth to the car with the many purchases. As Fran fit the box with the toaster into the back of the car, she said, "I could have gotten these things in Ely but it's been more fun shopping with you. Unless I get a car before moving, I might have to ask you or Don to help move my things. I hate to keep imposing on Tom. I should have thought more about my move."

"Oh, Fran, stop worrying. We'll help if Tom can't." Heidi thought to herself, nothing would keep Tom from it. "Besides, I loved guiding you through the domestic scene. We got most of the things we use, for my shower and wedding. They were all shipped here for us. Did you have a lot of things stored at your mother's?" Heidi was sorry as soon as this question was asked. A shadow of sadness seemed to cross Fran's face at this remembrance.

"Most of the little things we needed were arranged by our friends Susan and Fred. The few things I did buy were like everything else from that time, a bad memory. Susan and Fred took care of donating everything from the apartment to the Salvation Army. I only wish emotional baggage was as easily disposed of."

"I'm sorry, Fran, I didn't mean to spoil the day. It was a thoughtless question."

"Heidi, you are never thoughtless. It was a normal question. Nothing could spoil this day and the fun we have had together, choosing the new bright things I need for my new beginning. By the way, once I really get into cooking, I never really have done much; you and Don and Bryan will have to come to dinner at my apartment."

"I accept for all of us and hope it's soon. Don't wait until Bryan gets his teeth. That will take awhile."

"I might not produce a Julia Child wonder, but I assure you it will be before Bryan gets his teeth. I'll get a large supply of strained baby food, and if the main course doesn't turn out edible, he can share his with us," Fran laughed.

When they arrived home, Don said Bryan had been such a good boy that he had time to get dinner. He made his specialty—big baked potatoes topped with great chili. Heidi hugged him and proclaimed him the greatest guy on Earth. Fran said she would second that.

"I won't let that go to my head; you two are just tired and hungry." Don served frosted mugs of beer—very cold, American-style. Fran pronounced it one of the best meals she had ever eaten and hoped some day to be as good of a cook. "I have to admit, Fran, this is my only claim in the culinary department. You'll have to do better than this for Tom."

Heidi glared at him. Fran actually choked on a sip of beer; then said, abruptly, "Don, you are way off and certainly jumping to conclusions."

Don did look uncomfortable and said to Fran, "I'm sorry, forgive me, Fran. I seem to be having one of my foot in the mouth days."

Fran regretted her sharp response. She patted Don's hand, "I'll have to forgive anyone who fixed this great dinner, Don." Fran said lightly. "Cheers to the cook." The three clinked their mugs. The moment of tension was past.

As they were clearing the table, Fran said to Heidi and Don, "I don't want to wait until I settle in my apartment to treat you to dinner. Pick a great restaurant and make reservations for tomorrow night. Bryan is happy with me and I love caring for him. You two deserve a night out. No excuses, you must accept."

"No excuses offered, Fran," Don said with a big smile. "We accept."

Friday passed with out too much time left for Fran's thoughts to dwell on Tom. Heidi and Fran took Bryan along to grocery shop at Tesco. Fran found this English super market fantastic. The building was a charming, old English style. It was pretty to look at, not simply utilitarian. It was stocked so well; it outdid most of the super markets that she remembered from back home. Later in the day Fran did laundry, shampooed her hair and did her nails. The day was gone by then and it was time to baby-sit.

When Don came home from the base, he found Heidi ready. Her dark purple sheath silk dress accented her slim beautiful figure. She had put her long black hair in a French twist. Her gold and white costume jewelry was perfect. Don let out a long whistle and a WOW! He took her in his arms and said, "I'm going out with the most beautiful girl in England, tonight."

Heidi pretended a dismayed look. "Only in England?"

"Okay, okay," he gave her a quick kiss on the nose and said, "In the entire world. Your prince charming better get ready."

Don came downstairs, wearing his gray suit with a white shirt. His tie was navy silk with a red and white small leaf pattern. There was a tip of a matching silk handkerchief extending from the breast pocket.

Both girls gave him due admiration. Heidi touched him gently on his smooth cheek and said, "I'm going out with the most handsome man in the world."

They left in a happy glow. Fran was holding Bryan; she kissed his fuzzy head. "Do you know, little one, you have two beautiful parents?"

Fran suddenly realized how deeply she was feeling happiness for them. It was an open feeling, a giving feeling, a little part of the old Fran. At least, she thought, I can now feel joy for others; maybe someday I can unlock myself—for myself.

Chapter 18

Saturday morning, Tom woke very early before daybreak. Immediately, thoughts and worries flooded his mind. More sleep was impossible. He had been in touch with his mother often during these last few days. There had been no more calls from Brendan; worry over this was mounting. Tom felt torn between his necessity to be in London during this coming week and dropping everything to go to Dublin and begin a search for Brendan. His mother had urged him to wait the other week. "After all, there had been the one call telling me he was okay," Susanna had said. Actually, Susanna was trying to play down her own worry. She didn't want to make things harder on Tom, with all the difficulties he already had with the business.

Tom went to the kitchen and made coffee. He looked around this small, cozy kitchen; this home felt truly like his own. How deeply he loved Uncle Cliff and Aunt Berniece; he had stayed with them so much during his life. To them he was more like a son than a nephew. Knowing that his times with them would no longer be as frequent, there had been tears in their eyes when they told him how much they would miss him. Yes, he'd miss them, too. He thought, as he drank his coffee, about how he had wanted them to meet Fran. Be realistic, he told himself. The fun evenings he had wanted with Fran in London during the coming week were just a dream. How had this intense feeling for her happened to him so fast? No denying it—he loved her. He wanted very much to help her through whatever was crushing her; but I guess I'm not really important to her—friendship is all she wants. She hasn't fallen in love with me—face it, Tom. Well, at least not yet, he thought as he rinsed his mug and put it on the drain-board. I can't give up so soon. God knows I can't wait to see her this morning.

Tom arrived promptly at eight o'clock to pick up Fran. She was waiting in the doorway, looking beautiful as always. The day was sunny and clear even in this early morning. Fran was wearing a deep blue colored dress with a print of full-blown white roses throughout. Tom's artistic eye immediately saw the dress was the same shade of blue as Fran's eyes. He thought how I'd love to paint her just like this. This he didn't mention to Fran. He didn't want any personal comment to change the excited and happy smile he saw on her face. Instead he greeted her with a casual "Hi. I'm glad you're all ready. We'll want to have time to shop before I have to go to the shop."

Fran asked, "Oh, don't we have a little time for you to come in? I've been waiting to show you something."

"Sure, I guess we have that much time."

Fran in her excitement automatically took Tom's hand and pulled him on into the house. The moment their hands were locked, Fran felt a thrill she refused to admit. Yet, not wanting to seem rude didn't pull away.

Tom was delighted by this impulsive gesture and fully admitted the joy he felt in her closeness. So hand in hand they came into the living room. Don was watching the telly and holding a squirming Bryan. Don noticed the hand holding and smiled broadly as he greeted Tom. Fran, needing two hands to do so, picked Bryan from Don's arms.

Still holding Bryan, she said to Tom, "Come out to the table." Fran had displayed all the blue and white-striped pottery pieces. Her eyes still shone with pleasure and excitement as she said "Tom, this is just a little gift to say 'thank you' for all you are doing to help me move to Ely. I hope you'll enjoy it on your kitchen shelves."

Tom looked very surprised and a little embarrassed. "Fran, Fran, it's just beautiful. But you know I need no gift of thanks for the pleasure you've given me in allowing me to help you. Thank you so very much." He lifted the cheese keeper in his hands and took off the lid. "Hmmm, I can just see this with a good wedge of Stilton." He put down the keeper and admired all the pieces. "This is really what was needed on those shelves. All I can say is I'll treasure it and enjoy it always, knowing it's a gift from you." He took hold of Fran's elbow and was stopped from any thought of a thank-you kiss by a bouncing Bryan, still being held by Fran, who made everyone laugh by trying to pull Tom's nose.

Heidi came into the room and took Bryan from Fran. She greeted Tom warmly and said she would pack the dishes away for him to take on the next trip.

Fran hugged her and said, "You're dear, thanks so much. We do have to get started."

When they arrived at Ely they went directly to the furniture store. It didn't take long for Fran to decide on her bedroom pieces, in a French provincial style made of warm fruitwood. She followed the advice of the salesman in choosing her springs and mattress. "I can shop for the sheets and things later, Tom, I know we have to stop for lunch and you must get to your shop. To be honest, I can't wait to be in the Cathedral. It's almost a longing or pull to be there."

"We'll go to the Almonry for lunch. Then I'll go to the shop. You said you wanted to hear Evensong at five o'clock. I'll be back a little before and we can attend together. I love the service and try to make it whenever possible."

They hurried through a light lunch together. Tom had to be at the shop but it was Fran who seemed to be in a hurry to go across to the Cathedral. "You'll have a long time to put in at the Cathedral this afternoon, Fran. Would you like me to take you to the shop a little while, and then bring you back here? It isn't too far; you could even walk if you wanted."

Fran shook her head. "Time is never too long in the Cathedral. Besides, I'm really hoping that Ethel Fenman might be there today. I don't know why—but I feel I must talk with her again."

"If you see her, make her stay around to meet me. I'm getting curious about her. By the way, I did promise to ask people at the shop about her. I will today."

A feeling of expectation filled and puzzled Fran as she opened the massive doors. It being early afternoon, the Cathedral had many people taking tours. Fran walked from group to group looking hopefully for Ethel Fenman. Disappointed after looking through-out the entire Cathedral and even in the gift shop, Fran left the Cathedral and walked restlessly about the grounds, for about an hour.

Early that morning, the Cathedral housekeeping ladies, dusting the choir seats, would have been surprised if they could have seen the lady watching them with a tender smile. Etheldreda was once again in mortal form, waiting for Fran. Etheldreda was amused to find herself differently dressed today. The dress was simple, like the first but this one was a plain, soft peach color. She felt down over the soft fabric with her hands. This dress had a pocket on the side. She reached into it and found a fine white linen handkerchief. Whatever for? she thought to herself. Her long soft hair was neatly pulled back in one large, thick braid. She knew the difference was necessary because Fran, in seeing her, would wonder about her looking exactly as she had last week.

Etheldreda saw Fran when she first came in and watched her walk around the Cathedral. She knew Fran was looking for her but there were too many people about for her to approach Fran. She saw Fran leaving. This was not a concern; Fran would return, she knew.

Fran came back into the Cathedral and turned to her right. She walked toward the southwest transept to find the St. Catherine's Chapel. Her booklet listed it as being available for private prayer. She saw no other people around and desired the quiet.

Fran was almost startled when she saw Ethel Fenman standing in front of the St. Catherine's Chapel. She was looking directly at Fran with such a warmth and welcome. Fran was thinking she looks like she expected to see me here. Fran felt joy in seeing her. That emotion was mirrored in St. Etheldreda's face. Fran felt like giving a hug of greeting but stopped from doing so, remembering this was a reserved English lady, and they had only recently met. But Ethel Fenman reached out and took Fran's hand, saying, "I knew"—she caught herself—"I hoped you would be here today."

"Oh, I've wanted so to be back and mostly to see you. I've thought about you so much this week and the things you said to me."

"Have you? You have been in my thoughts too, very much. That you are a very troubled young woman was obvious to me when we met. How are things in your life now, Fran?"

Her almost motherly tone and her choice of words were of one older than Fran had at first thought her to be. "Ethel, would you have time to talk with me today? I know we only recently met and I have no right in asking you to listen to my problems. I can't explain why—but I've had such a feeling that if anyone could help me sort things out, you could. You probably think me presumptuous, or as we say back home, that I'm nuts."

Etheldreda put her head back and gave a silvery chuckle, amused at hearing the American slang. "No, Fran, I don't think you're nuts, nor presumptuous. I told you we were meant to be friends. What are friends for? Besides, I am a—temporary, what you might call, counselor here at Ely. I'll be glad to listen and I will try to help you. No—I *will* help you."

Hearing those words, Fran was filled with the same feeling of hope that had come to her in the early dawn on her first morning in England. What a strange premonition that had been, even stranger now that it was becoming a reality. She knew her help was here in the person of Ethel Fenman. Etheldreda glanced toward the West Doors. No one was there. "Let's walk down to the park behind the Dean's Meadow. We'll sit on a bench and have the talk we need. Let us be silent and meditate as we walk." She said this, fearing others might see Fran alone and talking as they walked. She knew the Lord would give them a time of privacy once they reached the park.

They walked past the Bishop's house and on through the Dean's Meadow and crossed to the park; it was quite deserted. They sat on a bench, in silence, for a few minutes. Fran was trying to assemble her thoughts; she didn't know how much of things past she should tell Ethel.

Ethel turned toward Fran and gazed directly into her eyes. Again in that motherly tone, she said, "Fran dear, talk to me—tell me of all that is troubling you. As I promised—I will help you."

At that moment all Fran's timidity and reserve vanished. She simply began to tell all about herself. She told of visiting England and the stay with Heidi and Don and baby Bryan. She tried to explain her feelings about this place—this Ely—and her decision to move here. She told also of Tom, how she felt toward him and how undeserving she felt of this wonderful man, if he should care for her. -She talked of her life before Jeff, of her dear parents, of her love of singing, her dreams and desires, the open nature she had once possessed. Then she related all that she had remembered during that afternoon in Heidi's garden, all that her life had held with Jeff, to this kindly and concerned new friend. Fran saw once again the vivid scene of Jeff's dead face and her lack of grief as she looked upon it. Fran spoke the words, "I have felt no grief or sorrow at his death. No sorrow that his life, his music was crushed out so terribly. I must be crueler than Jeff ever was." Fran was sobbing, her hands covering her face. "I don't deserve to be happy. I never will."

Etheldreda reached over and gently pulled Fran's hands from her face and moved them quietly to her lap. Etheldreda took her own fingers and tenderly wiped the tears from Fran's cheeks. Then she took the white linen handkerchief from her pocket and gave it to Fran. "Here, dear, dry your face and then you will listen to what I'll tell you."

Fran took the offered linen and thoroughly dried her face. At the touch of it she felt a comfort. She held it tightly in her hands and became composed.

When she knew Fran was ready to listen, Etheldreda said, "Jeff seems to have been a most troubled man—a man very unhappy with himself. What makes a person that way, we do not know. Sometimes a person like this does become selfish and mean and cold to others; they keep taking and never give. What causes this, or how guilty, or how responsible they are, is not known by even the saints in heaven. Only, our Great God knows this. God did give Jeff a wonderful talent for music. Jeff, indeed, gave joy to people through perfecting that talent. Jeff couldn't, though, find joy himself or care to give joy to others. Fran you must accept that Jeff is a child of God just as you are and I am. Perhaps in his last moments Jeff felt a deep sorrow for the hurts and wrongs he had done. Remember, Fran, Jeff's actions may have caused his accident but God is always in control of life and death. Had Jeff lived a longer life it might have added more misery for him or for others. As for his giving of music, the fact that it ended soon was not of your decision. It is not to be grieved for by you or anyone. Jeff's time to die was in God's hands, certainly not yours. Fran, leave Jeff to the merciful God."

Fran remained silent; her eyes searched Etheldreda's face.

"It would be most dishonest, Fran, for you to feel a sorrow at the loss of a person who was causing you to die."

"Oh, yes, Fran," Etheldreda continued, seeing the startled look on Fran's face; "your spirit was being killed just as surely as a body would be killed by daily doses of arsenic. Your loving, open self was being reduced to feelings of hate. You were being blinded to the truth of God's love for you. The song, the music in your heart and voice, was being silenced by emotional and physical tension."

"It's over now, Fran. You are to know you are called by God to be completely alive again. He wants you to know He loves you and expects that love to be returned to Him. He created you with a joyful spirit; it must not remain in danger of dying. Your own gift of voice and music must not be silent and unused. As life unfolds for you, accept and give with the alive spirit that is truly Fran. *Yes*, Fran—God requires this of you. Because He wants this of you, you can know that you *do deserve* any joy that awaits you. Learn from the past that storms in our lives do pass. Sometimes, a fierce storm can leave a path strewn with debris. One must have the strength to sweep it away so that the path is free again"

"I know, Fran that you have read about the life of St. Etheldreda. As a young woman she knew that God was calling her to become a nun. There were many times her spirit felt crushed because of the wants of others. Her dreams and desires were put on hold. Much of her life was spent in ways so different than she wished. Sometimes, because of the feelings and the true needs of others there was much conflict in her mind and heart. There were times of self-doubt and youthful longings for a different way. Yet, knowing clearly what God wanted for her life, she looked to the clean path that was right and took it. It is time, Fran, for you to do likewise. Think, Fran, of the warmth you do feel for your parents and dear friends in your life. Think of the countless creature comforts God provided for you. Think of the beauty that is everywhere in your world, of the beauty of your person and the many talents that God has freely given you. Let your heart swell with praise and thanks for all these things. If you continue to hold and hug close this sense of unworthiness in your heart, and don't acknowledge God's freely given love for you, the joy you do possess in these gifts will become impossible for you to feel. Your spirit will then be completely dead. You would become like Jeff. It must not be. Consider your path, what God wills for you and take it, Fran. Say it, Fran—I am deserving of the good things God wants in my life."

Fran's eyes were held by Etheldreda's while she was listening to this soft voice. Every word was penetrating her inner-most being. She felt the words to almost be an absolution. She felt every direction to be compelling.

Ethel stood up and looked down, smiling at Fran, "come, Fran, say it, say it.

"I am deserving of the good things God wants for my life. Oh, Ethel—" There were tears glistening in Fran's eyes. This time they were of joy.

Fran rose and they walked back toward the Cathedral. They did not talk. There was such a bond of friendship that the silence was comfortable, small talk was needless, everything had been said. Fran was clinging to the memory of each word that Ethel had spoken. They passed other people but of course they saw only Fran. When they reached the doors no one was about. Ethel put her hand on Fran's shoulder and said, "I must go away—and I will not see you again—for a long while. You will remember all I've said, I know."

"Ethel, of course I will. I can not even begin to thank you or tell you of my overwhelming gratitude for your help, or tell you of the peace I'm feeling because of you. I feel so close to you." Fran rambled on, feeling dismayed at the thought of not seeing Ethel again for, as she said, a very long time. "Tom is coming and we are staying for Evensong. I was thinking we could all go to dinner together, afterward. Won't you please stay and be our guest? I can't ever begin to repay you for what you have done for me. I'd like so much to be with you and try to do a little something to show how I feel."

"Fran, I really can't. Repay me by being the real you and be happy. Don't be unhappy about anything now, even at my going. In your future, if you ever do need special help, whisper a little prayer to St. Etheldreda here. God will hear your prayer and she will pray it with you. Now, go inside, Tom will be coming and it's almost time for service. God bless you, my dear Fran." They hugged each other for a moment, and then Etheldreda turned down the walk.

Fran entered the Cathedral and walked over to the statue of Christ that had attracted her attention on her first trip to Ely. This time her mind was filled with the reality of God's love for her and her heart held a joyous response. She put her right hand into the outstretched hand of the statue, feeling it to be a sign of her newly found trust. She heard the door open and her heart gave a leap when she turned and saw Tom. He came beside her, overjoyed at the radiant smile she gave him, and he sensed something different about her. "Did you see your mystery woman today?"

"Yes, Tom we talked and talked. She helped me straighten a lot of things out. I just can't explain how special she is. She said she was a kind of temporary counselor here at Ely. She told me she had to go away and I probably wouldn't see her for a very long time. I wanted her to wait and have dinner with us but she couldn't. I just came in and she was starting down the walk, you must have seen her, a pretty woman wearing a peach colored dress. She couldn't have walked that fast."

"No, I didn't see anyone around when I was coming in and I looked all about because I thought you might be outside."

"That's strange; I was in here for only a minute." Fran looked at the purse she was carrying and saw she was holding, with its handle, the large white linen handkerchief. "I forgot to give her back her hanky. I was crying and she gave it to me. I still can't believe you didn't see her."

"Well, my pretty one, I'm glad to be seeing you. I guess she will just have to remain the mystery lady."

"I can't think of her like that anymore, Tom. She is just the most extraordinary person I've ever met. I really needed her touching my life. Somehow, I know, it was only her presence and words that could have reached me and set my thinking in a whole new way. I thank God for her. I wonder what she meant by a long while? If she had family here she might be in touch and I'd find out when she is returning—if only I could find them. Did you ask about her at the shop?"

"Yes, no one there was familiar with her. Hey, maybe the Cathedral staff would know—if she had been a counselor. I'll inquire next week when the office is open."

Fran and Tom walked to the front of the Cathedral where the chairs were set for Evensong. Fran thrilled at the sound of the clear young voices. She hadn't enjoyed even hearing music for such a long time. Now, she let the beauty of it drench her spirit and offered it in thanksgiving for her newly found peace.

Chapter 19

—————⟫●⟪—————

They started the drive back immediately after Evensong, planning to stop for dinner on the way. As soon as they got into the car, Tom told Fran of his afternoon call to his mother. "Do you remember, Fran, I told you about my stepfather's son, Father Matthew McKenna, who lives in the States in Washington, DC?"

"Yes, Tom, I remember you talking of him."

"Mom called him to talk about Brendan. Of course, he's Brendan's half brother too. Well, good news! Father Matt said he had been going to call Mom to let her know he was coming to Ireland, this next Monday, and will be staying for two weeks. He's chaplain with a tour group from his church. When he heard of the trouble, he told Mom he would leave the group in Dublin, put on his casual clothes and with his Irish accent still intact, might be able to get a lead on Brendan's whereabouts. I'm so relieved. I was feeling guilty about not going over to try. But I really need to get things working well at the London shop this week, with the change in management. We haven't seen much of Father Matt but we are all very close in feeling. I was really like a son to Dermod and he was a wonderful to me. I think I had two of the finest men a boy could have in his life. I loved both of my fathers so much. Dermod, Mom, Brendan and I had flown to Washington, DC, for Matt's ordination. Brendan was only eight years old. Father Matt came over for our father's funeral, two years later. He has been over for visits twice since. He is a great guy, much like his father, warm, witty and peace loving. He looks like Dermod, too, tall and lean with sandy colored hair, Irish blue eyes and rugged handsome features. I'm anxious to see him; I'll go over while he's here. I feel hopeful he'll find Brendan and help to straighten him out. Then, we can all get together."

"Tom, I hope with all my heart that can be soon. I can only imagine the sickening anxiety that you and your Mom must be going through." Suddenly, Fran realized that she was fully aware of the pain and worry they were feeling. She had been sorry when Tom had looked tired and worried before, but her response about this problem with Brendan was one of personal detachment. Her words of concern were mainly polite ones, wanting to make Tom feel easier and happier, but detached nonetheless. Now, she knew her spirit was truly opened to others, to their sorrows and their joys. Now, instead of anger toward young Brendan she felt the concern and worry as Tom had. Yes, she was really alive again and whole.

After their stop for dinner, the drive together passed quickly. Tom talked more of his family memories. They were almost to Don and Heidi's house when Tom started telling Fran how he had enjoyed seeing Washington, DC. "We had two days of sightseeing after Father Matt's ordination. We saw many of the monuments and went inside the White House. We spent some time in the Mall area and had a little time at the Mellon Art Gallery. There were so many things to see and time was so short. We didn't get into any of the other Smithsonian buildings or the Capitol. I hope someday to go back and spend at least a week. I keep a "sometime list," and that's near the top. Have you gone to DC often, Fran?"

"I grew up in Pennsylvania, not far from DC. Yet, I was there to sightsee, a little, only once. I was about fourteen years old. You've seen DC as much as I have. You know, I'd like to go back again, too. Also, I'd like to see Mt. Vernon, George Washington's home. It's in Virginia, not far from DC. I think I'll put that on *my* "sometime list.""

Tom stopped the car in front of the house; he turned to Fran and said, "I hope seeing more of London is still on your "sometime list.""

"Of course, it is. I've seen so little, having just that one day so far."

As they walked to the door, Tom said, "I did mention, once, about having some free time while I'm there during next week. I had asked to show London to you. You didn't say yes but you didn't quite say no. I'm asking again, Fran, could we spend some time together in London, next week?"

"Tom," Fran paused a little as she looked at his dear face. Tom literally held his breath. "Tom, I would just love that."

Tom's smile was even broader than Fran's. "You don't know how happy that makes me. I'll be staying with my Uncle Cliff and Aunt Berniece. I know they would love you to stay with them but the flat is small. I think you would be more comfortable in a hotel and I will pay for that."

"No, Tom, I'll pay for the hotel—that I insist upon. It won't be a problem for me. I still have a while until my Ely flat is ready. I have time now to see more of London—a chance to do it with my favorite Brit makes it perfect."

Tom replied, "Thank you, Madam," in a staid, theatrical British accent.

They were both laughing when they opened the door. They found Don and Heidi at the kitchen table, having some cheese and crackers and wine. Scooby came and rubbed around Fran's ankles, then went to his food dish and began to eat. "I don't know what we are going to do with him when you go, Fran. He hasn't eaten a thing all day," Heidi said.

Fran went over and patted his head and scratched behind his silken ears. "Oh, I'll miss him, too. Gee, Heidi, I feel almost guilty; I'll be gone all next week, too, before my move."

Don said, "Not to worry, when cats get really hungry enough they eat. We'll just keep him happy on catnip. Tell us, pretty maid, where are you off to next week?"

Tom told of their plans. Don looked at Heidi and smiled. This time Heidi smiled back in agreement, with no sign of contradiction, to what she knew Don was thinking.

"We'll have to decide some things, how to get you there and where to stay," Tom said. "There's a nice small hotel called the Academy, on Grover Street. It's near the British Museum. I'll be tied up a lot in the daytime at the beginning of the week. Fran, you could spend some time there. Also, The Academy would be an easy place for us to meet as the shop is only a couple of miles away. It is a really pretty place with its patio garden; and the food is good there, too. If we're lucky and there is room, it would be ideal."

Tom called the Academy Hotel and told them a room for one week was needed through Friday night. They told him he was in luck. Someone had to leave earlier than expected and there was a single room available for that time and available that night. Tom cupped his hand over the phone. "Fran, they have a room. Would you want to drive on with me tonight? It would be much easier; you wouldn't have to take the train and cab."

Fran immediately got her Visa card from her purse and handed it to Tom, saying, "Sounds like a good idea. I'll go up and pack." She squeezed Heidi's hand, "You don't mind if I go off like this, do you? You know I'm happy being here with you."

"Of course, we don't mind. We're glad you are having some fun. Go now, hurry and pack."

"I won't be long." Fran almost ran from the room.

"Sit down, Tom, and have a glass of wine and a snack. When a woman says I won't be long, especially when they are packing, don't believe it," Don said, grinning.

Heidi put her hands on her hips, "remember, it takes me a long time because I have to pack for you, too."

"Okay, Hon, I'm chastised; that was a rather chauvinistic remark." Don looked at Tom and said, "Anyway, a good woman is worth waiting for."

Tom raised his glass, "I'll drink to that."

Heidi looked thoughtful. "It's so good seeing Fran exuberant—her real self again. Even while she has been seemingly happy with us, there had been an inner burden or torment that was apparent to me. It's gone—whatever it was is gone. Being with you, Tom, must be good for her."

"I can't take the credit for the change in Fran. I understand exactly what you mean. She seems free, as if a great weight has been lifted from her. She saw that Ethel Fenman, again, at Ely. Fran said they talked a long time. Whatever was said has almost worked a miracle. I still would like to meet that lady but she seems a hard one to pin down. She made herself available to Fran, that's the important thing."

A beaming Fran came into the kitchen. "I'm all packed and ready."

Don was washing the wine-glasses at the sink; he turned and said, "Well, I'll be darned. I told Tom he'd have a long wait. I apologize."

"You had better," Fran said, laughing. She hugged Heidi and Don and picked up Scooby and carried him as far as the door. "Now you eat and be a good kitty. I'll be back to see you soon." Scooby was not purring when Fran put him down. He turned and with his tail straight in the air, stalked away with the dignity a cat shows when it is very displeased.

The drive passed so quickly. Neither Tom nor Fran felt in the least tired, even though the day had been a long one. They talked of the countless things to see and do; deciding on the things Fran would do when alone and the things they would share.

"Fran, I want each evening to be special. I have some places in mind. Is it all right with you if I go ahead and make reservations at restaurants and plans for the evenings? You tell me, though, if there is somewhere you would like to try."

"Tom, it would be great if you choose. I love surprises. Besides, this is your territory and you know the best places. Tom, if you are going to have a lot on you this week, if you should feel tired, we don't have to do a nightly marathon."

"When I think of spending time with you, I know that tired won't be in my vocabulary this week."

Fran was delighted with the look of Georgian charm of the Academy Hotel. When Fran was checked in she looked about and enjoyed the cozy sitting room. She looked out of the French doors to the inviting patio. "I just love this place, I'm so glad they had room. Staying here will make the week perfect." Noticing that the hotel listed a live music program for one of the evenings, in the hotel's restaurant, Fran said. "We could eat here that evening—if you would like, Tom."

"That sounds good to me. I'm happy you like it here; I thought you would. I see the bags were taken to your room. I'll call you in the morning about the plans for meeting Uncle Cliff and Aunt Berniece. We'll have dinner together at Christopher's."

"I don't think I remember you mentioning a Christopher. Is he a relative, too?"

Tom grinned and shook his head, "No, Christopher's is a restaurant. It's not far from here. The dining room is very beautiful and the menu has a wide choice. I think you'll like it. I can't wait till Uncle Cliff and Aunt Berniece meet you. I think you'll like them, too."

"I'm sure I will, Tom. Despite your protestations you are looking very tired and I have to admit I'm beginning to feel that way, too." They walked across the small lobby to the entrance. Fran took hold of Tom's sleeve. "Goodnight, Tom dear, and thank you for bringing me this far."

Tom noticed Fran's more serious tone and liked the *dear* being added to his name. "Fran, I thank you for coming. I was driving here anyway; you have no need to thank me."

"No, no, Tom"—she took hold of his hand—"not thank you for the ride here—just thank you for your part in bringing me so far, not in miles, but in myself."

The entrance door opened. The incoming guests were quite apologetic at disturbing Tom and Fran. Not even the interruption could dim the look that their eyes expressed to each other. "Good night now, Tom, till tomorrow." Tom spoke softly, till tomorrow, dearest Fran."

Fran was shown to her room and walked decorously. Once alone in her room she whirled around in unmitigated joy, humming "I Could Have Danced All Night."

Tom was feeling no less happy. He wished his Aunt and Uncle would have been up to share his news of Fran's visit. However, the flat was quiet and he went quietly to his room.

Fran woke early but lay still for awhile, allowing the wonderful feeling of well being to sweep over her. She was thanking God for this new day, this new beginning. Her thoughts turned to her parents; it was early afternoon in the States, a good time to call. There had been a few calls since her coming to England; she had been concerned for them but really hadn't missed them. Now, she longed to hear their voices and share with them where she was and what her plans were for the coming week. The thought of how much they loved her wrapped around her. No matter how they had tried to tell her and show her their love, she had been unable to feel even that for such a long time.

The call was a long, happy one. Before Fran said goodbye, she told them how she loved and missed them and that even if she stayed in England she would plan to see them soon.

When the call was finished there were tears of joy glistening in Irene Colbert's eyes. Her husband Bruce gave her a hug and said, "Our little girl is back on track."

"I know she is. I haven't felt this happy in a long time, Bruce. I bet that Tom she spoke of has something to do with it." Irene laughed a little. "I'd really like to meet him. How would you like to go to England, Bruce?"
"Well, Irene, we might just do that. Maybe if Fran doesn't make it for Christmas, we'll decide to go then."

After the call Fran showered and dressed. The September Sunday was warm, so she chose her pale gray, short sleeve, raw silk dress. With it she wore the silver with dark blue stones necklace and earrings. These had been a gift for her twenty-first birthday from her parents. How close she felt to them as she put on this jewelry.

Tom called, telling her that they would be at the hotel at noon and go directly to Christopher's because they closed by three-thirty p.m. on Sundays. "After dinner, we might see St. George's Church and a few things close— maybe the Gardens at Russell Square. After that, Fran, Aunt Berniece and Uncle Cliff would like us to stop at their flat when we take them home. Is that okay with you?"

"Tom, I can't wait to meet them. The whole plan for the day sounds great. I'll be ready and waiting out front; you wont have the trouble of parking." Fran laughed, "Just look for the lady in the gray dress."

"I'll just look for the prettiest girl in the world. See you soon."

Fran glanced at the clock—two hours yet until I see Tom. She looked at herself in the mirror; "you silly thing," she smiled at her self and said aloud, "you're worse than a kid waiting for Christmas." She thought, that gal I'm seeing in the sophisticated looking dress must be someone else; she certainly doesn't look as giddy as I feel.

Fran went down to the pretty sitting room and chose a book about the British Museum from the well-stocked shelves. She got so lost in the wonders of the vast collection that the time passed more quickly than she could have imagined. She hurriedly replaced the book and went outside. It was only a few minutes until Tom was there.

Tom helped Fran into the car and his face shown with pride when he introduced Fran to his Uncle and Aunt. There was genuine pleasure in the meeting. The entire day was fun for all of them.

When they reached the flat, Aunt Berniece said to Fran, "Dear, please use our first names; Mr. and Mrs. Hart sounds so stuffy. Better still, call us Uncle Cliff and Aunt Berniece as Tom does. Would that be all right with you?"

"I should like that very much. For a long time I've thought of you as Aunt Berniece and Uncle Cliff because Tom has spoken of you both so often."

While Tom and Uncle Cliff looked over some paperwork at Cliff's desk, Fran and Berniece went to the kitchen and fixed a light supper. Aunt Berniece produced over aprons for both of them. "It wouldn't do to get a spot on that lovely gray dress and I'd hate to ruin mine." It was a two piece dress of sky blue with mother-of-pearl buttons down the jacket.

"I've been admiring that dress, Aunt Berniece, it's really lovely."

"Thank you, Fran. It's one of the few I've ever bought at Harrods. I felt today was rather special, a good time to wear it."

Berniece was such a pretty woman. She wore her glistening silver hair at medium length and softly waved and puffed to the side. She was small with just a little roundness, not really plump. Her eyes were blue. Indeed the dress was perfect for her. Fran had thought when she first met them what a beautiful couple they were. Uncle Cliff was straight and tall, the expression on his face warm and gentle. Tom was not quite as tall but there certainly was a resemblance to Uncle Cliff.

The supper was enjoyed in a totally relaxed mood by all. Fran truly meant it when she said she hated to leave, but felt Tom and Uncle Cliff needed rest before starting such a busy week. When Tom and Fran were leaving, Aunt Berniece gave Fran a hug and Uncle Cliff said to Tom, "Now don't be taking her back without another visit."

Fran reached for his hand and said, "Not a chance. This evening was fun; I want to come back."

When the door was closed, Berniece smiled at Cliff and hummed a few bars of Mendelssohn's *Wedding March*.

"Now, Berniece, don't be getting ideas. Tom hasn't said anything about that."

"Not yet, Cliff, not yet, however, I was thinking maybe I should have saved this dress for the wedding."

Fran insisted that Tom take her directly to the hotel. "The day has been wonderful, Tom, but I'm keeping in mind that this is a work week for you."

"Are you now? Well, remember all work and no play makes Tom a dull boy. Tomorrow night, my dear, we'll go out on the town and I'll refuse to watch the clock."

When they were in the lobby of the hotel, Tom said, "I'll be here at six tomorrow and after that—promise, no clock watching."

Fran smiled and crossed her heart, "I promise I won't."

Tom took hold of her hands, "Even one day seems a long time, Fran, till I see you again. You know that."

"Yes, Tom, it's the same for me." Again, their eyes spoke the feelings of their hearts.

Monday morning was gray with a little rain. Fran had a leisurely breakfast in the hotel restaurant before leaving for the museum. Her thoughts were filled with the pleasant memories of yesterday and the delicious anticipation of the evening to come. There was one disquieting concern that she simply couldn't disregard. She had never talked with Tom about her life with Jeff. Free as she felt now from that hold on her life, she could speak of it without the hurt or the guilt. She wanted to be open with Tom about all of her life; yet she hated to cloud the glowing feeling that now was theirs. Still, she resolved to talk of this soon.

When Fran returned from the museum there was a message waiting from Tom. "I'll see you at six. No need for fancy dress; nor any dancing or theater tonight. You were right, this 'dull boy' is feeling tired."

Fran laughed. Whatever they did was all right with her. Just being with Tom was perfect. Besides, she thought, her feet would be happy she wouldn't be dancing. She had spent six hours enthralled in the Prehistoric and Roman Britain Galleries. She planned to spend at least two more of her days at the museum; even that would never be enough time to enjoy the vast collection there.

The rain had cleared and, for September, the evening was mild. Fran thought of wearing her purple suit but chose instead, something a little more casual but very smart, a black and white zebra printed blouse and black slacks. With large silver earrings, she looked smashing as always, as Tom said upon seeing her.

When they were in the car Tom suggested his favorite Chinese restaurant, Fung Shing. "Is that all right with you, Fran?"

"More than all right, I haven't had Chinese for a long time, it sounds terrific."

During dinner the conversation mostly was of Fran's day exploring the museum. Tom was fascinated that she retained so many details for so many things. "It's been years since I've been in the museum. You make it sound so exciting. Maybe on one of your days there I'll make it for part of the time. I wish I could be there with you for all the sightseeing. But from the way you sound, I'd take a back seat to the collection. I'm afraid you wouldn't notice I was there."

Fran laughed, "Oh, I don't think that would be true, my handsome fellow. You would find no competition from the Lindow Man."

"Oh, thanks a lot. I can find a great comfort in that, *you wicked one.*" Fran grinned impishly.

It was dark when they left the restaurant. "Fran, I'm going to bring you back from Prehistoric Britain. You've got to see the wonderful modern Lloyds of London building. Seeing it at night is a must. It's not terribly far and the traffic is light tonight. It's the perfect time for doing it.

When they settled into the comfort of their seats, Tom turned on the car radio to the classical station. The Grieg *Piano Concerto in A Minor* was being played. When it was over the announcer said, "Our next selection is Beethoven's *Sonata No. Nine in A, Op.47*—known as the *Kreutzer Sonata.* The violin soloist is the late Jeffrey Amberson with Frederick Hendermer at the piano."

Fran's body stiffened. She felt icy cold. A wave of nausea went through her. Tom looked at Fran, his heart filled with concern. It was only then that he had realized who and what Jeff Amberson had been. As he reached to turn the music off, Fran's hand stopped him. At the first sweet, pulsating notes of Jeff's violin Fran closed her eyes and kept repeating in her mind Ethel Fenman's words, "it's over; it's over, Fran, it's over." With the first strong sound of the piano she thought of her dear friend Fred. How long since she had thought of him and Susan. Her being started to relax. As the instruments flowed together she thought of that first concert, the first time she had heard this work played by Jeff and Fred. Yes, Jeff's music was to live on in the recordings he had made; for this she was glad. She could listen now and be calm. Yes, thank you God, I am really free, she said in the silence of her heart.

She turned off the radio and looked at Tom's face, so dear and still so tense in concern for her. "I'm all right, Tom. I have wanted to talk with you about that part of my life. Now is the time."

They continued to drive toward the center of the city. Fran told Tom all that had happened but trying, as Ethel Fenman had done, to make excuses for the unhappy man Jeff had been. She told of her guilt over her lack of grief and repeated almost word for word the advice and direction Ethel had given her. "Now, I find that I can even hear Jeff's music with peace inside me, Tom, I'm free, truly free. She reached her hand to cover his on the steering wheel. Right now I'm very happy.

Tom sighed deeply in relief; his face was relaxed and smiling when he looked at her. "Right now, I'm very happy too, my precious."

They went into the hotel together. Tom took the coat Fran was carrying and put it around her shoulders. He held her hand and led her out to the patio. The night had become chilly and no one else was there. He wanted them to be alone.

127

"Fran, you surely know how happy I am that you are here. You must know how special you are to me." Tom thought he would risk saying that much. He wanted to say so much more, but still was almost afraid.

"Tom, you couldn't be as happy as I am being here. You are, indeed, special to me."

After the moments of closeness they had felt so many times, this almost awkward exchange seemed ludicrous. Their eyes met and they both started laughing. Soon the laughing stopped. Tom looked for a moment at that beautiful, tender, upturned face and softly said, "I love you, Fran, beyond my words, I love you."

Fran touched his face gently with her fingers, "I love you, Tom, with all my heart, I love you."

Tom took her in his arms and brushed her soft cheek with his lips; then, there was a promise of forever as their lips met together in that first kiss.

Chapter 20

Father Matt Mckenna reached overhead for his carry-on. The Aer Lingus flight from Washington, DC was soon to touch at Dublin Airport. He wanted time to change from the casual shirt he had worn on the flight to his clerical Roman collar. It would be better to be recognizably dressed for getting his pilgrimage group through customs and for meeting their Irish guide. He disliked changing in the cramped rest room of the plane. To make it a little easier he had worn his black serge dress pants on the flight. As he adjusted his collar, he thought, strange how it seemed to make him inaccessible to some people. He had thought when he first was given that collar that it was not just a sign of his calling but a sign, to all, that he was there to meet their needs. It often didn't seem to work that way, especially with teens and young adults. The few young people, from his parish, that were along on this trip had opened up and talked with him more during this flight than in all the time they had known him. They had talked of their faith and of their doubts and of sometimes seeing an ambiguity with the gospel of love and dogmatic rules. Some questions were hard. He hoped he had dealt with them well. One thing he knew, when he got back to his parish he'd spend more time in relaxed home visits and less time in pointless meetings and endless liturgical changes and discussion groups. These were always with the people who loved such things and attended any parish function available. These were the people whose spiritual life was not really changed by any of this. Yes, he'd seek out the infrequently seen young and go where he was truly needed in these changing times. Lost in thought, he took much longer than he meant in this limited facility. There was a knock on the door and an impatient voice said, "How *long* are you going to be?" The owner of the voice, seeing the collar, said in an embarrassed tone, "Oh, I'm sorry, Father."

Father Matt smiled and said, "Do please forgive me, my good man. I didn't mean to be so long." He put on his black coat as he returned to his seat.

When the group reached the hotel, Father Matt told them he would leave them in the good hands of their tour guide. "I'll catch up with you as soon as I can. I've some family business that I must see to. Please pray for a special intention. God bless you all along your way—and have a lot of fun."

The group expressed sorrow at his leaving and assured him of their prayers. With their happy excitement clearly showing, he knew they would get on very well without him.

He checked into the hotel and went directly to his room. He was tired and wanted to rest before calling Susanna and planning a course of action. He was hoping that Susanna would have heard from Brendan, that this worry was over. Tired as he was he simply couldn't rest and dialed Susanna's number.

Susanna had taken the day off so she and Matt could be in touch as soon as possible. Her worry had become so intense that had Matt not been coming she would have allowed Tom to drop everything and start a search for Brendan. She picked up the phone on the first ring. When she heard Matt's voice, she cried, "Matt, I'm so grateful you are here." He could hardly understand her words, her voice was shaking. This calm, courageous woman was truly at the breaking point.

"Susanna, I'll rent a car and come up to you right now."

"No, Matt," her voice was calmer. "Please start looking for Brendan as soon as possible. I did notify the Gardai but since Brendan left with his things and he had called me that one time, they won't classify him as a missing person. They will do nothing. I know—I just know there is something terribly wrong."

They talked for a few minutes longer. Father Matt asked about Tom.

"Matt, Tom would have come, he wanted to. However, he has been so busy with the changes in shop management; right now is a bad time for him to leave London. I insisted he should wait. Also, he mentioned meeting a girl. I get the feeling that she is rather special to him. I told him you were coming and that you would help. He is very worried too and sounded relieved. If you feel he could be of additional help, he will come over. We both felt with your being Irish that you might have a way of accomplishing more. When you find Brendan, maybe we can all be together before you go back. Oh, Matt, thank you."

Farther Matt felt anxiety that he wouldn't fulfill Susanna's expectations; her need was so great. "Susanna dear, I'll try with all my strength and pray with all my heart. Try—please do try to take care of yourself. I'll start looking today and be in touch with you."

Father Matt started out, still dressed in his black and collar. His first and most feared search began at the hospitals and ambulance services and the morgue; all the places the Gardai would have checked had Brendan been listed as a missing person. Everywhere, he was met with the deepest respect; every question was answered and every help given, but to no avail. He felt grateful for that. He hadn't thought to check the jail; that he'd do tomorrow.

Matt was pleased the hotel had a restaurant; he hadn't eaten since the light breakfast on the plane. The restaurant was not yet crowded. It was good to be quiet and alone. The tour group had departed in the bus for a drive around Dublin Bay and dinner elsewhere.

When he went to his room, he looked longingly at his bed. He hadn't slept on the plane and the day had been a long and taxing one. Still, he heard Susanna's pleading voice in his mind and couldn't give in to the tiredness. He showered and shaved and felt a bit better, glad for the two cups of strong coffee at diner. He put on his only pair of tan slacks and a dark blue pullover top and his tan, lined jacket. The evening was damp and chilly but he walked the short distance from his hotel to the Temple Bar area. There, among the crowd of young people, he thought he must stand out as a tourist. He felt so old and different as he observed them. There were many older people, obviously tourists, like himself. He walked through the maze of narrow, cobbled streets, trying to look at each young face. He hadn't seen Brendan for two years, but he couldn't have changed that much from his recent graduation picture of the spring. Matt thought he'd know him anywhere even if, God forbid, he had one of those silly spiked haircuts and earrings. It was late when he decided to go into some of the most likely pubs.

In the third and final one he ordered a pint at the bar and engaged the barman in casual conversation. He took Brendan's picture from his wallet and asked, "Have you seen this lad in here?"

The barman gave Matt a curious look but took the picture and studied it. "He's not one of the regulars that I know. He could have been in; there are so many I can't remember them all." He gave a shrug and handed the picture back. "It's half-ten, I'll be closin soon."

Matt returned to his room and despite his worry and disappointment of the evening, fell into a sound sleep.

When he woke the sun was bright through the window. It was ten-thirty a.m. He hadn't slept so late in years, even forgetting to arrange for saying his daily Mass. He dressed in his clerical garb and took time to say his daily office before going down for breakfast. His first visit of the day was the jail;

it proved fruitless. He checked at the docks but was unable to receive any information that would be helpful. Next he checked train stations and the main bus stop. He showed Brendan's picture to drivers of buses and taxis, everyone he encountered was respectful to this priest asking questions; all were sorry they couldn't help more. Matt ended his day's hunting for Brendan at some low-cost hotels, but to no avail.

He went back to the hotel room and put in a call to the nearby parish church. Matt explained his situation and was given permission to say the second Mass held each day, for as long as he was in the area. Next he put in the call he was dreading to dear Susanna. He had no small breakthrough of hope to give her; only the promise to keep trying.

After Matt told Susanna of all he had done so far, Susanna said she thought of a friend of Brendan's, that he had known from the summers spent in Connemara. "They were close friends and wrote some to each other once in a while. The lad's name is John Hobson. He and his sister lived with their very old maternal grandmother. I don't know her name or how to reach her. The thought just came to me that Brendan might have been in touch with John. Maybe he even went to Connemara. Brendan had mentioned a long while ago that the sister had moved with her husband to Dublin. I have no idea of her married name."

Father Matt made some notes while Susanna was talking. "Well, it's not much to go on, but then little threads can turn into cloth. Susanna, what is the name of the family that Brendan worked for and stayed with during the summers? They might know how to contact this John Hobson."

"Matt, their name was Hagan—Bart and Maggie Hagan—lovely people. But he died last winter and she sold the horse farm. That is why Brendan didn't plan another summer there. I have no idea where she is now. Of course," Susanna sighed, "Brendan said he was in Dublin with friends— so maybe thinking of the Connemara connection is useless."

"Any lead to follow is better than none, Susanna. I'm going to change clothes and have some dinner. Then I'm going to go back to where the young gather at Temple Bar. If I have no luck, tomorrow I'll see what I can do with the Connemara information. I know hour heart is breaking, Susanna. You're in my heart and prayers. I'll call you tomorrow."

Again, he started through the maze of narrow streets with their countless little shops and pubs; he went into many systematically. As he went into each he always managed to show the clerk or barman Brendan's picture. All were very busy, some were polite, and some were clearly annoyed. No one remembered seeing Brendan. On his seventh stop at the Elephant and Castle, the barman was extremely busy but took time to look carefully at the picture.

He looked at Matt, seeing the resemblance to the young man in the picture. "Might you be this lad's father? He looks like you."

"No, he's my kid brother Brendan. We haven't been in touch and I'm a bit worried for him. My good man, I know you're busy here but I'm askin if you would kindly keep a look out for him and if possible find out where he could be located. I'll check back—and tell him, please, to call his mom. I know it is a trouble; but it is important."

The barman smiled knowingly, "I have young ones of my own, often a worry to be sure. I'll try my best. Now, what will you be havin?

"Thank you much; I deeply appreciate your caring. For now, I'll have a pint of Guinness, please. Matt looked around again at the crowd of young people and kept watching the door, for new arrivals, as he sipped his drink. He had thought of asking some of the young customers in the pubs if they had ever encountered Brendan. He had decided against this just in case there was trouble and he would be talking to the wrong person.

Matt had spoken in as quiet a voice as possible, in this noisy room, to the barman and was careful in the showing of the picture. He hadn't paid particular attention to the young man seated on his left. The man had been there, eating a hamburger while reading a paperback book, when Matt sat down beside him. He took no notice of Matt. Matt glanced at him now and was surprised to see the intense stare directed at him. Before the young man, with the freckled face and flame red hair with a ridge of bangs, could look away, Matt smiled and said, "Hello."

The man said "Hello" in return, then turned away in obvious discomfort. He picked up his book, put money on the bar and left without another glance at Matt.

Knowing no behavior is strange in an Irish pub, Matt thought little of it. He sipped a bit more of his pint, paid for it and said good night to the barman.

Matt turned to his right and walked on planning to stop at other pubs. He never noticed Michael Griffith standing in the shadows watching the doorway of the Elephant and Castle. Michael fell in behind Matt at some distance. The crowd was thinning and he took care not to be seen should Matt suddenly turn. Matt made quick stops at two other pubs. Each time Michael found a place to hide and wait. Matt continued to the right and then made a left toward O'Connell Bridge. On the corner of the bridge he saw The Daniel O'Connell pub. The night had become really cold and he was shivering. A cup of hot, strong tea would go mighty good, he thought, and a sandwich before going back to the hotel. When he went inside, he thought this not a likely place to ask about Brendan. The few customers there didn't seem to be the young sort he had seen in most of the pubs. Yet, when he was served he showed the picture to the middle-aged waitress.

She smiled broadly when looking at the picture. "Sure, I've seen him, the young handsome lad. Not for a long while, though. Early in the summer he came often with a group of friends. Sometimes, late, when we weren't too busy—they'd get to feelin good and tellin stories and start to singin. When we felt it a bother to the other customers, we would have to stop them or ask them to leave. They were nice lads though—on the whole. There was one—he seemed a bit older—a big hulk of a man. He could be laughin and charmin and storytellin and then become almost glum and mean. The drink, I guess. Sean they called im. I don't remember the others names. There was one with bright red hair. He was always makin eyes at young Cathey—she worked here then. She'd have not to do with im. She's goin to college to be a doctor and has her head on straight." She handed back the picture to Matt. "Why are ye askin? Has ther been trouble? That bunch seemed to have some rebel feelins."

Matt explained about being Brendan's brother and not being in touch for a while and just wanting to see him. He added nothing else, knowing that the group wouldn't be back here. He feared more than ever for Brendan's well being. His thoughts were of the red haired young man he encountered at the Elephant and Castle. Questions raced through his mind like quick-silver. Was he the same man the waitress described? Did he know where Brendan was? Had he seen the picture? If so, why didn't he say? If there was no trouble—he would have.

Matt felt warmer when he came out of O'Connell's but very tired and not wanting the long walk back to the hotel. The buses ran late in Dublin; he still had time to catch one. Michael had wanted to tail him and find where he was staying; he had waited on the bridge with mixed feelings. He felt sorry for Brendan and knew this might be a way out for him; but it would surely be an end to the plans and Sean's rage wasn't something he was ready to face. Michael followed Matt to the bus stop. Matt was the only person boarding the bus. Michael almost decided to get on but not knowing if anything was learned at O'Connell's, the old hangout, felt he shouldn't take that risk. Matt would surely recognize him as the man in the pub and wonder. He walked back to where he had parked his car and drove to his flat.

John Hobson had moved in with him and was asleep on the pullout sofa when Michael went in. He shook John awake. "Get up; we've got to talk."

John sat up and looked at the tense expression on Michael's face. "What is it, man? You look like you've seen a ghost."

"I think I've seen worse than that. I've seen Brendan's brother and he's asking questions about him all over. I thought Brendan's brother was English and lived over there. This man was Irish, looked like Brendan and talked with the accent."

"Brendan has two half-brothers. Tom is English, he does live in England. Father Matt McKenna is Irish, his father was Dermod. Matt's own mother died and Dermod married Susanna who was a widow; Tom is her son. Dermod and Susanna's son is Brendan. But Father Matt lives in the States. What's he doin over here?

What he's doin is hunting for Brendan. Being a priest, everyone will be out for helpin him. He didn't have his collar on though, in the pubs. Sean's not to be likin this bit of news."

John looked confused, "Didn't Brendan go home? He planned to when he left me on Sunday. Is he missing?

Michael had forgotten that John wasn't told about Sean's finding Brendan on that Sunday night and taking him forcibly to the old cottage. He told John what had happened and that he believed Brendan to be still at the cottage, being watched by someone Sean knew. John wasn't told of Sean's persuasion with a gun nor of Brendan's being kept tied. Michael said Sean hadn't talked with him for a few days and as far as he knew Brendan was still at the cottage. Michael said, "Sean doesn't like me to go to his flat but I'm going, first thing in the morning. He'll have to know about this Father Matt thing. Besides, it's well into September and if we are to follow through with Sean's plans we had better get moving. I'd like to know what is going on."

Sean, so angry with himself over the escape, had not admitted it to anyone but Pearse O'Neill. He needed him to go down from Belfast and keep a check around Brendan's home. Back at the hotel, Matt was thinking, I'll check with the Connemara people tomorrow but it's not likely that Brendan will be found there. From what the waitress had said and of his encounter with the red haired young man, Matt believed Brendan to be mixed up in something here in Dublin. He decided to try getting Mrs. Hagan's number in Connemara, anyway, and checking there before calling Susanna. He was undecided about telling her of this night's happenings.

Chapter 21

Brendan woke early Wednesday morning; he felt stronger. He had been mostly in and out of deep sleeps, running high fevers and able to take only liquids through Saturday. Dr. Tim Madden had come by every day and Amy McGill had moved into the Quinn farm. Brendan had required constant care; Pat Quinn had helped through the restless nights of Brendan's fever. Dr. Tim said on Sunday that Brendan's lungs were finally clearing of the congestion. His mouth had healed enough to begin to eat. Amy and Pat helped a shaky Brendan walk about a little on Monday and Tuesday. Brendan's handsome face was returning to normal. Everyone was delighted that by Monday Brendan seemed to be really enjoying his food. Brendan talked very little, just accepting the ministering of these wonderful people. They didn't even know his name as yet. It wasn't until now that he felt the energy to tell them about himself.

Pat was the first to look in on him this morning. Pat stood in the doorway, his coffee cup in his hands, dressed to begin his day in the fields. The harvest time was beginning and he needed early starts.

Brendan was sitting with his legs over the side of the bed about to make a trip on his own to the bathroom. He was petting Ben's head, who was staring up at Brendan with big soulful eyes, his tail wagging happily. Ben had kept a constant vigil at the bedside. Brendan looked at Pat and smiled. "How can I ever, ever thank you? I would be dead without your help   and the others."

"Lad, it's seeing you getting better; that is the thanks. We'll talk about things tonight. Just tell me your name."

"I'm Brendan McKenna, Sir. My home is in Glaslough, Monaghan County."

Pat thought, the lad's quick enough on giving his identity. I'm sure he's not a bad one.

"Brendan McKenna, you take it easy now today. As I said, we'll talk tonight."

Amy and Anne came into the room as Pat was leaving. "You're lookin so much better. I'm so happy," Anne said exuberantly.

Amy McGill said, "Yes, yer lookin better but you're not to be over doin it, just yet."

Brendan remembered their names, having heard them when they talked with one another. "You're Anne, the daughter of the house, right? Is this your mother?"

"No." replied Anne, "My mom died when I was little. This is Amy McGill, your nurse. Dr. Tim arranged for her to care for you, -and what is your name?"

"I'm Brendan McKenna and I'm so very, very grateful to all of you— beyond the telling. When I'd wake and you were feeding me, I thought I was seeing an angel."

Amy McGill said, "You were close to seein angels, Brendan McKenna, and you'll be taken it easy till Dr. Tim says otherwise. Here, let me help you up."

"Thank you, but I really think I can walk alone today." Brendan stood and walked, showing no weakness, to the door.

"All right, but you get back into bed and I'll bring your breakfast tray yet this morning," Amy McGill said, in her most professional, take-charge voice.

Brendan grinned and said that sounded good to him.

Anne said goodbye to Brendan then cupped Ben's face in her hands, "You used to come part way to school with me, Ben, but you seem to have found a new friend. That's all right, you watch Brendan and don't let him over do—he can't play ball with you yet."

Anne left for school wondering about this Brendan McKenna and thinking they would soon know more about him and the trouble. It had been a week of thinking of little else. Her father had cautioned her not to talk to anyone about the young man. That was hard but she did not, even to her very best friend.

After Brendan was up for only a short while he returned to bed. It felt good to lie back on the soft pillows. Amy McGill was right; he wasn't up to much.

When Amy had removed his tray, he closed his eyes and tried to think things through. Should he go home? Would it be putting his mother in danger? His Mother—God, how she must be worried. Should he go to the police? It would be his word against Sean's and it still might not stop Sean's terrible plans for Ely. Ely, that sacred place—that beautiful Cathedral. Why would he have talked about that? When did he? Now he remembered with sorrow and self-loathing; it was early in the summer during one of those boisterous drinking evenings at O'Connell's. Sean and Pearse started telling their degrading and stupid anti-Protestant jokes. Brendan having had too many pints, wanted to be very witty. He said, "I've a shameful secret. I've got an English brother—a Protestant—who guided me through that big church in Ely. He showed me all through. Tell me, friends, do you not think he's tryin ta guide me down the wrong path?" The friends all had laughed in a drunken way, keeping up banter, all but Sean. Brendan remembered, now, Sean's looking at him thoughtfully. He recalled, too, that after the merriment died down, Sean had asked some polite and serious questions about Tom and Ely Cathedral. Sean had been so interested in the special harvest time that Ely celebrated. Brendan never could have thought that such a conversation would have sparked such an evil idea in Sean's mind. Sean had never mentioned Ely again, to him, until that day when he was a prisoner in the cottage. "Dear God, help me to stop it. *Forgive me!*"

He'd talk with Pat Quinn tonight. He knew he could be honest with Pat about everything; he'd trust him completely. Surely Pat Quinn could help him sort things out. His mind was tired; even to think about it all diminished the strength and well being he had felt.

That Wednesday morning, Father Matt returned to his hotel room after saying his morning Mass. He was able to get Maggie Hagan's new phone number in Connemara. She told him she knew that John Hobson had moved to Dublin and the last she heard, he was staying with his sister. The sister's married name was Barrett but she didn't have the address. As for reaching the grandmother, it would be quite useless, for the poor soul had no memory left for anything. She was now in a care home. Mrs. Hagan asked Father to let her know when he got in touch with Brendan. "I'm worried, Father, it's not like the Brendan I've known all these years to just go off and worry his mother. He was always a fine lad and like a son to us during those summers."

Father Matt promised her he would call and let her know. He felt badly when he hung up—just another person to be worried.

Matt spent the afternoon going to the addresses of Barretts he found listed in the directory. At first he had tried phone calls and ruled out a few. It was late afternoon when he approached the neat row house with a red painted door. He was turning to leave as there was no answer to his loud knocking. Coming up behind him was a beautiful young woman, extremely thin, with coal black full hair and intense blue eyes and finely chiseled features. From the description Susanna had given of John Hobson, Matt knew, he had found John's sister. He introduced himself and briefly explained the reason for his visit.

Joan Barrett asked Father to come in for a cup of tea. While Matt waited in the living room he saw on the table a framed picture of Joan with her younger brother John. She was several years older than John and had her arm protectively around him. Joan came into the room with the tea; she saw Matt looking at the picture. "That was taken a couple years ago, Father, I've always loved him so, ever since he was a baby—we were so close. A finer young lad you wouldn't be meeting." Tears were running down her face as she said, "he has become so different during this past summer. He had come to live with us with the intention of going on to Trinity College. All of a sudden that was off. He had always gotten on well with my husband Jerome. We both tried to talk with John—or more accurately, tried to get him to talk with us, but he just clammed up. Most of the time he spent away and would not tell us where he was going or about his friends. You had asked about Brendan; John did mention, early on in the summer, that he had seen Brendan, but that was just once. Anyway, John said he got a job—doing what, I don't know. He moved in with a friend of his—no name, of course, was given. That was Monday a week ago. He wouldn't leave an address or phone number with us. Oh, Father Matt, I've been sick with worry. If you find out anything, will you call me right away, please?" Father Matt promised he would; they talked a little longer while he finished the tea. He left the house thinking, another worried and sad person. Will these young lads ever know the agony they are causing? Well, whatever mess they are in, it seems to be based here in Dublin. He called Susanna when he got back to his room and told her of his day and promised to keep trying.

After his dinner at the hotel, he planned to return to Temple Bar and the Elephant and Castle Pub in the hope of another encounter with the red haired young man.

When he was almost finished with his dinner, his waiter came to him. "Are you Father Matthew McKenna? Father, an important message is waiting for you at the desk."

Matt quickly finished his coffee and went at once to the desk. "I'm Father McKenna; I understand you have a message for me."

"Yes, Father," the clerk said, "We have. A Susanna McKenna called, she had tried to reach your room directly; when she couldn't get an answer, she left the message for you to call her as soon as possible."

Matt thanked the man and hurriedly went to his room.

Susanna picked up the phone on the first ring. "Hi, Matt," Susanna said in an unusually happy, staged voice. "I've had a call from friends of yours. The Shaughnesseys. They want to see you while you're here on tour. You've caught me at a busy time. I'll ring you back in a little while. Bye for now," then she hung up.

What in the Dear God's name was that all about, he said aloud, his face in a puzzled frown. Shaughnesseys? I don't know any Shaughnesseys. Matt tried to read his office while he waited for the call but he had a hard time concentrating.

It was almost half of an hour until the phone rang; it was a collect call. After Matt accepted he heard Susanna's voice. "Susanna, what is going on?"

"Matt dear, I've driven into the hospital where I work to use a pay phone. It's a long story. Shortly after your call to me, a neighbor friend of mine came and said she got a call from a man, it wasn't Brendan. The man left a number and asked if she would give me the message to call him—when I was at work or shopping, but to call as soon as possible. I took it I was to call from a phone other than my own. I drove to the stores and called from a pay phone there. When I reached the number, a man said he was Pat Quinn"

"Your lad's all right, Mrs. McKenna," he said. "Hold till I give him the phone."

"When I heard Brendan's 'Hello, Mom,'—the relief and joy I felt—Oh, Matt, you know what I mean."

"Thank God!—Susanna, I can only imagine."

"Brendan's voice truly sounded like Brendan; not like the other call. He said he had been through a very bad time and had been very sick. But these people, the Quinns and a Dr. Madden and a nurse Amy McGill, brought him through this terrible time. He told me he came close to being involved with something horrible. 'I don't know how I was so stupid, Mom,' he said, 'but I'm back on track now.' Those were his exact words. He said he couldn't come home as he might be in danger, and worse, be putting me in danger. He plans to stay at the Quinns a time and that he didn't know just how he was going to handle things. Something about stopping some insanity that he knows about, but the less I know the better. He was grateful to you for all you've done and said to tell you he loved you. He also said that you are to stop now and not get somehow involved with certain people that might put you in danger. Matt, I'm relieved and yet worried as much as ever. I don't know what it's all about. I'm to send his I.D; he didn't take it with him when he left that Sunday. I'm to send it and a cashier's check, for Brendan has no money with him, to this Dr. Tim Madden at his office. Brendan said he talked things over with Pat Quinn and Dr. Madden and they thought that best. Brendan asked me not to try to contact them; he doesn't want to put them in danger. Something must be terribly wrong. Brendan wants me above all to be careful I'm not being watched. I'm to discuss none of this on my home phone. I'm to say nothing to neighbors or friends except that I haven't heard from Brendan, should they ask."

"Susanna, do you think this Pat Quinn and Dr. Madden are on the level?"

"Yes, Matt, I do. I didn't get the whole story, but from the way Brendan sounded and a few things he said about them; I really feel he's safe with them. I did check through the hospital to see if there was a Dr. Timothy Madden on the National Registry. There is and he is highly thought of. I know that, however these people came to be involved in Brendan's life, it was a blessing. Matt, please phone Tom at the London shop and tell him I've heard from Brendan and fill him in. If Tom calls me at home, I can't say. Matt, is there any way you can tell if your phone is being tapped if a device isn't inside in your own phone? I don't think anyone has been in the house."

"I don't know, Susanna, I'm not a person who's up on the technicalities of things. But I'll surely call Tom; I'd like to talk with him. It's been a long time. I'll call you tomorrow. Please try, knowing that God has helped so far and will continue, to get a good night's sleep. Be careful going home."

"I will, Matt, I haven't noticed anyone following me at anytime. Don't worry."

"Worry seems to be the name of the game these days, Mom. We'll all keep praying that this is soon resolved. I'll talk with you tomorrow."

Matt went through with his plans; he went back to Temple Bar and the pubs. He wanted more than ever to encounter the red haired young man again. But, of course, he didn't; he wasn't surprised.

Sean had called Pearse on Friday morning, after the escape, and had him drive down from Belfast to watch Brendan's home. Pearse had been in the area all that weekend. He had observed Susanna a few times thinking she looked worn and worried. On Sunday morning he had watched her coming out of church looking like she had been crying. He was sure she hadn't heard from Brendan. He reported this to Sean and told him he had to work on Monday and no, he hadn't put a tap on the phone. Sean was furious and raged at Pearse.

Pearse said, "Hold it, Man, I've got to work. You might be rollin in money—but I'm not—I have to work. If you still want me to do the job at the end of the month, I'll be taking off then." Pearse hung up as Sean was talking.

It was now a week since Brendan's escape. Sean had kept a check on the telly and newspapers to see if a body had been found. There was no news of such a thing. He thought, in Brendan's weakened state he might have died if he tried to go far. The gun, maybe, he was trying to recall the time of the fall, maybe the gun did go off and wounded Brendan. He hadn't found the gun. What if it was found near Brendan's body if he had died? No worry. It was an old one that had been around his father's house as long as he could remember. That's right—someone had given it to his father; it couldn't be traced to him.

He hadn't been contacted by the Gardai so he figured Brendan, if he was alive, hadn't been in touch with them. Sean had returned to the cottage on Sunday, thinking, Brendan might have come back for his bag if he was able. Maybe the bag had money in it he'd needed to get away. Sean found the bag still there. There was a small amount of money in it. He knew Brendan didn't have any money on him. Before leaving, Sean put the money in his pocket and the shaving things to throw away. He burnt the bag and clothes in the fireplace.

By this Wednesday morning he was beginning to feel a relief. He convinced himself that Brendan had died and the body just had not been found. Nothing ever could be traced to him. He was feeling free of that problem. Still, he felt a fear and a turning of his stomach when he heard a pounding on his door. Who the hell was there? Was it the Gardai? No one ever came to his flat. He didn't answer. Another pounding and Michael's voice calling, "Sean."

Sean threw the door open and hissed, "keep your bloody mouth quiet. What in the hell are you doing here?" Sean slammed the door behind Michael and locked it. "I've told you not to come here."

"You told me not to call, too. But I've something you should know and I've some questions to be answered."

"What's so damned important?"

"I was at the Elephant and Castle last night and sat next to a man askin about Brendan. It's his half-brother, a Father Matt McKenna, here from the States. He's all around hunting for him. I tailed him to O'Connell's. He might have learned something; he was in there a long time. When he came out he took a bus and I had to lose the tail. I didn't know if you would want a check at hotels for him; if you would want to keep a watch or do something about him."

"No, I don't think we'll bother about him. But we'll all stay clear of Temple Bar in case he got a handle there on one of us. I don't think he'll be findin Brendan."

Michael rubbed his stubble of red beard; he hadn't taken time this morning to shave. "Well, I doubt too that Brendan could be traced to the cottage." He looked at Sean and thought him to be taking this thing about Father Matt calmer than he had expected. "But what if the priest keeps nosin around and finds something out about us? Just how long do you think we can keep Brendan at the cottage? We'll be needin that place to make the bombs. Are we going through with it?"

Sean paced the room with his hands in his pockets jingling the keys in them, nervously. "I'll have to tell you there's no one at the cottage. The damned fool escaped last Wednesday."

Michael, who had been standing, sat down on the edge of the chair. "How the devil?—"

"Shut up, I'll tell you." Sean told of his beating Brendan's face and of Brendan's lack of food and weakened, shaky state. "He had to shit and I thought it safe enough to untie him. I had the gun on him." Sean described the scene in detail. "When he fell on me I think the gun went off. I couldn't find it when I came to. He couldn't have gotten far, especially if he was wounded. I've had a horrible week thinking somehow he got to the Gardai. But no one has come after me and there has been no news of a body being found. I've reached the conclusion that he must be dead somewhere in the fields or woods. There's not a damned way they could trace it to me if his body is found. I'm feeling free of the problem of Brendan at last. I knew he couldn't make it home but I had Pearse around there on the outside chance. Brendan's not been there." Sean breathed deeply in a show of relief and grinned. "I'm sure he's dead."

Michael stood and looked at Sean. He felt like he was seeing this man for the first time. Yes, they had been friends since boyhood; their mutual love of the old grievances and desire for retaliation had cemented their friendship. Hating a common enemy for a cause was one thing, but Michael was repulsed by what Sean had told him. He hadn't become so callused that he could accept a friend so abused and presumably left somewhere to die. Michael stared into Sean's eyes, "I think you are mad, Man, or sick."

These very words had brought Sean's rage at Brendan. Now, however, Sean controlled the inner rage he was feeling. He couldn't lose Michael or Pearse or Denis or John. He needed help to do what he had planned for so long. "Ah, Michael, I didn't know what to do." Lies came easily. "I did look for him a long time when I came to, before starting back. Then I went back and walked and drove about for miles. Maybe someone did take him to the hospital. I couldn't risk any of us by askin around, now could I?"

Michael wasn't impressed with Sean's insincere pleading tone. He didn't say anything in reply as he walked to the door.

Sean said, "We'll be meeting very soon for making concrete plans. I'll be in touch."

Michael pulled the door shut with a bang, thinking as he left; maybe I'll back out now: still he wanted to go through with the plans. Besides if I back out now, what's to stop Sean from killing me? I really think he would.

After Michael left, Sean thought, I'd better get things rollin before they all back out on me. He said aloud, "Brendan *is dead*. Get on with it, Sean."

He got ready to go to work at the boat repair; he was expected there today. He didn't need the money but he wanted to stay on their good side; he needed to take his own cruiser there for a once-over. It had to be in perfect condition. His plans wouldn't work without his boat.

Chapter 22

Michael went to work after he left Sean's place. His job in the offices of the ferry company demanded his concentration. Today he was simply unable to give it. His emotions were in control of his mind. He was filled with a loathing for Sean but mostly for himself. Why couldn't he just back out? Why couldn't he be through with it? Why not let go of his old hates—forget his own ax to grind?

That's what his mother would have wanted. She would have wanted him to have a good life, a peaceful, happy life. This need he found for revenge, she would have found to be an abomination. Yet, it was because of her, out of his loss of her, that this driving need to vent his anger and his sadness had grown. He was only ten years old on that day he, now, remembered scene by scene and word by word. He saw himself bounding through the door and tossing his school bag in the hall corner. He almost felt his young legs taking the flight of stairs, three at a time. His mother had been ill for sometime but was improving much. Soon she would be all better. He couldn't wait each day to burst into her room for her welcoming smile and kiss. He reached the door to her room; a room then filled with people, Kit Bradey, the neighbor who helped out and Dr. Conners and Father Paul. Kit Bradey was crying and put her arms about him. He could feel her arms, now, and his pushing her away. He had stood by the bed looking down at that stilled, beautiful face framed by her soft red hair, so much like his own. He heard in his ears his boyish voice screaming as it had that day. "Mom, Mom, open your eyes, it's Michael. I'm home, Mom—Mom." The truth had hit him. "Mom, don't be dead—you can't be dead." He felt his stomach tightening, the wretching starting. He felt Father Paul's hand on his shoulder and heard his voice as he had said, "She is with God, son."

He felt himself jerk away from Father's touch and saw himself running out of the room and down the stairs. In the front yard, he threw up until there was but dry heaves. He heard, now again, the screaming denial—"*No, No, No*"—emitted from his boy's throat.

Father Paul was then close to him; he sat down on the grass by the big tree and gently pulled the boy down beside him. Father didn't say a word but sat with him until he had cried all the tears that would come. He was still sitting by the tree while the funeral director came and took his dearest Mom. Kit Bradey had come to him and taken him next door to her house. Father and Dr. Conners were there with others. The house seemed crowded. He heard them talking about trying to locate his Dad. His dad, he never had been at home much. He had a selling job and was away a lot. Young Michael, of late, was getting the idea that he was away more than needed. There never had been closeness between them. His Mom was all to him. Then he heard the comments and saw the shaking of heads. A voice was saying. "It's a damned cursed thing, them only out for a bit of shoppin and to come to such an end. The shock of it too much for the poor darling girl's heart to stand; it surely killed her. Now, the poor lad's an orphan, or might as well be." He saw himself pulling at Father Paul's arm. "What is it, did someone kill my Mom?"

Father Paul told him that his grandma and his young aunt, his mom's sister, were killed in a happening in Belfast. As far as was known there had been an empty car bombing by the IRA. Some British soldiers chased some suspects and opened fire. Some people waiting for a bus were killed. His grandma and aunt were among them. Michael, now, remembered the look of deep sadness on Father's face when he said to him, "You know. Mike, your mother had some heart problems, made worse by her recent pneumonia, and her heart couldn't stand the shock of the news. She had a massive attack shortly after she was told. I was with her and so was Dr. Conners when she was told. Maybe she shouldn't have been. We'll never know. But she wasn't strong. -I don't think she would have had a much longer time here on Earth—even if this wouldn't have happened."

It had happened, and for young Michael, it was all the fault of the British being in his country. His Mother was taken from him, also his Gram and his pretty young Aunt Meg.

Now, he was remembering the years that had followed—years filled with his feeling of loss and growing anger. His father was home more often, but his interest in Michael didn't extend much beyond his providing; a rapport never developed between them. His father's elderly mother, his Gram Griffith, moved in with them. She was kind and took good care of his physical needs. He had felt more warmth toward her than to his father. Even before he was through school and ready to be on his own, her age was hard upon her. Her mind wandered and she grew quite remote. Shortly after Michael had moved out, she suffered a stroke and died. His father sold their house and moved away; Michael had no idea where. He heard nothing of him in years.

Sean had been his best friend during all those years. Sean was considerably older and through school long before Michael, but they had always hung out together. Michael had enjoyed the times they spent around Sean's father's business and shared Sean's love for boats. Then, too, Sean was always in sympathy to the bitterness Michael felt toward the English. When Sean's brother was killed in such a similar way to his own grandma and aunt, it furthered their anger and hate. It cemented their mutual longing for some show of revenge.

Now, Michael paced his office and stood staring out of the window, as he had done countless times during this day. Thoughts of Brendan tormented him and thoughts of young John messing up his life by being part of the plan. The lad didn't have a vendetta of his own. Michael remembered the first casual meeting of the two lads in a pub at Temple Bar. They were both so impressionable and eager to be accepted as friends, and to be included in evenings of boisterous jokes and songs. He thought of Sean as he was then; his charm and wit and persuasiveness, so lacking now, had played fully on Brendan and John. Michael was heartsick over what Sean had become. He was afraid for Sean and afraid of him. Yet, he couldn't rid himself of the desire to go through with the plan.

By the time Michael left his office, he had reached the decision to tell John everything he knew about Brendan and urge John to back out and go away.

Michael heard John coming into the flat. He called from the kitchen, "I've made some coffee; come have some."

John called back, "I'm going to shower first; I'm filthy. This job as a helper on a demolition crew doesn't leave you very pretty by the end of the day."

Michael came from the kitchen with a cigarette and a mug of coffee. He motioned to John to sit down on the plastic footstool. "John, I've something to tell you; the shower can wait." He got his pack of cigarettes and matches from his pocket and tossed them to John.

"What's wrong, Mike? Was Sean mad when you told him about seeing Father Matt?"

"No, the Father Matt thing didn't matter to him; it is way past being important. I'm going to tell you all I know of what has happened since Sean took Brendan at gunpoint on that Sunday night."

"At gunpoint?" John fumbled to light a cigarette.

"Yes, now be quiet and hear me out." Michael described in full detail the events of Brendan's abduction. He told of the cruel beating and the escape, as Sean had told it to him. "Even though Brendan did escape, it seems highly possible that he could have been shot when the gun went off. In any event, in his weakened state he couldn't have gone far. With no news in the media or from the Gardai, it's most probable that he's lying dead somewhere in an unused field. I'm giving it to you straight, John. Sean has become absolutely possessed. His hate has consumed every side of him. With his drugs and drinking, he is not even the man you once knew. Sean tried to tell me that he drove around some and looked for Brendan. I don't believe it; I could tell he was lying. Sean is convinced nothing could be traced to him if Brendan's body was found. He believes Brendan is dead and is, quite frankly, relieved and happy about it."

John's body shook. He covered his face with his hands. He had been trying to keep buried his feeling of misery over the estrangement with his closest friend. He had tried not to think of their parting on that Sunday afternoon. To hear that Brendan had been so vilely treated and probably *dead* was unbearable.

He stood and started to run from the room. Michael blocked his way and pulled John's hands from his tearstained face. "John, listen to me, and get out of this mess—*now*. There's not a reason for you to ruin your life—or lose it. It's different for me; it's too late. I've had too many years of living with hate, but I don't take friendship lightly. I'm sick to the core over Brendan and I'll not have you on my conscience. Leave now and go as far away from here as possible. Go back to Connemara. Go before Sean finds out you know of Brendan. To Sean all life is cheap—including yours. For both our sakes, leave now. For God's sake don't say anything to anyone that would set the Gardai on Sean. He knows where your sister lives. She might be in danger of Sean's revenge if he found his plans thwarted."

Michael stood aside and John left the room without saying a word. He knew Michael was right. He had to get away. To stay would further betray the friendship he had with Brendan. He had made up his mind to this before Michael's urging.

He showered quickly, and then packed his bag. When he was ready to leave, Michael was standing by the stove, frying some potatoes in a skillet. "John, you'll have some supper before you go?"

"No, I couldn't eat anything, but thanks. Thanks for a lot of other things, too; you are a good friend. What are you going to tell Sean?"

"He'll never know you knew anything about Brendan. I'll tell him something. I'll tell him you called a girl in Connemara who told you your grandma was dying. That when I got home tonight, you were gone and maybe you went there. That's damned far away and he won't be taking time to follow up on that. He'll go into a rage, but do nothing if he doesn't feel it a danger to himself or his plan. Remember not a word to anyone or it might be different. I think you ought to head straight to Connemara or somewhere as far. Do you have any money? I could let you have a little."

"I have some I saved and I got paid today. I've enough for bus fare and to run me a few days." John picked up his bag. Michael followed him to the door. "Michael, I wish you would get out, too."

"Like I said, it's too late for me."

"No, it's not Michael. You could."

Michael cut him short. "Don't worry about me, John. It makes me feel a little better just to know you're saved from this." As John was about to shut the door, Michael shoved some money into his hand.

"I can't take it Michael."

"Let me do something good, John. Try to think of me as not all bad. Goodbye, now and good luck."

John would always remember the sad look in Michael's eyes and the smile he tried to give as he closed the door.

John thought of going to his sister's for this one night, but quickly changed his mind. He couldn't keep up a pretense. His desolation over Brendan was so great. Any kindness from his beloved sister would break down his reserve and she would know the whole story; he couldn't risk her knowing. Oh, God, how he had let her down. How could he have been so stupid? He knew only one thing clearly; he could not go on to Connemara. He had to know what had happened to Brendan. If he was lying dead, John had to find him. He'd search the fields. He'd ask questions in Maynooth. If Sean found out, what the hell. The way he felt now, his own life didn't matter. His sister wouldn't know anything; but even if there might be a danger for her, he'd have to take that risk. He had to know. Brendan had to be found. He made his way to the bus station. Maynooth was a small place but big enough to get a room for a night. He was in time to get the last bus of the evening for there.

When the bus reached Maynooth, John asked the driver if he knew of an old cottage, a few miles on, into the countryside; it had once belonged to a man by the name of Devlin. The driver was young and didn't have knowledge of it. -John went into a small pub and asked where he might find a room for the night. He was directed to a small bed and breakfast, nearby. It was run by an older couple, the Murphys. At John's knock, the Murphys both came to answer the door. At first they were reluctant to admit him. He looked so young and slight and so tired that Mrs. Murphy's maternal instinct overcame her fear and she said, "Yes, we have a room."

Mr. Murphy said John would have to agree to have his bag searched. "One has to be careful these days. We usually take only guests with references or through an agency."

Mrs. Murphy looked embarrassed while her husband spoke to John. John said he understood and agreed to the search. With gratitude in his voice he thanked the Murphys for allowing him to stay. He felt very drained and suddenly he realized he was hungry. "If I could put my things in my room, I'd like to go back out to get a bite to eat. I haven't eaten since morning. I'll come straight back. I wouldn't keep you up."

"Lad, we were just havin a cup of tea in the kitchen. I've some cold beef and homemade bread for a sandwich. If that would do, you would be so welcome to join us," Mrs. Murphy said, her voice warm and motherly.

"I'd not like to impose, but that sounds so—wonderful. I would pay extra, of course."

"No need for that. If one can't share a bit of food with a tired young traveler, the world is comin to a worry way."

John followed the Murphys to the big, warm comfortable kitchen. They sat with John and drank their tea while he ate. Mrs. Murphy had fixed two huge sandwiches and a warmed baked apple, sticky sweet, seasoned with cinnamon and sugar. She put out a pitcher of heavy cream to pour on it. John was to remember always this delicious food, served with such kindness, as some of the best he had ever eaten. His strength returned and some of the wretchedness of his soul was comforted.

He told them about his growing up in Connemara and about his returning there. "I went to Dublin to attend Trinity College but that didn't work out for right now. Before I go on, I'm trying to locate a friend who might have spent a little while around these parts. Would you know of an old cottage, now vacant, once belonging to a man whose name was Devlin? I think it would be in the country, a few miles from here."

"Aye, I know of the old Devlin place," Mr. Murphy replied. "That's been abandoned for many years. Your friend surely wouldn't be stayin there. Good land with it; I never could understand why it wasn't sold. I've been told a nephew inherited but didn't do a thing with it. Is that the friend you're lookin for?"

"No, that isn't my friend. I was told my friend was visiting somewhere in the area of that place; he wasn't staying there. I don't have much to go on. Do you know anyone else that lives near there?"

"No, I don't know any of the farm people out that way. Wait—I do know Dr. Tim Madden's home is out there somewhere. He's on staff at the hospital here. I've been treated by him—a fine doctor. You could try to see him; he's busy but he's a friendly man and might take time to give you names of a few people in that area. There aren't many live around there and the farms are widely spaced."

"I wouldn't like to bother the doctor; but I might have to take your suggestion. Thanks for your help and thank you for the wonderful supper and your company; I feel much better than when I came. If I need to stay another night in Maynooth, would there be the room available for me, again?"

"Yes, Lad," Mrs. Murphy said, "but just for one more night. We have only three rooms and all are booked for the day after tomorrow."

"I'm sure if my friend is to be found, I'll know by then and be on my way to Connemara."

John spent a restless night and dressed very early. He took his small backpack to carry a bottle of water and sandwiches. His plan was to comb the country area. His heart felt like lead when he thought of what he might find. If he found nothing he would talk with Dr. Madden. He would have gone to the Gardai but was too afraid for his sister. If he would find Brendan's body, he would have to notify them. Then he would have something positive against Sean; Sean would have to be arrested and his sister would be safe. But, oh, God, please don't let Brendan be dead, John pleaded.

John went downstairs to find the Murphys already up. With the thought of the day ahead his appetite was gone. Much to Mrs. Murphy's concern, he didn't do justice to her hearty breakfast.

After stopping at the pub for his water and sandwiches, he caught the early bus that went out to the country. He told the driver he wanted off several miles out, in close proximity to the old abandoned Devlin place. He was glad the older man, driving the bus, knew where he meant. When he was leaving the bus, the driver told him it was about two miles up the old dirt road on his right. John asked if there were farms close by. He was told the nearest was down quite a way, across the highway to the left. The thud of the door closing on the bus seemed echoed by the heavy thud he felt in his stomach.

He didn't know where to begin. Hours later, he had walked many miles beyond the two; finally, John came insight of the old cottage. Either side of the dirt road had been searched, every rise and bog and ditch. Another hour was spent looking around and up beyond the cottage. The ground took a sharp, hilly turn upward; John felt it unlikely that a man so weakened as Brendan would have gone that direction. He went to the cottage and pushed open the door and surveyed the miserable place. Crossing to the hearth, he noticed something only partially burned. There were bits of gray nylon fabric; Brendan's bag was gray, it had to be his. He went outside and walked down the road, beyond the sight of the terrible place. He sat and drank some of his water but couldn't face eating. The calves of his legs were hurting; he rubbed them and rested for a short while. Continuing down the road and across the highway, he walked again through fields and inspected any place where a body could be out of sight. He searched on and on in the field parallel to the narrow paved road. Noticing brush and weeds by a short stone wall, he moved them and pulled at them. It was the exact spot where Brendan lay hidden until found by Anne Quinn. John walked through the field before turning up to the road; intending to look on the other side on his way back to the highway, to get the return bus.

When he reached the road he saw, far in the distance to his left, a house. It was very late in the afternoon and he was exhausted. He started walking back to the highway, but after a few steps, he turned and walked in the direction of the house. He still hoped that, somehow, someone might have seen Brendan and could tell him something. He walked to the house and passed the front. No one was about. A large black and white dog was stretched out on the grass; it stood and barked a little but didn't come toward him. John walked on and looked far to the back where a barn and some other small out buildings stood. He saw a man climbing down a ladder, with a bucket; apparently, he had been painting the side of the barn. The man handed the bucket to another man who had been holding the ladder. The painter disappeared into one of the small buildings; the other man started toward him, looking down at the ground as he walked. John started walking toward him and when he was half the distance, the man straightened and turned face on. John's shock was so great; his relief so overwhelming, that he couldn't utter a sound. He staggered and held onto a nearby tree to keep from falling. Brendan ran to him. As they faced each other, unashamed tears flowed down each of their faces. "Brendan, Brendan, God!—man, you're alive. I've searched the day for you, dreading what I might find." John was screaming words through his choking tears and hysterical laughing.

"John, *oh, my God*, John. I can't believe I'm seeing you." Brendan started to hug him but drew back, laughing through his own tears. "I'll get you all over paint, man; he was still holding the bucket. How did you know, John? What has happened?"

They sat down on the ground and John told all of what Michael had said to him. Brendan filled in all that had happened during his escape and his illness. He told him about the Quinns and their kindness to him. "I owe them more than I ever could tell. I wanted to do something around here to start repaying but they won't let me yet. This is my first day out. I was only allowed to hold the ladder. John, I'm so relieved that you have gotten away; that you finally know what Sean is like. I was heartsick to think of you being part of such an evil plan. You would have been killed or sent to your death if caught. If you would have escaped, after being part of it, the rest of your life would have been ruined. The Quinns have insisted I stay here where I am safe and until I can make up my mind what to do. I have to stop the terrible plan of Sean's from happening."

"Brendan, I still don't know just what Sean is planning. Pearse and Michael know I'm sure, maybe Denis. The plan for revenge was always talked about but I was never told what or how."

"I wasn't told either until Sean told me in, a drunken rage, when I was a prisoner in the cottage." Brendan told in detail what Sean had said about bombing Ely Cathedral. "I hate most that he thought I would betray my brother to help with his plan."

John looked horrified. "How could I ever have been such a fool not to have seen through him? I was building a hate in myself for no reason. I feel I'm as rotten as he is."

"No, you're not, John; Sean had a way about him. We were both green and felt free to do something different in our lives—free to be stupid, as we now know. We are lucky; we're out of it—except for stopping Sean's plan. Whatever happens to me, I've got to try. I'm going to fly to England soon, the early part of next week. I think the best thing is to get in touch with Scotland Yard. I'd like you to go on to Connemara and stay with friends where you'll be safe. Sean doesn't know you have any knowledge of the plan; he won't bother to hunt you down."

John started to speak but was interrupted by the black and white dog and a very pretty young girl running, from the back of the house, toward them. Anne called, "Brendan, you're not washed for dinner; it's almost ready." She came close to them and gave a puzzled look at John. Brendan had been going to stay away from other people of the village; who was this lad?

"John, this is Anne Quinn, the dear girl who saved my life. Anne, this is a long time friend of mine John Hobson. I'll tell you and your father all about his coming later. The poor man has been searching the fields for miles all this day, fearing to find my dead and decaying body. I know he's tired and hungry. Do you think there could be an extra place at dinner?"

"Of course, there will be. Hello, John," she offered her hand.

John removed his hand from the licking Ben was giving it and took hold of Anne's. "I'm happy to meet you, Anne. Thank you for including me at dinner." With all his tiredness he suddenly felt very good and very hungry and very glad there would be a place for him at dinner. He'd throw away those soggy sandwiches.

After dinner, Brendan and John talked at length with Pat Quinn. John had talked Brendan into letting him go along to England; that was decided. Pat said he would drive John into Maynooth for the night since the Murphys had held his room. John would return to the farm by bus in the morning;

and stay on with Brendan, in the small loft room that Brendan would use since his return to health.

John returned to Murphy's a much happier man. He did full justice to Mrs. Murphy's breakfast the next day. However, to be on the safe side, he said he hadn't seen his friend but that he didn't have time to stay longer and would be going on to Connemara. He promised to come and stay again if he ever found himself in these parts. As he walked to the bus, he was thinking of the trip to England and the reason for it. How soon would he be back this way? What all would happen before he was free to come back to Ireland? Standing with Brendan and doing what he knew was right gave him a strength. He was unafraid and happier than he had been since leaving Connemara. God—that seemed like years ago instead of months.

Chapter 23

Fran and Tom spent the remainder of the week in London in a glow that could light up a room.

When Cliff went home on Tuesday evening, after working with Tom all day, he said to Berniece, "You know, maybe you're right about Tom and Fran. Tom didn't say anything but he seemed to be in such a happy mood today; there must be something a foot. I know he is relieved that Father Matt is in Ireland looking for Brendan; but that's not the whole picture that has put him in this joyous state." Berniece responded with a hug for Cliff and a knowing smile, "I told you so."

Fran did more sight seeing during the day, but her mind was in constant happy anticipation for their evening together.

After their dinner that evening Tom suggested going to a great little place he knew, for some dancing. It featured a lot of older American recordings, including a few by Johnny Mathis, for slow dancing. Fran, while they danced, sang softly some of the words to "You Make Me Feel So Young. You Make Me Feel Brand New."

"You do, Tom, you know that." Tom pulled her a little closer and buried his face in her fragrant, soft hair.

For Wednesday evening, Tom had gotten tickets for the Royal Opera House and the new production of *Madame Butterfly*. Fran was delighted when Tom told her. Fran had done the role in the Conservatory production and was remembering it with joy. For such a long time she had shut even those memories from her mind and heart.

Now, on this beautiful morning, while she was getting ready to go shopping the gorgeous melody of the "Un bel di" was singing in her mind. Soon she was giving full voice to it and sang it through completely. Despite the fact that she hadn't sung for a long time, she was so happy and relaxed that her beautiful, young voice soared. She sang more wonderfully than ever before. When she opened her door to the hall, she found several people had gathered. When they saw her they applauded.

Fran was somewhat embarrassed. "I—I hope I haven't disturbed anyone, I just never thought about being in a hotel."

The couple she knew to have the room next to her assured her that it was indeed a great pleasure to hear her sing and hoped she would give them that privilege again.

Fran warmly thanked them and felt like she was floating, the distance of the hall, to the elevator.

Today, she would not go to the museum. It was not a day to be spent looking at the old and the saved. It was a day to be doing things as alive as she felt. Tom had asked her if she wanted to go to the opera in evening dress. He said he still had a tux at his Uncle's flat. Today, she would shop for an eye-popping dress, something that would dazzle Tom. She would have her hair done in an upsweep. She entered the formal dress department at Harrods, thinking I'll have to get something that fits well. I don't have time for alteration; maybe I can't be too choosy.

The first dress she was shown was a beautiful sophisticated black with gold dash beads. Fran told the lady she thought it exquisite but was hoping to find a dress of an intense color.

The clerk discerned Fran's exuberant mood. "I think we have found *the one*." She brought Fran a candy apple red satin, full-length sheath with a wide, low-cut front and back. It had wide straps that formed a suggestion of a sleeve at the shoulders. The neckline and over the shoulders were covered with a mixture of tiny seed pearls and crystal beads. It was perfect! The fit was beautiful in every way. The clerk was as delighted with Fran's joy over the gown as Fran herself. Fran was assured that it would be boxed most carefully and wrapped in tissue to prevent creasing. It would be ready for Fran to pick up when she was finished with her hair appointment.

Fran went to the coat department and chose a light cream, calf-length cape. She certainly couldn't use her all weather coat she had with her. Next stop was the shoe department where she found pale cream, high-heeled pumps and matching evening purse. On to the jewelry department, she saw, as if made for the dress, a small spray of little pearls and crystals to have worked through the side of her hair. She chose small earrings that matched. There was no need for a necklace; the gown was perfect without it.

She looked at her watch and decided she still had time to get gifts for Heidi and Don and Bryan. It didn't take long to find the cashmere, jewel-trimmed sweater for Heidi, a darling suit for Bryan, and a great tie for Don.

While looking at the ties, she spotted a dark blue and silver one that looked just right for her precious Tom.

She hurried to her appointment hoping her hair would be as much to her liking as the clothes she had chosen. Her concern was completely unnecessary. The softly piled hair with the spray of jewels worked through and the soft wisp of curls at the cheekbones was totally stunning—perfection itself.

She returned to Harrods where everyone was so helpful in arranging to get all her boxes and bags into the cab.

Fran sank back onto the cab seat and closed her eyes; a little tired but very happy and thanking God for her countless blessings, for giving her such joy. She thought of Ethel Fenman and wished she could tell her of this fun day and about Tom and all the delight that now filled her life. She would have told Ethel about everything and added what her heart knew, that the extra fun was nice, but if Tom and she could have afforded only an evening walk, hand in hand, she would be just as deeply happy.

After a quick dinner at the hotel, Fran tried to rest a little before dressing. Being too excited to sleep, she had to share the excitement of this day with someone. She phoned Heidi and talked until Bryan noisily informed them it was time for his supper. Fran meant it when she said how much she missed them.

A radiant Fran entered the lobby to wait for Tom. She had her cape just over her shoulders, revealing the exquisite red dress. When Tom came through the door, he noticed only Fran. He went to her and took hold of her small, gloved hands and drew them close to his chest. "I am the luckiest man in the world to be with the most beautiful and dearest woman in the entire world."

Her eyes revealed all the delight and tenderness she felt as she replied to his remark. "Tom darling, I don't know about your being lucky. All I know is that I'm with an extraordinary man who is very handsome in his tux. I might not be keeping my mind on the opera."

They were completely oblivious to the admiring stares from people in the theater lobby. The magnificent red and gold Victorian décor was a perfect foil for Fran's beauty. Tom thought how he would love to paint her, as she looked tonight, with one of the theater alcoves for the background.

The romantic, exciting evening was wonderful in all ways, a total enchantment, because everything they saw or heard or did was touched by the sparkle of their being in love.

When they were saying good night, in the empty lobby of the hotel, Tom said, "Darling, I'll pick you up here, tomorrow at noon. We'll have lunch and then we have some important shopping to do. Another thing, Fran, Uncle Cliff and I have made good headway with things and after a few hours on

Friday morning we will be all organized. Would you mind going back on Friday instead of Saturday? You mentioned that Mrs. Pickens had talked to Heidi and said the flat was ready for you now."

"Oh, Tom, that would be wonderful. I've had such a beautiful week that I haven't thought much about the move, but I would like to get settled. I haven't thought much about anything or anywhere this week because just being with you makes everywhere perfect."

Tom kissed her head and nose and they gently kissed each other's lips. The desk clerk discreetly seemed to be busy studying some papers.

"What do you have to shop for tomorrow, Tom?"

"That, my dear, I'll tell you when the time comes." Another quick kiss, with a most loving look and Tom left, saying nothing more.

Fran knowing, deep in her female heart, what was left unsaid and having to be vocal about some of the joy she was feeling, offered a loud, almost musical good night to the desk clerk.

He replied in a startled, rather prim way, "Good night, Miss."

The next day as they drove to the restaurant for lunch, Tom told Fran of his call that morning from Father Matt. "We talked a long time. Mom got another call from Brendan and we know that right now he is safe. "There is still something going on that we can't figure out." He told Fran of all that Susanna had told Matt. "I think I will fly up the first of the week. I want to see Matt and maybe by that time I'll think of someway to help."

Throughout the lunch, the conversation was light and filled with talk of the opera and the fun of the night before. The pretty but small restaurant Tom had chosen was quiet and almost empty when they were finished their leisurely lunch. Their corner booth was totally private. Tom became quite serious. Fran saw on his face the same tender, loving look it had when he left her last night. "Now, I'll tell you what our shopping is to be; depending, of course, on your answer to the most important question of my life. My precious Fran, will you be my wife?"

Fran blinked back the tears the overwhelming and solemn joy she was feeling brought to her eyes. She reached and put her hands in Tom's. "You surely know, my dearest Tom, my answer is yes."

Tom raised Fran's hands tenderly to his lips. The exquisite joy they were feeling caught them in a time and place away from reality. They were abruptly brought back when the stern looking waitress came up to the table and asked, in a matter of fact voice, "Will that be one check or two?"

That question and sudden change of emotion sent Tom and Fran into uncontrollable laughter. The unsmiling waitress looked disdainfully at each of them and asked. "Well?"

Tom cleared his throat and managed to say, "One check, please, my good woman."

"Thank you," she replied, "that's all I wanted to know." She put the check on the table and gave Fran, who was holding her napkin tightly against her mouth, one last scathing look and muttered, "thank you, come again," and hurriedly walked away.

"Hon, have I told you, I always knew I'd fall in love with a girl who ate her napkin?" Tom said, still laughing.

"Oh, Tom, now you know my guilty secret. I'm glad you approve," Fran said, giggling.

Finally, they made a desperate effort to control themselves and as they were leaving, Fran squeezed Tom's hand and said, "I'm going to love living and laughing with you."

Tom squeezed back, "I think we are off to a very good start. Of course, what that poor waitress thinks might be another story."

As they were leaving the parking lot, Tom said, "I'd like to buy your ring at Garrads; it's an old, old jewelers that has connections with the Crown, going back to 1722. In fact, they still do the upkeep of the Crown Jewels."

"Tom, that sounds like a terribly expensive place. I don't need a grand ring to tell me of your love."

Tom, keeping his eyes on the busy traffic, reached over and took her hand. "Fran, the grandest ring in the world couldn't say how much I love you. But I think I can get a nice ring, of good quality, within my budget at Garrads. They are family jewelers, too, and offer a wide range. So, don't be worrying your pretty head."

When they were inside the store, the clerk greeted them warmly; they were expected. Tom had called ahead to tell them the price range he wished to see. Fran grinned when she discovered this, and said, "You were pretty sure of yourself, Sir."

Tom raised his eyebrows, "Let me say—I was very, very hopeful."

The clerk brought the trays to the counter. There were many beautiful styles, some very ornate; but Fran was immediately drawn to the exquisite simplicity of a round cut solitaire, set in a narrow band of white gold. "I like this one, Tom," she said, as she lifted it from the tray. "To me it speaks of honesty, openness—and the sparkle is deep, so like the feeling we share."

Tom took and held the ring. "This would have been my choice, Fran."

"The lady has the best of taste," inserted the clerk. "This is indeed a very fine stone, *not* extremely large, but a most pure diamond. Its purity is perfect, creating its deep fire."

Ignoring the clerk, Fran and Tom gazed at each other while Tom put it on Fran's finger. By some little miracle, the ring was a small size and fit perfectly, no adjustment was necessary. Fran was delighted, "now I can just keep it on."

Still ignoring the clerk and all British reserve, Tom and Fran held each other closely.

The clerk cleared his throat discreetly, "Will you be intending to choose the matching wedding rings today?"

They made their selections of white gold bands; these were left at the store to be engraved when the wedding date was decided upon.

They left the store feeling that they wanted to shout their joy to the world. "Tom. I'm so glad we are going back tomorrow. I can't wait to tell Heidi and Don—but not on the phone. I'm so anxious to tell Mom and Dad."

"I know the feeling, Fran, let's call Uncle Cliff and Aunt Berniece and get them to join us for a celebration dinner. There's a restaurant called Rules, at Covent Garden. It's delightful and quaint; you'll love it. Even the menu is historic. Uncle Cliff's favorite is their steak and kidney and mushroom pudding. We should call right now and try to get a reservation." Tom made the calls and set the plans to meet at the restaurant at six o'clock. Tom came out of the phone booth and smiled at Fran, "I didn't say a thing about our news; I want that to be in person."

They got into the car and drove the short distance to Covent Garden. The remainder of the day flew. They saw some of St. Paul's Cathedral and watched some open-air entertainers perform under its portico. Just strolling around the Piazza and going into some of the many shops was fun. Fran found some just right little gifts to send home to her parents. Tom enjoyed the pleasure Fran showed for everything she did or saw. In this, she reminded him of his mother; Fran had the same alive appreciation of the beauty and charm of things great or small.

They sat at a little outside café for coffee. Tom told Fran he was anxious to tell his mother the news. "I have told Mom about finding this beautiful and special girl; but with the problem with Brendan, I haven't really kept her updated on how things have happened with us. I know she'll love you, Fran. I hope you can meet soon."

"Tom, from all you have told me of her and her life, I know she must be a very wonderful woman. I'm eager to meet her. I do so hope she will like me."

"Not a chance she won't, my darling. We'll go to Uncle Cliff's tonight and call your parents and Mom. I'm sorry we'll have introductions long distance, but it will have to do, for now."

"Yes, it will have to do, Tom, and I think it's a great idea."

After sharing an exuberant time and a delicious dinner, they headed for Cliff and Berniece's flat. Once inside, Berniece gave Fran and Tom a hug together. She stood back and looked at them, "Tom dear, you've always seemed like a son to us and now we feel we're getting the daughter. Your sweet mom Susanna is going to have to share her. Fran, I can't wait for you to know Tom's mother, she is a dear. You two will love each other. Well, best get on with putting those calls through. Fran, are you going to call your folks tonight. It's almost nine here and that will be two a.m. in the States."

"We'll call them first before it gets later. I don't think they'll mind waking up hear our happy news."

Fran heard the fumbling of the phone before her father's sleepy but anxious voice said, "Colberts."

A phone waking one at night usually makes a person think the worst. Fran hurriedly said, "Dad, Everything's fine. I hated to wake you but couldn't wait longer to tell you my news."

By that time, Irene was sitting straight up in bed, pulling on Bruce's arm and looking worried, "What's the matter?"

Bruce put his arm around her and assured her everything was fine. "Fran just has some good news." He handed her the phone.

Fran sounded so happy telling them. She "introduced" Tom and he talked with them for quite a while. When they hung up, Irene said, "Bruce, I feel very good about this. I remember when Fran told us her intention to marry Jeff she seemed thrilled—but after they were married she never mentioned once that she was happy with him or sounded happy. She always made excuses for him when he wouldn't take time to arrange a meeting with us. You know we never did talk with him—even on the phone. I always felt he thought himself too important to be bothered. When Fran came home to us after his death she was in a terribly unhappy state, that was understandable; but I got to wondering if that was the whole cause."

Bruce agreed, "I thought the same thing. Fran never talked of him or anything about him. At first I figured it was the shock of losing him in such a horrible accident; but as time went on I had the feeling we didn't have the complete picture. I'd bring things up sometimes about Jeff or the time she lived in New York but I'd just get a wall of silence from her. During all that time she was with us she was so different from what she had always been."

"I truly believe that is all in the past, Bruce. Our girl seems really herself again and very happy. Even with simply talking with Tom, I'm absolutely sure I like him. They haven't set a date yet for the wedding; but they both want us to be there."

"We had better put in for our passports, Irene; we want to be ready when the time comes."

"Bruce, I wouldn't miss the wedding for the world." Irene put on a little worried frown, "but you know I really don't like flying—and across the ocean! I'm not thrilled about that."

"Well, darlin," Bruce grinned, "we can't afford the *Q.E. II* and it's too far to swim so it will have to be a plane."

"In thinking about it, I'd rather be flying over the ocean for several hours than floating around on it for several days. Let's get up, Bruce, and have a drink to celebrate; I'm much too excited to sleep."

Before Tom called his mother, he said to Fran, "I know, Hon, you are eager to get your flat put together; but I'd love it if you would fly to Ireland with me to meet Mom and Matt. It would only be for a couple of days."

"Getting the flat ready isn't that important; of course, I'll go, Darling."

They called Susanna. Tom asked if she had heard anything more since he talked with Matt; the answer was no. "Mom, I have some happy news to tell you."

Hearing the joy in Tom's voice as he told her and the happiness in Fran's voice as they "met" on the phone made Susanna's heart feel lighter than it had for weeks. This special joy was what she wanted for her dearest Tom for a long time. "You're coming up next week? Oh, Tom, that's wonderful. Tell your dear Fran I can't wait to see her."

As they hung up, Cliff and Berniece came into the room with a bottle of champagne and stemmed glasses. Uncle Cliff popped the cork. "We have to drink one more toast this day." Cliff raised his glass, "To the engagement of this happy pair. May they know much happiness always and may their love stay as sparkling as the bubbles in this delicious champagne." Cliff actually smacked his lips in appreciation of the taste.

Fran laughed and said, "I feel so lucky in getting you two as family."

There were many hugs and kisses when Tom left to take Fran back to her hotel. When Tom returned, Cliff said to him, "Tom, you have done many wise things in your life. You've most always seemed to make good choices—and this is your best one by far."

"Believe me, Uncle Cliff, I'm in total agreement."

A little before noon, on Friday, Tom put Fran's things into the car for the trip back to Heidi's. "Luv, you have a lot more going back than what you came with."

"What I'm thrilled about taking back, Tom, is this precious ring I'm wearing. I simply can't wait for Heidi and Don to know about us."

"We'll make lunch a quick stop. I'm anxious to tell them too. When we set the date, they'll be the best man and matron of honor, won't they?"

"That's what I've been thinking. I can't imagine having anyone else."

They spent the drive making plans. Don wasn't home yet when they reached the house. "Do you want to wait to tell them together?" Tom asked, as they started up the walk.

"Tom, do you mind if we don't wait?—I just can't. Besides, Heidi is sure to see the ring. I don't want to take it off."

Tom grinned, "I really didn't expect you to, Darling. I was just teasing."

Heidi was picking up a smiling Bryan from his crib. She heard Fran and Tom coming in and called, "We'll be right down."

After the hugs, Heidi put Bryan down on a stretched out blanket on the floor. Heidi noticed that Fran and Tom had never stopped smiling or changed the excited look they had when she first saw them. "What's up, you two?"

Fran raised her left hand for the sparkling ring to tell their news.

Heidi's face mirrored their joy. "Fran, it's *sooo* Beautiful!—You know what happiness I wish for both of you. I'm not really surprised—maybe a little startled that this has happened so soon, but not surprised. I can't wait till Don gets home. Early on, he wanted to bet with me that you would fall in love. I didn't agree to bet against it, because deep down, I thought so too. When is the big day?"

"We are thinking of December, either the first part or the week following Christmas. We want Mom and Dad to be here. We'll have to work it out with them and Tom's Mom. There are so many things to decide. Of course, we are asking you and Don to stand for us; the time that would be good for you is important."

"Fran, we'll be honored and delighted; anytime you say will be great with us."

Tom brought the things in from the car while Fran started to help get ready for dinner. It was decided that Tom would put his dishes in his car and as many things for Fran as would fit. Heidi said she and Don would put the rest of Fran's things in their car and drive her up to Ely early in the morning. Tom had to drive to Ashwell right after dinner. He had gotten a call from the temporary chemist at the shop there, saying he had to see Tom about a few things. Tom would meet Don, Heidi and Fran at the flat in Ely on Saturday morning.

Fran had finished setting the table, when she saw him. He was sitting in the doorway, baring the path to the kitchen. He was staring at her, she thought accusingly, with big golden eyes. "Oh, Scooby, how could I have forgotten *you*?" She picked him up. His body was rigid. There was no purr to be heard; he was plainly angry with her. "Forgive me Scooby," Fran put her cheek on the top of his head and stroked his soft fur coat. Scooby would have none of it and jumped out of her arms and ran upstairs.

Tom had finished packing his car and was locking the door when Don pulled up. Don gave him a big, "Hi, how's everything?"

"Well, let's go inside, my friend, and you'll see."

Heidi and Fran came in from the kitchen. Don kissed Heidi, hello, and said, "What are you two grinning like Cheshire cats about? What's going on here?"

"Fran and I have a surprise, Don." Tom lifted Fran's hand for Don to see the ring.

"Oh, so that's it!—Well that's wonderful news, but I thought you said you had a surprise," Don said, laughing. "I'm so happy for both of you." He shook Tom's hand and kissed Fran's cheek. "You know, I feel kind of responsible for you two getting together. Always make each other happy; that's an order."

Fran smiled at Don and said, "Yes, Papa."

After dinner, Tom left. Fran and Heidi and Don talked the evening away; in and out of Fran's doing laundry and packing. Fran looked at Don who was on the floor playing with Bryan. "I'm so grateful that you'll take me to Ely tomorrow; but I don't like you to have to leave Bryan for a whole day."

Heidi and Don both assured her that Bryan would be in very good hands. Mrs. Cummings, their neighbor from next door, was going to care for him at their house. "She just loves him and Bryan is very used to her and is happy with her," Heidi said. "Besides, it will be fun for Don and me to have a free day; to be doing something different sounds great."

After getting ready for bed, Fran went over to the window. She thought again of that first morning's promise. How beautiful her life was now; her heart said a quiet prayer of thanksgiving. She turned around to see the dust ruffle move, revealing only two black velvet ears and nose and big golden eyes. Fran climbed into bed and stretched out. She was just dozing when—*thump*—up came Scooby. He found her bare shoulder and washed at it with a little rough, pink tongue then curled up close to Fran's back and purred a very loud purr. Fran patted his head. "That's the good kitty. I'm glad we're friends again. Sing me to sleep."

Chapter 24

Mrs. Pickens was looking forward so much to this day when that lovely Mrs. Amberson would move in. Even though they wouldn't be seeing a lot of each other—she would never dream of imposing on her tenant—there would be the feeling that someone else was in this big lonely house. My, she thought, sometimes I do feel so lonely. She was watching at the window when the car stopped, and was rather surprised when it wasn't Tom with Fran.

Introductions being made, Mrs. Pickens said to Fran, as they followed her upstairs, "Your beautiful furniture arrived yesterday. The men set everything in the most likely places. If you want it changed maybe your friends could help you rearrange things."

Nothing needed to be changed. The room looked just as Fran had pictured it. The rest of the flat was empty but so beautiful with the charming new paper and paint; everything glistened. Heidi and Fran were soon talking about curtains and a small table and chairs that would fit in the cheery little kitchen. Mrs. Pickens was deeply pleased with the delight Fran was showing about everything. There was a knock at the door. "That must be Tom," Fran said. "He planned to meet us here. Mrs. Pickens turned toward the stairs. "May I go, please," Fran asked?

"Why of course, you move much faster." Mrs. Pickens stepped aside.

Fran flew down the steps. The moment the door was opened they were in a warm embrace, glad to have a few moments alone.

Mrs. Pickens was followed downstairs by Heidi and Don. Don was saying, "We might as well get started carrying in Fran's things. Tom has a lot in his car, too."

Mrs. Pickens greeted Tom warmly, and said, "While you young people do the work I'll start water for tea." She turned to Fran and said, "I made some of the scones that you seemed to enjoy. I hope everyone will have some."

Heidi said, "Mrs. Pickens, Fran raved about your scones. That will be great." Everyone agreed.

Mrs. Pickens went into her kitchen humming and thinking to herself, I haven't felt so good in days. This is almost like having a party.

While the men brought the things from the car, Heidi helped Fran dress the bed and hang up clothes and put the other things Fran had brought where they belonged. It didn't take long. Fran still had much shopping to do.

After the delicious scones and tea, Heidi and Don left. They made plans to meet in a short while at the Cathedral. Tom and Fran stayed to talk with Mrs. Pickens.

Tom said, "Mrs. Pickens, we have happy news. Fran and I have become engaged to be married."

"I'm so happy for you and wish you both all the joy in the world. When, will this be?" "We are thinking of sometime in December. We haven't set a date yet." Tom noticed a dismayed look cross Mrs. Pickens's face.

"Well, I—I thought Mrs. Amberson wanted the flat for a longer time. I think our lease stated a year. You have your own house in Ashwell, don't you Tom?"

"Oh, Mrs. Pickens, I will be living here until the wedding and we should like to retain the flat here for at least the year. You know Tom comes up to Ely because of the shop; he often stays over in a small sleeping room over the shop. After our marriage he can stay here when necessary. Sometimes I'll be with him. Also, if it's all right with you, if my parents should visit from the States or Tom's mother from Ireland, they would have a lovely place to stay if they could use the flat. We wouldn't dream of asking you to break the lease. I love the flat and I'm looking forward to living here."

Mrs. Pickens face brightened. "That sounds fine to me. There is no problem with that at all. Mrs. Amberson, when will you actually be staying in the flat?"

"Tonight, this will be my first night here. Mrs. Pickens, will you please do me a big favor? Will you call me Fran?"

"I well indeed, but on one condition, you and Tom must call me Emma. When one gets older, so few call you by your first name. I really miss being called Emma."

"Emma," Fran said smiling, "I might be in and out today. Will you be here to let me in or will I get the key today?"

"I have your key right here in my pocket, M—Fran."

"Thank you, Emma, now I won't have to disturb you all the time." Fran and Tom said goodbye, making sure they said her given name.

As they were going out the door, Mrs. Pickens said to Fran, "Don't feel you would be disturbing me; if you should need anything when you come back please ask."

They met Don and Heidi at the Cathedral. Tom was to guide for a few hours. Heidi and Don went shopping with Fran for some groceries; then they went down to the riverfront to the former maltings. Many antique dealers had showrooms there. It was a delight to Fran to find this beautiful river, busy with colorful cruisers. She loved seeing the many different ducks on the green in front of the antique shops. It was hard not to linger there; she knew she would come here often. It was within walking distance of the Cathedral. Ely, she thought, Ely, I just love it here.

Fran said to Don and Heidi, "I'm anxious for the wedding and to be Tom's wife. I love him beyond words. But I'm going to enjoy this time of waiting on my own in this special place. Do you think that strange, Heidi?"

"No, Fran dear, I don't. If it had been anyone but Tom Hart and you, I would have thought the engagement was a bit soon. But knowing you both, we have no doubt it is the real thing. Still, having a little time to know even more of each other is important—and, Fran, the time on your own is special too. You never had that. You were away at school but that was so different." Heidi looked at her watch, "If we are to look for anything for your flat, we had better start." They went inside a shop. It wasn't long until Fran spotted the darling little round table with fancy metal legs and a glass top. The two chairs were ice cream parlor style of white metal with round padded seats, covered in a blue and yellow flowered print. "Don, could we get them into your car and take them with us? Would they fit?"

They each carried a piece to the car. Don worked until he made them fit. He looked at Fran and said, "Hey, there are only two chairs. I thought you were going to ask us to dinner sometime."

Fran grinned, "These are for my kitchen. If I don't get the table and chairs for the dining part of the big living room, by that time, I'll serve Japanese and use a crate for the table—we'll all sit on the floor. Don't worry, Don, I'll get you a soft pillow."

"I'll just worry about the cooking," Don said, grinning back.

"I'll serve a good wine anyway—and there's always take-out."

After the furniture was taken to the kitchen, Don said, "If you two are through admiring the breakfast set, we had better leave to meet Tom at the Almonry. Believe me, I'm ready for dinner. Those scones were a long time ago."

Tom and Fran said goodbye to their friends and walked back to the parking lot behind the Cathedral. They stood for a few minutes, quietly looking at the majesty of this great building. It appeared almost otherworldly in the deepening shadows of the evening.

Tom pulled Fran close, "I love this place more than ever, Fran, because it gave me you. It will seem like forever till I see you on Monday evening. I wish I didn't have to go back to Ashwell tonight, but I must. I'll be back on Monday in time for us to have dinner together. Would you like to go back to the Prince Albert?"

"Tom, I'd love that. I've wanted to go there again. Maybe we'll see May and we can tell her our news."

"May—who's May?"

"May is the sweet waitress at the pub. Something tells me, she will remember us and be happy to hear of our engagement. I still feel I want to tell the world."

Tom opened the car door for Fran, "I feel like that myself, darling, but the world's a big place; at least we'll tell May," he said laughing.

On the way back to Fran's flat, she said, "I'm so excited about our trip to Ireland. Will we flying into Dublin?"

"Yes, we have a direct flight scheduled from Stansted Airport; it's closer to Ely than Heathrow is. We'll be leaving Ely very early on Tuesday morning. When we reach Dublin we'll rent a car and drive to Mom's. I couldn't take the time now or we would have driven over to the coast and gone by ferry. That's a lot of fun. We'll put that on *our* sometime list; it's a joint one now."

They were at the door of the house, Tom held her for a minute, "Hon, I'm going to go on now."

Fran got her key from her purse. "Do you have time for a quick look at my big purchase of the day?"

"I'll take time for that." He kissed the tip of her nose.

Mrs. Pickens was in her living room watching the telly and crocheting. She heard Tom and Fran as they went upstairs. There was no way she could relax and keep her mind on her work or on the telly. She wished she could have talked plainly to Fran but she hadn't the time alone with her. In a few minutes she heard them coming back down. Tom had gone. She heard the door closing and was glad. Fran came to the doorway and looked over, smiling, "how are you tonight, Emma?"

Emma—oh, how she liked that. She was hoping the dear girl wouldn't be angry or resent her interference. "Fran, will you come and sit down for a few minutes, please? There is something we must talk about."

Fran crossed the room and sat on the soft, floral chintz covered chair.

Emma began, "I'm not at all comfortable about this. I like you and Tom so very much—but still—"

"Whatever is the matter, Emma? Don't be so troubled. Just tell me what it is." Fran felt completely puzzled.

Emma Pickens sat on the edge of her chair. She looked down at her tightly clasped hands, took a deep breath and looked at Fran. "This is difficult for me to say but I must. Until Tom and you are married, when Tom visits you in your flat, I want you to promise me that the visits will be just social—with no *staying together*. You know what I mean. I know many young people today think it is fine to live together before marriage, but I don't. Please don't be angry, Fran."

Fran couldn't help feeling amused but she held back any hint of laughter. She swallowed hard, not wanting to hurt this dear person in anyway. She got up from her chair and went close to Emma. Kneeling down by her chair, she took Emma's hands in her own. "Emma, I'm not the least bit angry. It just happens that Tom and I share your ideas completely for us. We really want to wait until we are married for that special privilege. So I can promise you that no matter how many times Tom visits or how long he is here, there will be no—staying together, as you call it. Our wedding night will truly be our wedding night."

Fran stood and Emma looked up, a little embarrassed, "Fran, I shouldn't have said—"

Fran smiled, "Now don't be troubling yourself anymore, Emma. I'm glad we've had this talk. Come upstairs and see my darling table and chair set. We'll try it out and have a cup of cocoa."

On Sunday, Fran walked about Ely, simply enjoying being there. She did go to the Cathedral for a short while on the outside chance that Ethel Fenman might have come back, although, not really expecting it, just hoping. Fran thought of walking down by the river and trying one of the restaurants there; but she didn't like eating alone. Emma, she thought, I bet Emma would love going out to a restaurant.

Emma was surprised at Fran's invitation. "Oh, my dear, I haven't been to a restaurant for a very long time. I used to walk as far as Alberts once in a while but even that is getting far to walk."

"We'll call a cab. It's so lovely by the river, and such a beautiful day."

"Fran, I haven't been down there in years. Mr. Pickens and I walked there often on Sunday afternoons. If, you're sure you want to be bothered with an old lady, I'd love to go."

"Friends are friends—age has nothing to do with that. I'm so happy you'll go with me. I'll call a cab, now."

"This is a special occasion. I want to change my dress; I won't be long."

Fran was going to say there was no need to change. Everyone dressed more casually today. She was wearing a cotton sweater with slacks. Mrs.

Pickens looked fine in her neat blue shirtwaist; she would just need a sweater. But Fran saw the excitement in Emma's eyes and said, "I'll change too."

Fran changed into her purple suit and high-heeled pumps. When she came down, Mrs. Pickens was every inch the proper English lady. She was wearing a silk, two-piece dress, navy colored with a small white print. On her head, was a small navy hat with a rolled back brim. She beamed at Fran as she pulled on her white gloves. "I'm happy to have the chance to dress and wear the string of pearls that Mr. Pickens gave me for our last anniversary." It was indeed lovely and Mrs. Pickens was delighted with Fran's sincere compliments.

During the outing there were a few people that remembered Mrs. Pickens and expressed pleasure in seeing her. The pleasure she was feeling far exceeded theirs. Fran took advantage of asking each person, they met, if they knew Ethel Fenman. The answer was always no. The little adventure was so enjoyable that Emma must have thanked Fran for "the wonderful day" a dozen times.

Fran went to the furniture stores on Monday morning. She saw things she liked but wanted to wait until Tom went with her to decide. Soon the flat would be his too.

She returned to the flat and packed her carry-on bag for the trip to Ireland. Writing to her parents and reading a little passed some time, but still it seemed to drag. Only two days apart and she couldn't wait to see Tom's dear face and feel the warmth of his arms around her. She went downstairs and looked into Emma's living room. She knocked on the door fame, waited and knocked a bit louder. Emma came in from the kitchen, drying her hands. "Fran, you should have come on in; you don't have to knock. Do you need something?"

"Emma, I don't want to be a pest. If you don't want to say yes to what I'm going to ask, it's all right, and I won't think anymore of it."

"Well, whatever is it, dear?"

"Your piano," Fran glanced in the direction of the big upright, would you mind if I played it sometimes?"

"You play, Fran? Oh, how wonderful! I play so infrequently anymore; only a little at a time because of the arthritis pain in my hands. To hear the piano really played again would be such a joy."

"My major was voice but I do play. Would you mind if I would sing too?"

Emma sat down on the chair and closed her eyes and smiled. She looked at Fran, "My dear girl, you never told me of your musical background. Sit down and tell me all about it and I'll tell you of mine."

Fran told Emma about her lifelong love of singing, her time at the conservatory, her dreams and plans and even of her brief marriage to the great Jeff Amberson, without dwelling on the marriage itself. "Now, Emma, tell me about Emma Pickens."

"A long lot of years ago, I played very well. I was not renowned but I frequently had the privilege of playing the great organ at Ely Cathedral. I accompanied wonderful soloists and choral groups. Music was a very important part of my life."

Soon Fran and Emma were looking through Emma's music cupboard and listening to each others memories and their musical likes and dislikes. Whatever Emma had been doing in the kitchen was completely forgotten. They took turns at the piano; Fran's beautiful soprano was singing a few measures every now and then. Upon hearing her, Emma said, "Fran, you should give a concert at Ely Cathedral. You shouldn't hide the gift you have. You know, I really believe that God sent you to live with me for a while. He surely knew I had been feeling so lonely and missed so the music in my life. To have someone to share a bit of that side of my life with is just glorious." There was nothing of the prim older women in Emma's face. There was a look of youthful sparkle in those clear blue eyes looking out of the small gold rimmed glasses.

The sound of the knocker startled them both. Fran looked at her watch, "I can't believe it is 6:30." It had been only three o'clock when she had come downstairs. "That must be Tom." Right now the most important part of her life was the man at the door. She flew to open it."

Emma gave them some time alone; when she went into the hall she greeted Tom with a hug and a peck on the cheek and said, "Thank you, Tom."

"What for, Emma?"

"For sharing your Fran with me." She went back to her kitchen, smiling and humming.

Tom and Fran walked arm-in-arm the short distance to the Prince Albert. They were pleased to find the booth they had first shared available. May, of course, remembered, as she thought of them, this lovely couple. She made an exuberant but sincere show of delight when she heard their news. She left the table and returned with three glasses of wine; giving them a beaming smile, she said, "Tonight, luvs, the drinks are on the 'ouse." She raised her glass, "a wish to both for all the 'appiness in the world, from everyone at Alberts, and especially from May." She finished her wine, "now, luvs, I'll take your order."

They lingered over their dinner. There was much to talk about. Plans were made for Tom to pick up Fran at four a.m. to leave for the Stansted Airport.

Back in her flat, Fran's thoughts were of the lovely day spent with Emma and the wonderful time spent with her precious Tom. She was excited over tomorrow's trip. How good life was for her now. Yet, suddenly there was a drop in her spirit; she felt a wave of fear, as if something waited to dim this joy she now had. She certainly wasn't afraid of flying; that she always enjoyed and felt it to be the safest form of travel. She told herself, this silly premonition was just that—silly. She was still not accepting that things could be good in her life. Thoughts of Ethel Fenman came and she went over in her mind all the advice Ethel had given. No, it was no longer a feeling that she was unworthy of good things. Still, the feeling of unease persisted. Was this unease something to do with Brendan? They had heard he was safe and in their own joy hadn't really talked of what was the underlying trouble. Whatever that was, it couldn't affect Tom and her, could it? Fran remembered Ethel saying, in the Cathedral, "If you ever do need special help, whisper a little prayer to St. Etheldreda here. God will hear your prayer and she will pray it with you." Fran knew she didn't have to be in the Cathedral or looking at a statue, a work of art, to pray. She asked St. Etheldreda to pray with her so that she might overcome her fear. It was like sharing a deep concern with a friend; sometimes that helps the worry to subside. Whatever happened, Fran felt comforted.

Chapter 25

Soon the plane would be landing in Dublin. The flight time had passed so quickly. The reassuring nearness of Tom dispelled any disquieting feeling that lingered with Fran from last night. Tom's face was radiant as he talked about the beauty of his home village in Ireland. "I can't wait to have you see the loveliness of Monaghan County, Fran. The Irish word is Muineachain, and it means 'little hills.' There are, indeed, many little hills with many beautiful lakes set in between. The Lough Emy is such a thing to see, a pretty picture, with its many wild fowls and gorgeous swans. Nearby, at County Cavan, is the place for fishing. Oh, the fishing is great there!—Fran, have you ever fished?"

Fran laughed and said, "*Never.*"

"When we come back again and have more time, I'll teach ye girl," Tom said, putting on an Irish brogue.

Still laughing, Fran replied, "Well, I love to eat fish so I might as well catch them."

"It's a lot of fun, Fran. Dermod would often take me fishing. He was a fine man." Tom sighed, "I still miss him." Tom was quiet for a few minutes, and then began again telling her his memories of Ireland. "Glaslough, where Mom's house is, is just a little bit north of Monaghan. It's a charming spot and surrounded by beautiful countryside. Like most of Ireland there are many wonderful historic churches around. There's a nineteenth-century gothic revival Roman Catholic Church in the nearby town of St. Macartans. It's a grand sight; you'll love seeing it; maybe not during this visit but sometime."

Fran squeezed his hand, "Did anyone ever tell you that you would be a great travel agent?" Sounding very American, she said, "You can certainly sell a place."

The plane landed smoothly. Tom had arranged for a car rental in advance; soon Fran and he were on the drive north. The day was fresh and clear, their mood one of happy anticipation. Fran's thoughts were of meeting Tom's mother. From all she had heard from Tom and Aunt Berniece, Fran was predisposed to love her. Also, she was looking forward to meeting Father Matt.

Matt had gone to spend some time with Susanna. There was nothing more to be done in Dublin to help Brendan. He decided to join the touring group in Dublin for the return home. He had kept in touch, calling them throughout the tour. All was going well, no problems with anyone. They missed him but he really wasn't needed. Susanna's need for his company was more important. He wanted to see Tom and meet his future wife. Although not blood relations, Susanna and Tom were his family and he loved them dearly as he loved his half-brother Brendan. During their lives, the times they got to spend together were few. Still, the bond of feeling was very strong. Susanna's frequent, warm letters and phone calls bridged the gap between the years and the ocean.

Tom and Fran drove off the main highway into a quaint village. Stopping at a local pub, they had sandwiches and wonderful iced white beer called Breó from Guinness.

"Tom, I've been hoping that something more might have worked out for Brendan and that he will be at home when we get there. We haven't talked much of him lately, but I do think of him. We haven't heard anything for a while."

"Hon, I think that is wishful thinking. It would be great and a big relief but as far as I know everything is still unsettled with him." They left the pub and headed back to the highway.

As they pulled into the driveway, Susanna and Father Matt hurried to meet them. After the first embrace and joy of the reunion of mother and son, Tom pulled Fran close to him and presented her to his mother and Father Matt. Fran's emotions were many; she thought how beautiful this woman is. Susanna's face radiated the happiness she felt in having her dearest Tom home. The worried and strained look her face had shown had temporarily vanished. Her warmth toward Fran was genuine and it put Fran totally at ease. Susanna was sure this lovely girl was perfect for Tom from all she had heard of her from him and Berniece and Cliff; now, seeing her there was no doubt. Susanna felt a love for her instantly.

They all lingered a long time around the large dark oak table in the charming dining room. Fran had admired the collection of beautiful Belleek. She was delighted by the stories of love Susanna told about each piece. Each was a gift, marking special occasions, from Dermod. Susanna used her best

Waterford crystal wine glasses for a special toast in honor of the engagement. Fran and Tom did justice to Susanna's luncheon; glad they had eaten lightly at their stop. Farther Matt said he couldn't resist a second helping of the apple crisp. Susanna smiled and said, "Matt you're like your Dad. That was one of his favorite things. In fact, the first day I met him, in Belfast, I had a freshly made one when he came to Dad's house to fix the kitchen sink. Every time I'd make it through the years, he would tease and say that's why he married me."

Father Matt smiled as he savored a bite, "Susanna, I think that would have been reason enough."

The relaxed happy mood was sustained and the conversation flowed. Fran and Matt talked of many things in the States. And there was much talk of Tom and Fran's plans. However, the tenseness returned to all their voices when their conversation inevitably turned to what was truly uppermost on their minds, the problem with Brendan.

Matt told all of his experiences in Dublin. He told of his desire to keep searching for the lad with the red hair that had followed him. "I didn't continue the search when Brendan asked that I stop. Not knowing what was involved and not wanting to make things worse for Brendan I did what he asked." He looked at Susanna with tenderness, "Mom needed my visit and we are waiting together for more news from Brendan. There has been nothing since the first call from the Quinns."

"Mom," Tom asked, "Didn't you have a number from that call, a number for that Pat Quinn?"

"Yes, Tom, but Brendan made me promise not to call more. He was so afraid of bringing danger there. I'm going to call tomorrow anyway. I just can't stand it any longer. Tomorrow morning, I'm going into the hospital; I'll use a payphone and call from there. Maybe Brendan will be able to level with us by this time. Just to hear his voice again would be some comfort. He said he would stay at the Quinn's until he decided what to do about the situation, whatever, in heaven's name, it is." Susanna got up and started clearing the table, unable to stay still longer.

Fran stood and helped carry things to the kitchen. Her heart was aching for Susanna. She felt in herself some of the same dark foreboding of last night. They placed the dishes on the sink and Fran faced Susanna; she wanted with all her heart to comfort her. "Susanna, I know you're a woman who prays. A friend I met at Ely told me, if I ever had a special need, to pray to the Lord and ask Saint Etheldreda to pray with me. Let's both ask her to help keep Brendan safe."

Susanna looked with tenderness at this lovely young woman who was to be her daughter-in-law and hugged her. "Fran, I can tell you that one prayer

I've made for a long time has been answered. I'm happy, my dear, Tom has found you."

Brendan had made his decision last week. He and John were in the Dublin airport waiting to board their flight to Heathrow; at the very time Brendan's family was together at lunch. Dr. Tim had driven them and Amy McGill had come along. Brendan and John both wore ball caps and very casual, almost sloppy clothes. It was a look that was a bit different for both of them. Dr. Tim and Amy waited with them, giving the appearance of a family. They would have been hard to recognize unless one was very close. Dr. Tim had insisted on this bit of disguise on the outside chance that, for some reason, Sean or the others might be around the terminal. There was no one of a worry at the airport. When they were soon to board, Dr. Tim shook their hands and said he hoped to see them again and admonished them to "be careful." Amy McGill stepped out of character from her brisk, practical self and hugged them both; but saying in a firm, authoritative voice, "stay out of trouble. See the proper authorities for help with your problem and don't be tryin to do anything brave and dangerous."

Brendan was trying to thank them once more and tell them how he felt toward them but Amy McGill cut him short, "now hurry—it's time to board."

When they were going to the parking, Dr. Tim looked at Amy, who was dabbing her face with a handkerchief; "you've become fond of young Brendan, I know, Amy."

"Aye, well he's so young. I guess with the nursing him back to health, my maternal instinct was brought to the surface. John is a nice lad, too. I'm worried for them. I wouldn't let them catch me snifflin. There was enough of that goin on this morning when Anne said her good-byes. She is so fond of Brendan but I think she felt toward him like a younger sister. But John, that's something again. He is not much younger than Brendan but seems much. There aren't too many years between Anne and John and I had the feeling they had eyes for each other. Just as well he'll be goin other places."

Dr. Tim laughed, "I don't know if you're sounding like a matchmaker or a chaperon. Maybe someday you will be a little of both. I think we'll see those lads again." Then, very seriously, with a glance at the airborne plane, he said, "I certainly hope so."

John's delight at being on the plane pushed the heavy purpose of their mission from their minds. While they were seated on the yet unmoving plane, John's eyes were on everything like a kid's. "I've never been flying before. This is my first time. You've been before, haven't you, Brendan?"

"Yes, many times. Mom and I would fly over to England; we have relatives there. They are Mom's relatives by her first marriage but we have always been close. When I was really young, we flew to the States for Matt's ordination."

"Clear across the Atlantic—were you scared?"

"No, I think I was too excited. Going and coming back were night flights. I slept most of the time each way."

The motor was running on the plane, John was listening. "Brendan, does it make that noise all the time?"

Brendan grinned and slapped John's knee. "It better had or we're in big trouble."

John, realizing what Brendan meant, flushed and burst out laughing. "I can't believe I asked that."

Brendan and John got their tickets for the Heathrow Express to London. Brendan was wishing he had called Uncle Cliff and Aunt Berniece Hart for some information on finding an inexpensive place to stay. He decided to call before leaving the terminal. They had always been so nice to him and he always thought of them as his uncle and aunt. There had been the same love shown to him as to Tom, when they visited. Aunt Berniece answered the phone. Brendan explained that he and a friend had some business in London and needed to be directed to a decent but inexpensive hotel. Aunt Berniece was stunned when she found the call to be from Brendan. He heard her saying to Uncle Cliff, "You'll never believe who this is. It's Brendan McKenna. Brendan, does your Mom know you're here? She has been so worried."

"No, Aunt Berniece, she knows I'm safe but doesn't know I'm in London. I thought it safer for her if she didn't know right now. It's a long story, Aunt Berniece. If you could please tell me of a place, as I said, respectable but inexpensive, I'd appreciate it."

"Brendan, dear boy, Cliff and I know the perfect place. I assure you it is respectable," she laughed a little, "and very inexpensive. No fee for the first year," again a little chuckle; "the name of the place is Harts and I think you remember the address."

"Aunt Berniece, we couldn't impose and besides, the situation I'm in—I wouldn't want to put you and Uncle Cliff in any danger—and, please, Aunt Berniece, don't call Mom about my being here."

"Brendan, London is a big place and whatever the 'situation' is, we'll worry about that if need be. As for you being an imposition, that's impossible. We will love having you and your friend with us;—we simply won't take *no* for an answer."

In fifteen minutes, on the Express, they were in London. The cab ride seemed too short for John who was stretching his neck to look out of the windows, continuing to enjoy all that was new to him. Soon, Brendan was in the motherly embrace of Aunt Berniece; John was given a welcoming hug as well.

Cliff and Berniece kept the conversation light and didn't ask any prying questions. They filled Brendan in about Tom and Fran's engagement. "Fran and Tom are in Ireland now for Fran to meet your mother and Father Matt. He is visiting there, too." Aunt Berniece couldn't resist adding, "It would be perfect if you could be there with them. Couldn't you let your mom know that you are here? She has been so worried."

"No, I got in touch with Mom. She knows I'm safe; I want to keep her safe. I've been mixed up with some really horrible guys back home. I feel she is safer if she knows nothing of my whereabouts for a while. So please don't tell her I'm here."

While Berniece cleared up after dinner, Cliff suggested a walk for the men. "I think it would do us good after that hearty meal," he said, while giving Berniece a hug.

Once outside, Cliff said, "Brendan, I want you to tell me what this is all about. I don't believe we would be in any danger over here. Maybe you are right about your mom; the trouble seems to have started over there. Aunt Berniece doesn't have to know the whole story if you think she would worry; but I insist you tell me everything. There is a small green ahead with some benches. This time of the evening we'll have it to ourselves."

They went onto the little park; as Cliff had predicted, there was no one there. They sat quietly on the bench for a few minutes. Brendan finally said, "all right, Uncle Cliff, I'll start at the beginning of how John and I got mixed up with this mess. I'll tell you all that has happened till now and what we hope to do to stop something horrible from happening."

Cliff listened thoughtfully without interruption. When Brendan reached the conclusion, Cliff shook his head, "Dear God!—Brendan, do you realize how lucky you are to be alive?" As he said this, he gently patted Brendan's back. He uttered not one word of criticism.

Brendan was so grateful for that; Uncle Cliff could have said plenty. His warped and twisted thinking of this past summer was so appalling to him that Brendan didn't feel he deserved this kindness, but he was thankful for it.

"Fellows, I think it's a good idea to take this matter at once to Scotland Yard. However, I'm told they get so many reports of dubious plans and threats that they just can't investigate all of them. There's a constant surveillance of the official IRA, of course, or of any known terrorists. How seriously they will take this threat, we'll just have to see. In any event, please, Brendan, don't you and John take any course of action that would put you in danger. It wouldn't be fair to your families. You will have done your duty by informing the authorities."

"Uncle Cliff, I can't promise. If the Yard won't try to stop it, I don't know what I'll do, but I'll have to try. I wouldn't want John caught up further but I feel responsible. Remember, I shot my mouth off about Ely and set Sean thinking of this plan."

"Brendan, if he had an evil design in him, if he was bent on doing damage to a site in England, he would have planned it somewhere without your talk of Ely. You've got to listen to me, boy."

"Uncle Cliff, I'll do what I can at the Yard." Brendan didn't add what was in his mind—"I'll stop Sean if it kills me."

Back in the kitchen, Berniece put in a call to Susanna. "Susanna, I just wanted to say 'Hello' to everyone while you're all together." When she was through talking with each member she asked to speak again to Susanna. "Susanna Dear, It's been great talking to all. There's a member missing I know, but I just want to tell you not to worry. Have some fun! Cliff is out right now—but love from both of us. Bye for now." Berniece didn't give Susanna a chance to respond. She hung up the phone thinking, I didn't break a promise, I didn't tell—but I think Susanna might get the idea. Her mind had to be put at ease.

Susanna put down the phone and looked at the others; she had a puzzled expression on her face. "Berniece sounded so silly, so joking and flippant about Brendan." Then a knowing smile crossed her face. "They've heard from him! That's it, or maybe he's there and she wasn't to tell me. She wanted to comfort me and knew I'd figure out what was behind the 'don't worry, have fun.' I'm sure of it."

"Mom, you're right; that's the kind of thing Aunt Berniece would do. She wouldn't tell if Brendan asked her not to; but she'd have to try to put your mind at ease. But *London*—what's he doing in London?"

Susanna said, "I will call Pat Quinn tomorrow. Maybe he will tell me something, or at the very least, let me know if Brendan is no longer there. Then, I'll be sure he is with Cliff and Berniece."

Despite Berniece's good intentions of easing their worry, the question as to why Brendan went to London was surrounded by a mysterious, unknown fear.

Chapter 26

Very early the next morning, while everyone was still asleep, Susanna drove to the hospital to make the call to Pat Quinn. She was on vacation but did take time to stop at her office to say a quick hello to her friends, then hurried to the public waiting room to use the pay phone.

Anne was just going out the door for school, when the phone rang. She ran back to answer it, wondering who could be calling so early. "The Quinn residence."

Susanna asked to speak to Pat Quinn. "I'm sorry; he's already out in the fields. This is his daughter; may I take a message?"

Susanna was about to ask for a return call, but maybe, she thought, this sweet-sounding girl would help her. "I'm going to ask a question concerning Brendan McKenna. I hope you can help me. This is his mother and I have reason to think that Brendan might be in London with relatives, but I'm not sure. Has he left your home?"

Anne was silent, what if this wasn't his mother? Could it be someone who found out where he had been and wanted to follow him? "Brendan McKenna, I know no Brendan McKenna. Perhaps he's someone my father knows. Call back about five o'clock."

"Oh, Anne! It is Anne isn't it? I know Brendan was staying with your family. I was given this number and allowed to call once. I talked with your father, Pat Quinn and to Brendan. He told me how you and your father saved him, how you and your dog Ben found him in the fields when he was sick." Susanna's voice was sounding like she was near tears.

"Mrs. McKenna, I know now that I'm speaking to Brendan's mother. I just had to be careful that it wasn't someone inquiring for an evil reason. I myself am not sure where Brendan and his friend John went. I believe my father and Dr. Tim might know. Some things they didn't talk over with me.

They did leave early yesterday morning to take a plane out of Dublin. Dr. Tim and Amy McGill, the nurse who cared for Brendan, drove them from here. I hope they are with relatives and keep safe. There are things I don't know but, whatever is wrong, I know it's not over."

"Anne, you mentioned John. Do you mean John Hobson? How did he make contact with Brendan there?"

"Aye, Mrs. McKenna, John Hobson. He found out from someone that Brendan had been brought to this area, and possibly dead. When John found that out and how bad the people were that they had been mixed up with, he left Dublin. He came and searched the fields for a full day, dreading that he might find Brendan dead. By luck or God's blessing, he found Brendan here. He stayed here too, for a few days. They decided to go off together. Beyond that, I don't know anything, truly. If Dad knows, where they are, maybe he'll call you. Brendan might not want you to know; but I'll tell Dad you called. Your Brendan is so nice—and so is John. I'm sorry I have to leave to catch my bus. Goodbye, Mrs. McKenna."

"Goodbye, Anne, and thank you so much." Susanna put her head in her hands and sobbed. She knew Brendan was found sick in the fields but what had led to this she hadn't known. If he was thought to be dead, something horrible must have taken place. Now he was safe; she must hold on to that. She pulled herself together and went to her car.

Susanna started for home, convinced now that Brendan was in London with John. Did she imagine, she smiled a little to herself, that Anne had a special fond inflection in her voice when she spoke John's name? She was glad Brendan was not alone in this. She had met John through the years and always liked him. What were they up to? "Ah, the plot thickens." She thought herself silly when the Sherlock Holmes quotation sprang into her mind. This business wasn't funny at all.

Susanna returned home to find everyone up and planning a picnic day at Rossmore Forest Park. She told them what Anne had said, not mentioning the horrible details. She didn't want to spoil their happy mood. All agreed that Brendan was most probably in London. Tom gave Susanna a hug, "Mom, I'm sure he is safe now. Today is beautiful; a picnic would do us all good. I remember the many times we used to take the forest walks with Dermod. I'd love to take those paths today with Fran. I've been sitting so much; my legs want to move. What do you say, Mom? Are you up to it?"

"Yes, I'm up to it. My legs agree with yours, Tom. I'd like a good walk. Fran, you'll love the park, and Matt, I know that it had been a special place for you."

Matt smiled, "Indeed, many a day I spent there, when I was a lad, with my mom and dad." He gave Susanna a hug and said, "I'll like going there with my second mom today."

"I love having three sons, Matt." Susanna looked at Fran and added, "It's high time I'm getting a daughter. Fran, do you think your mom and dad will share you?"

"I'm sure they will. I can't wait for you to meet them. Susanna, do you know what my parents said? They said, "It was wonderful having a daughter but it was high time they got a son."

There was much laughter as everyone finished the preparation. For a moment, Fran thought of the contrast with Jeff's life. Had he ever had a time of true fun like this? She doubted it.

Soon they were on their way to spend a wonderful day—the most relaxing one Susanna had in many months.

There was no thought of a relaxing day in the mind of Pearse O'Neill. He stood looking into the bathroom mirror. He smoothed back his long black hair and caught it in a rubber band in the back. He checked his dark beard; no, it didn't need a trim. The mirror reflected his dark brown eyes, the handsome strong face, but he wasn't seeing his reflection. He was thinking of the face he would encounter later that day. The big, pudgy face would be filled with rage—Sean's face, upon learning that Denis Fleming had firmly decided to leave the group. Pearse had been aware of a change in Denis. He had shown no interest, in fact he showed annoyance, if Pearse mentioned anything about "the friends." Denis had always seemed to look on the whole thing as something of a lark. Pearse never told Denis just what Sean's plans were and, since a major meeting had never taken place, Denis had no idea. He still thought they might be planning some disrupting show of defiance. Pearse really wasn't surprised when Denis told him last evening.

"Pearse, I no longer want to be involved with a hate-bent group. Most of Ireland is reaching another level. I want to be clean and get on with my own life. I've a good job now. I got a grand promotion with the computer company. I'm being moved to their northern office in Derry. I'll have to be moving out right away, in fact tonight. I'm sorry to be doing this to you, Pearse, but I'll be giving you an extra month's board. I don't want things hard for you. Surely, you'll find someone soon to help share expenses. Oh, and there's something else I've got to tell you, my Maggie said 'yes.' After I'm settled in Derry, we are going to be married."

Pearse was glad for Denis. He certainly hadn't tried to talk him out of the intelligent decision he had made.

When Denis left, he said "the next time you see Mike, Brendan, and John say 'hello' for me; there were some good times. Better not say anything to Sean, he'd probably just be mad." Denis laughed.

Pearse said he'd take care of it and wished Denis good luck. When Denis closed the door, Pearse said aloud, "Thank God—he doesn't know about Brendan or any of the horrible details."

Now Pearse was finishing his packing and wishing he could walk away as Denis had. It was too late for himself—the money, damn the money. Pearse had a less than adequate paying job at a shipyard. As a youth he had spent a short jail time because of some scuffle between a few IRA members and British soldiers. He wasn't really a member but had tagged along with some friends for an unofficial disturbance. However, it was enough for a bad record and to keep him from better employment. He made some money on the side, helping with some ventures of his uncle. His uncle was a militant member of the IRA and an expert at making bombs; Pearse had learned this skill from him. Pearse clicked the lock on his suitcase. Damn the day Sean had found out about him. At first, Sean was just the friend of a friend of his. That's how he met Sean; their association was strictly social. He had met Michael and the others through Sean while Sean fashioned himself as the life of the party. Sean covered the costs for Pearse and his friend Denis to come to Dublin on weekends for some fun. Denis thought Sean was just a kind of crazy guy, with more money than he knew what to do with, who liked to have a lot of friends around to agree with his ideas. Pearse had soon known, from the time Sean casually talked about making bombs and looked at him with cold, knowing eyes, that Sean had hunted him out and would eventually want something from him. Long before Sean had his exact plan in mind, he asked Pearse, "If bombs are needed, will you build them?" Pearse had tired to say he knew nothing about bombs. Sean had thrown back his head and laughed. "You're pullin my leg. Pearse, don't you think I know your history very well?"

"What would you be wanting bombs for, Sean?"

"I'll be telling you someday when I have it all figured out. I have a good place for you to build them."

"I have a job, man, I don't have money to be taking time off."

"Pearse, you don't think I'd be wanting your services for free?" Sean said in a mocking tone. Then he said in his most charming and persuasive way, "Seriously, Pearse, I'll need an expert bomb builder and a real helper in the business I need to do. Just how, just when, I don't know yet; but I want to know I can count on you." At that, Sean pulled out his wallet and put into Pearse's hands money to equal a year of Pearse's wages. "This is on account, for good faith. I'll give you twice that after we—" Sean's voice suddenly changed from charming to one filled with loathing. "—after we get even with the goddamned British swine. I'll pay you for what you need and any cost you have in securing the right supplies. Is it a deal?"

Pearse had looked at the money in his hand. He had wanted to be rid of that part of his life. He wanted to throw the money at Sean's face; but it was too much for him to resist. Saying nothing, he put the money in his pocket. There would be no turning back for him, ever. Sean would kill him in a minute.

Now, as Pearse turned the key to lock the door he had an eerie feeling that he might never be turning that key to open it again. He had taken off work for a month without pay. Sean would be paying for that. He drove away from his house thinking, that's me, bought and paid for by Sean Devlin. Sean's pawn, the silly pun came into his mind. He thought that's stupid just like I am. I'm on my way to do Sean's bidding, to build the bombs and God knows what else. First, I'll be havin to explain about Denis. *Damn.* Pearse gripped hard on the steering wheel at the thought of Sean.

The day in London was not the beautiful one that it had been in Ireland. The cold, gray drizzle matched Brendan's feeling of gloom. He hated having to own up to his stupidity to yet another person. He would be so glad when this visit to Scotland Yard was over. Cliff had insisted on going with them. Brendan was grateful for that. Cliff flagged down the black cab. Brendan and John got into the back; Cliff got up front with the driver. "Where to, Guv'nor?"

"New Scotland Yard—10 Broadway."

"No trouble finding that, Sir. We'll be there in short order. However, the traffic is rather heavy this hour in the morning."

Cliff and the driver chatted during the ride. Brendan and John sat in silence. Brendan was trying to collect his thoughts. He wanted to tell his story in a way that it would be taken seriously. John was absorbed by the sights of London and couldn't take his eyes from the windows. He momentarily forgot what their destination was. He saw the big double-decker buses with all the tourists gazing at everything as he was. Wouldn't it be fun to ride on the top of one of them; what a view of it all that would be. Then, he remembered he was not a tourist—not here to enjoy the sights. By the time the cab stopped at the Yard any lightness he had felt was gone. John, like Brendan, was tense and felt inadequate to the task before them. Seeing the three full blocks of buildings that was Scotland Yard did nothing to allay these feelings.

Cliff led the way, choosing to begin at the Criminal Investigation Department. They entered into a hallway and went into the first, stark office. A young man was busy over a stack of papers on his desk. He looked up with a small, polite smile and asked, "How can I help you? I'm Constable James."

Cliff introduced himself and the two young men. That Cliff was English was quite apparent to the constable. He soon found himself correct in his judgment that the young men were Irish; as Cliff continued explaining why they were there. "These men are from Ireland and they have a very disturbing story to tell. They have information of an intended violent plan against a site in England. Whom should we talk with about this?" Brendan and John were grateful for Cliff's calm initiative on their behalf.

Constable James studied the three men. They certainly looked serious. "I'll see if Sergeant Crosby is busy." He phoned and found the Sergeant was in his office. He briefly explained the situation. "Follow me. Sergeant Crosby can give you a little time right now." He led them down the hall to the Sergeant's office; the door was open. They entered and Constable James made introductions before leaving.

Sergeant Crosby's office was large with two chairs directly in front of his desk; a third chair was by the wall. He nodded, "Please sit down." He motioned to John to get the other chair, "Please bring it closer." The sergeant was middle-aged and just beginning to be a little weighty. With his thick, wavy, iron-gray hair, regular features and intense blue eyes he was still a handsome man. He had an austerity about him and his eyes seemed penetrating as he observed these three men. "Now, what is this all about?"

Cliff explained why they were there as he had to Constable James. He turned to Brendan, "Start at the beginning—just as you told it all to me last night."

Sergeant Crosby sat back into his chair and folded his hands quietly in his lap. He listened, asking no questions, until Brendan, with a little input from John, had told all that had happened from the beginning of their association with Sean and the others. Brendan and John didn't spare themselves as far as their participation with the group went. They told of their willingness, at first, to go along with what they thought would be disruptive but not violent demonstrations of protest. Brendan had to add in his and John's defense, that even if things had been just as they first thought, they knew now that they had been wrong and their whole involvement stupid.

Sergeant Crosby sat forward and folded his arms on the desk. He reflected on all he had heard while he looked from Brendan to John. He saw in both a sense of openness and a self-censure.

"The very fact that you lads are here convinces me that, as you put it, your 'stupid' days are over and any involvement you had with that group is ended. Indeed, both of you quitting the association before you knew anything of the dastardly move this Sean Devlin had planned tells me you have your heads on straight. Brendan, from what you said, I think you are lucky to be alive." He looked at Cliff, "What is your relationship with these men?"

"In an extended way, Brendan is a relative. His mother was married to my brother Jody Hart. He died and Susanna married Dermod McKenna; he is their son. Dermod was Irish and Brendan was raised in Ireland. I think of Brendan as my nephew. Our families have stayed very close.

"Now, this brother Tom Hart that you spoke of, Brendan, he is English and lives here. He is your half-brother, right?" Brendan nodded yes. "You said he volunteers as a guide at Ely Cathedral. Does he work?"

"He owns three chemist shops. One here in London, one in Ashwell, Hertfordshire County and one in Ely. He owns a house in Ashwell."

Sergeant Crosby pushed his forehead with the palm of his hand. He smiled and his face lost the look of austerity. "Ah, yes, the Hart Chemist Shop. He looked at Cliff. "Now I know where I've seen you. You are the chemist in the London shop. I've been in that shop often. I remember seeing Tom there too."

Cliff felt more relaxed. "I've retired from there recently. I've been trying to place you too, you looked so familiar."

"It's good seeing you, Mr. Hart. Good wishes on your retirement."

"Thank you, my wife and I are looking forward to a little travel time."

"Good. Now, to get on with the problem at hand. Brendan, do you have any photos of this Sean Devlin or of the other members?"

"No, I'm sorry; I never had any pictures of Sean or any of the others."

"Well, give me a description of each and tell me any background you know of them. Wait a minute." The Sergeant removed a tape from his recorder and called a typist. She came into the office immediately. "Please, do this right away, Miss Hill; I want a printed copy of this for these men to sign." He turned to his computer to enter what Brendan or John would tell him.

Brendan tried to comply, giving a physical description of each. He thought how little he really knew of them. He didn't know Sean's address and hadn't noticed Michael's when he went there. John spoke up; he had lived with Michael and knew his address but not the others. Brendan said Pearse and Denis lived near where his grandfather Peter Moran had lived in Belfast, but he hadn't paid attention to the exact location or address. He didn't know much background on any of them. He knew Sean had a cruiser he had talked about often. Brendan didn't know its name or registration but thought it was docked near Dublin. John said Michael worked for a ferry company but he couldn't remember the name.

The sergeant turned from his computer to face the men. "Brendan, you know a lot of these plans are just talk. I know you truly believe this Sean Devlin will try to carry out a bombing at Ely Cathedral. I'm not sure. It would take a lot of planning and effort. We are on top of a lot of threats coming from Ireland and the more radical members of the IRA. However, this has no connection with an official group, apparently. We do get many threats from hate groups or malcontents; we do our best and we have a huge staff but still we are over extended. All I can promise is that we will try. We'll contact Interpol—that's the International Police Organization—and check for fingerprints. We'll check with our Information Room for access to the distant computer center and maybe come up with something on Devlin's boat. The names of all will be checked against list of known terrorists. We can't spread any false alarms. No one has been officially accused of anything yet. So far, the intent to vandalize is only supposition and talk. I really don't know how far we can go on this. But I'll give it much consideration and try to do what we can within reason."

"When will you know if this horrible plan can be stopped?" Brendan's look was intense. "I know Sean means what he said. I know what he is like. *I know* he'll try."

"Brendan, I said we will try to investigate this threat. As I said, so far it is just talk and unless he has been accused of something else, Ireland will give us no help in pursuing Devlin or these other men. You have done your duty in this matter. All I can say is, I'll report what you told me and investigate where I can. Where can I be in touch with you if needed? Will you be staying with your uncle?"

"I don't know for how long. You could reach me through him. Is it all right, Uncle Cliff, to give your number?"

"Yes, of course, Brendan." Cliff looked at Sergeant Crosby, "I hope the young men will stay with us for a while." Cliff gave his address and phone number to the sergeant.

The sergeant stood with an obvious look of dismissal. Good-byes were said and the three left the office.

Berniece heard the door open. She came into the room and saw Cliff pouring three glasses of sherry from the decanter. Cliff crossed the room and gave her a little hug; but it was obvious they were all very subdued. Brendan especially looked drained.

"What's happened? Where did you go this morning?" Berniece spoke with deep concern.

Cliff looked at Brendan and John and then turned to Berniece and said, "We went to talk with the authorities at Scotland Yard concerning the troubles the lads have had."

"Scotland Yard!—What would the Yard have to do with the trouble you had in Ireland? Brendan, I've been trying to think of what danger you would be in over here and of your fear of danger to us by your being here. I simply don't understand it. Are people from over there likely to follow you here? Brendan, was it gambling? Did you get into debt and need money to pay them off? Uncle Cliff and I would help with the money and I know your Mom and Tom would help too. Don't be ashamed to ask if that's the problem. A lot of young men are foolish like that. We would help John too if there's a need."

Brendan shook his head, "No." He laughed weakly and said, "Thank you, Aunt Berniece, you are very kind and very sweet. I wish it was as simple as a gambling debt. It's nothing like that."

Cliff said, "Brendan. I think we had better level with Berniece; she is in the middle of this too. What she could conjure up might be more frightening than the truth. At least she will know the problem and will feel assurance of the Yard's help."

Brendan and John agreed. Brendan repeated the story from the beginning. Upon finishing, he thought to himself that he sounded like a recording. It came out word for word as before.

There were tears in Berniece's eyes as she looked into Brendan's. "Does your mom know how you were treated by this Sean Devlin?"

"Not everything, Aunt Berniece, nor does she know any details of Sean's plans. She only knows that I'm not a part of something terrible that I know about. Now, that you know everything, you must realize that Mom might not be safe if she had any information. If Sean finds out that I've talked, I don't know what he'll do. He is really evil or absolutely mad."

"He will be stopped, Brendan. The Yard is very efficient. They'll stay on top of this."

Brendan was wishing he shared her feeling of confidence.

Aunt Berniece put her hand on top of Brendan's. "You boys just stay with us until this business is over. You must not take any chances on your own."

Brendan did not reply. He knew that was a promise he couldn't make.

Berniece started toward the kitchen, "After a morning like that you all need a good hot lunch. To think, you left to face that ordeal having only tea and toast for breakfast." She pursed her lips and shook her head.

When she was out of sight, Cliff winked and said, "The maternal instinct."

John sighed and grinned, "Uncle Cliff, I'm glad she has it—I need it."

In Dublin, there was no comfort felt by the two men awaiting Sean's arrival. Michael had returned home, late, from the office. He had wanted to leave everything in good order as this was his final working day before starting his vacation. Vacation, he was thinking as he went into his flat, that's a laugh. A hell of a work is ahead of me. As the time was drawing near for the plan's execution, the whole thing was becoming less palatable.

Pearse had a key to his place and Michael found him already there, looking as glum as humanly possible. Pearse got up from his sprawled position on the sofa, "Hello, Mike."

"Pearse, you look as happy as I feel. What time did you get here?"

"I've been here much of the day; I left Belfast early. There were a few stops I made after I crossed the border. The contacts there provided me with the supplies to make the bombs; everything I need is with me. After that, I came straight on. I wanted to see Sean before our meeting tonight. I went to his place, against the big man's orders, but he wasn't there. There's something I have to tell him—something he's not going to like. I wanted to get that over with. Denis was smart and backed out. He still doesn't know what is really going on but he said, 'I want to stay clean and get on with my own life.' I was glad for him. Honestly, I wish I was in his shoes."

Michael gave a long, low whistle, "get ready for a visit from the raging bull. Young John is gone too. He never had been involved with anything and he had no need for personal revenge. I had to get him out. I told him what had happened to Brendan. When he heard of Brendan's beating from Sean he was desolate and he got the picture of Sean's true nature. It didn't take more to persuade him to go. Sean doesn't know this yet. I'm telling him tonight."

Pearse walked about the room, "My God, Michael, This is a good one. I'm glad I didn't see him this afternoon. Seeing Sean get a double dose of 'betrayal' will be something. You hit it with 'raging bull.' If I wasn't in bondage to that damned arse, the whole thing would be funny."

Michael seriously said, "There are only three of us to carry out the plan. It can be done but it might be harder on us. I'm damn sure Sean will never give up on it. Pearse, I'm sure that if the others hadn't backed out before knowing of the plan; once they found out they would have taken off. They never would have helped with it anyway. I'm glad for John and Denis. Poor Brendan, I try not to think of his horrible end. In the country like that, it could be months before the remains would be found. If he isn't dead, or if he would have been found, we would have heard of something by now; the Gardai would have had something in the news. I feel sick over it. It was I who helped Sean get him out to the cottage. I should have known what Sean was capable of."

"Well, you didn't know, Michael—you really can't blame yourself. Sean is due here soon and I need something to eat before he comes. I haven't eaten since morning."

"You're right, Pearse, We both need something to eat and a good stiff drink. We need to be fortified."

Sean parked his car a few blocks from Michael's building. The night was cold and it had stared to rain. He carried his umbrella down low over his face. When he reached the hallway to Michael's flat, he made sure no one was around before going to the door. He was still, as Michael had said, "paranoid" about them being seen together. He had agreed to meeting here tonight because there was no other place. Michael opened the door for him and was surprised to see a "smiling" Sean. Sean took off his dripping jacket and said, "Well, Michael my lad, this is the night—the night we finally set the plan on course. We'll be working out each flawless move. It's coming close." His eyes shown and his words were spoken with eager anticipation. He turned toward the living room and saw Pearse and his glance surveyed as much of the flat as was visible. "Where are the others?" His voice sounded, now, just loud and flat.

Pearse feeling a wave of hatred and a desire to burst Sean's bubble as soon as possible, said, "There are no others, Sean. There are only you and Michael and myself."

"What the hell do you mean? Where are Denis and John? Tonight the meeting is more important than any other damned thing they're doin. Are they coming late?" His voice was starting to bellow.

Michael said calmly, "John and Denis won't be here tonight or ever. They are no longer a part of it. John left over a week ago. I think he might have gone home. His grandma took bad; he left a note." Michael couldn't let Sean know that John knew about Brendan.

Pearse looked at Sean with unmasked hatred, "Denis got smart. He couldn't stomach being part of this any longer; even though he didn't know what was being planned. He moved out of Belfast. He's free—you haven't anything on him."

Sean was seething, instead of bellowing his rage, as Michael and Pearse had expected, he spoke low with a chilling intensity. "I'll take care of the shriveling bastards after what we have to do is finished. They haven't seen the last of Sean Devlin." He fastened his cold, icy look of hatred on Pearse. *You,* Pearse, remember—I know enough on you that someone else would take care of you fast, if I'd choose to talk." Sean was breathing hard and clinched his huge fists, "But I'd want the pleasure of that myself. You took my money. There'll be no backing out by you. You damn well better not try to scuttle the plan in any way or you'll never live to tell it."

Pearse shrugged his shoulders. "Don't worry, Sean, I know it's too goddamned late for me. Just so you remember when it's finished, I'm collecting."

Sean replied, with a sneer, "I remember our agreement—you get it through your thick skull— you see it to the finish or you'll be finished." Sean turned to Michael: "Are you wanting to back out too, my friend?" he said sarcastically.

"You know I have my own reasons for doing this, Sean. Don't be an arse."

"Did John know anything of the plan? While he lived here, did you run off at the mouth?"

"John knew nothing. He thought what was being planned were protest marches. He's very young, Sean. He probably wouldn't have gone along with things had he known."

"When I was the same age I wasn't such a gutless coward. I'm probably better off without him around. Still, when he turned his back on Sean Devlin, he was asking for a lesson in growing up." Sean hit one pudgy fist into his other palm, "Someday, and someday soon, that silly clown Denis, will be getting his. He won't be findin it something to joke about."

Michael opened three beers, and then said, "We had better get down to business. There are only three of us now. We've got to make some decisions, if we're doing it. My vacation time doesn't last forever."

They drank in silence. Sean asked for another beer. He calmed some but the feeling of elation he had exhibited when he first arrived did not return. Finally, he said, "Michael, yer right, we'd better start to chart the course. Get a pad and pen; each step has to be carefully thought out."

Michael stood with his hands in his pockets and laughed at this. "After I have this note written, do I have to chew it up and swallow it so no one will find it?"

Sean glared at him. "Get it, and the first thing on the list is for you to buy brown hair dye. With that bright red hair of yours, you look as Irish as Patty's pig. You'd stand out like a stoplight. Get a pair of dark rimmed glasses; not sunglasses, they make you look like you're trying to hide. Plain ones with dark rims—that should make you look different. Wear a dark business suit with a white shirt and tie; no sweaters, that you're so fond of wearin. You'll be thought to be a businessman or a teacher. I've been thinkin these little things out."

Michael snorted, "Aye, ye been doin a helluva lot a thinkin about me."

"That's another thing, Michael, try to watch the brogue a little. You'll be the one dealin with the English people. I know you can't change the sound of your speech, but try payin attention to the 'ings' and don't slur words together. I hate askin you to do it, but aim for the British English—damn them—and think before you speak."

"I do know how to speak correctly, Sean. I use proper pronunciation, daily, at work. My way of speaking is the least of your worries, or should be. Let us get this over with."

By late that night the plans were ready to set in motion. There would be more for Michael to see to, since Brendan, who was to have been the English connection, was no longer in the picture.

Chapter 27

Tom and Fran were on the drive back to Ely from Stansted Airport. "Tom, I wish I could have talked Susanna into coming over and staying with me for a while. I know she had a good time yesterday; I think she feels better with people around. I could tell this morning that the worry was front and center again, even though she tried hard to hide it. You know, Tom, I really care and I just love her already. Father Matt will be leaving in a few days. I hate to think of her being alone."

Tom smiled, "I'm happy you feel that way, Fran. I know Mom took you right to her heart. I'm also worried about her, very much. Maybe she feels that Brendan might return home even if he is in London now. She'd want to be there if he needed her. I'll call Cliff soon and see if I can find out more. Hon, I'll be busy at the shop all day, until late. I'll pick you up and we'll have dinner together when I'm through. If I find out anything in the meantime, I'll call you."

"I might be out for a little. I'm going to shop for a sofa bed. I was going to shop with you, but I know you're so busy and I want to have it if your Mom will change her mind and come over."

They had reached the house and Tom said, "Whatever you choose would be perfect. You have great taste."

"Well, of course, I do." She gave Tom a tender kiss. "I've chosen you." Caught up in the glow they felt for each other, their mood was lighter as they said goodbye.

Mrs. Pickens was not at home. Fran went directly to her flat and unpacked her things. She went into the kitchen and made coffee and sat at her darling table and looked around, delighted in her own little place. If it just wasn't for this thing with Brendan, absolutely everything in her life would be perfect.

She determinedly put the worry from her mind and savored the well being of the moment.

She was starting down the stairs to go shopping when the front door opened. Mrs. Pickens was saying goodbye to the neighbor who had taken her grocery shopping. When she turned and saw Fran, her face lit like a Christmas tree. "Oh, my dear girl, I've missed you." There were warm hugs and Fran helped carry the bags to the kitchen. Fran stayed and visited a while before going out. She knew Emma's "missing her" were not empty words.

When Emma was alone she said to herself, "Emma, you must not get so attached. Fran won't be here forever. Oh well, it's too late for that. I'll just have to deal when that time comes and enjoy not being alone for now."

Fran was thinking as she walked to the furniture store, of the many people she had in her life and how each encompassed her with their love and how the feelings were returned from her heart. Poor Jeff, she thought of him now as she had in Ireland. Her mind was filled with sorrow for him. He had never been open to receiving love from others and had none to give. How sad! She hoped that he had now found, in the mercy and love of God, the joy that was denied him in life.

Sean went early to the ship building yard. He had promised to work and then he wanted, once again, to go over everything on his own cruiser. Sean had her brought in from the dock for painting and an overhaul. Actually, she hadn't needed a thing. It was a standing joke among the others who worked there, the time he spent fussing with his boat. "She's his only love," one said. "He's too mean to have another." Sean paid little attention to the others but his eccentricities and temper were well known. "Too bad," it was said, "that he hadn't taken to the seafarin life; the poor chap might have been happier. We'll have to give him this—he knows all there is to know about boats."

Sean was aboard *The Paradise* late that afternoon. He was cleaning the cream colored, leather seats on either side of the red and chrome table. He heard someone calling his name. Looking down over the side, he saw it was Old Jack. What the hell's he doin here, Sean thought. Later he was very glad he hadn't asked in that way.

Old had become a part of the name everyone called Jack. He was skinny and wizened with skin the color of leather. Faded blue eyes squinted from his, never bearded, but always needing a shave, face. Countless years ago, as a young man, he had been a sailor on a cargo ship. He now spent part of each day wandering around the docks. Not getting in anyone's way, his presence was taken for granted at the dock where Sean moored his *Paradise*. Old Jack was happy to help anyone if given the chance. If there was anyone in the world that Sean always seemed kind toward, it was Old Jack—probably because of their mutual love of boats. Sean had even given Old Jack a few hours out on *The Paradise*.

Sean got off the boat and went over to Old Jack, "What can I do for you, Old Jack?"

"Well now, me matey, maybe 'tis me that's doin somethin fer ye. Been a long walk, could we find a bench?" Old Jack looked around. "Best no one to hear."

Sean and Old Jack left the huge building and sat on a bench in the front. Old Jack glanced about, seeing no one, asked, "Sean, might ye be in any trouble?"

Sean knitted his brows together. "No, what are you getting at?"

"I be down at the dock today—as is usual. Chris Plunkett were in charge. He said he had a quick errand and asked me ta stay and watch that no one would come messin around while he were gone. Soon this man showed up—wearin a suit he were an lookin important. He said he understood a Sean Devlin had the cruiser *Paradise* registered at that dock but he didn't see it. No, she ain't here, I said. He asked if ye had taken her out in the water. I don't know about her I said. When'd Devlin took *The Paradise* away? He said. She's not been here fer a long time, I said. I know, Sean, it were just last week—but I weren't fer tellin him nothin. Then he wanted ta know if I knew where he could find ye. I said, Man, I'm not be knowin a Sean Devlin. I seen the boat *The Paradise* here a couple a times—be a while ago. I wouldn't be knowin where she is now. He asked if there be someone else in charge. I said, he won't be comin back taday—I'm ta stay around and keep the boats safe. The chap put his papers back in his pocket and said he'd be comin back. When Chris comes back, I come straight here. Figured I'd tell ye this before the man comes back and talks ta Chris. When he was leavin he said he was from some kind of—some kind of a *pole*. Might just be one of them survey takers, anyways—I didn't tell him nothin and thought ye might want ta know."

Sean frowned, and then a look of alarmed comprehension crossed his face. "He said something about a pole? Think, Old Jack, did you hear anything else but the word *pole*?"

"Aye, ther be another part of a word—but I don't remember."

"Old Jack, try hard to remember. Did the word sound like *Interpol*?"

"That be it, Sean. Aye, that be it. Do ye know what he be talkin about?"

"Damn!" Sean's face was filled with fury.

"Did I do wrong, Sean? Are ye mad at Old Jack?"

Sean pulled himself together. "No, no, I'm far from mad at you, Old Jack. I'm beholden to you. You did the right thing coming to me about this. You've been a fine friend. You'll continue to be my good friend, if you don't tell of this to Chris or to anyone else. You keep it our secret. I think Chris knows where I've brought *The Paradise*; that can't be helped." Sean put his hand on the old man's arm. "Please, not a word about anything. If you hear anything else leave a message for me to get in touch with you at Barry's pub. I know Barry well and he has a tight mouth. Be sure to see Barry—no one else." At that, Sean took a sizeable bill from his pocket and put it in Old Jack's hand.

"Sean, ye needen't be buyin me friendship. I'll do just as ye ask. Ye've been a good friend to me all along."

"Old Jack, buy some Guinness. It's just to cover any inconvenience you might have. I know I don't have to buy your word. I simply want you to have a little gift. Now, best be going along. I've things to do."

Sean hurried back inside. Tim Higgins was there, having just disconnected a small sailing vessel from his tow. Sean had hired Tim to tow *The Paradise* here from the dock. "Are you signed up for anything, Tim?"

"No, Sean, but I'm through for the day. If you want *The Paradise* taken back to the dock, you'll have to wait till tomorrow."

"I'm needing a longer tow than that, Tim. I'll want her taken down to Wexford. I've some friends down there that have a place with a small private cove. I'm goin for a little vacation and will be wanting her there."

"Why not take her down on the water? It would be a lot easier and cheaper—quicker, too. I couldn't do a tow that far for a couple of days."

"I want to drive down; I want my car with me. My friend is needing my boat sooner than that, Tim. I'd want her taken down as soon as possible—like today."

"You're crazy, man. I'll not be towing a big thing like *The Paradise* that far anymore today. I said a couple of days. I'm not sure I want to do it then."

"I'll make it worth your while. How's four times your normal night towing fee?"

Tim looked thoughtful and said, "With a new baby coming at our house, I sure could use that kind of money. You must have money to burn, Sean."

"As I said, it's important to my friends."

"They must be mighty good friends for you to spend that. I'll go home and tell the wife and grab a bite to eat. I'll be back late this afternoon to get directions and my money."

"Tim, there's no need to tell the wife whose hiring or details. Keep it our business. The directions and a map will be on the boat, on the captain's seat, along with her papers. Here's half the money now. I'll be at Wexford when you arrive, the rest will be waiting for you."

Sean got the map and papers ready as soon as Tim left. He got off *The Paradise* and stood looking at her name. Hell, he'd hate to change it. For a minute he thought of painting it out now but the papers where all in that name. If Tim was stopped that night he'd be in trouble. The name would have to be changed and the phony papers taken care of later. He'd have to return to Dublin.

Sean left the building and hunted a pay phone. He was almost holding his breath when he called Phil Bailey in Wexford. Phil was quite surprised to hear from Sean. It had been a long time since he had even thought of him. Sean was relieved, beyond words, that Phil still owned the house and the grounds by the cove. Trying to sound casual, he said, "Would it be all right if I visited a short while and dock my cruiser at the cove? I'd just like to get away from the bustle of Dublin for a bit and I haven't seen my old friend Phil for such a long time."

"Sure, now would be a grand time, Sean. My wife and young ones are visiting with her mom in Cork. I took today off, myself. When will you be docking in?"

"I'll be starting down in my car in a little while. The cruiser is being towed down and will be there tonight. I should be there before it arrives."

"Why aren't you bringing her down?"

"I haven't had her out in a while and want to check some things out before setting her to sea."

"Whatever, Sean, but I think it would be easier to check her out there and bring her down."

"Phil, Id like havin my car with me; I might want to get around a little on my own."

"Well, that makes sense. You're welcome to come. I'll see you later today."

Sean hung up and gave a deep sigh of relief, thinking he was damned lucky that Phil was there and that he could go through with this quickly concocted plan.

He went immediately to his bank. He worried about being traced there, by this time, but there was no choice. Nothing was said there—so far, so good. Next he stopped at his flat and packed a few things; in minutes he left. He drove several blocks away to use a pay phone. "Michael, is Pearse still there?"

"Yes, Sean, he's here. Do you want to talk with him?"

"No, listen carefully, and do as I say. Pack your things. You won't be goin back. Tell Pearse to get all his stuff together. Both of you come in Pearse's car—don't bring yours. Meet me here; he gave Michael a street address. We'll talk then. Move it out *now*—be quick about it." He didn't give Michael a chance for reply. He went into a nearby pub. No one knew him there; he could relax a minute and watch for Pearse's car from the window and have a pint of Guinness.

Sean saw Pearse stop the car and get out. Who, the hell, was with him, getting out of the passenger side? The person turned and looked toward the window; he had short cut, dark brown hair and wore dark rimmed glasses. Oh My God!—It's Michael. Despite his inner tension, Sean gave a little laugh as he went through the door toward them. "It's a good job. It makes you look younger. I don't think I'd have known you, just seeing you on the street."

"I have to get used to myself. I feel like a different person. Sometimes I wish I could be a different person, like now."

"Don't be goin soft, Michael."

"Don't worry, Sean, I know it's too late for me to change."

"Get in my car—we'll talk there." Take your things from Pearse's car and put them in mine, Michael."

When they were settled in the car, Sean said to Michael, "Good thing you took care of the disguise. You'll be leaving for England later today or at least by tomorrow—or as soon as you can get a flight to Manchester. Pearse, you'll drive out to the cottage. You have all the supplies for the bombs, right?"

Pearse nodded.

Sean got out some money and gave it to Pearse. "Stop and get some food and things you'll need for stayin out there until you hear from me. Don't be goin into the town of Maynooth or be making yourself known anywhere. Stay put at the cottage. Just try to stay out of sight. Get into you car and get out of Dublin, now. Get your stuff and go straight to the cottage. There's been someone nosin around. Get going.

Pearse didn't ask questions. "I'll wait till I hear from you, Sean, before starting to build." He said goodbye to Michael and slammed the car door.

"What happened, Sean? Why the hurry? What did you mean by 'someone's been nosing around'?"

Sean filled Michael in on Old Jack's story. He told him what he planned for himself and the moving of *The Paradise*. "We have to be away from Dublin quick."

"Sean, how would Interpol have gotten wind of anything with us? Denis and John didn't know a thing that The International Police Organization would be interested in."

"There's only one answer, Michael." Sean's face reddened in anger at the thought. "That damned, filthy, son-of a-bitch isn't dead. *Yet*! He'll wish he had died at our first encounter. He'll pay—I'll find him, make no doubt. I'm thinking of the ways he'll pay. Damn him to hell—he'll be glad when he is dead. I can't waste the thought on him now, Brendan can wait. I have to keep my mind clear for what's to be done; everything will be harder—but it's going to be done. That's why your careful set-up in England is more important than ever."

Michael remained silent. He knew it would be harder. A feeling of fear, that he hadn't known, settled through him. Yet, deep inside, he was glad Brendan wasn't dead.

Sean drove to a dismal, decaying part of the city. They stopped in front of a dingy tobacco shop. "Get out, Michael, this shouldn't take long."

They entered the small, one room shop. Its few shelves were filled with the usual cigarettes and lesser priced cigars. Its one glass counter contained several cheap pipes and an assortment of pipe tobaccos. A man sat behind the counter, reading the paper. He stood and walked close to the counter. "Well, if it isn't Sean Devlin. Been a long time since you've been in. Who's your friend," he said, looking at Michael.

"This is Dylan Sanders; he's the one needing your services."

"Do you have a favorite brand, Dylan?" The man motioned toward the cigarette shelves. "Could I interest you in a nice pipe? Nothing like the pleasure of a good pipe smoke."

"You know damned well what we need Doyle. Dylan needs an identification card for some traveling and a driver's license. He lost his wallet and can't get official ones in time for his flight. I told him you could help him out"

"Sure, Sean, *he lost his*. You know that takes a bit of time even here."

Sean looked around the empty shop. "I think you have the time, Doyle, and could use a customer."

"Come on back." Doyle led the way through a curtained doorway into what was a combination bedroom, living room. He opened another door that appeared to be a door of a free-standing closet. However, it was the door that led into another small room. The new and expensive computer and camera equipment was in sharp contrast with the front shop and shabby living quarters.

Doyle looked at Michael, "What's your name again?"

He nearly responded with his real name. Sean came to his rescue: "His name is Dylan Sanders."

Doyle looked at Michael with a knowing grin, "All right, Dylan Sanders, let's get your picture." That done, Doyle asked what his address was.

Sean answered and said he lived in Kildare and gave a rural address that sounded logical for the area.

Doyle then asked Dylan's age, date of birth and occupation. Again, Sean answered, "He's twenty-seven, June tenth, and he's a free-lance writer."

"Well, he looks the part anyway. You seem to be doin all the talkin, Sean. Is young Dylan tongue-tied?"

"Just put down the information. That's all you need to know. Remember, you don't know anything."

"You know damn well, Sean, I never know anything. I don't dare know anything."

"I'll be having another little job for you, Doyle. I'll be back in a few days."

"Always glad to see you, Sean," Doyle said as he pocketed the money. He turned to Michael, "Dylan, you might want to dirty those things up a bit; they have older application dates. It would be better if they didn't look so new."

When they were back in the car, Michael read over the identification. "Why did you pick Kildare—and make me younger? A free-lance writer— that's a good one."

"You've been to Kildare a few times and you know something about it if anyone comments. You seem younger—and there's no business to be known of if you're a writer. I think I got everything shipshape, *Dylan*. Remember, Interpol is likely to trace Michael Griffith so, God, Man, keep up the cover—don't slip. I'm going to drop you in a couple of blocks. It's too late to get a flight today. Check into a hotel and get them to arrange the flight to Manchester for tomorrow. If they do it, you won't be needing a credit card; you don't have one now. I'm giving you a lot of cash. I got a bundle from the bank today. Oh, and stop at a bank before you take off and get some travelers checks. Don't go where you're known."

"I'm not stupid, Sean. I won't be going where I'm known and I won't be losing the checks or cash. I'll be needing a lot to set things up your way."

"I gave you plenty and there is no other way. We've got to stay covered. Before, I thought there could be an outside chance of questions, now I know, damn it! They'll be lookin for us. When you get to Manchester, proceed with everything the way we planned last night. I'll give you Phil Bailey's number in Wexford. If I'm not there leave a message where I can get in touch with you. I'll keep a check with Phil." Sean stopped the car, "goodbye, Dylan. Remember, Dylan Sanders from now on, including any messages at Phil's— use only first names."

Dylan Sanders—Michael kept repeating mentally. He wanted to sound natural when he went to the bank. There was one close by that he never had been into. The teller watched as Dylan counted out the money he wanted for the checks.

"That's a lot of cash to be carrying."

Michael thought the look the teller gave him was one of suspicion. "That's just it; my mom withdrew it from her account this morning to give to me. I'm going abroad and she knew I'd need it. I couldn't believe she had it all in cash. I told her I'd get the travelers checks right away; I wouldn't want that much cash on my person."

The teller nodded, accepting that as logical, "It certainly isn't safe to carry that much cash. You should explain that to your mother, for her safety."

"I have indeed. She simply hadn't thought it out. She herself hasn't traveled for years. She's quite elderly."

When the transaction was completed the teller smiled and said, "Have a nice vacation, Mr. Sanders."

Dylan Sanders then took a cab to a hotel near the airport. He checked in, and then asked that a flight be arranged to Manchester, England for the next morning. He went at once to his room and ordered drinks and dinner from room service. The extra charge was worth it; he felt drained. His room was large and had a telly; stretching out on his bed felt wonderful. Keeping out of sight is fine with me, thought Dylan Sanders.

Pearse had gone to the old cottage as Sean had ordered. He had stopped for many supplies that might make the stay there somewhat bearable. Opening the door, Pearse thought, making this place bearable is next to impossible. He had bought some blocks of peat to supplement the dwindling stack of wood at the cottage. The nights were getting colder and the dampness and musty smell were horrible. He was tempted to go into Maynooth and spend the nights at a hotel; but the fear of Sean's retaliation, should anything go wrong, held him to the place. In a different way, he thought, I'm a prisoner just like Brendan had been.

Sean, having parted with Michael, left directly for Wexford. He got there, hours before Tim Higgins arrived with *The Paradise*. He wanted it that way, not wanting Tim and Phil Bailey to meet. Phil had fixed them a light supper; they had a few beers and chatted a bit about old times. Sean forced himself to be sociable and feigned interest in stories about Phil's family. It took extreme effort to keep his mind off his plans, his problems and all the arrangements he had made that day. He was relieved when Phil said, "I'm sorry to break up the fine time we're having; but I have to get some sleep. I have to work tomorrow."

Once Phil had gone into his bedroom, Sean went outside to watch for lights on the upper road. For almost an hour, he paced the gravel road that ran past Phil's house and on down to the cove. He chain-smoked cigarettes. Since the incident with Brendan, he was trying to quit the strong drugs. He still drank heavily much of the time; but knew if he wanted to see his plan through he'd have to have his mind clear enough. Grinding another butt into the gravel, he couldn't help thinking, hell—I could use something tonight. Damn good thing I can't get anything around here; I've got to think how I can keep Tim Higgins's mouth shut about this trip. By the time he saw the head lights of the truck, he had figured out what to say. He walked up to meet the truck and help with Tim's turn around, so that *The Paradise* could be pushed down the long gravel road and set into the water. It was a stressful procedure. The road was narrow, scarcely wide enough for the large boat and truck, until it opened up onto the wider beach area. They finally maneuvered *The Paradise* into the water and pushed her almost to the end of the short dock. She had to be moored where the water's depth was adequate. They anchored her with a trip line with a buoy to the far end; Sean feared a rocky bottom. When they had her secured, Tim wiped his haggard face and said, "I'll never do another job like this for any amount of money. If you don't plan to be taken her home by water, Sean, don't even think of askin me."

"I'll not be asking anyone for that, Tim. I'm thinking of selling her to my friend." Sean gave Tim the rest of his money. "I realize what a hard job this has been, Tim, I thank you." He added to the amount agreed upon, and then he said, "Here's a bit more for a hotel rest before you start back. You do look mighty tired, man."

Tim didn't display any particular gratitude for the extra money. They both thought it was damn well worth it. "I'm surprised, Sean, that you're thinkin of selling *The Paradise*; you've always loved her."

"Well, there's one I've had my eye on, Tim. I'd like you not to be talking about your bringing her down tonight or anything about where she is—or of my plans for selling. You see, I had someone else that was interested and I don't want hard feelings. When this sale is settled in a couple of weeks, and I know you've kept quiet about all this, there will be a nice bonus. Is it a deal?"

Tim shrugged his shoulders. "Sure, Sean, it's no big thing not talkin about it, as long as I don't have to tow her ever again. Keeping quiet for a bonus, you said? Sean, you certainly must care a lot about your *friend's* feelings—or about something." Tim's look told Sean he was taking what he was told with a grain of salt. "Whatever, that's your business, Sean. I'll keep that bonus in mind. Now, if I can get my rig out of the mud, I'll be sayin good night."

By this time, Sean was too tired to worry about anything, simply too tired to care. Tim would probably keep his mouth shut, at least for a while, and buy him a little more time. It was so unlike him, nothing seemed to matter— he felt sick. He had this feeling now and then lately but had always dismissed it as just feeling damned tired. He went into the house, too exhausted to even get the beer he wanted. He went to the room he was given and fell across the bed sideways. His muddy boots and pant legs dangling on the floor. He meant to take them off but sleep came first. Waking in a few hours, he felt befuddled and his body was stiff and sore. He got up and changed and got into the comfortable bed. Now, though, his mind was awake. It was filled with his plan, his fears, his frustrations—and mostly his vengeful feelings toward Brendan. No sleep would come.

In Ely, in a small room over the Hart Chemist Shop, Tom Hart was also having a sleepless night. He had talked with his Uncle Cliff; his worry had increased since that call. Cliff hadn't admitted that Brendan and John were there. He had talked in a round about way; that confirmed Tom's belief that Cliff and Berniece were held to a promise. Cliff sounded strained and on the verge of saying more a few times during the conversation, but he always held back. Finally, he said, "Tom, I know you're busy but if you could drop in to visit us *soon*, we'd love to see you."

"I get your message, Uncle Cliff, and I'll be there just as soon as possible. Should I call first or just come?"

"Come without calling, that would be best, Tom."

"Give my love to Aunt Berniece. I'll aim at the day after tomorrow."

"Good, Tom, I'll tell Berniece when she gets back from the grocery store. Be sure to give our love to Fran." Cliff hung up; he heard the door opening. Cliff was glad the boys had gone with Berniece; he was alone when Tom's call came.

Tom was thinking about the call. It would be a good move to take Brendan by surprise and get to the bottom of this thing. He hated leaving Fran but Uncle Cliff hadn't asked him to bring her. Whatever was going on, Tom was sure Cliff thought it best he come alone.

Chapter 28

The next morning, the newly christened Dylan Sanders picked up his boarding pass at the airport. He had presented his identification. Before leaving the hotel he had thrown it on the floor and stood on it a few times and bent it a little, until it looked like it had been issued a while back and matched the time it was dated. He had done the same with his driver's license. Everything was fine; there were no questions asked.

The plane was airborne at the same time the man from Interpol was ringing the bell to Michael's flat in Dublin. Receiving no answer, the man went out of the building. Two children were playing while their mother watched. "Pardon me, Madam, does a Michael Griffith live here? Do you know him?"

"Only to say hello. He's lived here for a while. Mr. Griffith was here when we came; that was about a year ago. He is a nice man when you see him but as I said, it's only a slight acquaintance."

The little boy spoke up. "Mr. Griffith was off work yesterday. He said he was on his vacation and was goin away soon. I asked him where he was goin. He said to Australia to hunt kangaroos and koala bears and he was laughing. I guess he was happy about goin to Australia. I saw him leave with his suitcase and he was wearin a cap."

"Was it yesterday that Mr. Griffith left?"

"Yes, in the afternoon. He didn't take his car; some other man was with him and he was driving. Maybe he and the other man were going on a train or bus or maybe an airplane. Is Australia far?"

"Rather far, son, rather far," the man said, smiling. Odgan thought it best to keep things unofficial. He wrote on a plain card and gave it to the woman. It had a name and the personal number at a hotel on it. "Would you please call me if Michael does return?" He smiled broadly and in a warm voice said,

"Please don't mention I was here. I'm a cousin; my mother is his aunt and we would like to surprise him. We're visiting Dublin for just a few days. My mother hasn't been too well and it means a lot to her. Also, we wouldn't want him disappointed if he thought he missed us. So please call me first."

The woman looked at the card and returned his warm smile. "I'll call you first if I see him, Mr. Griffith; I see you name's Griffith, too."

"Yes, I'm on his father's side. It's been nice talking with you." He rubbed the curly head of the little boy and said, "Maybe someday you'll go to Australia." Clarke Ogdan got into his car, thinking, all in a day's work. On this job you have to have the gift of blarney. Griffith won't be back, if I guess right. He went with another man—interesting. Now, on to my second visit to the dock.

When Ogdan arrived at the dock, *The Paradise* was still not there. He looked around and saw nothing of the old man he had talked with yesterday. Going into the small office, he introduced himself to Chris Plunkett, not mentioning Interpol.

Chris answered questions in a friendly, direct way. "Yes, Sean Devlin has had *The Paradise* moored at this dock for a long time. Before her, he had a smaller cruiser here but I can't remember her name. No, Sean never caused any trouble around the dock. He is not too friendly but minds his own business. He really loves his boat. Yes, *The Paradise* was towed to the ship building yard about a week ago; Sean works there some. I guess he'll be bringing her back here; he's paid well in advance."

Finally, Chris asked, "Why do you want to know all this? What is your interest in Devlin and *The Paradise*?"

Ogdan had told the old man he was from Interpol yesterday. "Did the old man, who was here yesterday, tell you I talked with him and told him I was from Interpol? I don't remember telling him my name."

"Old Jack? No, he never said anything. He was alone for a short while. When I came back, he said nothing and took off right away. That was strange, too; he usually hangs around till late. He comes about noon everyday. Do you want to wait and talk with him again?"

"No, I won't wait. I see no need. If you do hear anything of Sean Devlin or *The Paradise*, anything at all, no matter how trivial it seems, please be in touch." He gave Chris Plunkett an Interpol card.

"I guess you don't want to tell me what this is all about, Mr. Ogdan."

"No, I'm afraid I can't do that. We might have gotten some wrong information but we have to check out a few things. Thank you for your time, Mr. Plunkett. Please, remember to call if anything comes up and please, keep this to yourself."

Chris looked at the card he was holding. "All right, Mr. Ogdan, I'll be in touch if there is anything at all. As I said, I really wasn't a friend of Devlin's—but I hope he's not in any trouble."

"I hope he's not, too, Mr. Plunkett." Clarke Ogdan left the office.

He was headed to the ship building yard and thinking, damn, why did I tell the old man I was from Interpol? He had though it might intimidate him and get more information from him. The old man had seemed unimpressed; actually he didn't seem to comprehend. Yet he had taken off somewhere in a hurry. Well, it was done—he couldn't change it. The old man had told him that he didn't know Sean Devlin. Ogdan was sure now that he did.

Clarke drove on to the shipyard and parked by the large old building. He entered and walked around looking at all the boats. *The Paradise* wasn't there. He went to an office at the far end of the building; he knocked on the closed door. The man at the desk looked up and saw him through the door's glass. "Come in—come in."

Clarke opened the door and asked, "Are you in charge here?"

"Aye, I'm Superintendent Bart Rooney. What can I do for you?" Rooney was a slender but muscular man. Clarke judged him to be close to fifty years. His short hair was bristly and gray as were his full mustache and short beard. He had an open, no nonsense look about him.

Clarke Ogdan decided to come straight to the point. "The name's Clarke Ogdan, Inspector from Interpol." He showed his I.D.

"As I asked, Mr. Ogdan, what can I do for you?"

"I'd like you to answer a few questions about a Sean Devlin. Do you know him?"

"Well, that's an interesting question. I've known him for several years. My partners and I bought this business from him when he sold it after his father died. He is an expert on boats and I'm glad he'll work here part time. Because of his liking for boats and enjoying using his skills, he agreed to that. He didn't want to be bothered with running the business; that is why he sold it. He certainly doesn't need the money, as far as for working; he just likes doing with the boats. Other than that, as far as 'knowing' Sean, as to what makes a man tick, I couldn't honestly say that I know him. Around here he keeps to himself and minds his own business. He isn't very friendly with anyone. Sometimes, his attitude doesn't sit well with the other workers. I've been told he has a wicked temper; but it's never been overt enough to be disruptive. On the whole, there has been a mutual understanding with Sean and the others to stay out of each other's way. You probably didn't want to know all that. What's really on your mind, Mr. Ogdan?"

"On the contrary, I appreciate having a little background on this man. Do you know where I can find him now? I understood *The Paradise* had been here, but I don't see her now."

"Sean is not here today. He was scheduled to work but I have had no excuse from him. He simply hasn't come. *The Paradise* had been here for about a week. She was here yesterday when I left, but she's gone now. I thought he might have had her towed back to the dock. You could try there; maybe that's where Sean is."

"No, I just tried there."

"I could see if Tim Higgins is around. He's in and out, land-towing boats. Sean had Tim bring *The Paradise* from the dock."

They went out to the work floor. Rooney stopped one of the men, "Gillen, did you see Tim Higgins today?"

"Aye, he's about to leave. He just finished undoin that sailer over there." He pointed to a small sailing boat with its masts tied.

They went over; Tim was already in his truck. "Hello, Tim, I'm glad we caught you. Get out and give us a minute, please."

Tim stepped down from the big rig, "Hello, Mr. Rooney, I'm mighty tired today. I won't be doin anymore towin till tomorrow." Tim saw the man with Rooney and thought I bet he owns a big one.

"It's not about towing for Mr. Ogdan, Tim; he wants to ask you some questions."

"Mr. Higgins, did you do any towing for Sean Devlin yesterday?"

Tim knew the night watchman had seen him take *The Paradise*; he couldn't deny it altogether. He thought quickly; he couldn't say he had docked her as usual, Plunkett would know he hadn't. There was someone on duty around the clock to track the boats. "I took her up to the north, by Meath. Devlin said he was meeting some friends there. He wanted to ship out from there with them. It was a small cove, not a public dock."

"Do you know the friends he was with?" Ogdan asked.

"No, they weren't with him when I met Devlin. We got her in the water, and then I left. That's all I know. Devlin doesn't say much. He's not real friendly."

Ogdan thanked Mr. Rooney and Tim. He gave them each a card, saying, "If you hear anything more from Devlin or have any information about *The Paradise*, I want to be told." He left feeling an extreme frustration. It had been a long morning with nothing helpful coming his way. Looking at his watch, he thought some lunch might revive his spirits.

When Ogdan left, Tim looked at the card and felt a knot tighten in his stomach. Casually he shrugged and said, "Interpol?—I wonder what that's about, Mr. Rooney, maybe drugs?"

Rooney said, "I don't know, Tim, Mr. Ogdan didn't say, but it must be serious. Interpol wouldn't be taking time with it if it wasn't." He turned and walked to his office.

Tim got into his truck, feeling miserable. He wasn't given to lying. Then too, if this were a serious matter, might the lie be found out—and could he be implicated in whatever illicit thing was going on? God, he wished he hadn't kept that stupid bonus uppermost in his mind. If he brought shame to his wife and young-ones, he'd not want to live. Then again, maybe he wouldn't live if Sean found out he told what he knew. He breathed deeply and decided, if he did hear anything else or found out what this was really about, he would contact Interpol and make a clean breast of it.

After his lunch, Clarke returned to his office. There was a fax waiting, informing him, that the inspector in Belfast had located the house of Pearse O'Neill. The neighbors said they thought he had been gone for a few days; his car hadn't been seen since then. For a short time, until further notice, there would be a watch on O'Neill's house. There had been a check on Denis Flemming. He had moved out before O'Neill had left Belfast. Flemming's Company had moved him to Derry. After talking with him, it was believed that his association with the group had been strictly social with no knowledge of the plan in question. He could be easily found should the need arise. Clarke laid the paper on his desk. He knew O'Neill had been the only one with a police record; that was from his youth. There was nothing else on file. The record wasn't enough to have his vehicle registered at the border for checking; there would be no help there. For what it was worth, he contacted the Dublin police and gave them O'Neill's and Devlin's and Griffith's car license numbers for a general watch. He really didn't expect return on that. Things were too indefinite to ask for roadblocks.

Clarke sat at his desk, drumming his fingers together. The only place he hadn't tried was Devlin's place of residence. He had been unable to find a listing for him and his mailing address just showed a G.P.O. box. Interpol didn't have a concrete reason to warrant a check on that. He called Bart Rooney. "When I was there I forgot to ask you for Devlin's home address or phone number. I need to have them."

"I'd like to be able to give them to you, Mr. Ogdan, but we have never had them here. Devlin calls us about his work schedule. That's the only contact with him. I know absolutely nothing of his living arrangements."

"Would any of the workers know?"

"I'm very sure they wouldn't, but I'll ask around. I'd let you know right away, but as I said, Sean was friendly with no one here."

Clarke hung up, thinking, it really didn't matter much. At this point, he felt sure that Devlin was not at his own place. He was convinced that Devlin was no longer in Dublin. Clarke hated having to send such a negative report to Scotland Yard. All that could be done at this time was to keep a watch on the water ways for *The Paradise* and have the airports checked for men fitting the descriptions the Yard had been given.

Phil Bailey returned home from work. Sean was nowhere around the house. He walked down to the cove. As he'd figured, Sean was there on the boat. Sean was on deck and called for Phil to come aboard and have a beer. Before boarding, Phil walked around looking at the cruiser. "She sure is beautiful, Sean," he called. "She really is a paradise." Then he noticed her name was painted out. "Why is she missing her name?"

Phil got aboard and Sean said, "It needed repainted. Then too, I'm thinking I might want to call her something else."

"Why, Sean? *The Paradise* was perfect for her."

"Well, I met a little lass, a while back, her name's Margo. I thought *The Margo* might be a nice name for the cruiser." Sean was thinking that's the kind of story Phil would buy.

Phil grinned, "You must be serious, man, to be taking the name for your beloved *Paradise*. Sounds like there might be a wedding I'll be going to."

"I'll let you know for sure, Phil, I haven't asked her yet."

"She might be impressed with her name on your boat—and say yes. It's about time you're settling down. Where's Margo from, Sean?"

"She's from Maynooth. But as for settling down, that's a long way off."

"Don't wait too long, Sean, a family is a wonderful blessing to have."

Damn, Sean was thinking, how long will this go on? He had picked the name out of the blue because a lot of boats had girl's names and it wouldn't be too distinctive. He had just been careful that it didn't seem particularly Irish like Bridget or Colleen. Now, in Phil's mind there's this girl and I'm stuck with this imaginary Margo. A long time ago, when he and Phil were drinking buddies, Phil hadn't been such a damned goody-goody. Sean was grateful to Phil for having him here, but he could hardly stand him.

They had their supper and passed another long evening that Sean forced himself to endure. Each time Phil would remark on something of his own marital bliss or family stories, Sean's future with Margo would be mentioned. Sean pleaded being tired as soon as was believable. "I'd like to go into town with you tomorrow, Phil. I'd like to look around Wexford a bit and be free as a bird for a while. I worked all day long on the boat."

"Did you get her all shipshape, Sean?"

"Yeah, she's all finished except for the painting of the new name. I have to get stencils. That can wait for a few days. I need a break. I'd like to go with you in the morning. I might decide to go somewhere by bus or train. Maybe

I can latch onto a tour group somewhere and see something different for a couple of days. That's why I'm not taking my car. I'll take a backpack with a couple of changes. If I have no luck, I'll call your office and come back with you. Will that be all right?"

"Sure, Sean, no problem, we'll leave about seven."

Sean felt relieved that Phil had accepted this story without question. He had to get back to Dublin and couldn't risk taking his car.

Tom was at the shop all that day. The other chemist was off and he had prescriptions to fill as well as dealing with the shop's business. He enjoyed seeing his customers; he had gotten to know them well and was truly interested in their needs. The day passed quickly; not allowing the time for Tom to dwell on the upcoming London trip.

When he arrived to pick up Fran, Emma opened the door. She greeted Tom with a hug and told him to go straight up; Fran was expecting him. The house was filled with wonderful smells, like an Italian restaurant. A smiling, flustered Fran threw her arms about him. "Avanti, Segnore. Welcome to Fran's Ristorante." A tape player was on the bare living room floor, loudly emitting "The Pines of Rome."

"Buona sara, Signorina, not only are you beautiful but you know the way to a man's heart is delicious Italian food."

"E'un piacera." Fran saw the questioning look on Tom's face. "It's a pleasure," she added.

"When did my girl learn to speak Italian?"

"Oh, I know only a little—molto poco—very little. I did a lot of singing in it, though. The most important word is *amore*."

"That, my darling, is the most important word in any language. Fran, I love you so very much." Tom held her close and kissed her.

The noise of a lid rattling in the kitchen broke the sweet moment. "Now, darling, go over and sit down. The water is boiling for the pasta. It will be ready in a few minutes." Fran motioned toward the front of the bare room. She had the little table and chairs from the kitchen placed by the window. The table was draped with a red and white checkered cloth; a lit candle rested in a bottle in the middle of the table. The salads and wineglasses were placed and a tray table held the red wine in a beautiful Italian pitcher.

When Fran came back from the kitchen, Tom was admiring the pitcher. "Tom, it's from Italy and I think it's rather old. I found it at the antique shop down by the river. I can't wait until you have time to go there with me."

"One of these days, Fran, we'll have more time for just the two of us. I hope to heaven it's soon."

The timer buzzed. Fran started back to the kitchen. Tom followed. "I'll help you."

"Tom dear, I can manage."

"No, Signorina, I will drain the heavy pot."

Fran laughed and handed him the potholders. "It's nice to be cherished."

Tom put the spaghetti on the plates. Fran ladled the thick red sauce with the green peppers and mushrooms. She handed Tom the basket of garlic bread and picked up the plates. She said, "This togetherness is a very nice thing—something I'll enjoy getting used to."

"For a lifetime, Fran?"

"Yes, precious, for a lifetime."

While they were lingering over their wine, Tom told Fran about Cliff's wanting him to go to London and that he was going tomorrow.

"Do you want me to come with you, Tom? I'd love to see Uncle Cliff and Aunt Berniece."

"Fran, I'd love you to come and I know they are anxious to see you; but I think Uncle Cliff thinks it best that I come alone. He didn't actually say, but I really believe Brendan is there. I'm just to drop in, unexpectedly. When we get all this over and done with, you and I will go down for a good visit. I hate for you to be alone so much. I'm sorry I have to go."

Fran watched the look of deep concern on Tom's face as he talked. "I understand, Tom. I think it is the best way too. I'll miss you, of course, but, Hon, I'm really not lonely. Emma is such a dear and I haven't spent much time with her lately. I've been on the go so much, shopping. By the way, I didn't tell you about the sofa. It's being delivered tomorrow. You'll love it. I want to look for a real dining table and chairs for this room. I do want to have Heidi and Don and Bryan up soon. My letters to Mom and Dad and everyone are long overdue. I did get a thank you off to your Mom and I want to call her and—"

"Hey, little girl," Tom interrupted her; he got up and pulled her from her chair. "Save a little of that time for missing me."

"That, Tom, is a constant thing. No matter how busy I am, I'll be missing you." She kissed him and they held each other tenderly. Fran looked up at Tom's face. "When will you be back?"

"I hope the day after tomorrow, I'm not sure. I don't know what I'm getting into. Whatever Brendan's trouble is, it's got to be brought to an end. Believe me, I'll be missing you."

That day, Dylan Sanders had landed at Manchester Airport. He rented a van for an indefinite time. Again, there was no trouble with his identification.

He sat in the van and studied the map for the best route south to Ely; there was a long drive ahead. He figured he'd stop at Peterborough; it seemed a good place to get a hotel for the night. That would leave a short distance to Ely on the following day. He stopped for a rest and some food at Leicester. By this time, he was feeling very tired and wasn't sure if the revenge was worth all this. There were still a couple of weeks until this would be done with. When he finally was stretched out on his bed at the hotel, he repeated to himself—a couple more weeks and it would be done with. Then, Michael wondered, would this act of revenge be *done with*—or would he be *done with*? Right then, it didn't seem to matter.

Chapter 29

Early in the morning, Phil Bailey and Sean were in the car headed to Wexford; Phil glanced at Sean and noticed the stubble of a four-day growth of dark beard. "Sean, are you aimin to grow a beard, or didn't you have time for shavin this morning?"

"I thought I'd give my face a vacation, too. I get tired of the daily shaving. Might just let it alone and grow a beard."

"Do you think Margo will approve? Some women don't like them."

Hell, Sean was thinking, the first thing in the morning—can't the man talk of anything else? "It's my face; she can take it or leave it. I've never catered to a woman before and I'm not about to start."

Phil heard the shade of anger in Sean's voice. It seemed to him that Sean was sounding a bit different from the man who talked of putting Margo's name on his boat. Phil didn't pursue the subject. "If you don't call and come back tonight, I'll look for you in a few days. Right?"

"Yeah, that's right, Phil. If you don't hear, I'll be back in three or four days."

"By that time Tess and the young-ones will be home. I can't wait to have them back. Joseph, being seven and Catherine, five, would love going out on your cruiser. Tess could come to and bring the baby. Danny is only a bit over two—he might like it, too. At least, he wouldn't be any trouble. We could have a picnic on board and make a day of it. Sound like fun to you?"

Sean could hardly get out a polite response to that. *Fun!*—It was the most miserable thing he could imagine. He tried to sound enthusiastic, "Yeah, the young-ones would love it. We'll make sailors out of them." Sean was thinking, I guess I'm damned lucky I got the boat down before the family was around to watch.

Phil pulled the car into one of the narrow lanes that lead into the little town of Wexford, just off Main Street. "Wexford is an interesting little place, Sean, you'll enjoy looking around. This is as far as I can take the car. There is no traffic or public transportation here, because of the narrow streets. Mostly there are walking tours. You will have to go north to O'Hanrahan's Bus Depot for a public bus. You could get a cab to there. As for connecting with a tour group, there are tours come for sights outside of the town proper, then do a walking through the town. If you see any, you could inquire. I think it would have been easier to have had you car."

"Phil, I just wanted to be free from studying road maps and doing a lot of planning for myself. Besides, the engine was missing occasionally on the way down. I want to check things out before taking the car into strange areas and have it let me down far from a garage." This was another story he hoped Phil would buy. Sean got out of the car and put on his backpack. "Thanks, Phil, for everything. I hate to be causin you all the trouble. I'll make it up to you."

"It's not that much trouble, Sean. Just remember, the family will enjoy a ride on *The Margo*."

Sean was hoping Phil would refuse, but asked, "Do you have time for coffee, Phil? There should be some places open."

"No, Sean, I still have a way to go and I've got to open my business. By the way," Phil grinned, "could I sell you some insurance?"

"I'll think that one over and let you know when I get back. Hey, old chum, thanks, again. 'See you later or in a few days."

Phil drove away. Sean gave a loud sigh and relaxed his face from the forced pleasant look it had during this morning with Phil. He went to a tavern and ordered a large breakfast. There was plenty of time to kill until the other shops were opened. He walked about the historic town, trying to assume the interested look of a tourist. Finally a small general store opened. Sean went in and was the first and only customer. The clerk asked if she could be of help. Sean put on his pleasant expression, once again. "Yes, my young sister is to have a part in a play and needs some gray hair color. She thinks there is a spray kind that washes out easily."

He was led to the hair care display. The clerk helped him find what he wanted. "We do sell this, mostly for costume type things. A little goes a long way. Of course, if she will be using it often, you might want more than one."

There were five cans on the shelf. Sean said, "I think my sister might need it several times; I'd better take them all."

"Where's the play to be, sir?"

"Oh, it's just a school play at New Ross." Sean figured that was close enough to be believable, but not right around Wexford. "I'll be seeing her today and promised to bring it." He saw a large soft carrying bag, "I'll take this, too." He gave the clerk a smile and paid for the things and got out as quickly as possible. A few doors down, there was a clothing store. Sean bought a collared shirt, a long gray sweater and black wool pants; clothes such as he had never worn, an old man's style of dress. He changed in the fitting room. His jeans and cream sweatshirt and all his things, including the spray cans fit well in the new bag; witch would go better with his new image than the backpack.

The clerk asked if there was a problem with the fit when he saw Sean come from the fitting room wearing the new clothes.

"No, I'm traveling and had a spill on mine. I'll be wearing these." Sean saw the man looking at his different bag and was thinking, I might as well make a reason for it. God! Everyone notices everything. "I bought a bigger bag up the street—so I could fit all my things together."

The man gave Sean his change and smiled, "Yer right, sir; too many things to carry can be a nuisance." Sean left before more friendly comments could be made.

Sean went into a different tavern and ordered a pint and drank it quickly, paid for it and went into the restroom. He was glad the room was for one at a time. After locking the door, he quickly combed the messy stuff through his hair and worked some into the stubble on his face. He put on sunglasses and looked into the mirror to check his disguise. The barman was busy with other customers; no one paid attention to him when he left.

He walked on until he saw the Talbot Hotel; going in, he arranged for a cab from there to the bus depot.

There had been no trouble at O'Hanrahan's Bus Depot. He hadn't thought there would be. The bus wasn't crowded; he was glad to have a seat alone. If there was a watch waiting at Dublin, no one would be looking for a gray-haired, older man. The Dublin terminal was a busy place; Sean was lost in the crowd. So far so good, but he'd have to risk a cab—he had to get the papers.

All went well. The cab dropped him several blocks from the tobacco shop and he walked the rest of the way. When he entered the shop, Doyle was busy with a man buying cigarettes. The man left and Doyle looked up from the cash register. "May I help?" He stopped in mid-sentence as Sean took off the dark glasses. "My God, Devlin, well, I've heard of people turning gray over night from shock; you must have had a big one," Doyle laughed. "What the hell are you up to, Devlin?"

"Mind your own business, Doyle. I need some of your special services."

Doyle walked to the door and locked it and turned the sign to closed. He led Sean to the back room. Sean asked for a pair of scissors. Doyle handed them to him, not asking why. Sean proceeded to clip at his short, thick, curly hair; till there was very little left. Doyle watched, making no comment. "Doyle, do you have any plain glasses?" Doyle opened a drawer and handed glasses to Sean. "Can I keep these, Doyle?"

"Yeah, you can keep them. I always keep a few extra on hand."

They went through the same routine as with Michael for Sean's identification. Sean Devlin became 45-year-old Ronan Farrell. He looked every bit of that. Actually, he looked like a much older man who hadn't aged well. Next, there were new registration papers for the cruiser with the name of *The Margo*.

When all was finished, Doyle looked hard at Sean. "Ronan Farrell, I know nothing of this." Doyle's usually humorous side was absent. "I can't imagine what the devil you're up to. By God, I wouldn't want to know."

Ronan Farrell worked the cards and papers as Michael had until they appeared used for a longer time. He walked several blocks to a car rental. There was no problem there. He was just a tourist getting a van for an indefinite time, for sightseeing. He drove away for the city and found a pub. God—how he needed a few shots of whiskey and something to eat before going on out to the cottage. He read a newspaper while he ate so no one would bother him. Before leaving he bought some beer and sandwiches to take with him.

He drove past the cottage, a good distance, and parked the van beside Pearse's. It was well hidden by a clump of trees and bush. Sean was sure no one ever came up the rutted, overgrown dirt road. The cottage was completely isolated and could not be seen until one would come up the road, miles from the highway. Still. He wasn't taking chances. He'd walk back to the cottage.

A weary, slovenly looking Pearse was at the doorway. He thought he heard a car pass; it was out of sight when he opened the door. He stood looking, ready to step back inside. To get out of this place a car would have to turn and come back. He saw a man walking down the road and he hurriedly stepped in and closed the door. He watched through the small front widow as the man came within sight. He was an older man with gray hair and glasses, carrying a bag, and he was coming toward the cottage door. Pearse decided not to answer if the man knocked; yet, any effort could turn the latch. Pearse was thinking, what the hell does he want? The man didn't knock but pushed open the door with a bang. Pearse growled, "Get the hell out of here."

A familiar and hated voice said, "That's a fine way to be talkin to a man in his own family home. Of course, I'm not a Devlin anymore. Meet Ronan Farrell, who has brought you some beer and sandwiches."

"Well, I'll be—" Pearse took in what he was seeing and burst out laughing. "Well, damn ye, Ronan Farrell, it's good to have a laugh over something." Pearse had grabbed the bag and opened a beer and tore into one of the sandwiches. "Everything I bought is gone. I was going into Maynooth tonight, despite your orders. I wasn't about to starve. This damned place is bad enough without being hungry. I want to get the bombs ready and go back to Belfast. After they are on the boat, you can take them across to Michael on your own."

"Don't even think it. You're coming with me. Dylan and I will be needing you."

"Dylan—Who, the hell, is Dylan?"

"Dylan Sanders is Michael's new name."

Pearse sneered and rolled his eyes.

"All this shit I'm going through is necessary now. As for your going back to Belfast, forget it. You can't now and probably never will. Things have changed." Sean looked very serious.

"What the devil are you saying? Are the plans changed? Why wouldn't I go back?"

"*No*, the plans haven't changed but working them has become much harder. Remember, I told you someone was nosin around. Well, that someone is Interpol. You're the only one with a police record; I'm sure your place is being watched." Sean told him everything as he had told Michael and all that he had done these last few days. "I'm going through with the plan. I've wanted it too long and too damned bad to drop it, whatever happens. If this cover works, I've got a plan to get us all away."

Pearse was silent. He was remembering the feeling he had when he locked his door in Belfast, that he'd never be returning. He looked at Sean and really felt like killing him. He was thinking, the promised future money meant nothing now. If the plan was stopped there would be nothing against them; the whole thing would blow over.

Sean turned and went out the door and into the falling down side of the cottage. He cleared away some old boards and took out a metal box he had put there a long time ago. In it was a loaded gun. He was glad he had forgotten it, when he left the place after Brendan's escape with the other gun. The gun fit well in the large pocket of the sweater. When he came out, Pearse was leaving the cottage with the hearth poker in his hand. "Where are you going, Pearse?" Sean asked in a cold, even tone.

"I'm not going to build your damn bombs, Sean. The money is no good to me now. I'll pay you back the other, if you live long enough to collect. You have no hold over me, now. Interpol knows about my record. I'll get away, if I have to use this on you." Pearse raised the poker.

"I thought you might try something stupid. You are wrong, Pearse, Interpol knows about your record, but they'd need to be informed about your uncle and all the times things weren't recorded about Pearse O'Neill." Sean lunged toward him and with his bull-like strength sent Pearse sprawling to the ground, knocking the poker from his hand. "I don't think you have thought it all through." Sean whipped out the gun. "Now, if you don't want to end up dead and put your uncle away for the rest of his life, you'll play along. This bomb called Sean has a very short fuse. I'm bigger and stronger than you and *my friend* will always be with me." He put the gun into his pocket and patted it.

A dejected Pearse went back into the cottage. He knew if he tried anything he'd be dead on the spot. Worse, life for his uncle would be all but over. He had no choice but to go along. Afraid of a search at the border, he hadn't brought his own gun.

"Now, my friend," Sean sneered, "you and this old man are going into Maynooth. I'm not too well known there and no one has ever seen Ronan Farrell. You will stay in the car while I get supplies. If I find you gone, your uncle is on a hook right away. I can't cope with anything else and won't think twice. We'll take my rented van; they might be looking for your license. Before we leave, heat some water and cut and shave that beard and cut off the damned pony tail." Sean looked worried for a minute. "One thing I hadn't thought of was someone coming around this place. Brendan would have told about it. So far they haven't. You didn't notice anyone around, did you?" Pearse shook his head, no. "Well, when you're through shaven put out that fire; then get all your belongings. We'll put everything in the van and get away from here as soon as possible. While we have to be here tomorrow, if anyone comes around," Sean touched his pocket, "I'll just have to take care of them. Nothing is going to stop me now."

Pearse left with Sean, looking younger and very different with short hair and being clean-shaven. His face was smarting; it hadn't been shaved in years.

At another time Sean would have made a smart remark about Pearse's red face but he felt too tense to bother. They drove in silence to Maynooth. Pearse was surprised when Sean told him to drive into a hotel parking lot. When the car was stopped, Pearse looked at Sean and saw his face was contorted in pain. Sean fumbled in his other sweater pocket for a roll of antacid tablets. He took some and sat still, breathing deeply. "Damned indigestion, it's been getting me of late." After a few minutes he said, "We'll get the supplies in the morning. Pearse, your name is now Richard Farrell." Ronan Farrell checked in at the hotel, getting adjoining rooms for himself and his son Richard.

On the way to the rooms, Pearse asked, "Are you still feeling sick? Is that the reason we're staying at the hotel? I thought you'd have us sleeping in the van."

"I'm not feeling good; but that's not the reason we're staying here. We have to be away from the cottage as much as possible. Besides, I wouldn't have felt safe sleeping with you in the cottage let alone in a van. I'll feel much safer sleeping in a locked room by myself. If I find you gone in the morning, your goose is cooked. The calls would be made. I'll give up the plan rather than let you off."

Pearse responded with hate showing in his voice, "I've gotten the message, father, just shut up."

Sean locked the door to the adjoining room. It had been a very long day, he was dead tired, but sleep didn't come for a long time.

Angry and frustrated as Pearse was, he felt grateful to sleep in a real bed, in a decent room; after the several days in that God-forsaken cottage. Thinking, there's not a damn thing I can do, he stretched out and was soon asleep.

Shortly after Pearse and Sean had left for Maynooth, Clarke Ogdan drove up the dirt road and stopped in front of the cottage. The cottage door opened without trouble. There was nothing about and the hearth was clean. Yet, the musty air still had a trace of a smoky odor; someone had been here not long ago. He looked in the part where the roof was half caved in. There was a mess of filthy, moldy canvas sticking out from the caved in part. It must have been old sails from a boat. Nothing looked as if it had been disturbed in a very long time. Clarke got into his car and followed tracks up to where a van was hidden. He had Pearse's license number and knew the van was his. The van was locked but nothing, apparently, was in it. There were tracks beside it that were reversed and going back down the road. He figured Devlin had picked Pearse in his car and they were long gone. Damn, he was thinking, if only the information from the Yard had originally included the story of McKenna's being held a prisoner here. Then, he would have known about this place and been here two days ago—and maybe run into them. This information hadn't been given with the sketchy request through Interpol. He had followed up on all the information he had been given; still he wasn't satisfied and couldn't get this business out of his mind. He had taken it upon himself to call Scotland Yard and talk directly to Sergeant Crosby, who had made the first report. Maybe it was just curiosity, on his part, but he wanted to know more of the reason for this inquiry.

He went back to his hotel from the cottage, feeling more frustrated than ever. There were other cases he needed to work on; yet, this one wouldn't leave his mind. No use going back to the cottage again; surely, they wouldn't be returning there. Yet, he wondered. Of course, he couldn't request a stakeout; no one in charge would go along with it. There wasn't the money or the people to spare on this type of report, which was based on hearsay.

Dylan Sanders checked out of his hotel early. He paid his bill with travelers checks and got a few cashed, wanting to have more English money with him. Before driving to Ely, he took time to study the currency, not wanting to appear fumbling when he bought something and call attention to himself. Looking over his map, he decided the most direct route would be using some of the secondary roads. The day was cool but sunny and the small villages nice to see. He had never come over to England. Always, he had nursed his hatred for this country and anything to do with it. Yet, as he drove along, seeing much of its charm and its people going about their daily lives, he felt a small degree of sadness that those early feelings had shaped his being and brought him to this point. He remembered Sean saying, "Don't be goin soft, Michael." No, damn it, he wouldn't be goin soft. So much hate was still there for the British Government and the sorrow it caused to his country and his own life. He had come too far—it was too late to change.

He reached Ely and drove around the small town. He went down by the River Ouse and around the small business district; the Cathedral was most frequently in view. After parking the car in the lot to the east of the Cathedral, he walked for an hour along a route that skirted the Cathedral, like any other tourist. A stranger would not be noticed at Ely; obvious tourists were everywhere. He didn't go into the Cathedral; that would wait for another day. The realtor's office had to be found. Hopefully, he could find the kind of place Sean needed for their stay here.

The door of the Milford Reality jingled as Dylan Sanders entered. The small front office was empty. Dylan began looking at the photographs of many houses with short descriptions attached. A slim, pretty, but very business-like young woman came from an inner room. "I'm Elizabeth Milford. Do you see anything there that is of interest to you?" she asked, looking at the wall board with the photos.

"I don't think so. I don't see anything that looks like a small country property; a rather private place, that's what I'm hoping to find, a place to rent not to buy."

"*No,* there is nothing like that shown there, Mr.—"

"Sanders—Dylan Sanders. I'm new to the area and would like a place as I described for a short while. I'm a writer and want a quiet kind of place."

"What do you mean by a short while, Mr. Sanders? Would you like it furnished or unfurnished?"

Michael knew he couldn't say that less than two weeks were needed. "That's a bit indefinite, a month or two, and I'd like it furnished, if possible.

"Mr. Sanders, we might have something listed such as you need but that would require a large deposit and at least a six months lease. The only thing I could arrange for a month or two would be a flat, one that is to be sub-let. Your best bet would be a country bed and breakfast. I know of two that would give you a great deal of privacy and would take someone on a monthly agreement."

"I'd rather have a place to myself. You said you might have a listing requiring a longer lease. If need be I'll sign a six months agreement, Miss Milford."

"It's Mrs. Milford. My husband and I own the business together." She sat down at the computer; at last, she said, "Nothing is showing, but there are a few listings yet to be entered. I'll look through this folder; George might have added something recently." She pulled a paper from the file. "Mr. Sanders, you are lucky. This sounds perfect. It's a small house—almost buried in the woods. The owner wants to rent it furnished for the next six months. He's going to a warmer climate for the winter. You would have to sign a lease for that long. However, if you keep in touch we should be allowed a sub-let, if someone else would be interested, just so we keep the place occupied while he is gone. Would you like to see it?"

"Yes, could I put a deposit on it now? I'm really interested and I wouldn't like to lose it."

"Mr. Sanders, you might not like it when you see it." Elizabeth Milford laughed a little. "I promise you, no one will get a chance to rent it before you."

"Could I see it today?"

"I'm afraid that isn't possible. My husband is away; he will have to take you. I don't think I could even find it. It's really off the beaten path. Would you like to make an appointment to meet my husband, here, tomorrow morning? Would ten o'clock be all right?"

"That will be fine. I'll see you tomorrow at ten. Thank you Mrs. Milford." Dylan Sanders left the realtor's office with high hopes that he had found the perfect place. As far as the lease, after two weeks Dylan Sanders wouldn't be around to care. A feeling of ice water coursed through his veins. Would Michael Griffith be around—anywhere, ever again? Would he ever be going back to Dublin? All this effort was just to finish their plan. But then—what? Sean had said "he had a getaway plan," but how and to where? Dylan Sanders drove south toward Cambridge until he found a hotel for the night.

Chapter 30

Tom left Ely before daybreak and drove without a stop to Uncle Cliff's in London. He tried to open the door of the flat, but it was locked. The door had never been locked during the day unless they were out. That seemed strange to Tom; Uncle Cliff knew he was coming. He knocked. Instead of Aunt Berniece opening the door at once, he heard her voice asking, "Who is it?"

"Aunt Berniece, it is Tom."

The door was thrown open by a smiling Aunt Berniece. "Oh, my Tom, I've missed you." The warmth of her hug felt wonderful.

Brendan and John had been watching the telly. Brendan jumped up, he swallowed hard. Of all the people he was embarrassed to see, Tom was at the top of the list. Tom had always been a great brother and was never critical of him. Yet, this time might be different. In Brendan's eyes Tom was perfect; every thing he did was right. Tom would never have pulled a stunt like he did. Brendan need not have worried. Tom embraced him and, with deep love showing in his face, said, "You're really here, thank God!"

"I'm so ashamed, Tom, I've been so stupid. I've worried Mom and everyone so."

"Brendan, calm down, nothing matters but that you're safe. We'll work whatever through. I still don't know much." Tom turned to John and warmly shook his hand, "It is good seeing you again, it's been a long time, John."

Uncle Cliff had stood in the background giving Tom and Brendan time to meet alone. Tom felt a firm pat on the back, "It's mighty good to see you, Tom, and we've missed you around here. I really glad these other lads came. Aunt Berniece needs someone to mother." Cliff grinned at Berniece.

"Aunt Berniece, you can mother me right now," Tom said, as he squeezed her hand. "I didn't stop to eat on the way down and I'm starved."

"Tom dear, I'll put on fresh coffee and a large portion of beef and potato pie is still warm in the oven, we just finished eating. Come out into the kitchen and visit with me—you men can talk later."

"I was surprised to find your door locked, Aunt Berniece," Tom said, as he pulled his chair close to the kitchen table. "At first, I thought you weren't here."

"Oh, the boys thought it unwise to leave it unlocked. They really are afraid for us. They think there's a chance of them being followed here. I don't know; I doubt it. Anyway, I couldn't hear of them leaving us. They are waiting for word from Scotland Yard; they've been to see them—enough of that, Cliff and the boys can tell you later. How's our darling girl? I wish she could have come with you."

"Fran sends her love to you both. She really wanted to come, but Uncle Cliff sounded like he wanted me to see Brendan alone and help if I could. Fran and I will come for a fun visit when this problem is resolved." Tom told Berniece all about Fran's flat and the great Italian dinner she fixed for him. "Aunt Berniece, everything was so beautiful and truly delicious."

"I'm sure it was, Tom, Fran would want it perfect for you. But you know when two people are so much in love, sharing a crust of bread can seem wonderful." Berniece pinched his ear and chuckled.

Tom enjoyed his lunch and talking with Aunt Berniece about the pleasanter side of life. "Aunt Berniece, you'll have to give Fran your recipe for that beef and potato pie. That's one of my favorites." Berniece beamed.

Tom returned to the living room. The telly was still on, with none paying any attention to it. Brendan was standing, looking out of the window, his body slumping. Tom took hold of Brendan's shoulders and pulled them back and gave him a few firm rubs over the tense muscles. "Try to relax a little."

"That feels good, Tom, I'll give you exactly five hours to stop that."

They both laughed a little. Tom continued the massage for a while.

"Now, Brendan and John, it's time I hear the whole story. Don't hold anything back."

Cliff, said, "I'm going to help Berniece in the kitchen." He went from the room thinking, the lads might be more comfortable talking alone.

They talked for a long time. Brendan and John told it all, once again, and answered any questions Tom raised. Tom was told in detail of their contact with Scotland Yard. "Now, we are just waiting to hear from them." Brendan shrugged his shoulders. "I honestly don't know how much they'll follow up on this. I know Sean is hell bent in doing what he wants. The weekend after next will be the harvest festival at the Cathedral. If the Yard can't stop it, nothing or no one will keep me from stopping him." Brendan's face was set with an angry, determined look.

John banged his fist on a table. "I agree with Brendan; I'm with him all the way. We'll do whatever it takes."

"Brendan, that's still a way off. Calm down, you two, and be patient until the Yard calls. They are not fools. They will try. Also, I'll be in touch personally with the Ely police. They know me and will take seriously what I tell them. I won't have you putting yourselves in danger."

"If that's what's needed, Tom, it will have to be. It's through me Sean got this damned idea."

"He would have come up with something just as horrible without your silly talk, Brendan; maybe something even worse or harder to stop. Quit blaming yourself."

"Tom, you never would have gotten your life messed up. You never would have hurt anyone. You've always been perfect."

Tom laughed. "Far from it!" Then, he looked serious. "I think it's time I told you something about myself. Something I don't like remembering. Brendan, I did hurt someone I loved very much, by remarks of the stupid hatred I was feeling, when I was just a little older than you are now." Tom looked at Brendan who was again pacing around the room. "Sit down, I'll tell you about it; even Mom never knew this. I was brought up in England until I was twelve, as you know. I'm English on my father's side and part on Mom's side. England is my country. I came back to college here and there were many visits back before that. You came along for many of the visits with Mom and Dermod. After his death those visits were less frequent for you. Every one of the Harts loved you, just like Aunt Berniece and Uncle Cliff do. They felt no difference; to them you are family. Yet, you are mostly Irish and Ireland is your country. Despite the fact that we had such intelligent parents and extended family, that held no feeling of prejudice, we were both affected by "the troubles." We had divided loyalties because of the conflict and voices of people not as wise as our parents. Sad to say, the difference in the persuasion of religion is often brought into play to serve greed and political strife. When one is very young, it's easy to feel mixed emotions when caught up with the two country's problems. Countries so close together and who share so many things the same, yet have the tragedy of the hate." Tom gave a little smile. "I didn't mean to get so long-winded, but I just wanted you to see, I do understand—and perhaps make excuses for myself and how I hurt Dermod."

"Dermod—Dad?" Brendan looked at Tom in astonishment.

"Yes, Dad!—I had come back to England and started college. At the midterm break, I came home. You were just about five; you wouldn't remember that time."

"I remember some of your visits home, Tom, and how I always missed you when you would go away."

"I missed you too, Brendan, I liked having a brother. Wrong tense. I *like* having a brother, a brother I love very much."

John had been listening in silence and was eager to hear Tom's story. He spoke up, "Tom what happened between you and Mr. McKenna?"

"Well, on my second day home, Dad closed his clinic and we took off for a day of fishing at one of the beautiful lakes. I really didn't want to go. I had read the paper that morning; it gave details of a violent protest in Belfast. A young British soldier was killed and his body dragged into an alley. His head and face were smashed after his death. That soldier, I had met often in England. He was my friend, an older brother of a classmate of mine. My heart was so full of misery for his family. Suddenly, all the stupid anti-Irish sentiments, spewed by some of my older, newly found friends, incredibly seemed truth to me. Dad saw my brooding, silent mood and asked if I didn't feel well. I told him what I had read and in a torrent of rage screamed anti-Irish and anti-Roman Catholic idiocy. That had to hurt him very deeply. I deserved his full anger, but he showed none. He said, 'I'm deeply sorry for your friend and for his poor family and for your grief.' He put his arm around my shoulder and said, 'You poor lad.' I shook off his arm and stood away. What I wouldn't give to feel his strong arm about me now. Then he said, as he gathered up our fishing gear, 'it's not a good day for fishing, Tommy, we'll start for home'. Neither of us talked on the way."

"Mom was shocked to see us back and looking strained, I'm sure. Dermod could have told her how stupid *this* son had become; but he said he thought he had a bit of cold that had settled in his back and didn't want to stay in the damp. I remember he gave me a little smile when Mom got him a heating pad. He dutifully put the unneeded pad behind him and told Mom, 'That feels good.' I didn't even have the decency to tell him how sorry I was, during the remainder of that stay. I was sorry and ashamed. Deep down in, I knew what I had spouted was a lot of rubbish, but I was too mixed up and stubborn to admit I was wrong. Dad was so kind during that time and never mentioned that day again."

"I returned to England earlier than was needed, staying in my room at the school. Some of the guys hadn't gone away for the break. I started spending time at the pubs and did my share of being cynical about everything and told bigoted jokes with the rest of them. Of course, I had stopped going to church altogether. In my book the Roman Catholic and the Church of England were both filled with hypocrites. Had I allowed myself to remember, for a moment, the countless truly good people I knew, that were members of both churches, and the true Christian message I heard when attending either, I'd have had my head on straight sooner."

"I got a twelve-page letter from Dad, not in the form of a lecture, but filled with good sense and logic—and love for me. I didn't read beyond the first page for about a month. I tossed it into my desk drawer. I wanted nothing to change the mind-set I was in. I knew that letter would contain truth I couldn't ignore. Every time I was in my room I'd think of that waiting letter and resented it. I even thought of destroying it, unread. I thank God I didn't. The state I was in mentally, of course, carried through with the work I was doing—or not doing—at school. The next grading period found me failing in everything. I was not surprised, but felt miserable. After an evening with *my friends* at a pub, trying to forget my problems, I went back to my room and fell into a drunken sleep. It was afternoon when I woke, missing my classes, of course. I showered and changed my stinking clothes. There would never be another night like that night; that much *I knew*. I thought of Dermod's letter and pulled out the desk drawer. All the contents fell to the floor. I stood there looking at the mess and thinking it was like I was. I had fallen from all the good in me. My life was now simply a mess. I picked up the letter and read it through over and over. My thinking became rational for the first time in months; as I accepted the logic of Dermod's words and I cried at the compassion he showed to me. That evening, a note was sent to me from the Dean's office. I was not permitted to finish the term."

Brendan and John listened quietly and watched the sadness in Tom's face as he recalled those memories.

"I called home; I talked to Mom for a few minutes but couldn't bring myself to tell her anything about what had happened at school. I asked to talk with Dermod. I usually called him that. He wanted that before he married Mom; he had said to me, 'Tommy, Mr. McKenna is much too formal for good friends such as us. Call me Dermod.' But he was really a dad to me—one of the best. Anyway, I told him everything and tried to thank him for the letter and to tell him how desperately sorry I felt for the pain I had caused him. He was silent for a while and then said, 'Tommy, go stay with your Uncle Cliff and Aunt Berniece. I'll come to you as soon as I can.' In a few days he came over and met me here. It was agreed that I would live with them and work at the shop until the next term. He went back to the school with me and arranged for my return in the fall. I'll never forget that special time with him. Dermod and Uncle Cliff helped me to really grow up. So, you see, Brendan and John there can be set backs for anyone. You have to allow yourselves to mature and make right choices then—and to forgive yourselves. Brendan, I still have Dermod's letter. I think you have already found, in yourself, its logic, but I'd like you to share that part of your Dad.

It's at my house in Ashwell; sometime soon, I'll get it for you. First, we have to finish with the danger you're in. My problem was not as terrible or as far reaching as yours. I just wanted you to know I understand how it is, when you are young. Anyone can make a far from perfect time for themselves. Mom still doesn't know the details of that time. Dermod smoothed it over, saying, I had been sick and fell back in my studies and that he felt it was a good idea for me to take time off until the next term. He was so great. Since he can't be here for you now, I'll try to fill his shoes the best I can." Tom put his hand on Brendan's shoulder.

Brendan got up and hugged Tom. "Now, Tom, I know you're perfect."

Tom laughed and gave Brendan a fond punch on the arm. "That makes two people who think that; my Fran is under the same delusion. Brendan, I can't wait until you meet your future sister-in-law. Now, there is someone who's perfect. I'll tell you all about her at dinner tonight. I think we all need to relax while we wait to hear from the Yard. We'll go out to a restaurant. I'll go tell Aunt Berniece she's off kitchen duty tonight."

Before leaving the room, Tom turned to Brendan. "I'm very aware that throughout hundreds of years the Irish people have suffered great injustice and misery at the hands of the English. But things are changing; Ireland's economy is changing. The mind-set of clinging to old hatreds, on both sides, must change. I said I feel England is my country, yet Ireland is very dear to me. There is much I love about her and I do remember my ancestry on the Irish side. Maybe the right thinking people of the younger generation will heal the wounds. Yes, Brendan, I'm a bit Irish and you're a bit English. Sure'an we're a bloody good mix." Tom smiled at John, "That's not meant as an insult to a purebred."

"I'll not be takin it as such," John grinned back.

Chapter 31

Dylan Sanders checked out of the hotel and headed back to Ely to keep the appointment at the Milford Reality. He wasn't feeling at all comfortable with the acting that he had to do. Mr. Milford might not be as easily convinced—still he had to go through with it.

George Milford got the papers and keys ready. He was hoping this Mr. Sanders would like the property; not too many people were interested in such an out of the way place. "What's this Dylan Sanders like, Liz? Did you think him reliable?"

Liz looked up from her computer keyboard, "Yes, George, he seemed very pleasant and sincerely interested in finding just such a place. He's a writer and wanted something remote and quiet. I told him there would be a large security deposit in advance. That didn't seem to be a problem."

"Did he say where he's from?"

"No, come to think of it, he didn't say—and I forgot to ask him. But I'm sure he's from Ireland. He didn't speak with a brogue, but he had that soft rise and fall to his voice. I just assumed he was Irish. He's a good-looking young man, but there was something about his looks that was interesting. I couldn't decide what it was while he was here. After he left, I got to thinking about it, and it struck me. His hair is brown but his skin is very fair with a sprinkling of freckles; the look of skin you usually see with red hair. Not that it matters." Liz laughed a little, "It just made him look a little different."

"No, darling, his skin doesn't matter. If he's a good tenant and careful with the property and has the money, he'll do fine. I haven't had high hopes of getting anyone in that place."

The door opened, Dylan Sanders was there, right on time. Elizabeth introduced George and Dylan. While they were talking, she found herself studying Dylan's hair roots. Seeing none, she walked around the office so she could see the back of his head for a few stray hairs. His neck was clean-shaven, recently too, the fair skin was very reddened. Picturing him with red hair, she thought, how much better he'd look. The two men left and Elizabeth got busy and gave no more thought to Mr. Sander's choice of image.

Dylan said he'd take his van and follow George Milford, saying that it would make him more sure of the way. He was glad that sounded logical to Milford; he didn't want to keep a conversation going or answer possible questions on the drive.

The drive on the busy road wasn't a long one, about a half an hour. They turned onto a narrow paved road for another ten minutes. They didn't see any houses until they arrived at the small bungalow. It was surrounded by trees with a little clearing around the house. A small creek flowed through the woods at the rear of the house. Dylan felt a great relief at seeing it. At least this much was working out; it was perfect.

George Milford turned the key and motioned Dylan inside. Dylan feigned interest as the rooms were shown and the features of the kitchen and bath and laundry area were made note of. It was a nicely appointed place but that really didn't matter to Dylan. He was just in a hurry to have this showing over but did remember to ask if the water and heat were turned on. George Milford told him the owner had left just a few days before and as yet the utilities hadn't been disconnected; all was ready for moving in. "The phone had been disconnected, Mr. Sanders, you will have to see to that."

Dylan said, "There is no problem there; I'll probably get a cell phone. Can I sign the papers now? I'm sure I want the place."

"Mrs. Milford did explain to you about the lease and security deposit?"

"Yes, I'm prepared to sign, and I have the money with me."

"Since you drove yourself and I have all the papers with me there is no need for you to return to the office. You can just stay on if you wish." The business being completed, George Milford gave Dylan the key. "I hope you like it here, Mr. Sanders, and I hope you won't miss Ireland too much."

Dylan was a little surprised at the assumption of that statement, but knew it would be ridiculous to refute it. "With school and traveling as a free-lance writer, I move around a lot. I haven't been back to Ireland for a few years." He hurriedly said, "Mr. Milford, thank you for all you've done to help me find the place I need. I have many things to do to get moved in and I think I'd better get on with it."

They went out of the house; Dylan locked the door. "Thank Mrs. Milford for me, please; she was very helpful." He started walking toward his van.

Mr. Milford called after him, "Of course, I'll tell her. If you need anything else, call or stop at the office."

"Thank you, I will." Having said that, Dylan started the motor and went down the narrow road in the direction they had come. When he reached the main road he took a different way. He didn't know where he was headed but he wanted to avoid another meeting with the Milfords; it was hard to keep up the pretense.

George returned to the office. Liz looked up from her desk. "Is Mr. Sanders coming? Did he like the place?"

George sat on the edge of the desk and put the signed papers and money in front of her. "Yes, it was all taken care of at the house. He paid the security, half in cash and half in traveler's checks. I don't know, Liz, he seemed pleasant enough and said the place was perfect for his writing, but he really seemed to be in a hurry for something. He didn't pay much attention to the house. Oh well, I guess the quiet location was all he was interested in. You were right about him—being Irish. But because of school and his writing he hasn't been back for years. I was going to ask what kind of writing he was planning to do here, but he hurried away, saying he had a lot to do before moving in. That makes sense. Yet, I think I'll keep an eye on that place for a few days."

Dylan eventually returned to the town of Ely. He cashed more checks at the bank and located the telephone systems dealer and got the phone. A long time was spent getting food and small household needs. There had to be enough to last through the stay for the three of them. He was thinking, at some point he'd have to seem like a tourist and get familiar with the Cathedral and the grounds around it, but not today; he wanted to get settled. He told himself it was needless to feel so uncomfortable about being seen by the Milfords or others that he had dealt with. As a newcomer, it would be an ordinary thing for him to want to see the area. Still, he would try to avoid conversations with anyone.

On the drive back, a worry came to him. What if Milford comes checking around out there? He'd think it strange if he didn't see a computer or at least a typewriter and some papers about. Well, I'll take care of that in the morning; all the frozen food couldn't hold for more shopping today.

Dylan put everything away, filling the empty refrigerator and cupboards. He looked around the pleasant, well-equipped kitchen; then walked through the other rooms. It was nice, not fancy, but comfortable. The walls were light throughout and the many windows showed the loveliness of the outdoors from every room. How different from living in a town house or a flat; he was thinking, how great it would be to live here. In the small den were bookshelves and a kneehole desk with a padded chair. The desk was against a wall, forming an L with the computer desk. He hadn't noticed that before. The computer monitor had been turned to the wall, the word processor covered. There was a large note attached to it with the words "Kindly Do

Not Use." Dylan said aloud, "That takes care of that." I'll have to get my typewriter; I'm glad there's such a good desk for it. He turned on the three-way lamp that was near the desk. Good lighting, too, that will be great for working. Oh God!—What the hell am I thinking? The typewriter will only be a prop for this make-believe I'm living. There is no Dylan Sanders who is going to write. He walked over to the window that faced the front yard and stared out at a beautiful tree, circled with still blooming pansies, planted by the man whose home this was. A deep sadness enveloped him. No, there was no Dylan Sanders, the writer, only Michael Griffith a terrorist. For a few moments he had almost forgotten.

Ronan and Richard Farrell left Maynooth after they shopped and had breakfast. Sean had been quite confident that his disguise would fool anyone. He had totally enjoyed putting Pearse through the farce, as his son. Pearse had said as little as possible. He knew he had to endure it. Sean's hand was frequently patting the gray sweater pocket. Sean would never leave his guard down—no matter what they were doing.

Pearse stopped the van by the cottage. Sean told him to carry in the few things from the store. "I'll take the van up, but I'll be right back. Don't try anything funny or your uncle won't be a happy man."

"I'll be here, Sean. *Damn you to hell*, I'll be here."

Sean sneered and called from the van, as he started the engine, "You're a fallen angel too, Richard."

Sean returned to the cottage. "I left our bags in the van. We'll be stayin at the hotel again tonight; I had them hold our rooms. Today, the bombs will be made, my skilled son. Tomorrow morning we'll come back here and put them in the van and get started for Wexford and get them onto the cruiser. We're pullin out of here early. We'll have to hold somewhere till late at night. I don't want Phil and his family around, watching. Another thing, they know me there. I won't be Ronan Farrell, but you'll keep the name Richard Farrell and just go along with anything I say. We'll ship out from there early Sunday morning, if Michael has been in touch. I've got to talk to him before we can start over. Now, back to the task on hand. You said you had everything you needed, Pearse, what have you come up with?"

"I've given it a lot of thought. Considering the amount of handling, anything has a degree of danger. The safest I can come up with is my own recipe. Basically, I'll be using stable dynamite, the kind with the plastic charge. It is more resistant to sweating the nitroglycerine. A sudden impact won't set it off. From what you said, you want four to position in the church. Is that right?"

"Do you think four will do it? I want real damage to be done."

"Yes, but not positioned as you first thought, hiding them in the fall flower things. It would blast and weaken the stone at the base of the lantern but the wood starts much higher. It might not be possible, without much larger bombs to cause a fire there. That building is primarily stone. I've read about the place. Taking more bombs or larger ones would require more time to position than what we will probably have."

"I'm not thinking now about the harvest festival, except for the time. I just thought that might work if Brendan would have gone over early and wormed his way into helping with things. He could have hidden charges in a couple of them and maybe found a way for us to get some higher. It doesn't have to be that way now. Where do you think would be best?"

"The wooden choir stalls—there would be a lot of damage there—especially if gasoline could be poured about before the blast. That old wood would go up like crazy." Pearse showed Sean a picture of the choir stalls. "See, they are on both sides of the aisle, east of the octagon. That wooden carving reaches way up and around the organ pipes. It should get them too."

"Would one on each side be enough?"

"With the gasoline, absolutely, but I thought you wanted four."

"I do. I still want to put the other two at a couple of the octagon pillars. You said it would blow some stone and weaken things. We'll use two there."

Before closing the book with the pictures of the Cathedral, Pearse looked for a minute. "Sure'an it's a beautiful place." He closed the book abruptly and heaved a sigh.

Sean gave a sneering smile. "Now, you're surely not feelin soft about a building, *son*, after knowing you've helped to kill people with your bombs."

"Since I'm feeling all but dead inside, it isn't likely I'd care about anything. Let me get on with it. All the makings and the small kegs and packing for the bomb are hidden in the other room."

"What kind of fuses are you using?"

"Radio fuses, they can be used from some distance and they don't need a line-of-sight connection. They can be detonated from miles away, but you can't see through a stone building. We'll have to be closer. I'll be installing a new safety device to block a premature detonation from interfering signals. These things were hard to get and, as you know, damned expensive."

They went out the door and into the other room of the cottage. Pearse started to put out the things he needed. They had been well hidden beneath a pile of old canvas and boards that had looked undisturbed for years. Sean asked, "How far away can we be to set them off?"

"As close as possible, within a block or two. I'll have to know the layout around the place to be sure. When will you be talking to Michael?"

"Not till we get to Wexford. He's to leave a number down there for me to reach him. I hope to hell he's found a place to stay."

Pearse continued moving the large pile of musty, filthy canvas from the hidden metal box where the dynamite had been stored. He turned to Sean, "Are you planning to stand all day and watch me?"

"No, I know better than to think you would blow yourself up just to be rid of me. I'm going over to put some more of that junk through my hair. It's starting to wear off. I'll be around, in and out, so don't try anything funny." Sean still had his hand over the bulge in his pocket.

"We've been through that, Sean; just shut up and *go*."

When the bombs were finished and packed as safely as possible for transporting, Pearse went over to the other side of the cottage. He tried to open the door and heard something heavy pulled from the inside of it. Pearse hadn't seemed as threatening as yesterday; still, Sean wasn't taking any chances.

"What the hell was that all about, Sean?"

"I wouldn't have wanted a surprise visit, especially from you, son."

Pearse didn't reply. He crossed the room to where the old enamel basin and a bottle of water were on top of a small, rickety bench. With the cold water he washed as best he could and ran a comb through his short hair.

"Feel better, son?" Sean asked, with mock fatherly concern.

"If you don't want this water thrown in your face, Sean, you'll shut your big ugly mouth. When are we leaving for Maynooth?"

"Are things well hidden over there?"

"Yes, I even tried to arrange things so that the dust didn't looked disturbed."

"Okay, take everything out of here. Throw the rest of that water out. This place makes me nervous; we're leaving now. We'll get here early tomorrow, load the bombs, and start for Wexford."

Sean had thought about taking Pearse to Doyle's for a change of identification, but he didn't want to go into Dublin again. Pearse would be having no need to show his I.D. After it was all over—hell, that was Pearse's problem. If it would cause a problem for Michael and himself, he'd just take care of Pearse; it would be as simple as that. He fingered the gun, almost lovingly. He firmly believed he would find Brendan and kill him; another one wouldn't matter.

It was mid-morning in London, and the three boys, as Berniece referred to them, were helping to clean the flat. At first, Berniece had protested, but they were convincing of their need for something to do.

Cliff had gone for a walk, needing to post some long overdue letters to the family in North Yorkshire. The family had expected a visit from Cliff and Berniece. He wrote, explaining they had unexpected, out of town visitors. Of course, he didn't say whom, or give any indication of trouble; no need to worry anyone else. They all loved Susanna, dearly, and her Brendan was loved by all from the time he was a baby.

When Cliff returned, Tom told him, "The Yard hasn't called. If they don't today, I hate to pester them, but I'm going to call tomorrow. This waiting is wearing everybody down."

"I agree. Tom, it's time we know something."

"Are you going to be here the rest of today? You could take the call and Brendan could call back. Would you mind?"

"Yes, I'm going to be here the rest of today. Yes, I'll take the call if it comes. No, I don't mind," Cliff said laughing. "What do you have in mind, Tom?"

"I thought of taking Brendan and John sightseeing for a little while. Brendan saw something of London when he was much younger and John has never been here before. I don't think John was ever out of Connemara until he went to Dublin this past spring." Tom smiled ruefully, "Too bad the poor lad didn't spend his time seeing the sights there. Anyway, he thinks it would be fun to ride on top of the red tour bus."

Tom's suggestion sounded great to Brendan and John. They were, indeed, getting cabin fever; that along with the big worry and the waiting was hard to take. Last night's restaurant dinner had been their first time out since their visit to Scotland Yard.

They got goodbye hugs from Aunt Berniece and left the flat. Once out in the bright, crisp air, they were all feeling free as schoolboys on a picnic.

The bus tour took them past the major sights of interest. They did a hop-off at Parliament Square and walked about The Houses and the clock tower and across a bridge, over the river Thames. They walked around Westminster Abbey and had some lunch from a food cart on the grounds. Tom glanced at his watch, "We don't have time to do a tour of the Abbey today. We'll go inside for a quick look. I'll bring you back sometime; it takes hours to really see it all." Having done that, they got back on the bus and headed to Madame Tussauds. John had told Tom how much he wanted to see the wax museum. He had heard about it, when a small child, from his father who once had visited London.

After the tour, Tom took Brendan and John to a man's clothing shop. "I noticed when you fellows were doing laundry this morning that you didn't bring much over with you. Both of you get some things you need. It'll be an early Christmas present from me."

"Wow! Tom, I'm not saying no. Thanks, big brother, we've been having to do laundry everyday."

"I don't feel right about this, Tom." John looked a bit reluctant. "It's different for Brendan. He's your bro—"

Tom cut him off, "I've just adopted you, brother John." Smiling, he gave him a slight punch on the shoulder, "Now go and enjoy getting the things you need."

On the way back to the flat, the lightheartedness of the day seemed to vanish. Brendan was wondering if the Yard had called. John looked thoughtful, "Tom, is Ely Cathedral anything like Westminster? It's certainly a grand, beautiful place."

"Not really, John. They are both wonderful in their special ways but different in their style—and besides Westminster Abbey is larger. Actually, much of Ely is a little older. The site of Ely Cathedral has been a place of faith since 673, when Saint Etheldreda built a monastery there." Tom was feeling at peace while even talking of it. "There was a Bishop Gunning of Ely who wrote a famous prayer speaking of Ely. The bishop is buried there. He wrote, 'It has the power to move all sorts and conditions of men.' I find that to be true."

Brendan said, "I was through it that one time you took me, Tom. Remembering it now, I think I know what you mean. I can't believe I made light of it and joked about seeing it. Oh, dear God. Sean must be stopped." There was a cry of agony in Brendan's voice.

Brendan's spirits fell further when they reached the flat. Cliff told them there had been no call from the Yard.

"Relax, Brendan," Tom said, seeing Brendan's distressed look. "We'll call first thing tomorrow. Speaking of phone calls, I haven't talked to Fran since I arrived." He went to his room to make the call. How he missed her—it would be wonderful just to hear her voice. Yet this call would not be an easy one to make. He had been having fearful thoughts and he intended to be remote with her. He was determined—*no matter what*—to ensure the safety of his precious Fran.

Chapter 32

Fran had kept busy at many things, as she had told Tom she would; but nothing stopped her from missing him. He told her when he called last night that he still didn't know when he would be back. She had asked if he had found out what the problem with Brendan was. He had said yes and that it was serious. Beyond that, he told her nothing. She was beginning to feel left out of something that was important to Tom. It wasn't a good feeling. They had been so close, so open with each other. Then too, he hadn't returned her words of love when he hung up the phone. She forced herself not to feel hurt by that. He was probably very tired or had other people in the room; still that was so different for him. He sounded a little cold. She could have no idea of the worry that was growing in Tom.

The thought had come to him that if Sean got to Ely before trying to follow through with his plan, he would seek revenge. If Brendan couldn't be found, Sean could easily track him down; worse, if Sean found out about Fran, she might be in danger. Tom was already thinking that he'd have to keep Fran out of this completely and that would mean out of his life. He knew the only way possible would hurt her deeply, but he had no choice.

Tom had spent a restless night; he couldn't dismiss the sound of hurt in Fran's dear voice when he couldn't confide in her. He kept hearing her sweet tenderness: "I love you, Tom." How he longed to respond to that love, but in loving her, he knew he couldn't. This morning, he felt miserable and hoping with all his heart that the Yard would now be in charge of the situation; then his plan to keep Fran safe wouldn't be necessary.

The time seemed to drag. Tom had to know something. At nine o'clock he called and asked to speak with Sergeant Crosby. After giving the reason for the call, he was put on hold for a very long time, or so it seemed. Cliff was sitting on the edge of his chair. Brendan and John were standing close to him, watching him with tense expressions. Aunt Berniece was in the doorway, drying and re-drying her hands on a dishtowel. They weren't making the waiting easier. Finally, someone was, again, on the other end of the line. "Yes, this is Tom Hart, as I told you; I'm calling for my brother Brendan McKenna. Sergeant Crosby had talked with him and with John Hobson and my Uncle Clifford Hart. I know Sergeant Crosby, too. He is familiar with a serious problem and we have been expecting to hear from him." Tom looked at the expectant faces. "Crosby's on another line. They'll put me through shortly." "Yes, Good morning, Sergeant. You were planning to call today? Do you know something? Would you like us to come down to your office? You don't feel that to be necessary." Tom listened and made notes of what Sergeant Crosby was telling him. "Yes, Sergeant, if we think of anything more we would certainly call. If you would know anything more, will you please call us right away?"

Tom hung up the phone and looked over the tablet with his notes. He motioned for Brendan and John to sit down. "Well, I'll tell you what Sergeant Crosby told me." Tom told them every detail of the report from Interpol regarding every move they had made to make direct contact with Sean, Michael and Pearse. "They had no luck; those three have completely disappeared. They found Denis Flemming. His company had him move to their northern office in Derry. He told them he was through with any associations with Sean or the others; that their hate filled talk had finally seemed repugnant to him. He said there had been talk about some kind of protest but he had no knowledge of any plans having been formulated. Interpol believed him. The very fact that he was so easily found, while the others weren't, was convincing."

John said, "I believe Denis. He always seemed to take everything lightly, not serious at all. That used to make Sean mad. That didn't bother Denis; he didn't care what Sean thought."

Brendan said, "I believe Denis, too. I can't see him going along with it, if he would have known. Man, I'm glad he's out of it. What else did the Yard say, Tom?"

"Interpol followed up a lead they were given that Sean had taken *The Paradise* to Meath and shipped out from there. There was a watch on the waterways—but it's a big sea; so far, nothing. There were descriptions sent to airports and ferry lines for personnel awareness. However, no one had been officially stationed anywhere. There aren't enough people and there isn't enough money, since it is still in the threat category. There are no leads to narrow things down. This could change if they get a fresh lead, by chance. Crosby said there is concern because it looks mighty suspicious that all three men can't be found. He thinks it backs up your story and that something is going on. But for now, with the Yard and Interpol, it's a wait and see thing. As they said, they haven't any leads."

Brendan stood, "I know what I have to do." His face was rigid as stone.

"Brendan, I will go back to Ely and alert the local police; I know they will listen to me. I can't imagine how Sean will try to pull it off; but I have a gut feeling, with them all disappearing, that Sean is going to try. You know, if he gets over here, he's going to be looking for you. Time is getting short, so he won't waste it coming to London. You and John must stay here. Let the authorities at Ely do what they can."

"If he can't find me at Ely, I'm sure he can find Hart's Chemist Shop and you, Tom. We're going to Ely, Tom, and we're going to stop him. If he has to have his revenge, I'll be there for that. I'd rather be dead than have you hurt. I'll not have you pay the price for my stupidity. John and I are going back with you."

"No one has to die, Brendan. The police will be involved. You and John must stay here. I won't take you back. I'm not going to take chances; I'll take care of myself." Tom was talking a lot surer than he felt. He didn't say anything to Brendan about his fear for Fran. Sean mustn't find out about her. "I'm leaving tomorrow. *Alone.*"

Brendan did not reply, but looked knowingly at John.

Tom went into his bedroom and began writing:

Dear Fran,

I'm not sure when I will return to Ely. The problem Brendan had was mostly financial. He owed someone money. Things have been worked out.

I'm having a really good time here. I ran into some old friends and we've been doing a bit of the town.

Fran, I don't know how to say this, but I think I need this free time. I've been doing a lot of thinking about us. I'm reaching the conclusion that I made some decisions too soon. Even if I come back to Ely, I'd rather we didn't get together for a while. I don't want you to go to the shop. This whole thing will be embarrassing to me.

Please don't think too unkindly of me. I'm just an old bachelor who can't help himself. I really thought I could settle down and be the person you needed. I find that impossible.

I know a lot of people in Ely and I'd rather you didn't talk about me. I wish, now that I know what I really want, that you had never moved to Ely. I wish you would go back down with Heidi until we do get together, if you want to give the ring back.

If you stay in Ely, I ask, again, please don't go to the shop and don't talk about me with anyone. It's a small place, and if they form a bad opinion of me, my business would be finished.

Please don't call down here or at Mom's. I'd rather everyone think this a mutual decision.

I'm really sorry, Fran. You thought you knew me but you didn't. You deserve someone good. I hope he comes along.

Sometimes I wish it could have been.

I'm sorry,

Tom

Tom knew Fran's pride would have her do what he asked. She would talk to no one. He also knew that if she were told any of the truth, she would stay close to him—*no matter what.* He couldn't take that risk—he just couldn't.

Tom sealed the letter; deciding to post it overnight mail. He felt sick to his stomach, knowing the deep pain it would cause her. His whole being ached with love for her. He missed her beyond the telling. All he wanted in his life was to make her happy always. Would she ever believe him again, when she did know the truth? She had been so hurt by lies in the past. Still, he had to take that risk.

Tom went into the kitchen; Berniece and Cliff were starting to prepare lunch. They saw the serious and sad look on Tom's face. He asked them, "If Fran should call here, would you please do exactly what I think best?"

"Berniece and I will do whatever you ask, Tom, you know we will. What is it?"

"Tell her you don't know where I am, that I've gone out for the day with friends. Say nothing, absolutely nothing, about the situation with Brendan. Don't discuss it or me in any way. What I'm asking is for her safety." Tom had to swallow hard. "It is very important that you do as I ask. I'm sending a letter, filled with lies, and it will hurt her deeply. If Devlin does show up at Ely, he must not be led to Fran through me. I believe, from what I've heard of him, that his revenge could extend to Brendan's family. If he heard of Fran, she could be included in his venting of his hate. Fran mustn't learn the truth."

"Isn't there any other way, Tom? I just can't think of Fran's being hurt. She loves you so."

"Aunt Berniece, there is no other way. If she knew, she would insist on being with me constantly. She would have no fear for herself. I cannot have her in danger from a mad man. I'm leaving today for Ely. After I post this letter, I'll start directly. I put my case in the hall. I will not take Brendan and John with me. *Make* them stay here. They're watching the telly now;

I'll just tell them I'm going to post a letter, when I leave." He gave Cliff and Berniece loving hugs. "I'll be in touch. Call me on my cell number if you hear anything else or if you need me."

When Tom left, Cliff put his arm around a crying Berniece. "Let's wait a while for lunch, Berniece; I feel like I have a rock in my stomach."

Pearse and Sean put the containers carrying the bombs carefully into the van. They hid them well, beneath their clothes and soft bags. Pearse got into the driver's seat as Sean had ordered. "We'll be heading southeast and stay away from the main highways as much as possible. It'll take longer, but then we have a long day to put in. I don't want to be at Phil's place till late but we can't hang around here. Let's get moving."

"Even going back routes, we'll not take long to go to Wexford, Sean. What the devil are we going to do with the rest of the day?"

"Well, I thought it would be safest just to play tourist. We'll stop at the Irish National Heritage Park; it's near Wexford and it has a café—we've got to eat."

"A heritage park—you're not serious?"

"Yes, damn it, I'm serious. No one would be looking for us in a place like that. After it's closed, we could spend a few hours at a pub; we're not known and we wouldn't be conspicuous during the evening—or we could go to a movie. We can't just keep driving around. If push comes to shove, we'll find a secluded place and sit in the van. The important thing is to get to the boat late at night."

"Whatever we do, it'll be another long, stinking day with you, Sean, and so it doesn't matter much."

Sean ignored the remark. Most of the drive was spent in silence. To both, the day seemed painfully long.

It was after eleven p.m., when they passed Phil's house on the way down to the cove. Sean was annoyed when he saw a light still showing from the house. "Damn, I hope they stay put."

They reached the boat and quickly unloaded their supplies and the containers with the bombs onto the dock. "Get them on the boat, Pearse. I'll show you where they are to go in a few minutes. I have to take care of something first. He started the smaller generator that provided power for light and other needs while docked. Next, he went into the small bathroom that contained a shower and the basin and the head. *The Paradise* was well equipped.

When he returned to the deck, his hair and beard were black again. The gray sweater had been replaced with a dark blue jacket; the gun was carried in its pocket. Pearse and Sean had finished storing everything when they saw

Phil approaching, carrying a torch. He called up to the deck, "I thought I heard someone coming down the road. I wanted to check that no one was messing around your boat. I wasn't expecting you back so soon."

The two men came down from the deck. "Thanks, Phil, for watching out for the boat. I had gone back to Dublin and ran into my friend Richard Farrell. He brought me down."

The introduction was made and Phil asked if they were planning to stay at the house. "Tess and the young-ones are home but there's a couch in the living room and a pull-out in the den. If that would do, you're very welcome to stay."

"Thanks, Phil, but we're staying on board tonight. We have light and heat and everything else we need."

"Come back to the house for a while and have a drink. Tess and I were up and she's anxious to meet you. The young-ones are asleep, of course."

"It's late, Phil, I don't want to be a bother this time of night. Richard is tired. He did all the driving," Sean glanced at Pearse.

Pearse spoke up, "It's not that late for a short visit and that drink sounds good, Phil." Pearse was thinking that to be with anyone beside Sean would be wonderful. He wasn't going to pass up the chance.

Tess greeted them warmly. She was a truly gracious woman and an attractive one in a very natural way. Her long brown hair was held back by a thick rose-colored band that matched the soft, tailored robe she was wearing. She had no makeup but a touch of lipstick, and needed none. Her gray eyes exuded warmth, as did her soft, full mouth.

Pearse looked at this lovely room and at the delightful lady pouring the drinks. He noticed the warmth of exchange between Phil and Tess. He drank his first drink quickly and accepted a second, trying to vanish the thoughts of what he had missed in his life. Sure, he had messed up a little in his youth but why had he kept things going that way? There had been no homes remotely like this one in the slum neighborhood of his childhood. He couldn't blame his mom and dad for all of his rotten decisions. But they always seemed so unhappy. They tried to stretch the little money his dad earned; yet it couldn't begin to meet the family's needs. His parents may have been married, but if they ever had love for one another, it had been killed by their world-weary lives. Never had he or the six younger children seen their parents giving loving looks to one another, or even kind words. He had seen nothing to aim at. There had been nothing to encourage him to seek better. Lately, he hadn't even thought of how life could be; how it could have been for him. He was lost in his thoughts and didn't hear Tess ask, softly, "Are you tired, Mr. Farrell?"

"Richard," Sean spoke loudly, "You seem very quiet. Are you going to sleep?"

Pearse abruptly returned to the reality around him. He stood, "I guess I am feeling tired. It's been really nice meeting you, Phil, and Tess. Thanks for the drinks." He turned to Sean, "I'm ready to head back to the boat."

On the way back, Sean glared at Pearse, "You were the one who wanted to go up to the house and there you sat like a bump on a log."

"I got lost in my thoughts after seeing how nice it is to live like normal people. What's it to you, Devlin? I didn't think you would care about the social graces."

"I know how to act if it serves my purpose. If people can be useful to me, I'll show them any side they need to see. That Tess is some attractive woman."

"A woman like that would soon see through your act. A woman like that wouldn't wipe her shoes on you."

They reached the boat and went straight to their separate, small staterooms. Both were glad to be rid of each other's company. Sean locked the door and put the gun on top of the little, built-in set of drawers; and thinking, how damned tired he was of keeping his guard up around Pearse. He might be looking younger than his Ronan Farrell character, but now he felt twice as old. Damn it, Brendan! He'd pay for making things so hard for Sean Devlin. By hell, he'd pay.

Tess sat on the edge of the bed and kicked off her slippers. Phil was lying on his side, admiring the pale cream skin of her back and shoulders and how beautifully the little slip of a silk gown clung to her firm, slender body. Life was wonderful! She was back. He reached to pull her close but the look on her face told him her thoughts were not on him. She slid under the cover. "Those friends, of yours, are interesting. The younger one, the good-looking one, was so quiet. He looked like his thoughts were a million miles away."

"I'd never met Richard Farrell until tonight. You're right, that's how he did seem. He said he wanted to come up to the house as soon as I asked them. Funny, he did seem remote once he got here."

"That Sean Devlin—I guess it's not very charitable of me, just meeting him, but I can't say I like him. Oh, he tried to be so friendly and so charming. That's what I felt—he was just trying, simply putting on an act. I'll be glad when he's gone."

"Sean was a drinking buddy of mine, along with a few others, years ago in Dublin; he was always a bit loud. I didn't think much about him one way or another, back then. You know, Tess, I really was surprised when he called and said he wanted to get together. It has been years since I'd even thought about him. I have been thinking that the real reason he came was to keep his cruiser here and that he wants to ship off somewhere from this point. I wouldn't know why. Anyway, he seemed friendly enough and said he just wanted a vacation from the bustle of his life in Dublin. Still, he has been doing things in a strange way. Do you think he's involved in something illegal?"

"I wouldn't know, Phil, but there's something wrong with him and I'll be glad when he leaves. You had said about going out on the boat with the children. I don't want to—I really don't. Something tells me, Sean Devlin wouldn't really want to either."

"You're probably right, Tess. The more I think of it, the less appealing it is. I just want him gone and to have you and the young-ones to myself."

Tess rolled over with her back close to Phil. She felt his warm breath on the nape of her neck. In that delicious moment all thoughts were of the joy at being back together. She turned over for the sweetness of his mouth on hers. Nothing else in the world existed but the love they shared

That night, Dylan Sanders was trying to block from his mind what the next week would bring. That morning he had gone into Ely to buy the typewriter and the things needed, if one was going to write. He tried not to look in the direction of the Cathedral when it came into view. The very sight of it was causing a most uncomfortable feeling of guilt to surface within him. The grounds had to be studied. A tour of the building had to be done. Once again, he put it off. He told himself it would be better to do it tomorrow with the larger crowd of Saturday tourists.

He had returned to the house. Soon the den was looking like an office; made to look like he planned to begin *his work*. He placed a dictionary and a thesaurus and some historical reference books in full view. Having done that, he really didn't know what to do with the rest of the day. He walked out around the house and noticed that the grass could use a cutting. There were taller weeds near the house and pathways that needed to be trimmed. He had seen a mower and clippers and that sort of thing in a small porch, off the kitchen. Always, he had lived in the city. When he was young and lived in a row house, the neighbor man had taken care of their small yard. After that, Michael had lived in flats. He didn't know anything about mowers but went to have a look. The mower was rather new and he found the operating instructions on a shelf.

He took the mower outside and when he got it to turn over, he said aloud, "Nothing to it." It was fall but the sun still gave heat to the afternoon. It felt *wonderful*. The freshly cut grass smelled *wonderful*. He was focused on what he was doing. He was feeling *wonderful*. Just for today, he was thinking, I'll be Dylan. Just for today, this will be my house, my yard, my mower, my clippers and my weeds. He trimmed the tall weeds and raked the cut grass and the few leaves that had fallen. He looked up at the turning leaves. His spirit fell. How he wished he could be here for the raking when the trees were bare. He was kneeling, pulling weeds from the pansies when George Milford drove up.

George looked around, "You have everything looking great here, Dylan."

Dylan stood and brushed the earth from his knees and thanked George for the compliments for his efforts. "What are you doing out this way, Mr. Milford?"

"Oh, I had to be close here and thought I'd check to see if you needed anything—if everything was working all right." George was feeling a little embarrassed that he had come to check on Dylan Sanders. All the work that was done proved to him Sanders was a serious tenant.

Dylan figured the real reason for Milford's visit and was glad he seemed so impressed. Maybe now, he was satisfied and wouldn't be coming back next week

"Come in and have a cold drink with me. I've worked up a thirst. I'm dusty; we'll go in the back way."

George Milford looked about and saw everything clean and neat. "Have you started your writing, Dylan?"

Dylan shook his head, no. "I just got my typewriter this morning. Come see how I've rearranged the den a bit." They crossed the hall to the den. "This is a great place to work. All I need now is to get inspired. I need to get down to business, but I couldn't pass up the beautiful day. I had to get outside." They had their drinks and Dylan said, as George Milford was leaving, "I want to thank you and Mrs. Milford, again, for helping me find this place. I like it and I'll have the solitude I need."

As George drove away, any nagging fear of his was completely gone. He really liked Sanders. He wouldn't be bothering him again. No need for that. Besides, the man clearly wanted his peace.

Chapter 33

Saturday morning, Dylan hated the thought of putting through the call to Sean. What if he simply didn't do it? What if he didn't go over to the coast to get Sean and his bombs? Sean would rent a van and bring them himself. He'd be madder than hell and hunt him down. It wouldn't end. There was no doubt in Dylan's mind that Sean would have his revenge and kill him, no matter the consequence. He knew he couldn't just go somewhere else. How far could he get with the phony identification? Then too, there was the lack of money. What Sean had given him was gone. There was no way he could get his own money from the bank in Dublin. Well, he had agreed to this and had done his share in causing the plan to work. Why the feeling of guilt now? They wouldn't be killing anyone. It was only a building. Hadn't he wanted to get even, somehow, all of his life? He tried to stir up the feelings of hatred that had long been a part of him. Those feelings were gone; the whole thing seemed repugnant to him. He wanted another life, another chance. But it was too late; his course was set.

Tess and Phil were getting the children's breakfast. It was cozy and warm in the bright kitchen, a sharp contrast to the cold and gray of the day. The phone rang. It was the call Sean was expecting from Dylan Sanders. He left the number for Sean to return his call. That ended the relaxing morning. "Hold that second cup of coffee, Tess, I'll have to get dressed and go down to the boat to get Sean."

"Ask when he's planning to leave, Phil. I hope it's soon."

"Me too, Hon."

Seven-year-old Joseph looked up with his cocoa-smudged grin and his eyes dancing with excitement and tugged Phil's robe sleeve. "Is that the man who's going to take us on his boat? You said he would, Daddy. I want to go on the big boat."

Phil and Tess stared at each other with a parent's look of "how can we tell him 'no'?"

"Well, I thought he might, Joe, but the weather is cold and gray and it is going to rain later. It's not a good day for boating. I think Mr. Devlin has to go away soon and I don't think he'll be having the time since it can't be done today."

Joseph looked disappointed and glared out the window. "Why does it have to rain today, Daddy?"

Phil gave him a hug and winked at Tess. "We can't help the weather, Joe."

Joe left to join his sister Cathey, who was playing in the living room. Tess grinned at Phil, "Did you ever see such a lovely dark day?"

"It surely got us off the hook." Phil went to get dressed for the walk to the cove.

When he reached the boat, he found Sean busy stenciling *The Margo* on the stern. "Good morning, Phil," Sean called down from the rope ladder. "I'm trying to get this done before the rain starts."

"Hope you make it," Phil said, looking up at the dark sky.

"I want to take her out early tomorrow. This is my only chance; it's to rain hard later today. Richard's in the cabin. Do you want to come aboard and have coffee with him?"

"No thanks, Sean, I've had mine. I came to let you know that there was a phone call a short while ago. Someone named Dylan left a number where you could call him."

"Thanks, Phil. I'll finish this and Pearse can paint it in. I'll be up to the house soon."

"Pearse—who's Pearse?"

Damn! Sean thought. "Oh, that's Richard's first name. He doesn't like it. I knew him, when he was a kid—everyone called him that. He always goes by his middle name Richard now. Sometimes I forget."

"Sean, you come when you want. It's getting breezy, I'm going back." Phil pulled his jacket collar up about his neck. He was wishing he had listened to Tess, when she wanted him to wear a hat.

When he opened the door, Tess put her warm hands on his ears, "Next time listen."

He smiled, "Yes, Mother. This'll warm me up." He gave her a lingering kiss.

It wasn't long until Sean was knocking. He had left *Richard* to finish the letters. Sean had been surprised that Pearse had been so willing. Despite being in the cold, he was glad to have something to do. Anything, to keep his mind focused for a while, blocking out the reality of the mess he was in, was good.

Phil told Sean he could make his call from their bedroom phone. "That way, the young-ones won't be interrupting and you can have some privacy."

"Thank you. You and Tess are grand hosts." He smiled at each of them. "You think of everything." Sean put on his most charming side.

When he closed the door to the room, Tess smiled at Phil with a knowing look and said, *sotto voce,* "He's just too much."

Michael picked up the phone and heard Sean's voice oozing leftover charm, "Dylan, my friend, how are you?"

"I'm here, Sean. I've got the place as you wanted. I suppose you have instructions for me."

Sean heard the curtness in Michael's voice. "You don't sound in a very good mood, Dylan. Have you had trouble?"

"No, Sean, or at least not the kind you want to hear of. I'd rather call the whole damned thing off."

"Don't be an ass. We've gone too far; don't even be thinking of it." Sean's inner rage started to boil. "Now listen well." He told Michael where and when he expected him on Sunday night and what the plans would be after that. "There's to be no backing out, Michael, no double crossing me. I've always thought your friendship special but that wouldn't get in my way if you'd try anything. What in the hell has happened to you?"

"I'll be where you said on Sunday night." Michael put the phone down with a bang.

Sean slowly cradled the telephone. His emotions of rage had turned into feelings of flatness. His life long dreams of friends with a common cause, carrying out a great plan of revenge, what had happened to that? He felt so alone. Am I the only one who can remember why it has to be done? Michael—of all of them—Michael. The hell with him. By God and by Hell, I'm going through with it. I remember, even if they don't. He thought of Brendan and John, Denis and Pearse, and now Michael. Some gone and the others wanting to be. He remembered Brendan calling him *mad* and the time Michael said it. Was he? *No,* it wasn't him; it was them, the damned bastards, and the rotten cowards. He had his head in his hands when he heard the doorknob turning. He heard Tess saying, "No, Catherine, you can't go in. Mr. Devlin is making a phone call. Come along."

Sean shook his head as if to clear his mind. God, he had to go out and seem friendly to the pack of them. He had wanted to do something. It was hard to think. Yeah, that was it. He wanted to leave money for the call and for a time on a cruise boat for the young-ones, since he didn't follow through with a ride on his boat. No one was going to get the chance to think Sean Devlin was stingy with his money. Phil had been good to him and wouldn't just take money for his trouble; Sean knew that. He pulled himself together and went into the living room. All of the family was there. Sean handed Phil the money, "I want to leave this for the phone call, Phil." Phil demurred. "No, I insist." Sean laid money on an end table. He looked at the children. Joe and Catherine were watching him intensely. "Your Dad and I had talked about a ride on my boat. I'm sorry that didn't work out. I'm leaving some money for all of you to go to Rosslare Harbor, or somewhere, to take a nice ride on a big boat sometime."

Joe said, "Sometime when it isn't raining, Mr. Devlin. I'd like that. Thanks, Mr. Devlin."

Tess said, "You don't have to do that. The children understood that a ride on your boat wasn't possible."

"I know I don't have to, but I really want to have them enjoy a ride on a big boat. There's nothing as much fun." For the first time, Tess heard sincerity in his voice. Sean shook Phil's hand. "I want to thank you, old friend, and you, Tess, for all your hospitality." Phil and Tess assured him he was welcome. To Phil's surprise, Tess asked Sean if he and Richard could come up to dinner. What surprised him even more was the look of warmth and sincerity when she issued the invitation.

Sean was surprised too. He had felt a bit of reserve toward him from Tess. "That's very kind, Tess, but I've a lot to do today. I want to check my van a little and go into the car rental with Richard to turn his in. It's a rented one. Then I have some chart work to do. We'll be leaving early tomorrow to cruise down around St. George's Channel and on to Baltimore. I think Margo's visiting an aunt there. I might see her. I'm not sure. I probably won't be seeing you before we leave. Thanks for the invitation and everything." He was about to close the door when he turned and said, "Phil, I'll have to leave my van here for a few weeks. I'll pick it up as soon as I can. Is that all right?"

"Sure, Sean," Phil laughed; "I won't let Joe drive it." He rubbed his fingers through Joe's hair.

Joe looked at Sean and said, adopting a serious tone, "I won't drive it, Mr. Devlin. I'm too little."

Even Sean had to give a real smile. "Okay, Joe, enjoy the boat ride."

The door closed, Phil turned to Tess and said, "I was surprised at your invitation. I thought you couldn't stand him. Did you think you should invite him because of the money?"

"No, Phil, that had nothing to do with it. I rather surprised myself. My dislike suddenly turned into pity. I can't say that I like him more but

I think his life must be miserable, somehow." Tess looked thoughtful and was frowning. "He's probably caused the misery for himself. I don't think he is really serious about Margo. He doesn't talk like a man who really cares. Maybe he's lonely and won't admit it. I don't know what it is. He looked angry and a little confused when he came out from the phone call. I feel he's in some kind of trouble and I believe he's the cause of it. I pity him anyway. Life must be hard for such a person and I wanted to do something kind."

Phil reached down and picked up the baby. "You know, Danny, that mother of yours is a very special lady." He smiled at Tess, "I'm very happy that special lady is my wife."

Sean returned to the boat in a foul mood, thinking of Michael. He took care to color his hair and beard and changed to Ronan Farrell before leaving to return the van. With the cold hard rain that had started, Sean felt safe that the Baileys wouldn't be outside seeing the "old man" in the van. Still he was relieved when they had driven beyond the house.

Fran was measuring the wall space in her living room. Today she intended to make final decisions on the sofa bed and dining set. She heard Emma calling, "Fran, there is a letter for you. I'd bring it up, dear, but the steps would bother me a bit today."

"I'll be right down, Emma." When Fran reached the top of the stairs, she saw Emma holding the letter high and smiling.

"It's a letter from London."

Fran almost flew the rest of the way. She wanted to dash back and read the letter at once, but she took the time to give Emma a hug and asked if her legs were hurting today.

"A little bit, Fran, it's the change in the weather. The old arthritis is acting up. Let me know how Tom is doing."

"I will. I'll be down later for tea." Fran hugged the letter as she ran to her flat. She sat down at the kitchen table and opened the envelope; then she held the folded sheets to her lips, thinking, his dear hands held them. She began to read. Her hands started to shake and her body felt ice cold. The tears that came were scalding against her cold cheeks. She crumbled the letter and threw it across the floor. What seemed an eternity ago, Jeff had crushed her, but Tom—not Tom—not Tom, she was moaning aloud and choking on the tears. She stared at the ball of paper, hating the evil thing. She walked throughout the flat, time and time again, feeling numb and murmuring, it can't be—it can't be. She went back to the kitchen, feeling it a dreaded place, and forced herself to pick up the horrible thing. She read it over, and then again. Her face registered a look of understanding as again she read the pages. Then she sighed in relief, and was quite calm. She smiled a little.

If it hadn't shocked her so or if it hadn't been written for, God knew what, serious reason, it would almost seem funny. The whole letter was simply a lie. She reread the line, "You thought you knew me but you didn't." Oh, yes, she had no doubt in the world, she *did* know her Tom. This was not Tom in this letter. That side of Tom that he tried to present in the letter simply didn't exist. Even the words and the phrasing of the composition were almost silly. Tom had tried hard to make this believable; he couldn't, not to her. She did know her precious Tom. Her relief in recognizing the truth and knowing that, of course, he loved her, was giving away to worry. Why? She didn't believe that Brendan's problem was, as Tom said, solved. All the many weeks of worry and what little she knew from their visit with Susanna were proof that the problem was a terrible one. She knew the reason Tom had lied and hurt her so was an effort to keep her away from this horror. Maybe to keep her out of danger. She couldn't imagine what or why. How like him, even to sacrifice himself in her eyes—to put her first. That ridiculous letter, now, only caused her to know and love him more. Fran got her stationery and returned to the little table and wrote her answer to Tom. She sealed the letter and didn't affix a return address on the envelope. He wouldn't receive it until Monday and wouldn't then, if he wasn't back at Ely. Still, she wanted to post it right away.

Emma heard her coming down the steps. "Fran dear, I had the water on for tea but turned it off when you didn't come. Do you want me to start it now?"

"Emma, I got involved in answering Tom's letter and forgot about the tea. I'm sorry."

"If I had a letter to write to my sweetheart, I'd forget about it, too," Emma said with a smile. Then she came closer to Fran and noticed the eyes, still red from crying. "Is everything all right? I don't want to be nosy, but your eyes are so red."

"It's my sinuses. The weather bothers your arthritis; with me it's my nose. I just sneezed about twenty times." Fran hated even a little fib. Well, it really wasn't a fib, she thought. She did have sinus reactions to the changes in the weather. Today was a cold, damp one. Fran glanced outside, "It is yucky. That hot tea will be good after going out to post this letter."

"Yucky—that's a good one." Emma delighted in Fran's occasional American slang.

After having tea and hot-buttered cinnamon toast with Emma, Fran went back to her flat. There was no desire left for shopping; she couldn't concentrate with the worry that was building within her. The day was yucky indeed. The rain had started, but she had to do something. She put on her thick-soled, leather, tie shoes; she called them "her uglies." Wearing her warm raincoat and with a scarf tied over her head and her umbrella held low against the wind, Fran was on her way to the Cathedral.

She went through the huge West Doors and stood for a while near the back. She had no idea if Tom was back, and doing tours today. If she saw him, she wouldn't approach; she would do as he had asked and stay away from him. Because of the weather, there were fewer tourists than usual for a Saturday. She saw one guide with a few people and one apparently waiting for something to do. Unless he was far at the other end or in the Lady Chapel or through the Norman nave, Tom wasn't there. She walked through, carefully looking as she reached those areas, satisfied; Tom was not at the Cathedral today.

She went to the shrine of Saint Etheldreda. Some of the candles were burning on the small rack. What had Ethel Fenman said about lighting candles at the time of prayer? The words returned to her mind. "It was like taking a little gift to a friend when you asked a favor. It was your response to the friend, not theirs to you. The prayers were heard and the friend or Saint you had asked would pray with you, but not because of the candle." How perceptive Ethel Fenman was; Fran missed her and longed to talk with her. Of course, she couldn't mention Tom and the problem. She had to abide by what he asked, but Ethel's presence would be a comforting thing to her now. She lit some of the candles and put an offering in the slot of the little box. For a long time, she stood, praying for Brendan, for Tom and his family and for herself. She looked at the statue of St. Etheldreda, asking the help of this saint in heaven. Silently, she told all she knew about the situation and that terrible things must be happening that she didn't know. She talked it all out, as she would have to Ethel, had she been free to do so. Deep within, a hope, a sense of trust replaced the worry and fear.

She lingered in the Cathedral, freer in spirit, to once again enjoy its great beauty. Walking toward the choir stalls, she saw a young man whom she had noticed with the tour group. He was standing, alone, looking up at the organ pipes. Turning, he glanced at everything around him. She couldn't help seeing the sadness on his face. Fran watched him as went back to the Octagon; he stood in the center, his head bent back for the longest time. He seemed to be staring at the center of the dome to the carving of Christ. Fran had walked closer to him, close enough to share a comment on the beauty of this place; but was sorry that she had invaded his privacy. When he lowered his head, there were obvious tears on his face. She said, "It is beautiful and overwhelming, isn't it?"

"Yes, yes, it truly is." Abruptly, he turned and walked quickly back to the West Doors. When he reached the doors, several people were standing in the back. He opened the doors and was struck with a gust of wind and pelting rain. A matronly looking woman said, "You can't go out in that, young man. We're all waiting it out. When it comes this hard, it won't be long."

Dylan Sanders stepped back in and walked toward the nave. Fran was coming back the aisle toward the door. "No use, Miss, it's a deluge out there," he said in a soft Irish voice.

"I had been debating about staying for Evensong. This makes up my mind." Fran turned to start down to the front. She looked at the man, "Have you ever been to Evensong? It's a beautiful service. Come up to the front; it's about to start."

He said nothing and Fran went on. Glancing back, he saw the people still waiting. He didn't want to stay, but he felt so tired. Chairs were now positioned in the front; for that reason alone, he went up to wait out the storm. He sat down in the back row of chairs. He closed his eyes; when he did, the carving of Christ that he had stared at so long was almost visible. When he opened his eyes, the young boys, in their red robes, were positioned in the stalls. As he watched and heard the innocence of these young voices, he was hoping for them that they would never know the hardness of heart that was his. He was hoping that they'd never have the miserable life he was living, hoping that they would never have the reason to feel as he had felt, since his childhood. Memories began to fill his mind of his school days. There had been a boy's choir in his parish church. He would have none of it; even though his Gram and Father Paul had always been on him about it. He *had* believed when he was little and went to church with his Mom. After she died, he didn't believe in anything. He had paid attention to religion classes in school so he'd get passing grades. That's all they meant. Through the growing years at school, he and Sean would not go to Mass. They couldn't stand the many sermons about forgiveness and peace and loving, even, our enemies. Sometimes, they would go into the back of the church after Mass so Father Paul would see them and think they had been there. There had been times he'd have to go with his Gram; then he'd take Communion so he wouldn't get in trouble with her or get Father Paul on him about that. He'd think of something else while receiving. They couldn't make him believe. Now, the words *unworthy reception*, *sacrilege* surfaced in his mind. He closed his eyes again. The thought of that carving of Christ was there as if he was still staring at it. He was remembering words that he had heard so long ago. They seemed connected with the picture in his mind. "For I have not come to call the just, but sinners." Was there hope for him? Was the belief so long denied really a part of him? This place! What was it about this place? Sean had asked what had happened to him. He couldn't explain it to himself, let alone to Sean.

The storm had abated by the time the service ended. Dylan Sanders left the Cathedral. He knew it wasn't just the name Michael Griffith that he had left back in Dublin. The person bearing that name was gone. He was wracked with mixed emotions and indecision.

Tom had been at the shop all day Saturday. He kept a lookout for anyone fitting the descriptions Brendan had given. But he had to give his assistant at the shop a break; he had taken over so completely while Tom was away. Tom planned to guide on Sunday and on all the afternoons of the coming week. He felt sure one of the three would be looking around the Cathedral. On Monday he would be talking with the local police. Tom was feeling sick about the letter to Fran. If only he had thought of some other way. When he was driving back, from London, the idea came to him too late. He could have called Don and Heidi and asked Heidi to pretend to be sick and in need of Fran's help in caring for Bryan. Fran wouldn't have refused. Heidi and Don would have agreed without knowing the details; knowing he would never have asked such a thing if it hadn't been extremely important. Now, it was too late. Fran probably had the letter. What was his precious one going through, because he had been so stupid? Why couldn't he have thought of this alternative before? Fran would have told him why—"He was just no good at lying." He simply wasn't a devious person and couldn't concoct falsehoods so easily. Of course, he couldn't know this and was suffering horribly at the thought of her unhappiness and at the thought of the loathing she must be feeling for him. All of this day and the next he was locked in a sadness such as he had never known before.

Chapter 34

—————➤●◄—————

Berniece and Cliff were returning from church on Sunday morning. "The boys are so down and so restless, Cliff, I've been thinking, we should take them to see something interesting, to help get their minds off the problem for a bit. I thought the British Museum might be nice. We could eat there, too. Or there's the Theatre Museum; the boys might really like that. What do you think?"

"I agree; we should find something for them to do. They're like dogs on a leash. I feel sorry for them and frankly, Berniece, they're getting on my nerves. I think your idea is a great one. Maybe we can talk them into it."

The flat was quiet; there was no sound from the telly. Cliff called, "Brendan, John."

Berniece went to the small room the boys were sharing; the door stood open. A quick glance showed her their belongings were gone. Cliff found a note on the table. "Oh, Cliff, they're gone. I don't mean out; I mean they're gone."

"I know, Berniece." He handed her the note.

Berniece pulled out a chair and sat to read it. She already felt weak with worry. "Cliff, we promised Tom we would make them stay. We shouldn't have gone off to church and left them alone."

"Now, Berniece, they are young, but they are grown men. We couldn't possibly have kept them here. Read the note."

Berniece sighed, "You're right, Cliff." She put on the glasses; she wore on a gold chain around her neck, and began to read.

254

Dear Uncle Cliff and Aunt Berniece,
We hate worrying two of the most wonderful people in the world.
You have been so kind to us and we can't begin to tell you how grateful
we are. We really have no choice but to go to Ely and try to help end this
horrible thing. We know Tom did what he thought best by not taking us;
but we truly have to do this. We have just enough money for bus fare and
will go to Tom when we arrive. He'll have to listen to us then. Again,
we had to do this. Please don't worry. We'll be in touch soon. Thanks is
a very little word, but we really mean it.

Love, Brendan and John

Berniece put the letter down and removed her glasses. She reached for a
paper napkin to wipe away the tears that were starting. "Don't worry, don't
worry, they say. Oh, Cliff, there's nothing we can do but worry."

"We can pray, Berniece. Now, try to think positive. Tom will be there
and in charge of things. The police will be aware. Maybe that Sean Devlin
won't even make it to Ely." Cliff was holding Berniece tightly in his arms and
trying to believe what he was saying.

Way before daybreak, Ronan was up and showing Richard his work
chart. "We're going straight across to Cardigan Bay and we'll be going into
the Port of Aberystwyth to arrange for mooring there for tonight. The cruiser
will stay there for a week. There is a small cove, a bit north, between Clarach
and Glan-y-nor. The depth seems good enough to anchor in for a short time.
This will be after dark. We'll be meeting Michael there and transferring
the bombs to his van. He'll drive inland a piece to Llangollen and stay at a
place there tonight. We will return to Aberystwyth and spend the night on
board. I'll pull up anchor in about fifteen minutes. The water isn't a great
depth here but I used the large storm anchor and it should be easy to break
away. It shouldn't give us any trouble." Sean returned to the cabin and pulled
out a drawer from under his bed. He removed a metal box and took out the
large amount of money he had stored in it. He put the notes in two pockets
attached to a canvas belt and tied it around his waist. It had been safe enough
while the cruiser was here; form now on he'd have to keep it on him.

Day was just breaking when *The Margo* was putting forth onto the open
sea. It was promising to be a calm and clear day, quite different from the
wind and rain of Saturday. The weather would be causing no problem.

Dylan Sanders spent a long and horrible night, in and out of restless sleep.
He tried desperately to stifle the guilt—to quiet the nagging conscience, to
erase the effect of his visit to the Cathedral. He'd have to be logical, these

feelings were not. He'd not let old superstitions or other people's sentimental piety overtake him at this time in his life. If he wanted life, he couldn't double-cross Sean. As for the Cathedral, it was only a building filled with art for art's sake, nothing more. There could be no more indecision. He wouldn't go to the police but start over for Sean as he had agreed.

It was very early in the morning, but he had to get away before another surge of doubt clouded his thinking. Dylan looked over his maps before going out to the van. Aberystwyth, on the west coast of Wales, seemed almost directly across the country from Ely. To take a route using all major roads would seem to take him out of the way. He chose to use some secondary roads as well as some local ones through smaller towns. With stopping to eat, he figured the drive would be at least seven hours. He'd go directly to Llangollen and check into his hotel. After that, while it was daylight, he'd drive to the coast to hunt for the likely cove near Glan-y-mor, where Sean wanted him to be, late that night. Sean had cruised around the area before and seemed to know what he was doing; but the directions, he had given on the phone, left something to be desired. Dylan folded the map and told himself it would be a hell of a lot easier to find the place in daylight. After finding it, he'd go back to the hotel and wait.

The day went as planned, except for one thing—his nagging conscience and doubts rode with him the entire way.

Driving to the small stretch of coast where the cove would have to be, he found only one where the depth of the water looked adequate for a boat the size of *The Paradise*. It would have to be brought close enough to unload. There was a short old wooden dock, probably used for fishing, which would help. It had become cold and the water looked bleak in the growing dusk. It was a desolate spot but it couldn't compare with the desolation he was feeling.

Alone in his hotel room the remembrance of his experience at Ely Cathedral completely possessed him. There was no pushing it from his mind, no turning back from the change that enveloped his spirit. He had made the wrong decision in coming for Sean. He couldn't go back to Ely now; there wasn't the money for enough petrol for the return. He had to get money from Sean for the expense of the hotel. There was no choice but to see it through. But once back in Ely, he'd go to the police. Even if it meant going to jail—or his life—he'd have to stop this madness. Instead of fear, he felt calmer, with a peace that he couldn't begin to fathom.

It was ten o'clock when Michael drove the van as far as possible on the soft, sandy beach. The cruiser was there, showing dim lights. Michael walked out on the dock, close to her. Even with the dim light the name *The Margo* was visible. He was surprised at that but knew, without doubt, it was *The*

Paradise. For a minute he was startled when an old man with gray hair and beard came into view. "Dear God! Sean."

"Who'd ye expect?"

Michael looked at Sean's bloated face. It looked mean and tired—and old, old beyond the color he had in his hair. He was thinking of this friend and the younger years; the time when Sean had another side, before he had allowed the hate filled part of him to completely dominate his being. Michael knew there would be no sharing his own change of heart with Sean—no convincing this man, maddened with hate. Michael felt a pity for him.

"Well, what the hell are you starin at? The rope ladder's over the side. Get up here. Pearse will get down and take them from us. Then, we'll carry them to the van."

When the containers with the bombs were carefully hidden in the van, Sean looked at Michael, "Dylan you've been very quiet through all this. I expected a bit of excitement about coming this far. What happened to the fun times? Come on board. We'll have a drink and a toast for a successful mission."

"I'm dead tired, Sean. It was a long drive—and a long day. I want to go back to the hotel. Oh, and you'll have to give me some money for that and for petrol to get back to Ely."

"I gave you a bundle. What the hell did you do with it?"

"Airline fare, van rental, large security for the house, among other necessary things. I wish I would have used it to get as far away from you and this mess as possible."

Sean's face was full of rage. "You've really shown your true colors, you damned coward." He hit Michael's face hard with the flat of his hand. Michael didn't retaliate in anyway. He calmly looked into Sean's eyes. Michael's expression was one of sadness and pity.

Sean had his hand in his pocket, about to remove the gun—but he didn't. He was held by Michael's stare. He was feeling confused and sickened. Anything close to a caring in his life had been for Michael. Michael had taken the place of his younger brother. Michael, whom he had made his ally for his cause, that special person that knew his need for revenge. Now, feeling this betrayal, Sean lost his look of rage and coldly said, "Michael, I'll not let anything stand in my way. You and that damned bastard Pearse had better pull it together if you want to remain on planet Earth. Tomorrow morning, at nine, park at the Marine Hotel. Don't go in. We're staying aboard tonight but we'll be there to leave. How much will the hotel bill be?"

Michael told him.

"Do you have petrol to get back to Aberystwyth in the morning?"

"Yes, but we'll have to stop soon on the way back."

Sean gave him just enough money for the hotel and a small breakfast. He turned and started up the rope ladder. *"Be there, Michael."*

Michael returned to the van, thinking of the monstrous things that were behind him as he drove. Pearse had told him they had special safety devices and that he was keeping the detonator with him. Still, Michael felt the worry. He parked the van at the far end of the lot as far away from the hotel and other cars as possible. "Dear God," he said as he locked the van, "don't let people be hurt by this." He stood looking up at the star filled sky and realized that was the first prayer from his heart since childhood. His guilt for being part of this thing was crushing. Yet, with all the change within him and his resolve to end this horror, he couldn't bring himself to end it this night. Clinging to a vain hope that he might find another way, he couldn't summon the courage to contact the authorities here at Llangollen.

Tom had asked to guide at the Cathedral on Sunday afternoon. He searched each face he saw for anyone resembling the description of Sean, Pearse, or Michael. He stayed for Evensong and stood near the back of the chairs to study all attending. No one had been there that day, he was sure. He left the Cathedral, thinking he should go somewhere for dinner; but eating alone, without his Fran, was not appealing. Actually he didn't feel hungry at all. There was a coffeepot and some snack food at his room over the shop; that would do for tonight. He walked the few blocks to his shop; it was in the middle of a block. When he reached the corner, he saw in the dusk two figures standing in the doorway. He thought he should turn back but went a little closer. He then knew who was there and hurried toward them. "Didn't I ask you to stay in London?" Brendan and John's tense looks gave way to smiles when they saw Tom's grin as he took hold of their heads and mockingly bumped them together. "What am I going to do with you?" Tom was serious then. "I'm not angry. I guess I respect you both for wanting to be here and help with this thing. Have you had your dinner?"

"No," John spoke up. "All our money was spent on bus fare. We've been here for a good while. We haven't eaten since early this morning, before we left."

"I haven't had anything since this morning either." Tom was glad they had come. Frankly, it was good not to be alone. "I'm starved too. We'll get in the car and drive to a restaurant by the river. We'll get some real food. The only thing upstairs is a bit of cheese and some biscuits."

As they enjoyed dinner, Tom reported that he was absolutely sure none of the three were at the Cathedral that day. They made plans to go together to the local police the next morning. After dinner, Tom got Brendan and John settled in a hotel. They wanted to stay in his small room. "We'll sleep on blankets on the floor, Tom." Brendan argued, "I don't want you to have the expense of a hotel."

Tom said, "If you are seen at the shop, it might put my shop, or worse, my staff in danger. Even with me I'm worried about that. With you there the risk would be greater if Sean did come around. One of those bombs might find its way there." Brendan and John saw that logic and agreed about the hotel.

Back in his room, a very tired Tom was feeling a little more relaxed. He was glad that the guys had come. It took his mind off the situation with Fran for a short while. After the sleepless night before and the long day that had ensued, sleep came easily.

Chapter 35

—Monday—

Tom opened the shop; he had to stay until eleven o'clock when Henry would be there to take over. He had told the boys to meet him at the police station at eleven-thirty. There were a few customers and he had calls to refill prescriptions but the morning seemed to be dragging. The early post came and Tom began sorting the mail. The fifth piece of mail was a very pale peach colored envelope. The writing was Fran's. Tom held it for a few moments, dreading to open it; thinking of how she must despise him. Slowly he slit the envelope and unfolded the peach colored paper. He was stunned at her salutation and sat down on his stool behind the counter. He continued to read.

Darling Tom,

I don't believe a word of the letter I received this morning. You, my dearest, are a man of many talents, many abilities. However, there is one thing you are not at all good at—the questionable art of lying, even in a letter. The silliest line in the letter was "you thought you knew me." Tom, I <u>do</u> know you! That is a fact. For a short while, I was hysterical and stunned. Then, I knew it just couldn't be.

I know I'm not wrong in my conclusion that something horrible is continuing with Brendan's problem. For some reason, even at the risk of sacrificing yourself in my eyes and causing me pain, you felt you had to keep me away from it. You must believe that to do this, I have to be kept away from you. I wish with all my heart that you would let me be with you in this worry, whatever it is. I love you so deeply and want to share with you, "for better or for worse," even before we marry. (No, Silly, I'm not giving back the ring.) Seriously, Dear Tom, I will respect your wishes and won't be in touch. Of course, I'll talk to no one of this. I hope you

260

will change your mind and will allow me the right to know whatever devastating thing is happening in your life. I'm not afraid for me, as you must be. I'm so afraid for you. Whatever is wrong, it must be terrible.

Maybe I can only help by doing as you asked. You surely know I'd do anything in God's world for you. All I can do now is be patient and pray. I love you so.

Forever, Your Fran

He read and reread the letter. How could he have thought the Fran he knew so well wouldn't see through that stupid lie? Yes, they were really one in spirit, so close, so beautifully close. She, indeed, knew him so well. He felt weak with relief, happier than he thought he had a right to be. He vowed never to hurt her again. Total honesty still couldn't come, but he was grateful that she accepted the need to wait without questioning. They must keep apart until this was over. She had to be kept safe.

He wrote an answer at once. Every line of this letter showed the real Tom, Fran's Tom. From the depth of his being, his love flowed in every line. How he longed to see that precious face and hold her in his arms. Knowing she was waiting with love for him and understanding was so much more than he had hoped for. Dear God, please let this soon be over, he fervently prayed.

Tom and the boys met at the police station. Tom and Constable Dixon greeted each other warmly. They had known each other well for over a year. They told Constable Gerald Dixon everything and all that Scotland Yard had done about the situation. He was horrified at the thought of Ely Cathedral being in danger of a terrorist attack. "You think it likely, if they get over, for the action to be this Friday night; after the preparation for the harvest weekend. People are usually about the Cathedral all that evening. There are the animal stalls to be positioned and the animals to be brought in, and of course, the fall decorations. There would be no way anything could be hidden in the decorations before."

"No," Brendan said, "not now. No one in the group is helping with them. That was supposed to be my job. But it won't stop Devlin trying to go through with his plan to blow up the place. The very fact that he can't be found is a sure sign that he's planning to try somehow. He really has become a madman, totally focused on his revenge."

"You feel he will try to have revenge on you too, Brendan? If he is like you say, he probably will. It would be wiser if you stayed out of sight. We will be on top of this. We haven't a big staff; Ely is a small town. Not much goes on here. We do have patrols and we'll follow up on everything and have a large guard around the Cathedral on Friday. Tom, I think your idea is a good one, to be a guide during this week. You might just spot them. At least one of them will be seeing the place before. Hopefully, we can get a lead and stop this before the involvement is inside of the Cathedral."

Brendan said, "John and I would know them. Tom might not. He knows only their descriptions. We should stay at the Cathedral, too."

"No, I don't want that and I'm sure the Bishop wouldn't. With this man having a personal revenge toward you, he might try to kill you on the spot. We want to avoid desecrating the Cathedral. He probably wouldn't try anything on Tom, there. Tom, don't wear your name pin; tell the groups only your middle name. That way, none of the rotters would know you were Brendan's brother. Call right away if you think any of them show up. Brendan, I still think it better if you and John aren't around, even outside the Cathedral. Of course, I can't stop you. But don't go inside."

Tom said, "I think that's a good idea, Jerry. You might ask at hotels; I don't think, though, they would stay at one nearby."

"I'll be checking anyway and I'll give descriptions at petrol stations and a few other places. The patrols will be on a constant lookout. With this being a place of so many tourists, it would just be luck if we got an early lead. But it will be stopped. We wouldn't let it happen." Jerry Dixon looked at Brendan. "I'm glad you escaped from Devlin with your life, Brendan, for your sake and the sake of your family, but also, that you could warn us in time to stop such a terrible thing."

"Jerry," Tom asked, "Are you going to tell the Bishop and alert anyone else at the Cathedral?"

"Not just yet, Tom. I'll wait a little. I want to catch those terrorists. They might panic at the Cathedral and close it to the public; it might just prolong this action of Devlin's. I'll be in touch with the Yard immediately. I wonder that they didn't notify me. I guess, with Interpol not coming up with anything concrete the Yard felt the plan hadn't progressed and Devlin wouldn't be showing up here. You said there was an ongoing lookout for *The Paradise* and personnel checking at the airports. Hopefully, something has turned up." He looked at his notes. "You haven't been in touch with the Yard since last Thursday, right?"

"Right, Jerry, but I think I'd have heard from them through my uncle in London, had there been any news."

Jerry Dixon got up from his desk. "Well, we'll do the best we can here and be in contact with you, Tom. I know you will call us at the least thing."

Michael met Sean and Pearse at the Marine Hotel as planned. Sean got into the back of the van so he could watch both of them. He still didn't trust them. With both of them wanting out of the caper, he was starting to fear for his life; he kept the gun on his lap during the long drive.

The morning was gray and chilly when they left Aberystwyth. Sean growled, "Remember, if we stop I'm Ronan Farrell and you are Richard Farrell my son, Pearse. We are with Dylan Sanders. Don't let it slip."

Dylan looked at Pearse and grinned. "*Son*? He looks old enough to be your grandfather."

"Shut up, you damned bastards could make anyone look old. What happened to the good times?"

Dylan said, "These aren't good times, Sean. Just shut up yourself."

Despite the gun on his lap and the tension he felt, the ongoing silence and the motion of the car caused Sean to sleep some of the way.

"How the hell did we get into this mess, Pearse? I can't go back to Dublin. Maybe you'll never be able to go back. Sean fed me the desire for vengeance for a lot of years; I bought it. I've seen things differently, but far too late. How did you get involved?"

"Money, Michael, it started with the need for money." Pearse told Michael all about Sean's first approach to him and what Sean was holding over him. It was good to talk with someone. He missed Denis and talking of normal things. He found himself telling Michael about his boyhood, his family and what caused his life to go so bad. "It's too late for me, too, Michael."

Michael said, "It's never too late for a change inside, Pearse." He was thinking, it's not too late to stop this thing. By God, I'm going to try.

They drove to the house by a route not taking them through the town of Ely. When they reached the house, Sean looked around. "You've had it nice here, Dylan, while I've had to go through all sorts of things to keep the plans moving ahead. No wonder you're getting soft, playing the 'English gentleman.'"

Michael didn't respond to Sean's gibe. "I got groceries in that will be enough for several days. If you want anything cooked, you'll have to do it. I did the driving."

Sean said, "Give me the van keys. I'll be in charge of where it goes." Michael tossed Sean the keys. "Is there another set?"

"No Sean, the rental gives you only one. Don't lose it."

Pearse was looking into the fridge and cupboards. "I'll cook, Michael, you know, that's one thing I've always liked to do."

Sean sneered, "Yeah, Richard, you're good at putting things together."

Pearse ignored Sean and his double-meaning comment, and said, "Michael, I think had I been better directed as a lad, I might have become a chef. What a nice life that would have been. You shopped well, Michael. We're well stocked."

Sean sneered again and left the room.

Pearse cooked noodles and made a sauce with milk, cream cheese, onions, flaked tuna, and pimento stuffed green olives. He layered the noodles and sauce with good Munster cheese and put freshly toasted buttered crumbs on top. It was wonderful to be doing something normal. When it was baked and they were eating, Sean lost his sneer.

"Maybe you should have been a chef, Richard; this is one of the best damn things I ever tasted."

Michael said, "It is truly delicious, Pearse."

Pearse took a second helping, "well, that's one thing we all agree on."

Sean returned to his annoying self during the evening. Michael had said he had been to the Cathedral but had no information to give of the entrances that would be more accessible for them to use. He had no practical details needed for the plan.

When Sean went to the bedroom he'd use alone, he asked for the key.

"There aren't keys to any of the inside doors, Sean." Michael got the message. Sean didn't feel safe with them. Michael looked at Sean and calmly said, "I'm not a murderer. I don't kill sleeping men."

Pearse said, "I might like to but what would I do with your stinking body? If I did, it would probably backfire on me—as everything always has in my life. Of course, if you want to feel safe, you could lock yourself in the van. It gets damned cold at night, though. Then too, the bombs are there and I have the detonator."

Sean slammed the bedroom door and Pearse and Michael heard him dragging the heavy furniture to hold it shut.

Clarke Ogdan, after a restless night, sat at his desk in his Interpol Office. He was investigating other cases and had been extremely busy since his check at the old cottage. Yet, on this Monday morning he couldn't get this Sean Devlin thing and Ely out of his mind. His concern for this had been the reason for his troubled sleeping. He had been raised in Cambridge and visited Ely many times; there were many fond memories of the place and the Cathedral.

There had been no sightings of *The Paradise* or of Devlin's car license—nothing more of any of them. If Devlin's plans were working out, Friday night was to be the attack. Ogdan had been told not to spend more time on such a sketchy thing. With only the word of informants to go on, there couldn't be an all out manhunt; Ogdan would be wasting his time. Still the thoughts came, all were missing, Devlin, O'Neill and Griffith. They were still gone from their jobs and homes. He had checked that out again. Deciding to take it as his own responsibility, he requested the news services to do a missing person bulletin on the three, giving their descriptions.

The bulletin was aired that evening. Tess Bailey was curled up on the sofa with Joe, helping him with his spelling homework. Phil was on the floor, being pounced on by Cathey and Danny. Phil left out a grunt, "Careful, Cathey, you're a bit heavier than Danny." She giggled and started pulling his hair. The telly was on with no one paying attention to it. Suddenly, Tess said, "Quiet."

A missing person's bulletin had come on the news. The first listed was a Michael Griffith from Dublin. The second was a Pearse O'Neill from Belfast and the third was Sean Devlin from Dublin. The description of each was given, but no other details. A number was given to call if anyone had information on any of these men.

Joe had been listening as had Tess and Phil. "That's not our Mr. Devlin is it, Mom? He was here. He's not missing."

"Probably not, Joe. Don't worry about it. Mr. Devlin was here, so it couldn't be him. Now, run along and get ready for bed. Your spelling is all finished."

Tess joined Phil who had quietly gone into the kitchen. "You do think it's him, don't you Phil? It certainly was his description. It didn't say he was actually being hunted for any reason. Do you think he's connected to the other two?"

"I'm sure it's him, Tess. Sean called the guy with him Richard Farrell. However, I had forgotten that when I went down to the boat he called him Pearse, once. Sean gave me a story about Pearse being his name but that most people called him Richard, his middle name. I do think Richard Farrell is Pearse O'Neill."

"The bulletin said Pearse O'Neill had long hair and a beard. That would be easily changed. You are going to call that number, aren't you, dear? Do you think their families are worried about them?"

"No, Sean Devlin has no family around that I know of. I don't know about the others, but I don't think it has a thing to do with their families. If the reason is a serious one for their being hunted, they could be traced here; that worries me. I don't want to be held for being a part of something. Devlin's van is still here. I'm sure the cruiser was noticed while it was moored here. That Margo bit, I'm sure, was a crock. There is some lowdown reason *The Paradise* became *The Margo*."

"Phil, I agree, we haven't any choice. We have to call. I didn't catch the number. Did you?"

"No, I was too shocked. I'll call the station and get it."

Tess went to check on the children. When she had them tucked in, she came back to the kitchen. Phil said he had gotten through to an answering service and a call would be returned shortly. Even as they talked, the phone rang.

Clarke Ogdan asked, "Are you the gentleman who called concerning the missing person bulletin?"

"Yes, and to whom am I speaking?"

"This is Clarke Ogdan of Interpol. Please give me your name, Sir, and any information you might have on the whereabouts of any of the people mentioned."

At hearing the word 'Interpol', Phil shut his eyes, then, looked at Tess with an expression of, 'it's worse than we thought.' He took a deep breath and answered. "This is Philip Bailey from Wexford. Can you tell me what this is about, Mr. Ogdan? Is Sean Devlin in serious trouble?"

"I'm sorry I can't give you the details, Mr. Bailey; he may or may not be. Some questions have been raised about a situation of importance. We would like to be in touch and talk with Sean Devlin or the other men. Do you know where they are right now?"

"No, the last I saw Devlin and O'Neill, was on Saturday. It's a long story. I don't know Michael Griffith."

"Are you a close friend of Devlin's or a relative?"

"No, I'm not a relative—and I couldn't say I'm a close friend."

"Mr. Bailey, would it be terribly inconvenient for you to see me tonight? It would run late; it's about a two hour drive. I really would like to talk with you."

"That would be all right, Mr. Ogdan." Phil gave the directions to his house.

Tess and Phil spent a tense evening. Tess tried without much success to concentrate on knitting a sweater. Phil tried, intermittently, reading or watching the telly. Frequently they would find themselves back at the speculation of what it was that Sean was involved in—why he was being hunted by Interpol.

It was late when they heard the knock. Clarke Ogdan showed his identification to Phil. Phil's demeanor and the sincere graciousness that was a natural part of Tess's character impressed him. Being a good judge of personalities, he knew immediately that these were good people. He could trust what they would tell him and be trusted with any information he would give.

He thanked them but refused the refreshments he had been offered. "You said on the phone, Mr. Bailey, that your recent association with Devlin was a 'long story.'" He took out a notebook and briefly reviewed its contents.

"If you start at the beginning and mention anything you might know, even if it seems trivial, I would appreciate it.

Phil did as he asked. Starting, with knowing Sean years ago, in Dublin; and the surprising call after many years of not being in touch. He told everything he could remember from the first visit and of the late night arrival for the second stay. Tess and Phil recalled each detail of their encounters with Sean and Pearse and their personal reactions to them.

"We have had a watch for *The Paradise*. No wonder she wasn't seen," Ogdan said, when he learned of the name change.

Tess said how sure she was that there was no Margo in Sean's life. "He only wanted *The Paradise* to have a different name."

When they had covered everything, he checked his notes and dates. Ogdan said, "The call to you, from Sean Devlin, was on the day I started looking for him. He had to have had an informant. It had to be an old man from the dock Devlin used for *The Paradise*."

Phil asked, "Couldn't you give us an idea of what this is all about? Is it drug running?"

"No, that's not the trouble. Scotland Yard informed us that Devlin might be planning a terrorist attack at a site in England. The story was told to them by two men, not much more than lads. Devlin had tried to entice them to be a part of his hate group. They had backed away even before knowing the seriousness of his plan for revenge. The Yard took it to be important but as Devlin and the others weren't part of an official group, and nothing had actually been done; they allowed only a small amount of time and money for investigation. Nothing has turned up since the first thrust, but it's worried me. I took it upon myself to do the missing person bulletin. Now, with this new information from you, there will be a greater intensity to the investigation. You said, Devlin tried to be friendly and appreciative of your kindness; but if for some reason, and it's not likely, he shows up here again—don't let him know you were in touch with us. He mustn't think you know a thing. I think he is really a man maddened by his desire for revenge. He could be dangerous to you or your family, if he thought you knew." Clarke Ogdan picked up the framed picture of the three smiling children. "Don't let them out of your sight until this is resolved."

Tess put her hand to her mouth and said, with a voice choked with emotion, "Oh, Dear God, I won't"

Phil shook his head, "I can't believe I was so stupid, so taken in, and helped them get away."

Clarke felt deeply sorry for them. "Don't blame yourself in any way. You were dealing with a devious, cunning person. People who aren't that way have a hard time recognizing it in others. I really don't think he'll be back. I didn't want to worry you more. I just want you and your children to be safe. As for his getting his van, that would be after the fact. We'll have him before then, rest assured."

Before leaving, he said, "I'll be in touch when I know anything to put your mind at ease. I'm sure it will be soon." He gave them a warm smile and closed the door.

Phil and Tess held each other closely in silence, hoping to comfort one another with a sense of relief that never came.

Chapter 36

—*Tuesday*—

On Tuesday morning, Cliff and Berniece were at Paddington Station anxiously awaiting Susanna's arrival on the express from Heathrow. They had wanted to go to the airport to meet her plane but Susanna was insistent; taking the express would make it easier on them and wasn't trouble for her. It had been well over a year since they had seen each other. There was much joy in this reunion.

Berniece and Cliff were both concerned when they saw her. Her still beautiful face showed the signs of strain. Susanna was always slender but now, she was extremely thin. Her smart looking, woolen suite hung much too loosely on her thin frame.

On the short ride to the flat, Berniece sat in the back so she and Susanna could talk. Susanna reached over and squeezed her hand. "It's so good to be with you two; I've really needed this. Being alone with the worry has become unbearable. When I first decided to come over, I thought I'd be seeing Brendan here. Tom called me and said Brendan and John are with him in Ely. I wanted to go there but Tom said I absolutely must not come. He sounded tense and didn't say much beyond that. The call was a short one. Berniece, do you know what is going on? Please, please tell me if you do."

"We're almost home, Susanna dear, we'll get you settled in and have some lunch. We'll have lots of time to talk."

Berniece and Cliff kept the talk light during lunch. They reminisced about their young lives in the Yorkshires. Susanna enjoyed talking about Jody with them. "This is the first food I've enjoyed since Matt, Tom, and Fran visited me."

Cliff said, "I'm glad to hear that, girl." He grinned, "With Berniece's good cooking, you'll get a little weight back on."

Berniece winked at Susanna, "I'm certainly going to try."

"Having the good cooking and the beautiful company, I'll try to cooperate. I've been pinning over every skirt I own." Susanna started to help clear the table.

Berniece followed Cliff into the living room. "Do you think we should tell Susanna all we know? Cliff, I do. She pleaded with me to tell her."

"You don't think she'll worry more?"

"Cliff, I don't think she could worry more." Berniece returned to the kitchen. She and Susanna chatted while they did the dishes. "Susanna, has Father Matt called since he went back to the States?"

"Yes, frequently, he is such a dear person. He sometimes calls me Mom. We are very close. Also, I've gotten some calls from the young girl Anne Quinn. The Quinn family took care of Brendan when he was so sick."

"Oh yes, I know, Susanna. In fact, the boys mentioned them, a lot, when they were here. They talked about a Doctor Tim Madden and Nurse Amy McGill. They must be fine people." Berniece chuckled a little, "John talked of Anne quite a bit and said how pretty and sweet she is. I got the feeling he is kind of 'sweet' on her."

Susanna smiled, "I think the feeling is mutual. She seemed particularly interested in news about John. I had none to give except that he was safe in England with relatives. I know she wanted to write to him but no one was to know exactly where they were. Berniece, please tell me what it's all about. You do know, don't you?"

"Come into the living room, Susanna. Cliff and I will tell you everything." Nothing was held back. Susanna was told of the early involvement with "the friends" and Brendan's horrible days of being Sean's prisoner and the details of his narrow escape. Susanna's body shook and tears streamed down her face as Cliff described that time. Berniece sat on the sofa beside her and put a comforting arm around her. Cliff told of how Brendan found out the terrible thing that was being planned and all that had taken place since then. Now, Susanna knew why Tom didn't want her at Ely. She gave an understanding nod, "I am sure that Tom told Fran not to write or call. She had wanted me to visit; then her calls and notes stopped. I was puzzled and a little hurt. Fran had seemed so warm and loving toward me. Oh, that poor girl—what must she be going through?"

Susanna stood and paced the room, almost screaming the words, "I'm going to Ely. I'll stay at a hotel but I'll see them and be with them."

Cliff put his hands firmly on her shoulders. He calmly but firmly said, "*No*, Susanna, you are not to go to Ely. Tom is seeing the police there. They will be on top of everything. Your going would make more of a problem and much more worry for all the boys. Tom is not going near Fran. He is trying to keep her apart from all of this. Devlin, from all we know, is mad with revenge toward the English and anyone who crosses him. The danger is real but you can't stop it. You being there would make things more complex. You are not going."

Susanna looked at Cliff's mouth set firm and the tender anxiety in his eyes. She nodded and softly said, "You're right, Cliff. You are absolutely right. I'll calm down"

"You've a right not to feel calm, but I'm relieved you'll listen to reason." He gave her a hug.

Berniece took her hands. "Susanna, maybe we shouldn't have told you. Our thoughts are so consumed by it. I don't think we could have pretended any longer."

"I needed to know. Knowing it all doesn't make the worry worse than it has been. I'm grateful to God that my Brendan is not a part of this man's hateful plan. I'm in agony over the danger he and Tom are in, but it would be unbearable for me if Brendan was a part of this terrible revenge. We'll just have to pray and trust. I'm with you and that helps."

Michael was drinking his morning coffee and thinking. Sean would probably go to the Cathedral to see, for himself, what was needed. He hoped it would be soon, Sean had the van keys and there was no way he could get them and drive off himself. The walk to Ely would be a long one but if it proved necessary, he'd do it. Surely, Sean would go in soon; once there, it would be easy to give him the slip and go to the police. That was not to be today.

That morning, Sean had run from his bedroom and directly to the bathroom. He emerged, glowering at Pearse and Michael. "What the hell was in that food you cooked last night, O'Neill? I'm sicker than a dog." He looked even more bloated and his skin had a yellow cast.

"Michael and I ate the same food, Devlin. We're fine. Could it have been the full bottle of whiskey you took to your bedroom last night? How much is left?"

Sean didn't answer and once again barricaded himself in the bedroom. Picking up the bottle, he saw it contained about an inch. "*Hell*, he thought, I often drank that much and more. It never used to make me sick—but lately, it seems to be doing me in a bit." This time, though, was the worst. He still felt sick and had real pain; it hadn't been that bad ever. He threw himself back across the bed and eventually fell into another deep sleep. It was late afternoon when he woke; too late to get to the Cathedral. He came out of his room to the smell of spaghetti sauce cooking; to him it was sickening. "I'll not be eating anymore of your damned cooking, Pearse."

"No one said you have to, Sean. Get your own grub."

Much later that evening, Sean fixed, for himself, toast; his hand shook when he poured hot milk over it.

Early that morning, Clarke Ogdan had informed Interpol and Scotland Yard of the latest development. There was a watch on the water for *The Margo*. Requests were sent to the ports along the West Coast of England and Wales. If nothing showed there the ports of the south and east would be notified.

Clarke Ogdan was out of his office until mid-afternoon. When he returned, there was a fax waiting for him. A report had come in from a port at Aberystwyth. *The Margo* was in dock there. The rent had been paid for a week. The man who arranged for it was a Ronan Farrell. He was traveling with his son Richard Farrell. The papers for *The Margo* seemed to be valid as was identification for Ronan Farrell. The younger man, the son, had misplaced his, but as they were going to stay on board the night they docked; the promise to locate it and show it in the morning was accepted. After arrangements had been made, Farrell took *The Margo* out and returned late that night. Ronan Farrell didn't fit the description of Sean Devlin, other than being a large man. Ronan Farrell, according to his identification was older. His appearance, as remembered by the people who had dealt with him, was of a much older man with gray hair and beard and wearing glasses. All about him seemed much older than a man in his thirties. Richard Farrell was remembered as young and good looking with black short hair. Possibly fitting the description of Pearse O'Neill. Only two men were seen. Neither Ronan nor Richard Farrell had been seen all of Monday or Monday night. There was no one aboard when *The Margo* was checked on before the report was received. Following the report, a thorough search was made but nothing of a suspicious nature was found on board.

"Damn," Ogdan said. Of course, it's Devlin and O'Neill. They were in Ely by now or on their way. He contacted his home office and Scotland Yard; both had been informed of the report from Aberystwyth. There was no question in anyone's minds that it was Devlin and O'Neill, despite the disguise and phony papers. It was agreed that Griffith had to already be in the country and, no doubt, met them on Sunday evening to unload the bombs from *The Margo*. Probably they traveled to Ely together.

When the official business was finished, Clarke phoned the Bailey home. He hung up feeling the first bit of lightness that day. The relief in Tess's voice, when he told her Devlin was no where close to Wexford, seemed to make all his efforts worth while. Her sincerity, when she spoke of her concern for the people of Ely and the Cathedral, was good to remember. There were nice people out there, people like Phil and Tess. Sometimes it was hard to remember that; with a job like his where he was always thinking of rotten scum like Devlin.

Constable Dixon was at his desk, drinking a cup of hot, strong tea, when the phone rang. Sergeant Crosby was calling from Scotland Yard. "Constable Dixon, I want to discuss some new information we just received concerning the threat to bomb Ely Cathedral." He described in detail all that was now known. "I have two questions; have you come up with anything there? Do you think you need anyone sent up from here?"

"No, we haven't come up with a thing. We might need someone; I'm not sure. Give me another day or two." He explained all the moves they were making, "I'll keep you updated if anything gives us a lead. I appreciate your direct interest, Sergeant."

Jerry Dixon put down the phone. He tipped back in his swivel chair and put his feet on his desk. This was his best thinking position. Having heard this latest information, he felt sure they were in Ely now. In Ely—but where? He had hotels checked over a large radius, also petrol stations. The patrols were on constant lookout and had thoroughly checked any abandoned buildings or shacks. He'd have them hit every place again. The old descriptions had been given; that would have to be updated, also the names they were using now. Of course, there could be another change in appearance. There were so many vans, with plates from all over. He'd order the patrols to stop any van whose occupants, even vaguely, resembled the descriptions. This was only Tuesday; he still wanted to keep trying before alarming anyone at the Cathedral.

He picked up his cup and started to sip; he looked at the cup as if it was at fault, blimey—how he hated cold tea.

Once all the directives were set in motion, he left the station and headed toward the Cathedral. He found Tom standing near the entrance. The tours were finished for the day; it was almost time for Evensong. "Have you found anyone you suspect today, Tom?"

"Jerry. I'd have called, if I would have. There were only a few people today. We had a busload of tourists, mostly Americans. There were a few older women from a garden club. I'm sure none of the three were here. I'll be here till the doors are locked and then tomorrow all day."

"I have some new information, Tom." Jerry updated him on everything, giving him the new descriptions. "I don't know anything about Michael Griffith—no new description. He probably met them and is with them."

"I'm sure, as you are, that they are in Ely now. As I said, I'll be here all day tomorrow."

"Be careful, Tom, and be in touch at the least suspicion. Try to get Brendan and John to stay holed up at the hotel."

"All I can do is try, and of course I will." After the service, Tom met Brendan and John. They had spent the day walking the area and the grounds. They readily agreed with Tom's suggestion of a dinner at a nearby pub.

Chapter 37

—————

Fran spent the last few days in ceaseless activity. She had shopped and chosen the furniture. It would be delivered this Wednesday morning. All the curtains and drapes were hung throughout the flat. Her letters to Fred and Susan Hendemer and to Dean and Marion Ratchford were mailed. Now, she could remember them as just the dear people who were so kind to her. She was truly fond of them and wanted to be in touch. The time was past when thinking of them brought only the bitter thoughts of Jeff to her mind.

Fran had called Heidi on Tuesday. Heidi said Don and she talked about coming to Ely to see her and Tom on the coming Saturday. Heidi laughed, when she said "Don wanted me to ask you, 'when were you going to cook him that dinner you promised'?"

Fran longed to see them; it was hard saying a visit would have to be put on hold. "Tom's so involved right now and won't be here. I'll talk with you next week; maybe, we can plan then."

Heidi hung up feeling a little disappointed. She thought of the call throughout the day. When Don came home, Heidi said, "Fran called, she sounded bright and happy talking about her shopping for furniture—a little too bright—a bit put on. It doesn't suit for us to go this weekend."

"Fran often sounds bright and happy, why would she put it on?—Why can't we go, this weekend?"

"That's just it, Don. When I said about coming, Fran's voice changed, she sounded a little tense. She quickly said Tom was involved and wouldn't be there and that she'd call and *maybe* see us the next weekend. She seemed in such a hurry to say goodbye. I have a feeling something is wrong. Fran didn't go on about 'her precious Tom' as she usually does or didn't say anything about wedding plans. We usually talk a little about that, too."

"Hon, you're probably reading more into things than you should; Fran could have been busy. As for Tom, he does have a business—three shops to see to."

"I don't think Fran was that busy. She made the call to me. Tom doesn't have much to do with the London shop now, from what Fran said, a while back. Oh, Don, I hope Tom and Fran aren't having a fight."

"I really don't think so, Heidi. That would surprise me almost as much as our having a fight." Before she could say more, he planted a firm kiss on her mouth—"and that, My Darling, isn't at all likely." Don looked thoughtful, "Heidi, has Fran said anything about the problem Tom's brother had? When they were here, I remember, Tom was worried about him. He didn't go into details; I had the feeling he didn't know exactly what was wrong at the time. Do you think that could be what Tom is involved in, trying to get Brendan— isn't that his name?—straightened out."

Heidi said, "Yes, Brendan—that's his name. You might be right, Don. Fran has never talked about the trouble at all. Come to think of it, that seems odd. I had forgotten about it all together. Well, I hope it is something beside Tom and Fran having trouble between them. I remember what Fran has been through; I wouldn't want to see her hurt again."

"Heidi, stop worrying. Tom Hart is head over heels in love with Fran. He'd never do anything to hurt her. I'm sure of that. There is one thing I'd like you to worry about," he said, seriously.

"What, Don?"

"Dinner," he grinned. "I'm starved."

At that moment, the youngest member of the household became very vocal, letting them know Don wasn't the only one that was starved.

Michael woke to the sound of cupboard doors being banged in the kitchen. Sean was feeling better but shaky. His hands had trembled when he tried to light a cigarette. He growled when he saw Michael in the doorway. "I've looked in every cupboard; I need a drink. You said you got supplies. Where'd you put the liquor?"

"You drank the bottle the other night, Sean. There's a little red wine in the fridge. We had some with dinner last night. There isn't anything else."

"Damn it to Hell! I need a drink, not that water you call wine."

Michael started to make coffee. "What you need is some food and coffee."

"I know what I need. Don't take forever with your damned breakfast. You and Pearse get moving. We're going in to get the layout of the Cathedral. Since you were on holiday," Sean sneered, "and didn't bother getting what was needed." Sean stormed out of the kitchen.

Sean went into his bedroom. He dressed in his old man clothes, transferring his gun from his robe pocket to the pocket of the long gray sweater. His hands shook as he combed gray hairspray through his hair and beard.

Sean walked through the house, impatiently waiting for Michael and Pearse to get ready. He found a little guidebook in the den on Ely. He studied the map on the book. He went over it with Michael and Pearse, trying to judge the distance from the parking lot to the Cathedral. "I'll look around the outside and see how close we can get with the van. Today, we'll park in that lower lot down from Broad Street. You two will go inside and hunt for the best entrance to use. It'll have to be opened from the inside. Michael that will be your job. You'll have to find a place to hide before the place is closed on Friday. It shouldn't be hard to keep out of sight in a place like that."

Michael knew that he had to gain Sean's trust, if he was going to get away from him. He said enthusiastically, "Yeah, there are so many side altars and alcoves; I have an idea already. I did spend a good bit of time there. Hiding shouldn't be a problem. The main thing today is finding the door that will be closest to the van. You're right, Sean, it will probably be bolted from inside: I'll have to be there."

His own excitement was carrying Sean away. He readily thought that Michael was feeling the same. "Sometime after midnight, you will open the door. Pearse and I will carry the bombs and gasoline and place them. We'll all get the hell back to the van and drive as far as we can—and still have the detonator work. Then, we will simply drive back here. No one will ever know. We've covered our tracks good. We'll lay low here for a while and stay out of sight. Dylan Sanders has a right to be here."

Sean smiled in arrogant confidence. "Yes, they'll never know. I've outsmarted the stupid English. What do you think, Michael, will it work? It's good to hear a bit of excitement from you."

"It's a great plan, Sean. I had been a little tired but now that it's so close—we've wanted this a long time—might as well enjoy it."

Pearse was quiet through all of this. Michael's response to Sean was very surprising to him. In fact, it wasn't at all believable.

Sean looked hard at Pearse. "You've had nothing to say. Do you have anything to add?"

"Sean, do you really believe that no one will be around watching the Cathedral? Do you remember that Brendan has informed about 'your plan'? Do you remember that there was a search for us?"

"Yes, damn you; I remember what the goddamned sneak did. But I've outfoxed them. They couldn't be knowing we're here. As I said, we've covered our tracks well. I thought out everything. They won't be spendin time and money with nothin to go on. If anyone is around the place, I'll take care of them." His pudgy hand moved to his pocket. Confidence was being replaced by agitation and his hands were shaking. "Now, Pearse, getting back to the plan, do you have anything to say?"

"Not really, Sean. The main thing is being able to get close enough and, of course, to have enough time in the building to remove the safety devices. It should work without a hitch. We should have time to be headed back here before they have a chance to think about a chase. Good plan, Sean." Pearse went along in Michael's manor.

Sean, in his conceit, easily took the compliments to be genuine. Elated by his mad desire for the completion of his plan, Sean's worry over their loyalty to him had diminished.

They were about to get into the van. Sean looked at Michael while his shaking hands gave him the keys. "Damn, don't you ever look in a mirror? Can't you see your damned red roots have grown in? Pearse, you are going to have to go into the stores. I want a good supply of whiskey and you'll have to get dark brown hair dye for Dylan Sanders. A stupid thing like your red hair roots might be noticed," he said, glaring at Michael. "You're known around here."

Sean got into the backseat. He was glad the van had darkened windows at the sides. The bright light bothered him. God, how he wanted a drink.

Pearse got the hair color as Sean had ordered and several bottles of whiskey. Sean opened a bottle and had enough to steady him by the time they reached the parking lot. Sean took the keys from Michael. "We'll separate; you two go into the Cathedral."

Sean looked up at it, feeling nothing but hate; wishing he could blow the whole damn thing. "We'll meet back here as soon as you finish. Get in your mind what is needed and don't drag it out. I'll walk about the area—and you, he glanced at Michael, "try staying away from anyone you might have met. Try not to talk with anyone."

Pearse and Michael crossed Broad Street and walked up the path past the Cathedral and on up to the Great West Doors. Sean walked down toward an area called the Park. He figured he'd look around there and at all of the buildings and places on the south side of the Cathedral; then he'd go around the front and check the north side on his way back to the van.

Pearse and Michael stood in silence for a few minutes. They were looking down at the maze at the western entrance to the Cathedral. "Even the floor is beautiful, Michael."

"Aye, Pearse. I read in the little booklet that this maze is supposed to confuse evil spirits."

"I think, perhaps, it already has, Michael."

Michael watched Pearse's face as his gaze swept the great length of the nave, the rounded Norman arches and the beautiful painted ceiling. It was obvious from the look on this handsome face that Pearse was captivated by the beauty of this place.

There was a tour forming. Pearse went alone to the small table and paid their admission charge. He returned to where Michael was waiting. "Pearse, take the guided tour. I won't take it with you; its better if we aren't seen together—Besides, I shouldn't get close to other people—my hair, you know," Michael grinned. You'll have to stray off a little. I'll be around and watch for you. When you reach the south door, hang back from the group."

Tom was not the guide for this tour. He had just completed one and walked toward the back. Carefully, he studied each person ready to begin the tour. There was definitely no one that could have been Devlin in any disguise. There was a man about the right age for O'Neill—short dark hair, good looking, with no beard. Of course, that description could fit any number of men. Tom observed his manor. The man seemed very interested in what was being shown. He was frequently in conversation with a middle aged American couple; sharing a mutual appreciation for what was being described. Tom had gone close to hear their remarks and soon dismissed him as just another pleasant tourist.

Tom walked back toward the west tower. He saw a young man, wearing a suit, looking at a folder. The man turned into the southwest transept. Tom walked at a distance behind him. The man went into the Saint Catherine's Chapel; it was the one available for private prayer. The man knelt on the priedieu, his head bent and his mouth resting on his clinched hands. Tom backed out quickly. He couldn't get so paranoid that he'd disturb a person in prayer. This man surely couldn't be a terrorist.

Michael was praying. He hadn't even been aware of Tom's watching him. "Dear God, I'm new at this—but I know what I have to do. Help me, please. I feel rotten about Pearse. If I go to the police, I know he's done for, too. Give me the strength to do what I must." He left the chapel and went down to the south door. Just inside, Pearse was waiting. They inspected the door.

Pearse said, in a flat voice, "It's bolted on the inside and its heavy. Someone would have to be inside."

Michael said, "Pearse, you had better catch up with your tour. I'll meet you in the choir stalls. I'm going over to the loo, it's outside by the Almonry." He couldn't risk telling Pearse the truth. He simply didn't know if Pearse would agree or how much the promised money meant to him. He was thinking, if Pearse would come with me, things might go better for him— even with his past record and actual building of the bombs, again, maybe not. Michael was hoping that Pearse would escape if the plan were stopped. Whatever—Michael knew he had no choice.

Pearse rejoined the tour. The group stayed at the Octagon for a long time. The guide explained the details of this magnificent and complex structure. Pearse's gaze was drawn upward to the carving of Christ. He was remembering all the statues and pictures he had seen, of this Jesus, as a child. His mom had taken the children to church, sometimes. Church and his family life at home didn't seem to match. He had no way of knowing the misery in his mother's heart as she tried to do a yearly confession of the times missed, of her anger and feelings of rebellion. The pattern never changed; it couldn't change for her, with her miserable life and drunken, abusive husband. Pearse had stopped going to church when very young. It meant nothing to him. He remembered their dire poverty. All was blamed on "the dirty Protestants— the rotten English," words bellowed from his father's mouth that reeked of whiskey. It was no mistaken religious zeal or political loyalty that got his own life messed up. It was money—always money.

The tour went on to the Lady's Chapel. Pearse looked at the carving of *The Sinister Green Man*, whose mouth seemed to spew evil. It seemed to him a depiction of Sean—and yes, of himself.

Pearse went on to the choir stalls marveling at the beauty that surrounded him. The rich carving, the great organ pipes, the grand carving of a peacock, all was wonderful to see. He turned toward the Presbytery with the breathtaking beauty of gilded work. *No!* He couldn't let bombs destroy any of this place; bombs his own hands had built. He'd stop it if Michael and the police couldn't. Yes, he knew where Michael had gone. The truth he saw in Michael as if he had spoken it. He just hoped Michael hadn't encountered Sean outside and that he had the chance to get on with it.

Michael went out of the west door. There was no sign of Sean. Quickly, he turned to his right and headed to High Street. He had studied the map; there was no problem walking the distance to the police station. He walked rapidly but no longer did he fear meeting Sean. Sean wouldn't have come out to the main street. Still, his heart was pounding. The fear of what he was letting himself in for as well as the concern for Pearse was sickening. There was no turning back; no turning from this resurgence of faith. Even in the midst of his troubled thoughts there was a small core of joy.

Michael entered the station and approached the uniformed officer, seated behind a desk. "I'd like to speak with the person in charge."

The officer looked at this young man, neatly dressed in a suit. "Constable Dixon will be here later." He was about to ask if he could help him, when he noticed the red rim of hair at the base of the brown. He had just been reading the descriptions of the wanted men; something clicked. The man's accent was surely Irish. "What is your name—and your business?"

Michael answered, giving the name of Dylan Sanders. "It's a matter I'd rather talk over with the person in charge. I'll wait."

The officer stood and studied the man. He didn't seem to be a threat in any way. His clothing fit tightly; he was sure the man wasn't armed. Maybe he had been wrong. He couldn't go accusing someone with out a reason. Why would Michael Griffith have come here? If the man hadn't said he'd wait willingly, he might have taken the matter further. "You can wait. Constable Dixon shouldn't be too long. Right this way, please."

Michael was shown into a small, windowless, holding room. It was empty except for two chairs and a small table. The officer returned to his office, closing the door behind him. Michael heard the key turn in the lock. He sighed and was thinking I'm a prisoner already.

Constable Dixon answered his cell phone. He heard the perturbation in the voice of his clerk. "Chief, get back to the station right away. I'm not sure but we might have one of the men; the red haired one—Griffith." He was looking at the report on the desk, "Michael Griffith—I've got him locked in the holding room."

"What happened? How was he caught?"

"He wasn't caught. He came into the station and said he wanted to speak with the person in charge. He said his name was Dylan Sanders but I think he might be Griffith."

"Did you talk with him? You can't keep a person locked anywhere without a reason."

"He wanted to wait for you. I didn't tell him I was locking him up. I just locked the door. I think I've reason enough. This guy's got red hair—at least at the roots and he's Irish, without a doubt. He's staying locked up till you get here."

"I'll start right now and be there in a half an hour." It seemed a long wait for all of them.

Sean had walked into the Park. He thought, at first, it might be a good place to bring the van but it wouldn't work; it would be too far to carry the bombs for only the two of them—*damn* the others. The detonator might not work from that distance anyway; no use wasting time down this far. He was about to go right toward the south side of the Cathedral when he looked upward to a knoll, identified on his map as Cherry Hill. Coming down from the rise were two men. He moved out of their sight behind a clump of trees and shrubbery. He watched them as they reached the flat area of the park. Rage welled inside him as he recognized them. "Those damned, filthy bastards," he muttered to himself, Brendan and John—looking for me. Well, you'll find Sean Devlin and be damned sorry you did. He was in an agony of indecision. If he overtook them now, would his plan be finished? Which meant more to him? Which revenge would be sweeter? His gun didn't have a silencer; how far could the shots be heard? He hadn't seen anyone else around, but there might be. If he waited till his plan was accomplished and hunted them down, he could make them suffer longer than just the shooting. That was what he wanted for these damned cowards. He'd let them go this time.

Brendan and John moved on toward the Cathedral where there would be other people. He couldn't let them see him there. He'd have to come back another time to find the place needed. Sean felt like a volcano about to explode as he walked back to the van. After slamming the van's door, he reached for the bottle of whiskey. Even that did nothing to calm his rage, to quiet his utter frustration. Now, he was wishing he had taken the pleasure of killing them on the spot.

Pearse came up to the van and got into the driver's side. "Where the hell is Michael? You took long enough. Do you have everything for the inside figured out?" Sean rambled on "we're going through with it tomorrow night, not Friday. Brendan and John are here. They probably have them expecting it will be Friday because I had planned it for the time of that damned festival. I asked you, do you have it figured out?"

"Yes, Sean, I have it figured out. Do you have things figured out? Things might not go so well with Brendan and John here."

"I just said we're moving it up. It will work tomorrow. As for those two bastards, I'll hunt them after it's all over. That'll have to wait—but by hell I'll get them. Why isn't Michael with you? Where the hell is he?"

"He left the Cathedral to go to the loo. He didn't come back."

"How long has it been? Damn you—did you look for him?"

"It's been a while, quite a while, Sean. I didn't see him around when I was on my way back," Pearse answered calmly.

"Those goddamned bastards have seen him and turned him into the police. Get the hell out of here. Move it! They'll be looking for us. Go, far away from this stinkin place—just get out of town. There's no going back to that house." Sean's face was filled with rage and fear.

Pearse started the van and left the parking lot. "Where do you suggest we go, Sean?" Pearse asked in the same calm voice.

"Damn it, use your head. Go north on the lower roads then go northwest till we find some place to hide the van. I'll have to think things through. You can't go east, stupid, you'd run into open, flat marshland."

"I'll do the best I can; I don't know anything about this place." Pearse was wishing he had gone with Michael and taken the consequences.

They were well beyond the outskirts of Ely when Sean broke his brooding silence. "Don't you have anything to say? You're damned calm about this."

"What can I say, Sean? You're the one who has always had all the answers. It's your plan, your problem. You figure it out."

"Damn you to hell, I'll tell you this—I've come this far and nothing's stopping Sean Devlin."

Pearse didn't comment. He had gone through a small, old country village and onto a narrow lane that seemed away from everything. He drove off the lane and down a slight embankment. The place was a wooded area, with a creek about two hundred feet down from the road. Pearse pulled the van into a thicket of trees. "This is the best hiding place I can find, Sean. If you don't want us to use all our petrol, we'd better stop here.

Sean had continued his drinking throughout the ride. His feeling of rage was somewhat numbed. He saw a bag on the seat beside him. "What's all that stuff?"

"That's the hair color you had me get for Michael and shaving cream and a new razor. I got those for myself, and a pair of scissors. My hair needs another cut."

"No food?"

"We planned to go back to the house, remember?"

Sean sat in the van, the bottle again in his hand. Pearse walked down by the little creek. He wanted away from Sean to think, to try and formulate a plan of his own. He thought if he could get the safety devices removed he might just be tempted to blow the van and Sean with it. He looked at the long stretch of trees with their dry leaves. Doing that would start an enormous fire; it was stupid to even think of it. He'd wait—there'd be a way.

Constable Dixon arrived and went directly to the holding room. "Know anything else?" he glanced at the clerk as he took his keys from his pocket.

"No, there's not been a sound out of him. I haven't checked."

Dixon turned the key and threw the door open quickly, not knowing what to expect.

The man was sitting, very still, on the straight back chair. The fair, freckled face that looked up at the Constable was showing terrible tension. The sherry brown eyes showed deep sadness, certainly not the face of a terrorist. "I'm Constable Jerry Dixon," he said in a kind voice and closed the door. You wanted to talk with me? What is you name?"

"I'm Michael Griffith, Constable Dixon. Have you had information about a plot to put bombs in Ely Cathedral?"

"Yes, Scotland Yard had informed us. We have believed the men involved were already in the country and probably here in Ely. We have, of course, been doing a search and have patrols and others on constant watch. Believe me, we won't let this happen. Now, as I recall the name of Michael Griffith was given as one of the three men wanted. Are you that Michael Griffith?"

Michael breathed deeply, "Yes, I was involved." He closed his eyes for a moment, "I can't believe, now, how I could have been. I reached a decision after spending time in the Cathedral that no matter what happened to me I had to stop this horrible thing from happening. I was at the Cathedral again today, but my intent to come here was made several days ago. I had to find a way to get away from Sean Devlin. When I left, Devlin was looking around the grounds and Pearse was taking a tour of the inside. I doubt they will still be there. They were probably gone before I got here. We had rented a house but I don't think they will go back there, with my being gone. Sean might figure something went wrong and it wouldn't be safe to return."

Dixon asked Michael for the location of the house and the description of the van and number. He left the room and gave directives to the clerk. "Call all the patrols now. We might soon get the other two." He gave the van number and its description. "Tell the patrols to watch for it as they proceed to this location, he gave the clerk the note. "Be sure they all stay together. Those two might be dangerous." Dixon picked up the report from the desk and returned to the room. He sat down behind the table and read it. Finally, he looked at Michael, "this last report was that Devlin and O'Neill came across in Devlin's cruiser, now named *The Margo*. You weren't seen with them. When did you come over?"

"I flew over earlier and rented the van in Manchester, then drove here. I was using the name of Dylan Sanders, following Sean's orders. I rented the house where we would stay during the time needed. It's a long story."

"Why don't you tell me how this all started? Knowing the information given by the two young men Brendan and John, I'm curious. I want to know your story and why you're turning yourself in. I want to know every move that's been made since this started."

Michael talked about everything pertaining to Sean's plan. He tried to describe how Sean had been in the early days of "the friends" and how possessed he had now become. He told how he really had been afraid Sean would kill him if he had backed out. Michael tried to explain how he had tried to quiet his own conscience by telling himself the Cathedral was only a building and no people would be hurt. He mentioned how Pearse, even though he made the bombs, now had no wish to go through with it, but feared for his life; also there was something Sean held over Pearse that might cause harm to another. Michael didn't know what that was about, only that a problem existed. He answered the many questions he was asked.

"What made you have such a change of mind, Michael? It couldn't be out of fear of being caught; you wouldn't be here if that was it."

"As I told you, I wasn't thrilled with doing something this extreme when it first started. I think, though, the first time my anger and stupid hate was pierced, I began to detest the idea. That happened as I drove through the English countryside and towns. I began to see the people in a rational way—not as hated enemies. Then I dealt with lovely people like the Milfords at the realty—I wished I was Dylan Sanders, living a normal life. Mostly, though, it was the Cathedral. Every time I would see it in passing, it seemed like a living, breathing thing accusing me. I finally forced myself to go inside. I was struck by its beauty but mostly by a feeling I can describe to no one. Memories surfaced within me. A God I had rejected for so long was making Himself known to me. That night I couldn't sleep; I fought with myself about going over to the coast to get Sean. I told myself to be logical—that this feeling was just so much superstition. Then too, I didn't have the money to get away and I still didn't have the courage to come here. Anyway, I went. However, that night at the hotel, before driving back, I knew I could fight it no longer. The truth—the grace—or whatever one would call it, made me know, beyond a doubt, that I'd get away and go to the police. I had to stop it. That's why I'm here. I don't know what's going to happen to me." He looked at Constable Dixon and gave a small but honest smile, "I feel a freedom inside like I've never known."

Dixon had watched every expression on Michael's face. He believed him. He liked him. Before he could comment, his cell phone rang. He silently listened, then said, "I didn't think they would return there but keep a patrol close to the house but out of sight. I don't they'll risk coming back since it's been this long. Keep watching for the van. I have no idea where they might head. Go anywhere you think likely. Check wooded areas and petrol stations outside the area." He clicked off the phone and stood, running his fingers through his hair and yawning. They had been sitting in this small, stuffy room for a long time. "Let's go into the front room and get some coffee."

The officer at the desk looked puzzled as Dixon and Griffith stood by the small table pouring coffee. He was thinking Dixon was certainly acting casual with this guy. Wasn't this guy a terrorist? He studied Michael; he didn't fit his idea of a terrorist. Of course, he had never come up against one before.

As they had coffee and munched some plain biscuits, Dixon said, "I hate to do this, Michael, but I'll have to arrest you. You'll probably have a court hearing, maybe a trial, I don't know. By your own admission, you were part of a violent threat, by citizens of a foreign country, against a site in England. That is serious. I don't know what you'll have to face, but I haven't a choice. You'll have to be held. I personally feel you've done more good than harm. I'm rather sorry I have to do this."

Michael sounded Irish as he said, "Don't be feelin sorry. I expected an arrest. You've no choice; besides, I've no money and nowhere else to go." Michael became very serious. "If Sean would happen to see me anywhere, he'd kill me for sure now. I'll be safer locked up."

Chapter 38

—Wednesday Evening—

Late that afternoon, after officially arresting Michael, Jerry Dixon returned to his office. He placed a call to Scotland Yard and asked for Sergeant Crosby. He was glad to know the Sergeant was not yet gone for the day, he liked dealing directly. Upon hearing all the events of the day, Crosby deemed it inappropriate, due to the nature of the crime, for Michael to be kept at Ely. It was arranged for him to be taken to London and incarcerated there until further consideration. Sergeant Crosby insisted on sending extra patrols for the manhunt. He wanted to have a media approach but Jerry Dixon pleaded with him to hold off on that. Jerry still wanted the situation to be kept as quiet as possible. He had been firm in his request for silence from all at his station. Crosby finally agreed to Dixon's reasoning.

Jerry was putting on his coat and was about to leave to see Tom at the Cathedral when George Milford came through the station's door.

"Hello, Jerry," George smiled at his long-time friend. "What's happening around here? I went out to a property I've rented to Dylan Sanders. I found a patrol car with your men. They wouldn't let me near the place."

"There's a lot 'happening' as you put it. I'll fill you in because of the property involved. I'll ask you to keep it to yourself for a day or two. It's a long story. If you don't have plans, come with me to the Cathedral; I have to talk with Tom Hart there."

"I'll give Liz a call and be with you in a minute." George crossed to the office desk and picked up the phone.

Liz answered, "Milford Realty, may I help you?"

"That sounds very interesting but I'm rather busy right now. What do you have in mind? A massage—or a candlelight dinner or—"

286

"Oh, you silly! I'd be glad to help with all the wonderful suggestions." Her voice sounded deliciously warm and inviting.

He could picture the grin on her face. He could still picture a grin when a more practical voice said, "However, if you are Mr. George Milford, calling to tell me he will be late, there will be no help available."

"Yes, Darling, I will be late. I'm at the police station with my friend Jerry Dixon and we are going to meet Tom Hart. Jerry has something to explain to me about a problem with one of our rental properties. See you later, Luv."

Liz frowned as she put down the receiver. How dare George sign off without telling her everything. What would be Jerry Dixon's concern over one of their rental properties? She turned off the lights, put the closed sign on the door and lowered the thermostat. While doing these things, her mind was consumed by that curious statement—a problem with one of the rental properties. She was wondering as she drove from the parking lot, what had Tom Hart to do with this? He had bought his small shop through them over a year ago. That wasn't a rental. His fiancée was renting directly with Mrs. Pickens; that flat hadn't been through Milfords. What had they rented lately? That's it! Liz said aloud. Dylan Sanders—who was he really? Why was he dying his hair? She always wanted to know that. She wished George had asked her to come along. Nothing happened out of the ordinary, very often, in Ely. She could hardly wait for George to come home—and it wasn't for a romantic evening. Satisfying her curiosity was uppermost.

Evensong was over. Jerry and George met Tom, as he was about to leave the Cathedral. "A lot has happened today, Tom. Did you see any of them here?"

"No. Why? Do you think they were here, today, inside the Cathedral?"

"Yes, two of them were inside. Devlin was outside for a while, on the grounds."

"Jerry, I can't believe I missed them. I've been here all day." Tom closed his eyes and shook his head. "I know now who they would have had to be. There was a young man, nice looking, and seeming like such an ordinary tourist. He was talking with others of the group; I dismissed the thought, of him being O'Neill, at once." There was no one with red hair. That was the only description on Griffith. But he had to be the young guy pretending to pray in the chapel."

"You're wrong there, Tom. He wasn't pretending to pray. I promised to tell George what's going on. Let's go have a bite somewhere quiet while I run this through once."

"I'm meeting Brendan and John outside, Jerry."

"Good, we'll all go together. That will bring everyone up to date on what has happened." They met the boys and Jerry asked, "Does anyone have any ideas about a place where we could have some privacy. My wife's having card club or I'd take you to my place."

George spoke up, "if you all would be satisfied with sandwiches, we could go to my place. Liz will want to know, too, because of the property being involved." George looked beseechingly at Jerry. "I couldn't keep anything from her anyway. If it's secret stuff, she'll keep it to herself."

Liz had changed from her business suit into a lounging outfit. It was comfortable but smart looking, with velvet leopard print trim. She heard George coming, and quickly turned off the telly and looked over the sofa toward the entrance hall. She had heard George talking with someone—there were four other men. Dear God, how big a problem is it—and how could it involve them? She said, "Hello, George" and with a slight smile and nod acknowledged the others. Her expression was somewhat tense. "What's the trouble, George?"

"Relax, Liz, you've no trouble. All we want is sandwiches and some coffee; you don't have to cook dinner for five." George grinned and gave her a peck on the cheek.

"Well, it's good to know that," she grinned back. "That's not what I meant, though." She looked serious again.

"Jerry tells me there are problems but it really doesn't involve us. Because of the property, he is going to tell us what is happening." He made introductions to Brendan and John. "Of course, you remember Tom Hart; Brendan is Tom's brother."

Liz responded with the usual pleasantries; then said, "You know, I'm dying to hear what this is all about."

"First, Hon, we'll get something to eat, and then we'll hear what Jerry has to say."

They were stunned when Jerry began by telling them that Michael Griffith, known to the Milfords as Dylan Sanders, had come to the station and turned himself in. Brendan and John told of the situation from its beginning. George and Liz hung on every word. Jerry told them of Michael's conversion and repeated all that Michael told him that day. After they talked out everything, John said, "Michael is being taken to London late tonight, right?"

"Yes, he is to be transported by Scotland Yard."

"Could we see him before he leaves? We were friends, you know. He was very kind to me."

Jerry looked thoughtful—wondering if such a thing would be permissible. He was still in charge; what would it hurt. "Yes, John, you may see him. I think it's a good idea. I really like the man and believe what he told me. I feel sorry for him."

"Jerry, could George and I see him, too? I felt so sorry when you told us how Michael wished he could have been Dylan Sanders, living the life he was pretending."

"Sure, the poor guy needs to feel he has some friends and support. Let's all go now."

Michael was sitting on the side of the cot. His eyes were closed; an unopened magazine was on his lap. He heard people approaching and looked up, expecting to see the guards from Scotland Yard. His surprise and joy were evident when he saw John and Brendan. Jerry unlocked the cell and John went in and hugged him. "Michael, I'm sorry, but I'm glad. You're safe and through with Sean."

Brendan hugged him, "That goes for me, too."

Once they were all inside the cell, Jerry locked it and left them. Michael was introduced to Tom, who shook his hand warmly, "You've done a fine thing Michael. I hope the bad times can soon be over for you."

Upon seeing the Milfords, Michael said, "I'm sorry for having deceived you and for all the trouble it will have caused. When I can get my money from the bank in Dublin, I'll pay the extended rent."

"George and I aren't concerned about that, Dylan—er, Michael," Liz spoke. "We'll get another renter. We know the whole story and feel as Tom does. We just want you to know you'll have friends here in England. We'll keep in touch. London isn't that far away."

George shook his hand and said, "If it can be of any help, I'll certainly tell them what a good tenant you were, how you worked to improve things about the place." George sounded a bit stilted and self-conscious. "I wish things were different for you. If you'll let us, we'll keep in touch like Liz said."

Michael, close to tears, tried to thank them. "I need all of you so very much. I don't deserve it but I'm so grateful for your kindness."

Liz tried to lighten things by reaching and running her fingers through Michael's hair. "You'll have to promise me one thing, Michael. You have to let that red hair grow in and keep it that way. With your fair, freckled face, the brown just didn't work for a handsome Irish man. I always knew it was a dye job."

Michael gave a little smile, "Sure'an that's a promise, Mrs. Milford."

"Good—and the names are Liz and George from now on."

Jerry returned and unlocked the cell. "You'll have to leave now. The detail from the Yard has arrived."

When the friends had gone, Michael asked if Sean and Pearse had been found.

"Not yet, Michael, but I feel it can't be long. Good luck to you." Jerry offered his hand, "I'll be in touch too."

Pearse had stayed down by the creek a considerable time. He was hoping Sean would go into a deep sleep so he could carry out the plan he had decided on. When he went back to the van, Sean was awake and feeling miserable. "I need food—my stomach hurts like hell.

Pearse opened the divider between the front seats. He tossed back two packs of snack crackers. "Here, I just remembered I bought these on the way from the coast."

Sean devoured them greedily. It didn't ease the pain that was building; it wasn't from hunger. He kept drinking, hoping it would numb him and the pain. For awhile he felt that he might throw up; but the booze **took** over and he fell into a deep stupor.

Pearse tried, but failed to rouse him. Satisfied that Sean would be out for quite some time, Pearse carefully set to work. He took the keys from Sean's breast pocket; Sean never stirred. He thought of taking the gun, but Sean's hand was clinched firmly around it, inside the sweater pocket. He wouldn't risk that now.

He unlocked the back of the van and removed the bombs and carried them, still in their secured packing cases, close to the creek. Slowly and skillfully he removed them and dismantled each of them. He gently submerged the dynamite into the flowing creek and did the same with the rest of the makings. His relief was overwhelming. What would happen to him no longer mattered. The knowledge that no one or no thing would, ever again, be destroyed by his bombs was wonderful. Now, he'd go back to the van and risk getting the gun from the sleeping Sean. *Sean was no longer asleep.*

The pain had been too intense to allow a prolonged sleep. A drug stronger than alcohol would have been needed for that. Sean had forced himself from the van and started walking toward the creek; he saw Pearse putting something into it. Scattered on the ground were the packing and containers that had held the bombs. The rage and agony of frustration was far worse than his physical pain. *His plan was dead.*

Pearse never heard Sean as he moved closer. Pearse was standing, lost in a thought that had come to him suddenly. He couldn't imagine why. He was remembering himself as a small child, crying. His mother had knelt to him and taken him in her arms. He heard the gruff voice of his father. "Don't be makin a damned baby out of him." His mother held him even more tightly and kissed the top of his head. He could almost feel her comforting arms around him. He didn't hear Sean coming nearer. Sean reached into the gray sweater pocket. One sharp sound broke the silence.

Sean walked on and stared with hate at the dead Pearse. He kicked at him and kept kicking until the lifeless form rolled over the slight bank and into the cold flowing water.

Slowly, he returned to the van. Not one small shred of remorse was felt for the horrible deed he had done. The cold drizzle that had started with the coming of evening wet the gray sweater; it hung heavily on his slumped body. So maddened was he with rage that he was totally unaware of his physical pain. He lumbered into the van, dropped full length onto the seat, and reached for the bottle. Finally, in a complete mental fog, he succumbed to a heavy sleep.

Chapter 39

—————

—*Thursday*—

Early Thursday morning, Sean awoke in a confused state. His first awareness was of his pain and then of his shaking with cold. The damp, cold clothes still clung to him. He didn't know why they were wet. Where was he? Moments, seeming like forever, passed until the remembrance of what had happened came into his mind. His first coherent thought was one of cruel amusement. He had gotten even with Pearse.

He sat up and cursed as he looked down at the floor. The last bottle of whiskey had slid from his hand when he had fallen asleep. The bottle was empty. There was a spot on the floor as wet as his sweater.

He tore off the sweater and wet shirt. Cursing aloud, he rooted behind the seat and found an old pullover shirt he hadn't taken into the house. Pearse's oversized jacket was on the front seat. It was tight on him but it would have to do. Still shaking with cold, he started the motor. After awhile, the heater warmed the van. Finally, the shivering stopped. His pants, which hadn't been as wet, were almost dry. He was able to think now and make his plans.

He had to get back to Ely. Brendan and John would be there, he was sure, and probably that brother of Brendan's. Sean's face looked as dark and evil as his thoughts. I'll make them pay. *Damn*—Sean Devlin will make them pay. He looked at the gun he had tossed on the seat. It had only three bullets in it when he had taken it from the cottage. One was gone. If I wouldn't have been forced into doing things so goddamned quick, I'd have had more ammunition and all kinds of guns with scopes. There hadn't been the time to get them from the special sources that he knew about. He couldn't risk buying them on the public market after he knew he was being hunted. Then again, he wasn't planning to gun down anyone but Brendan—just a bombing of that damned Cathedral. There were still two bullets. By Hell—he'd get his satisfaction in using them. That was all that was left for him—all that was important now.

It was full daylight. He pulled the van's mirror down. It wasn't the gray hair and beard that caused the few moments of concentration that his jumbled, mad mind would allow. This face looking back at him was a stranger. It didn't look at all like the Sean of six months ago; that face used to have a rugged charm, no longer. He'd have to change his disguise. He opened the brown bag and took out the shaving cream and razor and scissors. Trying to ignore his pain, with his shaking hands he cut his hair and beard; then shaved until his pudgy face and huge head were smooth. He looked totally different.

He knew he couldn't risk taking the van close to Ely. To get a public bus he'd have to be near a village. Surely, no one would be expecting him to be on public transportation. It would have to be later in the day—closer to dusk. The day was gray and cloudy; maybe a fog would set in. That might help, he was thinking, he wouldn't be so noticeable.

The waiting seemed like forever. Pain and hunger and the great need for a drink were torturous. The pain at times was so severe that he thought he should drive to a hospital and give himself up. That thought was immediately pushed from his mind. His desire for revenge was even greater than his misery.

The day was long. He once went down to the creek and walked about two hundred feet down stream. There he saw Pearse's body. The clothes had caught on some large tree roots. Pearse was held there; his unseeing eyes were open. Sean looked down at him, sneered and spit in the direction of the corpse.

Throughout the night the patrols had kept up a relentless search but to no avail. The day shift would begin and continue the hunt with intensity. Jerry Dixon had moments of doubt—maybe he should have made this public. He couldn't believe something hadn't turned up by this morning. He decided to wait one more day. He couldn't imagine how Devlin and O'Neill would do it. Getting back to Ely without being spotted would be almost impossible. Yet, Jerry had this gut feeling that Devlin would surely try and that it would be tonight. In utter frustration, Jerry banged his fist on the desk and said aloud, "Devlin, I'll be waiting for you."

Tom also was filled with frustration and fear. Devlin would never give up, and he was devious enough to try anything to get his revenge, if not on the Cathedral, on Brendan. Brendan and John would not stay at their hotel. They, too, were sure that Sean wouldn't quit. They spent the day intermittently checking the grounds and questioning at businesses, hoping to come up with some leads. Tom spent the day at the Cathedral. He doubted Sean would try coming inside but Pearse might return, still thinking he wouldn't be known.

George Milford stopped to see Jerry that morning, "I'm taking the day off to ride around and hunt."

"George, we can use another patrol—we need all the help we can get. Just don't try anything brave, understand? Simply be in touch if you spot them."

George held up his cell phone and grinned, "I'm better with one of these than a gun."

Despite all the effort, by late afternoon, nothing more was known.

Fran took her breakfast cocoa and toast into the living room and turned on the telly. There was nothing on to hold her interest; she soon turned it off and took the unfinished food to the kitchen. It was getting increasingly harder to keep her positive attitude, to keep that firm trust and faith. The things she had needed to do, that had kept her busy, were completed. Planning for the wedding or even thinking of the future was impossible. She thought, Dear God, will there really be a wedding? Will we have a future? Will I ever see my dearest Tom again?

She knew that staying alone so much was not a good thing; but she was finding it harder to spend time with dear Emma Pickens. Emma had noticed the disquiet in Fran and, although not wanting to pry, had warmly questioned what the trouble was. Several times Fran had come close to confiding in this dear friend. She had promised Tom that she would not discuss the problem; and that was to be respected above all else.

She stood for a long time at the window, thinking, how she would love to go to the Cathedral and perhaps encounter Ethel Fenman. She couldn't go—Tom had asked that, too; she was to stay away until she heard from him. Moving away from the window, she ran her fingers through her hair. That was one thing that needed doing. She looked into the mirror; her hair really needed a trim. There was a shop just a few blocks away. If they could take her today, it would give her a reason for going out and seeing other people; she needed that even more than a hair-do.

Fran ran down the steps, hoping that Emma might know the name of the shop. Emma was dusting her living room. She gave Fran a delighted smile, "I'm just about to stop and have some lunch. Will you join me, Dear?"

"Thanks, Emma, but I had some cocoa and toast. I'd like to get an appointment for a hair trim. I saw a shop a few blocks from here; a small building, painted cream. It had white ruffled curtains at the windows. I don't know the address or the name. Would you know it?"

"Oh, yes, Fran, it's called Sarah's Shears. Sarah Lowell is the owner. She has two girls working with her. It's usually easy to get an appointment— unless it's a Friday or Saturday. I've a standing one on Wednesday; my friend Ruth does too, she drives me. Your hair always looks so lovely, Fran. I never thought to tell you about Sarah. Let me call for you."

"Emma, that's a wonderful idea. With you being a regular, they might try to squeeze your friend in today."

Emma hung up the phone and smiled at Fran, "Sarah said one of the girls will be free if you can go right away."

"Thanks, Emma, I'll get my coat and I'm on my way. I'm sorry about lunch."

"Don't worry about that. We'll have hot tea together when you get back."

"I'll take you up on that. It's such a cold gray day; I'll need it."

The distance was short but Fran was glad to be inside the bright, warm shop. "Welcome to Sarah's Shears," a pleasant, middle-aged woman shook Fran's hand. "You're Mrs. Pickens's friend, right?"

"Yes, I'm glad you could take me."

Fran was introduced to a thin young woman whose name was Tracy. She told Fran, "I'll have to work you in with some waiting. I'm timing a perm on another customer. Is that all right?"

Fran assured her it was. There was a slender, very neat young woman in the next chair. Her hair was soft, natural blond and parted on the side; it was straight and gently curved in at the middle of her neck. The simple style was smart and suited her well. As she was finished and getting down from the chair, Fran smiled and told her how much she liked her hair.

"I've worn it like this for years; it's easy to keep." She stopped by Fran's chair. Fran was alone. Tracy had gone to the rear of the shop to check on the lady getting the perm. "I heard your name. You're Tom Hart's fiancée, aren't you?"

Fran was surprised, but of course, there were many friends of Tom's at Ely who might know about her. "Yes, yes, I'm Tom's fiancée." It felt good just saying it.

"I'm Elizabeth Milford." Then she added in a concerned voice, "How are you holding up?"

Fran was puzzled and trying to think of a response.

Liz Milford said, "You must be so worried for Tom and his brother." Liz had assumed that Fran would know everything.

At that Fran was truly startled. She glanced up and saw Tracy approaching with the other customer. She said, "Miss Milford, I'm very deeply concerned but I can't discuss it now."

Liz noticed the others coming. "Of course, I understand. Hopefully, the worry over this horrible thing will soon be over. I'll look forward to seeing you again, Fran." Liz left the shop.

Fran's thoughts were filled with anxiety and questions throughout the afternoon. She made an effort to be pleasant and interested in Tracy's light and constant chattering. Her hair turned out lovely; Fran thanked her warmly and tipped her well.

Fran was truly relieved to give into her thoughts and feelings when she left the shop and started the walk home. Who was Liz Milford? Why would *she* know all about the problem? Had she been a "special" friend of Tom's before they met? She didn't doubt Tom's love for her or his reason for not telling her. Still, it wasn't comforting to think there was a woman he would turn to and confide in—someone he needed in his life when he had a problem. Yes, she was feeling a little jealous—if that *was* the case. She wanted to be all things to Tom, the very soul mate that she had believed herself to be. More than this, though, was the sickening worry for his safety. Liz Milford had called the problem a horrible thing. She had indicated that Fran had every reason to worry.

Emma opened the door, "Hello, Dear, your hair looks lov—." Emma noticed the tears.

Fran closed her eyes and patted Emma's arm. "Sorry, Emma, I'll have to skip that tea." She ran quickly upstairs.

Emma stood watching, her own heart heavy. She had come to love Fran like the daughter or granddaughter that she never had.

Late that afternoon, Sean drove the van up to the lane. He headed toward the country village he remembered coming through; passing some farms, he knew he was coming closer. He pulled into a field that seemed overgrown and neglected. There was no place to really hide the van but he couldn't drive any closer to the village. It would be a long walk—his lumbering, shaking body was telling him it was impossible. He wouldn't give in. One more push, he told himself, would see his revenge completed. He didn't give a damn after that.

It seemed to him like he had climbed Mount Everest when he had walked the level mile to the center of the village. The small houses were built close together. The petrol station and other small businesses took up less than three blocks. Dusk had not set in but it was so gray and foggy that it may as well have.

Sean longed to sit on the steps of a deserted small shop. He was forcing himself to think coherently; that wouldn't be good—it would call more attention to him. Food might help him but he couldn't risk going for it or prolong his time in the village. He dare not ask at the petrol station about a bus. Even a fool would know that they had been alerted.

Sean noticed an old man in scruffy clothes going back and forth from a feed store to a dilapidated pickup truck. When the man had made the final trip and all the bags were thrown onto the bed, Sean walked over to him. In a croaking voice he asked, "Mate, is there a bus that comes through here that could take me to the dock at the River Ouse in Ely?"

The man's eyes, set close over a beaked nose on his skinny face, looked hard at the big, ugly, bald man. The farmer's mouth was pulled in a straight, tight line. He looked as if giving anything, even information, was more than he desired to offer. Finally, the lips parted, "Not now, it's too late in the day." He moved to get back into his truck. Sean blocked his way.

Sean's head was reeling. He was making an effort to bring forth some of his old persuasive charm; it wasn't working. Still, he had to think of something. Desperately, he said, "I have to meet some friends there. They have a small cruiser moored there and are expecting me tonight. My car is in the garage for repairs. I've got to get there. Could I hire you to take me?"

"No, man, I'm tired. Try over at the petrol station; ye might get a young fellow who hangs around there to do it."

"Do you think he'd do it for a hundred pounds?" Sean fumbled for his wallet and took out the amount.

The dim eyes opened wide. "Ye must want to go there mighty bad."

"I do. My friends expect me tonight. I don't want them to push off without me. I tried to get in touch with them and couldn't. Do you think someone would do it for that? I'll pay first."

"Gawd, man, I'll do it for that. She's old but runs good," he said, patting the truck.

Sean got into the truck. The old leather seats were worn hard and flat; but for once, Sean was grateful for something. He could have stood no longer and he had that dreadful pain in his stomach.

The man said, "Ye and yer friends must be mighty rich—what with cruisers and all."

"Yeah, you have to put a lot of money into having a cruiser." Sean's thoughts were of his *Paradise*. "I had a lovely one once—a real beauty." He fell silent. He'd never see her again. That was over; he had lost it all. There was only one thing left for him—this night for having his revenge. "I'm tired, mate. I had to walk a lot when my car let me down. I'd rather not talk. I need rest."

"That's fine with me, man. I won't disturb ye."

Sean dozed, off and on. He kept his hand over the gun in his pocket just in case the little guy got greedy.

Sean woke shortly before the ride was over. The pain was still there but he felt stronger. He got this far. He could make it through this night.

"Where should I drop ye, man? We're well into Ely now, close to where ye wanted."

"Turn down Broad Street and drop me where it intersects with Jubilee Terrace. I'll walk the rest of the way down to the Quay. I'm not sure of the exact spot where the cruiser is moored. I might have to ask someone. It's a small area—won't be any trouble findin it." It took every effort to think all of this out but he hoped to sound logical to this guy. He didn't want to waste any energy he had left walking up from the Quay. He needed to be close to the park, down from the Cathedral.

It was dark and quite foggy with the river being so close. Sean glanced around when he got out of the truck. No cars were seen. No one was about. Sean mumbled, "Thanks," as he closed the door.

The old man muttered, "It's been nice doin business with ye," and he drove away.

Sean went into the park area where he had seen Brendan and John yesterday. Was it only yesterday? It seemed to him an eternity. They'll be here sometime helpin in the search to find me. The damned fools. He was hoping it would be here—an easier place to stay hidden. If they don't show, I'll do my own search They'll find me then—and it will be tonight.

At the same time, Tom, Brendan, and John were at the Almonry. They were just about to leave when Tom got a call from Jerry. He told them to come to the station; he had some news.

When they entered Jerry's office, he remarked that "we have only one now to worry about." The three sat down. Jerry put his arms on the desk, leaning over them. "We got a call from Scotland Yard about an hour ago. The van was found abandoned in a field in a farm area to the north. They are well equipped with powerful searchlights, so they decided to continue the search. I got a second call right before I phoned you. They found a long strip of woods and a place where one could drive into it. On a hunch that someone could have hidden there, they investigated. Tire tracks led them to the empty cases the bombs had been packed in, and then they found a body in the creek. There will be an autopsy, but the police are sure death was from a gunshot wound to the back. They are bringing him to the hospital morgue now. I'd like you to come with me for identification. I think it must be Pearse O'Neill from the description. Devlin had not been found."

Brendan and John were visibly shaken after the ordeal of identifying Pearse. John's voice cracked when he said, "Pearse wasn't all bad. That he destroyed the bombs proves that."

"I'm sure he wasn't, John," Tom said. "No one is all bad."

"Except Sean Devlin," John responded.

"Even there, it isn't up to us to judge. From all I've heard by now, he is truly mad—unable to be different. There was probably a time when he could have chosen not to feel his hatred and taken another course. God alone knows the capabilities of a mind. Sean must be completely insane. Surely, he'll be found soon—and hopefully, before his madness destroys anyone else."

Jerry said, as they reached the parking lot, "I'm keeping all my patrols on duty around the Cathedral, in case he gets back. Frankly, I can't imagine how he'd do it. All methods of public transportation have been alerted early this morning. Of course, he could have hitched a ride. But that isn't likely; most people don't pickup strangers these days." Jerry looked deeply distressed, "Tom, I thought I was doing the right thing by not going public. The Yard wanted a broadcast. I talked them out of it. I didn't want the reason for the hunt to be spread and to have the Cathedral become a focal point for negative publicity. I'm not sure it was the right thing to do. If they could have been caught sooner, maybe Pearse would still be alive. Now, the general public might be in danger from Devlin."

"Jerry, I think you had good reasons for wanting to handle things your way. A lot of people wouldn't have heard a broadcast so they wouldn't have known anyway. Devlin will stay focused on the revenge he's after. I don't think the general public will be in danger. As for Pearse, it's very sad but we don't know if there could have been a different ending for him. If things had been made public sooner, the Cathedral would have been closed. Michael might not have had his time there—the time that changed his life. That would have been a really sad thing."

Jerry smiled a little at Tom. "Well, that's a point. I'll have to hang onto that, thanks, Tom. Maybe we'll get a call soon announcing that they've caught him; they are still combing the area and doing a thorough check of the neighboring village. Let's hope."

Tom said, "Jerry, drop Brendan and John at the hotel." Tom looked to the backseat, "I want you to stay put there until this is over. The patrols are riding around the area. There are other police around the Cathedral. They'll spot Sean if he shows up."

"The grounds are big; it will take a lot of people to cover them, Tom. John and I are going to be there; it's our responsibility."

"It's your responsibility to think of your families," Jerry said. "Listen to your brother and stay away from that madman. I have men on foot there, but I can't imagine that he'll be near the Cathedral now that his plans are ruined. He could be hunting you on the streets. Do us all a favor and stay at the hotel—in your locked room."

"Jerry, we all agree, Devlin is mad—mad enough to try some kind of vandalism at the Cathedral. I just know he'll be driven to go back there. He could even hide somewhere and maybe get into the Cathedral to get at Tom tomorrow, if he can't find me tonight. I can't let that happen." Brendan's voice rose in emotion. "I won't let that happen!"

"We won't let that happen. I'll keep men around all night and tomorrow if he hasn't been found." Jerry pulled up in front of the hotel, "Now get out and go in—and stay there."

"Please, for Mom's sake, listen to Jerry." Tom added, "Alert the desk clerk that if anyone comes looking for you—you're not there. Ask them to notify the police at once." Tom looked tense.

Jerry said, "Better yet, I'll put a plainclothes man on duty there tonight, just in case."

Once inside, Brendan said to John, "We'll go to the room and get the big heavy-duty torch and the cell phone we bought. We'll be gone before Jerry's man shows up. Devlin will head to the Cathedral; he'll get there somehow. He'll have his revenge. If he can't get us it will be someone, even if it's a guard. This mess is still my fault and I'm not ignoring it. Not having a gun, all I can do is call if we spot him." As they left their room, Brendan said, "I'm scared, and I'm not pretending I'm not. John, you don't have to come."

"Dear God, Brendan, do you really think I'd let you go alone? This mess is as much mine." They were on their way before Tom and Jerry Dixon reached the Cathedral.

The Cathedral was open and light shone from its stained-glass windows. Some members from the harvest committee and workmen were there. The stalls were being put together in the center nave. All the animals would be brought the following evening when the decorations of wheat, fruit and flowers would be placed.

Standing and watching the happy activities of those busy people was a lady in a dark raincoat. The coat's hood covered the light yellow hair. Her shoes were low and sturdy. She looked on as the metal pipes and fencing were assembled. What a pleasure these people seemed to be having at this simple task. She thought, too, of the many people who would see these symbols of the harvest and of the feeling of gratitude that might be inspired by these efforts. Though she walked among the workers, she was not seen.

What was her purpose here now? As yet, she did not know. She turned and watched the bishop as he came through the West Doors. He, too, walked past and was completely unaware of her presence. He greeted the workers warmly. "Have you come to help, Bishop?" asked one of the men, grinning.

"No, I'm afraid I'd get in the way. You'd throw me out," the bishop returned the grin. "I'm meeting someone here soon."

Jerry and Tom came through the West Doors. The bishop went back toward them. Jerry had told the bishop that he must talk with him about something important.

The bishop motioned to his right, "We'll go into the gift shop. We can talk there without interruption." The woman went along unseen into the shop, knowing she would soon learn the reason for her presence.

The bishop closed the door, "What in the world is this about, Jerry? I've noticed a frequency of patrols around the streets close to the Cathedral. Also, I know that Tom," Bishop turned to Tom and smiled, "has a business to run and a life of his own, yet he has practically lived here this past week. I've observed his brother and his friend, time and time again, on the grounds. Young fellows might enjoy the grounds once in a while, but not everyday. If you hadn't called me, you would have gotten a call soon. All this has to do with this something *important*, right? What is going on?"

"Bishop, first off, I want to say we wouldn't have allowed any danger to come to the Cathedral or to anyone involved with it. That's been the reason for the close watch. You weren't told of a threat that had been made because I wanted things to run normally here in the hope that we might be led to and able to catch the perpetrators. Also, had this been made public, the Cathedral would have been in the center of disruptive media publicity. The danger to the Cathedral is now over. However, there is still one man we are hunting. I think the man is in fact mad. There are patrols out, some from Scotland Yard. Men are on the grounds now, close to each entrance. Tom and I will stay in the Cathedral while the people are working. Will they be long tonight?"

"No, they should be done shortly." The usual pleasant, benign expression on the bishop's face was replaced by one of consternation. "Are you certain the committee members and workers will be safe going to their cars?"

"Absolutely. We'll keep a close watch."

"Jerry, you told me your reasons for not telling me about this. I think, perhaps, I should have been told. Again, maybe your reasoning was right. I might have handled things differently and unnecessary panic might have prevailed. But now I'm insisting you tell me everything. Tom, are you and your brother helping the police in this matter? How did you get involved?"

Tom said, "Jerry, you go out to the nave with the workers. I'll tell Bishop the details."

Etheldreda was thinking to herself, am I here to help Tom? If the Cathedral is no longer in danger is it something to do with Tom because of my special involvement in Fran's life? That knowledge was as yet not given. She would stay and listen. She must know.

The bishop looked so strained and tired. There was one chair behind a small desk. "Tom, I hate to take the only chair but right now I feel the need to sit."

"I was about to suggest that you do just that, Bishop, I am going to give you an outline of what has brought us to this night. When the man we are hunting is caught and we have time with less strain, I'll tell you all the background of this matter. I want Jerry Dixon to tell you about the young man he talked with and what moved him to go to the police station. Tonight we haven't the time. I'll fill you in, quickly; I might be needed."

Tom explained for a while. It was hard to condense the story. The bishop asked questions and alternately nodded his head between disbelief and understanding.

Tom persuaded the bishop to return to his home, accompanied by himself and a police officer. They were leaving the shop when Jerry met them. "I got a call from my man at the hotel. When he got there he tried to call the boy's room. They weren't in. He was told by the clerk that they had gone to their room and returned to the lobby in no time and left."

Tom heaved a sigh, "Oh, Dear God, I know they're here somewhere on the grounds. If Devlin has made it here tonight, there's no question that they're in danger."

Jerry said, "Let's get the Bishop home. All the workers have gone, and the doors are in the process of being locked. We'll start looking for the boys."

Etheldreda knew what she must do. She must find them. How she could help? She would know when the moment came. She ran from the Cathedral at once.

Sean had gone into the park and tried to stay hidden within the trees and shrubs. He sat on the ground, weak and befuddled. He looked up at the Cathedral. The lights were on—*damn it*, maybe there is a service in progress. He couldn't get closer if there were a lot of people. He couldn't risk being caught until he found Brendan and John. He'd have to stay and watch to see if the lights went out. Then he'd start his hunt. He felt horrible. A string of cursing spewed from his mouth. The waiting seemed like forever. Yet his feverish desire for revenge so penetrated his whole being that this final test of his endurance was bearable.

Brendan and John reached High Street. Seeing the lights in the Cathedral, Brendan said, "If he is around, he won't be close." They cut down the darker area of the Almonry and the paddock. There were several cars in the parking lot. "There's too much going on around here; if he's here, he's hiding down further."

John said, "It's so dark with the fog setting in; he could be anywhere, even by one of the buildings or walls. It wouldn't be hard to hide in a place like this."

"He could be hiding close, but off the grounds, waiting for things to calm down around here. John, let's look around those buildings on the other side of Broad Street. They crossed and searched there for a while. Their torch was making little dent in the darkness. They continued down Broad Street. Turning to their right, they were back on the tip of the Cathedral grounds. Still searching, they made a curve around the buildings of the Resource Center.

They stayed out of sight as they saw one of Jerry's men coming out of the Porta entrance to the park. He turned and walked up The Gallery Walk toward the Cathedral. "He was probably looking for us, Brendan. I guess Devlin isn't in the park or he would have seen him."

"In the dark he could have missed him and Sean would have stayed well hidden. If Devlin sees us, he'll show himself."

"I'm not exactly thrilled at being the decoys, Brendan."

"I have the phone ready. One push of a button will contact the police. Sean is big and powerful but he doesn't move fast. We can outrun him. I've got to find out if he's here and end this."

They entered the Porta that led to Cherry Hill and the Park. They did not see the lady in the dark coat running down the pathway at the edge of Dean's Meadow. She was running quickly toward them.

John kept the torchlight close to the ground. Its light could penetrate the fog for only a few feet. The fallen leaves were slimy and the ground slippery and uneven at the base of the small hill. John swung the light higher in an effort to search. The beam revealed the huge form, not three feet away from them. Sean's heavy breathing was the only sound to be heard. A look of evil triumph was on his face. His hand held his gun at the ready. He reached and sent the cell phone crashing from Brendan's hand. "Running won't work—a bullet travels fast. I can't wait to pull the trigger." Sean grabbed the torch and illuminated his foes. "I want to enjoy the looks on your faces, you damned filthy bastards. Aren't you the lucky ones? You've found Sean Devlin." The light was full on Brendan. Sean's sneering look of triumph was gone. It was now one of seething hate and was focused completely on Brendan. John took that instant to throw himself at Sean's feet, hoping to pull him down.

"You stupid fool. You're like a kitten attacking a lion," he sneered. He gave a brutal kick to John's head, never taking his eyes nor his gun off of Brendan. An unconscious John lay at his feet. Sean pointed his gun at Brendan's face.

Brendan knew there was no escape. He had brought John here. His mother and Tom would be devastated in their grief. Why hadn't he listened? The hate he was feeling wasn't for Sean but for himself.

The moment had come. The trigger was pulled—but the shot was low, resulting in a wound to Brendan's leg. "Hell! Who?" Sean looked to his right, stunned. There was no one there. But someone had pulled his arm down. Where did they go? What was happening to him? It must have been a nervous twitch. Or was it?

Seeing Sean's confusion, Brendan made an effort to lunge from his crouched position. His leg was painful and bleeding and wouldn't support his weight.

Sean glared down at Brendan and pushed him flat with his foot. Again, he pointed the gun. "This won't miss." *But it did.* The gun fell to the ground, the bullet discharged into the dirt. Sean screamed in rage as he jerked around to look for the person who had grabbed his arm with such force. Still, he saw no one. He clutched the long handle of the torch in both hands and dropped to his knees. He raised the torch with the intention of bashing it hard at that hated face. Standing close in front of the prone Brendan was a woman wearing a dark, hooded coat. She just stood there looking down upon Sean, with a calm and sad expression. Sean fell back and screamed in fear. Still clutching the light, he scrambled to his feet and ran the length of the Park to the Dean's Meadow. He flung himself to the ground. "I'm going mad. I'm imagining things." Hot tears of rage washed down his cheeks. He pounded the ground with his hand. Nothing went the way I'd planned, he said to himself. Why would I run and leave Brendan alive? Maybe John was dead. Maybe Brendan would bleed to death. Sean longed to know, but shuddered in a fear such as he had never known. He couldn't go back there.

The pain was growing more intense. He looked up toward the Cathedral. The lights were out now. Maybe someone would be there. He had to get help. He didn't care about anything except getting rid of the pain. Damn—he wished he had that last bullet to use now.

Tom had seen the bishop to his home. He began searching for Brendan and John on the north side and in the area to the east. Once the Cathedral was locked, Jerry sent some of his men to search the west and the lower area to the south. He went to search around the buildings at Firmary Lane, still feeling it unlikely that Devlin could have gotten to Ely. Just in case, he wanted Brendan and John found. The fog wasn't helping anything.

Sean forced himself up and staggered on through the Meadow, across the path and on toward the Cathedral. He reached the south side at the place by the Prior's Door. Stopping for a minute, he tried to breath as deeply as the pain allowed, while gripping hard the handle of his torch.

Tom had come around from the east side and was walking the length of the south side. He saw the beam of light, and, thinking it was one of Jerry's men, called out, "Wait up." The man didn't answer. Tom called again, "It's Tom Hart. Are the boys found?"

Sean snapped off the light and stood quietly waiting, forgetting his pain, his weakness. Maybe the revenge he wanted could still be his. He was standing on the grass, close to the path that butted against the door. He took a few steps back to the side of the path.

Not seeing the beam of light, Tom assumed the man hadn't heard and had gone on to the front of the Cathedral. He continued walking rapidly along the side of the building.

Sean raised the torch in both hands. His arms ached with tension as he held the heavy torch. He was ready.

Tom never saw Sean through the fog. He was directly in front of him. But an instant before the blow struck its target, a woman's voice screamed, "Tom!" He jerked to his right out of Sean's way. The force that was to have crushed Tom threw Devlin off balance. His foot caught on the brick walk. His body plunged forward as he fell. The extraordinary force smashed his head and face hard against the Norman carved stone of the Prior's Door.

It all happened so fast. Tom grabbed the torch that had fallen at his feet. He turned the beam on the dead man that he knew had to be Sean. He was startled to see a woman kneeling by the body. She seemed to be tracing the Sign of the Cross on the top of his blood-covered head. She was praying. Tom stood silently and watched, weak and trembling with shock. Who was she, this woman in the dark coat? When she raised her head, her hood fell back showing her light hair. She turned to Tom and said. "He is dead. It's over, Tom. Go for help."

Tom's eyes were riveted to the dreadful scene in front of him. He was unable to move.

"*Tom*, it's over. Just go." The woman spoke louder. She stood and repeated her admonition. "Go."

Tom rubbed his hand over his face and then looked into this woman's eyes. Her look was of sadness and deep concern and yet there was a warmth and peace. Whomever she was, he somehow felt in awe of her. He said nothing and handed her the torch

She gently touched his hand. "You keep it, Tom. I don't need it."

Tom went to the front of the Cathedral. His mind was reeling. That woman called my name, but I don't know her. She saved my life!

As he rounded the corner, Jerry called, "Tom, I've been looking all over for you. The boys have been found."

Tom looked terrified, "Where—where are they? Jerry, tell me, are they all right? Sean was here!"

"Take it easy, Tom. They are going to be fine. Hurt a little—but okay. The ambulances are on the way. Dear God, Tom, you look terrible."

Tom took hold of Jerry's jacket sleeve. "Are you telling me the truth? Are they all right?"

"Tom, *believe me*. I'll take you to them right away."

Tom stood back, shook his head as if to clear it, and swallowed hard. "Since they're not in danger, Jerry, it will have to wait. Call another ambulance or a hearse, I don't know. Sean Devlin is dead—by the Prior's Door."

"My God, Tom! When did you find him? Did you kill him?" Jerry stopped talking to make the call.

"I didn't kill him. He tried to kill me and he fell."

"Are you sure it was Devlin?"

"Yes, he didn't have hair or a beard—but it's him. Right now he's a bloody mess." Tom tried to fill Jerry in on the way things had happened. "The woman who screamed my name and saved my life, Jerry, I don't know who she is. Maybe you'll know her. I guess she was staying with the body."

They reached the Prior's Door and the body. The woman was gone. Tom shone the light around and called, "Hello? Madam? Lady?" There was no answer. "That's strange. She seemed so caring; I'm surprised she didn't stay."

Jerry shrugged his shoulders. "Some people don't like to be involved with the police. She probably thought she'd have to answer questions."

Jerry's phone rang. He listened for a while and finally said, "It's a little late for that information. We know he got to Ely. He's dead. Meet me at the hospital morgue in a little while. We're at the Cathedral waiting for a hearse to take away Sean Devlin's body. It's all over but the paperwork." Jerry looked at Tom. "That was a call from the Yard patrol, telling us that Devlin had managed to hitch a ride to Ely. They were doing a door to door search at the village, when an old man came into the petrol station. He started bragging that some bloke gave him a hundred pounds to get him to Ely."

They heard the ambulances coming. "Jerry, I'm going down to ride with Brendan."

"Go ahead, Tom. I'll see you at the hospital."

Tom ran out the front and down the Gallery Way. He reached the entrance of the Porta as the two stretchers were being brought through. The waiting ambulances were parked close by. Their bright lights penetrated the darkness. A breeze had started, bringing a warm current of air; the fog was dissipating.

Tom's spirits rose when he saw Brendan look up at him. "I'm okay, big brother. I'm sorry I didn't listen. I don't know what saved us. I guess a miracle." He winced in pain. "Have they found him?"

"He's dead, Brendan. It's over. We'll talk later." Tom kissed his forehead.

John tried to prop himself up. "I'm okay. Just my hard head hurts."

"Be still, mate, till after the x-rays." John was gently pushed down by the medic.

Tom looked at John and patted the hand on top of the stretched white sheet. "You listen to them and take care. Remember, you're my 'little brother,' too." Tom gave him a reassuring smile.

John closed his eyes, "Tom, we sure were lucky."

"Lucky and then some, John. Indeed, it is a miracle that we are all alive." The ambulance with Brendan was ready to leave. Tom got in. He asked the paramedic, "How bad is it?"

"All we did was stop the bleeding. We'll know more when we get him to the hospital."

Brendan was still, his eyes closed and his lips pressed hard together, enduring the pain silently. Tom held Brendan's hand during the ride, murmuring almost as a litany, "It's over—thank God—it's over—thank God."

Chapter 40

Brendan was rushed into surgery, and the bullet was removed. Tom was told there was some damage beyond a flesh wound, but he was assured that eventually Brendan's leg would be fine. John's x-rays showed no internal swelling or bleeding. The external swelling was being treated with ice. He would be watched carefully at the hospital for the next twenty-four hours. Tom stayed until Brendan was coming out of the anesthetic. Satisfied that all was well, he started down the corridor. With his phone in his hand, he eagerly called his mother with the good news.

"All is well," he reported. With unabashed tears of joy running down her cheeks, Susanna thanked God for Brendan and Tom's lives.

As he prepared to call for a cab, Tom saw Jerry coming toward him. "How's it going for the boys?"

"Thank God, Jerry. They're going to be all right."

"Tom, you'll never believe this. They did an autopsy on Devlin. He had perforated stomach ulcers. Without immediate treatment, he would have died from that. Also, he had very advanced cirrhosis of the liver. Even with good care, he wouldn't have made it long."

Tom shook his head in disbelief. "You'd wonder how he could have forced himself to do what he did. I remember Brendan saying, 'Sean was like a mad dog with a bone. When he hated someone, he just couldn't let go.' I guess that kept him going."

"I'm through here, Tom. I'm heading home—thank the Lord. I'll drop you off to get your car."

"Jerry, take me directly to where I want to go." Tom swallowed hard to keep the emotions of relief and happiness in check. "I was beginning to think this time would never come."

Jerry grinned, "I don't have to ask where that is. What are we waiting for?"

Jerry pulled the car in front of Mrs. Pickens's house. Tom was out of the car before it fully stopped, "Goodnight, Jer," he said, over his shoulder.

Jerry chuckled and drove away. Lord, it was good to feel relaxed.

Tom was surprised to see lights in Fran's flat and in Mrs. Pickens's lower level. Tom glanced at his watch. It was past one a.m. He couldn't wait any longer to see Fran. He couldn't worry about being polite. He banged the knocker loudly. Mrs. Pickens was up, trying to watch a little telly. She was too worried about Fran to sleep. She timidly went to the door. It had to be trouble at this hour. She opened the door a crack. "*Tom!*" She threw the door wide open.

Tom almost picked up the little lady who was wearing a long blue flannel robe and danced her around, kissing her cheek, "How's my second favorite girl?"

Emma was laughing but tried to sound scolding. "Tom, you naughty boy, where have you been?"

Tom stood still and looked toward the top of the stairs. He was overwhelmed by his emotions. Was this really happening? He was seeing his precious Fran.

After that moment of sheer disbelief—realizing that Tom was really there, in her presence—Fran started down the stairs as Tom started up. Their eyes locked with a mutual look of love. Then came the wonderful instant when they were locked in each other's embrace. After a long tender kiss, Tom cupped her face in his hands. "I'll explain it all to you, Fran. I had to keep you safe. Being away from you—oh, Fran, it was awful."

"For me too, Tom." It seemed like forever. They kissed and hugged joyously. Fran stepped back and studied Tom's face. "My darling, you look so very worn and tired. I've the sofa now. Come stretch out."

Tom called down. "Emma."

Emma came back out into the hall. She had stepped into her living room.

Tom looked down at her with a teasing grin. "Emma, I absolutely promise, I'll not be *naughty*. There'll be nothing improper, but I'm going to stretch out on that sofa and stay the night. I'll explain what's been going on tomorrow."

"Bless you, Tom dear, you do look so tired. I'll make you some scones in the morning. Get some rest now." She went back into her rooms, grateful that she could give into her tired old body and go to sleep. Whatever it was—it was over. All was right for her Fran. Emma hadn't felt so happy for a week.

"Tom, I'll start some coffee and fix something to eat." Fran looked at him. His eyes were closed, and his hand trembled as he touched her cheek. The memory of this night filled his mind. A delayed reaction to what this night had held was now consuming him.

Tom went to wash his face and hands while Fran went into the kitchen. He washed with a fury as if wanting to cleanse away the horror of this night. He stretched out on the sofa. Fran had a warm blanket there for him and a soft pillow. He put his head deep into its softness and closed his eyes. But the picture of Sean's crushed, bloody head—and Brendan's pale face after his surgery—would allow him no rest.

Fran found Tom sitting up, his face in his hands. She put the tray on the coffee table and sat beside him, holding him in her arms in a comforting way. In silence for a long while he absorbed her caring. Finally, he straightened and looked at her lovingly, "I needed that. Brendan was hurt but he's in no danger and he's going to be all right. I spoke with Mom, and she'll be coming later today. Fran, what took place tonight by the Cathedral—I would be dead if a woman hadn't screamed my name."

At those words, Fran's body quivered and she felt faint. Tom continued: "I turned quickly to see who it was. I hadn't known Sean was behind me. He was ready to bash my head with a heavy torch. My move broke his balance and he fell with a terrible force headlong into a stone doorway. His head was crushed—it was horrible. For a minute, I was confused as to what had happened—the fog was thick. I picked up the torch from the ground and turned it on him. There was a woman kneeling by him, praying. She looked at me and said, 'He's dead—it's over, Tom.' She called me by my name again. She really had saved my life. Fran, I don't know her."

"What did she look like, Tom?"

"I'm not sure. I can't explain, I don't think I'll ever forget the expression in her eyes." Tom was frowning, trying hard to recall. "It was so foggy, but I think she had a dark coat and she was small—quite small. She had light hair, I think. It was all so confusing. Somehow, I had a thought that she was young—then again she seemed much older." Tom shook his head. "I'm not making sense. How can a person seem ageless? Yet in all the confusion that impression crossed my mind. I thought she would be there after I got Jerry Dixon, but she didn't stay."

Fran stood and hugged her arms tightly to her chest. "Tom, the person you have just described is Ethel Fenman. She must be back at the Cathedral."

"She doesn't know me. What would she be doing there that late at night?"

"What would anybody be doing there at that time of night, Tom? She is the kind of person who would help anyone in need. She wouldn't be afraid to stay where there was trouble. Oh, Tom, I'm sure it was Ethel Fenman."

"Darling, I can't imagine how she would have known about the situation. Whomever it was, I'd like to see her and try to thank her."

"Oh, so would I, Tom, *so would I*." She sat close to him, looking at that beloved face, her heart bursting with gratitude.

"I'm too spent to tell you the whole story tonight. Just know that it's over. Tomorrow, I'll tell you and Emma everything." He took a few sips of coffee. "Thanks, dear, for getting this." He glanced at the tray. "I—I just can't eat right now. This week has been such a strain and tonight a horror." Tom took a deep breath, "Thank God, it's finally over."

"I think it's best, Tom, that you do get some rest. Knowing the whole story can wait; you're here, and that's all that matters." Fran picked up the tray to return to the kitchen. She couldn't resist asking, "Tom, please tell me one thing, who is Liz Milford?"

"Liz Milford?" Tom looked puzzled. It took a minute to remember. "Oh, she's George Milford's wife. They own a realty business. Why, Fran?"

Fran couldn't help it; Tom's reaction to this brought a happy smile to her face. "I just happened to meet her. Now try to get some rest. Goodnight, My Darling." She kissed the top of his head and left the room.

Tom didn't know what Liz Milford had to do with it, but he certainly enjoyed that typical Fran smile. He felt a bit more relaxed and it wasn't long until he fell into an exhausted sleep.

He woke to hear Fran busy in the kitchen. Thoughts of last night flooded his mind, but this morning he could cope. He folded the blanket and stood back to admire the new sofa he hadn't noticed last night. He looked at all the beautiful new things—the lovely drapes, the picture—and called out to Fran, "Hon, you have everything done up so lovely."

Fran came into the room and into his embrace. She kissed his slightly bearded cheek. "Good morning, My Dearest." Her smile was as radiant as the sun that was shining through the windows, casting a puddle of light around them.

He buried his face in her sweet-smelling hair. "Good is an understatement for this morning, My Precious Fran, the night—is truly over."

Epilogue

—*Six Years Later*—

It was early afternoon. Fran finished clearing away the few things left on the dresser; everything else was packed. She sat down on the big soft chair in the pleasant hotel room. Giving in to its comfort, she closed her eyes, grateful for the little time of rest. The wedding yesterday had been beautiful. She was thinking, how ironic—no, not really—just life as it is with its ups and downs, hills and valleys. Poor Sean, that's how they all referred to him now; despite or because of his sad life and the horror he had caused, there had come such joy. If Sean hadn't set in motion the events of that terrible time, would Anne and John have met? The Quinn's farm, west of Maynooth, had nothing to do with Trinity College in Dublin. Had John's plans not been interrupted by that episode with Sean, would he and Anne be on their honeymoon today? Fran doubted it. John had returned to Ireland and stayed with his sister Joan and her husband Jerome Barrett. At Trinity, John had majored in agriculture and animal husbandry. Pat Quinn was indeed a happy man; John and his dear Anne would be staying on the farm with him. John was like a son to him already and had such good ideas for expansion. They all had so much to look forward to.

Fran got up and moved to the bed, standing quietly for a while, looking at the sleeping, beautiful, three-year-old girl. She spoke her name softly, "Mary Audrey, Mary Audrey." The child stirred a little but did not wake. Fran tenderly stroked the soft dark brown bangs and short bobbed hair that framed the sweet round face. Fran glanced at her watch and said to her precious daughter, "Just a little while longer, Darling, then you will have to wake. Daddy, Gram Susanna, and Uncle Brendan are waiting for us." The three were having a last visit in the adjoining room before Susanna and

Brendan returned to Glaslough and the Hart family took their flight home to England.

Fran returned to the comfy chair. Her thoughts drifted back to the lovely wedding of six years ago when she became Mrs. Thomas Hart. It had been a simple one, early in December, following that troubled fall. Her parents were there, along with Susanna, Brendan, and John. The faces of all those dear ones who had been there filled her mind. Uncle Cliff, Aunt Berniece, and Emma, of course, were there—and the Jerry Dixons and George and Liz Milford and a few other friends, including May Chittenden from the Prince Albert Pub. Dearest Heidi and Don stood for them as planned. Their joy over the wedding was only a little less than that of the bride and bridegroom. Fran was remembering how stunning Heidi had looked in her dark green velvet dress. She had worn a soft cream colored wool dress with matching fur cuffs. It was chosen to go with the gorgeous cream wool cape that she had bought on that happy day in London. Fran gave a contented sigh. The wedding was a beautiful beginning to the tremendous joy that was theirs—and had been theirs during these wonderful years.

Fran chuckled when she thought of her mother; by now, Irene had lost her fear of flying and delighted in each trip she and Bruce made to England. Even though they were an ocean apart, Tom's family and her parents had become fast friends. The one deep grief during the past years was the loss of dearest Uncle Cliff. Aunt Berniece moved from London to the flat in Ely. Tom and Fran had retained it although they had moved to their home in Ashwell. The happy couple and various members of their families had stayed there from time to time, much to the delight of Emma Pickens. Emma was getting frailer and had help come in each day, but was still amazing for her age. She loved having Berniece living there. For Berniece, it was such a blessing to feel needed. Without her beloved Cliff, staying in London was unthinkable. The frequent visits with Tom, Fran, and their darling little Mary Audrey helped, too.

Brendan had followed in Dermod's footsteps. He was a veterinarian and had started his practice in Glaslough; as yet, he was living with Susanna. However, as best man, when he had toasted John and Anne, he let it be known that he was hoping to find his "colleen" soon and know the happiness that was theirs.

Fran continued in her reverie, remembering their "sometime list" and all of the things from it that they had done. There had been their honeymoon trip to Washington, DC. They had seen so many things in Ireland and England. To Emma's great delight, Fran had given a beautiful and well-received concert in Ely Cathedral for the benefit of their maintenance fund. There had been trips to Florida to see her parents and visit with Heidi and

Don; they were back in the States and stationed not far from the Colberts. Mary Audrey thought of them as Aunt Heidi, Uncle Don, and big cousin Bryan. On one of their trips to Ireland, they had crossed on the ferry. That was the time Tom took her fishing. Not being squeamish, she had even baited her own hook. She remembered with a smile that she had caught a fish. Oh yes, these years had been richly blessed for her with the truest of loves and so many memorable times.

Fran's thoughts returned to the present and to the two guests that had come form the States to attend yesterday's wedding. It was so wonderful seeing Father Matt; they hadn't been with him since Mary Audrey's christening. Then, he had come on the flight with Fran's parents; it was so good having all the family together. Dear Uncle Cliff was with them; that was the last family time he was to share. Brendan was the Godfather and Liz Milford was Mary Audrey's Godmother. The Milfords and the Harts had become the closest of friends.

The occasion of John and Anne's wedding was Michael Griffith's first trip back since his move to the States. Yesterday's reception seemed to all of his friends to be a celebration of Michael's new life. Since the horrible plot had been aborted, there had been no trial. The Explosives Act of 1883, which had never been used to prosecute anyone, certainly was not applicable in Michael's case. With his complete renunciation of the plot and willingness to cooperate with the defense, had it been necessary, he was totally exonerated— a free man at once. He had returned to Dublin just long enough to settle Sean's estate. Michael was shocked to learn that he was the soul beneficiary. He contacted the authorities and paid all costs accrued in the investigation. With the sale of *The Paradise* and Sean's other assets, the amount of Michael's inheritance was sizeable. He made a large contribution to the Youth Center in Belfast and insisted on helping John and Brendan with their college costs in retribution for all they had suffered. Father Matt had taken him under his wing and helped him get settled in the States. There, Michael spent the remainder of the money on his education. He was now teaching in a school for troubled youth. Yes, Fran thought, what great good had come from that terrible time. What ultimate purpose there must have been? Surely, there would be mercy shown to the tragic, demented Sean Devlin. Fran was wishing that there would have been more time to visit with Father Matt and Michael; their flight back to the States had been early that morning.

The door opened. "Fran dear, I think we'll have to wake our sleeping princess." Tom went over, sat on the bed, and kissed the soft pink cheek. "Gram Susanna and Uncle Brendan are ready to take us to get the big airplane."

Mary Audrey sat up and threw her arms around her daddy's neck. "Are we going home now, Daddy? I want to go home—I miss Scooby."

"Yes, Mary Audrey, Scooby will be glad to see you, too." When Heidi and Don left England, four years back, Scooby had come to Ashwell to live with the Harts. Tom grinned at Fran, "Sometimes I think I play second fiddle to Scooby with both you girls."

Fran leaned over and kissed the top of Tom's head. "Don't bet on that." Tom was suddenly being hugged by, as he called them, the two prettiest girls in the world.

Susanna and Brendan came into the room. Fran smiled at Tom. "Should we tell them now?" Susanna looked questioningly at each of them.

"Big news, Mom. You're going to have another grandchild. Tom, Jr., is on the way."

Susanna hugged Fran. "Oh, My Darlings, I'm so happy. You know already, it's a boy?"

"Yes, I've had the sonogram. Since we have our little girl, we thought it would be fun to know."

Brendan said, "A boy—so that's the news. I knew there was a baby on the way."

Fran asked, "Did Tom tell you before?"

"No, dear sister, I couldn't help noticing yesterday at the reception that you were a bit rounder and had a certain glow about you. Remember I'm a medical man," Brendan laughed.

"Oh, you, what would you know? A vet is hardly an obstetrician."

"No, but I kind of know the signs." Brendan grinned, "Then too, there were those kinds of secret sharing looks you and Tom kept giving each other. When you were dancing, I heard Tom ask if you were feeling tired and telling you not to overdo it." Brendan gave Fran a squeeze. "I better get busy with my life, if there are to be cousins for your brood."

Fran gave him a beaming smile, "You know, I enjoy having a brother."

They were through checking out at the desk, when a happy, good-looking, slightly older couple came to check in. Fran noticed them but, of course, couldn't know that their lives, too, had been forever changed by the happenings of six years ago. The couple checking in was Mr. and Mrs. Clarke Ogdan. Clarke, who thought he was a confirmed bachelor, had gone to visit Phil and Tess Bailey to tell them how the Devlin case had been resolved. Tess's older sister Patricia was visiting at that time. She was much like Tess, possessing the same warmth and charm in such a natural way, a woman of discernment and honesty. Their attraction was immediate; their wedding had taken place three months after that first meeting. Clarke had found a happiness he never dreamed could be his.

How wonderful it felt to Fran and Tom to be back in their home in Ashwell. Every room was furnished now; all the touches were making it a comfortable, beautiful background for that precious love that made the house a home. Fran smiled as she came into the living room and looked at her portrait above the mantel. Tom had painted her as he remembered from the evening at the Royal Opera House in London. The red and gold Victorian décor of the alcove was the background. He had painted her face with a beauty that she never saw in herself. How blest she was.

Tom had gone on to the shop after telling her she mustn't carry the heavy luggage he put in the hall. She kissed him and said, "I promise."

Mary Audrey was having milk and cookies in the kitchen, where the blue and white-striped pottery gleamed from the open shelves. She stopped munching to ask, "Mommy, will we soon go to Ely and see Aunt Berniece and Grandma Pickens?"

"Yes, Mary Audrey, hopefully, next week." Fran watched as she continued to nibble the cookies and thought of how they had come to choose her middle name. Fran had first suggested Ethel. Tom felt it sounded like an old name for their little baby girl. At the suggestion of Etheldreda, Tom had said. *"Now, Hon,* don't you think that's a little much?" Then they thought of Audrey, a name they both liked. Tom had reminded Fran that Etheldreda had been called Saint Audrey for a period after the Norman invasion. So, Mary Audrey it was—a very happy compromise.

Mary Audrey was quite finished with her cookies and was carrying a grouchy looking Scooby in a loving but, what must have been for him, an uncomfortable way. "Let's take Scooby out and have him chase a string in the grass, Mary Audrey. He likes it when you play with him." Mary Audrey gave him a firm hug and a kiss on his velvet ear and put him down. He went with them through the back door and dashed ahead to hide under a bush. Mary Audrey forgot about catching Scooby when she saw her sandbox; she had missed that, too.

Fran walked up and down the little brick path, feeling such contentment. She looked up to the sky and remembered the first early morning in England and her feeling that somebody somewhere would help to guide her. That somewhere she found was Ely. Fran was always eager to return. Ely Cathedral still pulled at her like a magnet. Often she would go and stand quietly by the statue of Saint Etheldreda and remember Ethel Fenman, her special somebody. Fran knew now that she wouldn't see her again. Deep in her heart, although she never mentioned it—even to her precious Tom—she had become convinced that the woman sent to guide her and to save her Tom had been, indeed, the Saint from the Fens.

- The End -